Just a tou[...]
a question. When her mouth opened beneath his, he groaned at the rush of warmth that flooded his body. His hands left her hips to frame her face. He angled her head to deepen the kiss and she responded with the same rising desperation he felt. He'd known it would be like this, touching her. As if opening a floodgate, and he'd only wanted to be standing on solid ground first. He was just beginning to realize that there was no solid ground where Janie was concerned. He'd been falling since the moment he met her, and it didn't seem as if he'd be hitting bottom anytime soon.

He'd been wrong, dead wrong, to take her back to Columbus Junction, but she'd survived it. Survived that place, Gideon, everything life had ever thrown at her. He could feel her pulse thrum beneath his thumb where it rested on her elegant neck. She gasped for air and he gave it to her. She was solidly, thrillingly, electrically alive, and he just wanted to rest in the knowledge of it for a while.

She pulled away, and though her eyes were lust-darkened and her face flushed, there was still a shadow of doubt in her eyes. "Back in Columbus Junction, I thought... What changed your mind about me?"

"Nothing, sweetheart. My mind's been made up for a good long while about you. I never wanted to get in the way of what you wanted. Didn't want to be a temporary comfort or another burden you had to carry. But don't be confused about where I stand. *Hate* is the last word I'd use to say how I feel about you." He touched a finger to her swollen lower lip. "You can turn me away but it'll be your choice if we walk out of here right now, not mine."

For a moment, he thought she'd do just that. The possibility that he might have missed his chance with her locked the air in his lungs. He couldn't remember ever being this nervous, not the first time or anytime since. When she turned her head to kiss his palm, the tightness in his chest eased and he reached to pull her closer.

"You won't regret this."

Also available from Eleri Stone and Carina Press

The Reapers Series

Reaper's Touch
Gun Shy

The Twilight of the Gods Series

Demon Crossings
Witchbound

The Lost City Shifters Series

Mercy
Redemption
Rebellion

The Spellcraft Series

Threads of Desire
The Shape of Temptation

ELERI STONE

GUN SHY

carina press®

carina press®

Recycling programs for this product may not exist in your area.

ISBN-13: 978-0-373-00283-2

Gun Shy

Edited by Kerri Buckley

This edition published by arrangement with Harlequin Books S.A.

www.CarinaPress.com

Printed in U.S.A.

Dedication

To Katie Marie

GUN SHY

ONE

LYLE SPAT OUT a mouthful of dust and lifted his face. A pair of hawks circled gently overhead, black specks against the crisp blue sky. It was the kind of late autumn day that should be spent baling hay, sipping cider or making fence before the frost set. No sign in that beautiful calm heaven of the hell surrounding him down here. Not even a cloud to show how fiercely the wind was blowing.

With the sound of gunfire still echoing in his ears, he holstered his revolver and looked over the field to make sure that all of his men were accounted for. The rocky ground at his feet was littered with the bodies of about a dozen Reapers. All of them disabled for the time being, none dead. Their one injured Ranger, Garrett, was already in the medical tent with Doc. Cam had seen him there. Four scouts checking for tracks to be sure there were no stragglers and the other Rangers were in the field making sure none of the Reapers would give them trouble until transport arrived.

Only a year ago, they'd have been running cleanup by now, lopping off the heads of the dead before they resurrected. Now, they shot the Reapers to disable them and then worked in groups to shackle and load them onto reinforced wagons. They'd cart the snarling, stinking bunch back to the fort, tie them down, inject them with the cure and then stand back to see if they survived. Close to half didn't, but the ones who pulled through seemed to recover fully.

The Rangers gave the survivors a change of clothes, a pair of boots and money for their next meal. And then they sent them on their way. Doc worried about what happened to them after that, but Lyle had never been able to muster up much sympathy. Life was hard. It was hard all around. This was his job—bullets, blood, chains. He didn't have the time or the energy to worry about what happened to former Reapers once they left the fort.

He turned at the sound of his name to see Cam about fifty yards distant, waving his arms and standing right next to the medical tent.

"Damn."

He set off at a jog, weaving between the downed Reapers, careful not to come within grab range of any of the twitching bodies. Garrett had been with the patrol for nearly twenty years, a good run. Most didn't make it that long. He was far too experienced to have made such a stupid-ass mistake, assuming the Reaper with the head wound wasn't a threat. He'd hurried. Hadn't waited for Cam to cover him and when he reached for the thing's legs, the Reaper came to. They were ravenous when injured and this one had taken a shot to the gut. It needed meat to heal itself and Garrett had practically served himself up on a platter.

Lyle tried to read the news on Cam's face as he approached. Hands planted on his hips, legs braced, Cam looked ready for a fight. Seemed he was always ready for a fight these days. Could have been any number of things that had set him off. The scowl was reassuring. That was anger, not grief, and Lyle took it as a good sign.

Cam waited until Lyle was within earshot before speaking. “Talk to him.”

Lyle looked at the tent. The flaps were down, rope ties dangling, thudding against the post in a drumbeat. A gust of wind pushed at the canvas and just as abruptly bowed it in the opposite direction. “To who? Doc?”

“He’s gone soft in the head.” Cam removed his hat and shook the sand off the brim. “You have to talk some sense into him. He’s as bad as Abby. They’re Reapers, not fucking people. Not yet. Maybe not ever again.”

“What are you talking about?”

“I’m talking about Doc sawing off Garrett’s damn hand that’s what I’m talking about.”

“Stand aside and let me see what’s going on.”

Cam hesitated, looking as if he’d like to say more, but then jerked the flap of the tent back. Lyle ducked inside and paused while his eyes adjusted to the dim light. It was almost shockingly quiet inside the tent with the heavy canvas blocking the brunt of the wind. The walls were moving, sucking in and out with every gust. It was like being inside a pair of bellows. Lyle stifled a cough. Doc looked up sharply at the sound. “What the hell are you doing here?”

“Apparently, I’m talking sense into you.”

Doc snorted and set back to work. “That’ll be the day.”

Garrett was stretched out on a wooden plank, moaning softly in his drugged state. Lyle dodged a swinging lantern and came to stand beside the table.

“How bad is it?”

Doc swiped sweat from his brow with his forearm though it wasn’t particularly warm inside the tent. The scent of blood made the air seem thick.

"He'll lose his hand," Doc said flatly. "The rest will heal eventually so long as there's no infection."

In the past, they'd have just hacked a limb from a newly slaughtered Reaper and attached it to the wound. The same parasite that made men turn into Reapers gave them an amazing capacity to heal themselves. You only had to place the severed limb to the site of the wound and it would bind itself to the host. In a normal man, the parasite healed the wound but turned the man into a Reaper. Because Rangers were immune to Reaper infection, the parasite-laden blood could only heal their bodies, not take over their minds. Rangers had been patching themselves up with Reaper flesh for the better part of the past century, but that was before the cure.

Lyle's whole life was split in half by that one point. There was everything that had happened before the cure and the uncertain, still fucked-up world they were trying to figure out now.

"All of the Reapers are salvageable," he told Doc. None of them had been accidentally decapitated this time around. The Rangers were beginning to perfect the new art of capture. He met Doc's sharp gaze and said what they were both thinking. "Half of them won't survive the cure."

Doc's mouth tightened and he shook his head. "Trouble is telling which half. I can't cut off one man's hand to replace another's."

That was the thing though, wasn't it? "There was only one man injured today. A dozen Reapers. One man."

Doc gave him a look. A whole lecture in it though it lasted all of a heartbeat. Lyle swore under his breath. "I hate this."

The expression on Doc's face softened a bit. "No one likes it. We have our orders and they're sound. You know they are. You signed off on them same as I did."

Lyle gestured toward Garrett. "Do you need someone to hold him down?"

As if he could hear them talking about him, Garrett cried out and swung his injured hand onto his chest. Lyle turned away from the blood-soaked rag covering the mangled stump. Doc hesitated for a moment and then nodded. "Nobody squeamish this time."

Lyle turned and left the tent. Waving Jess over, he pointed. "Doc needs you."

Jess's face paled. "You want me to help with Garrett? Lieutenant, I don't think—"

Lyle shoved him toward the tent. "An order, Jess. Don't test me, not now."

He didn't wait to make sure Jess obeyed him. He didn't have to. Jess would follow orders now and make him pay later with surliness and dragging feet.

Cam whistled from a dozen yards away. "Over here."

Lyle jogged over to where Cam squatted beside a dying Reaper. The shot that had taken the Reaper down had gone right through his skull so he likely wouldn't be rousing anytime soon. The meat was still fresh. Lyle looked at the layers of dirt. The red stain around his mouth. His matted hair long and tangled. Years. It took them years to look like this. Decades, even.

"No one's looking for this one," Cam said. "Not anymore. There's not one person left alive to mourn him if he never comes back. He's as good as dead and buried anyway."

Somehow, that seemed sadder to Lyle than the loss of a hand.

"Lieutenant," Cam snapped. Pissed—he only used the title when he wanted to get under Lyle's skin. "You need to make a decision. We're running out of time."

Lyle rubbed the grit from his eyes with the heel of his hand. "Damn it."

Cap would have his head for this. "You have the knife?"

When Cam nodded, Lyle grabbed on to the Reaper's shoulders even though it made his skin crawl. Trying not to think about the gritty, oily, bug-ridden flesh he was clinging to, he pressed the full force of his weight down. "Go on. Do it."

Cam didn't hesitate. Not that he enjoyed this any more than Lyle did. Cam wasn't a bloodthirsty man, would likely be puking into the bushes as soon as he walked away. But a weak stomach had never stopped him from doing what needed to be done. It didn't stop him now.

Lyle ignored the sound of flesh parting beneath the blade, the bone snapping. He closed his mind to the wrongness of it all. Later, he'd chew it over and maybe figure out what he could have done different. For now, he focused on holding the thrashing Reaper steady enough so that Cam could finish the job.

It seemed to take an eternity but was probably only a matter of minutes. By the time the arm came off, they were both covered in warm blood and Cam had turned a shade of green that paled only where his lips were pressed tight together. Wordlessly, Cam handed Lyle the limb and sat back on his heels. His hands were shaking and the knife slipped from his fingers to fall to the ground.

Leaving Cam to deal with the mess, Lyle brought

the Reaper's hand to the medical tent himself. Doc already had Garrett's arm strapped to a length of wood. Jess stood near his head, looking green but ready to hold Garrett down when Doc began to cut. Lyle threw the arm on the table and took Jess's place. Jess looked as though he might weep with relief when Lyle told him to leave.

Doc stared at the arm for a moment and then glared at Lyle. "Where did you get this?"

"What the hell kind of question is that? You know exactly where it came from."

Doc swore even as he grabbed the limb to examine the cut. When he saw the raggedly sawed tissue, he cursed again. "Our orders are to inject Reapers with the serum, not use them for parts." He grabbed hold of a short-bladed saw. "We're saving them now, in case you hadn't noticed."

"I noticed." Lyle lifted his chin toward Garrett. "Save him first."

Doc set to work, measuring the Reaper's arm against Garrett's and marking both. He cut through the flesh and bone with all the delicacy of a butcher. Lyle was aware that most people found the whole process disgusting but he'd always been more fascinated than appalled. This procedure in particular, watching as the hand from a Reaper reached out to attach itself to a Ranger's bloody stump… No matter how many times he saw it, it always seemed like a miracle to him. A prayer fell from his lips as the wound begin to heal. A little disconcerting, that. It reminded him of the time his friend Rachel had let him press his hand against her pregnant belly and the babe picked that moment to roll over. This was a different kind of miracle but a miracle just the same.

He looked up to meet Doc's glare.

"I'll have to report it."

"I know."

"You've seen enough of them healed now you know the cure works. We're already sending them out into the world with nothing but the clothes on their backs. How about we let them keep all the parts they were born with?"

"Report it. I'll take what's coming to me. I did what I needed to. I expect you'll do the same."

With a dramatic sigh, Doc grabbed a rag to wipe the blood from his hands. Lyle braced himself for a lecture but it never came. Instead, Doc sat down without a word, his back to Lyle as he set to work cleaning off his tools. Doc could be as pissy as a farmwife when crossed but he'd get over it. Eventually.

Taking his silence as a dismissal, Lyle left the tent.

Cam was waiting for him outside, sitting on a rock with a flask of whiskey in his hands. He stood up as Lyle came toward him. "Doc give you trouble?"

Lyle shook his head. "Not much. Come on."

He led Cam back to the Reaper they'd harvested the hand from. Already, the blood flow had slowed to a trickle. Not because he was out of blood but because his body was beginning to repair itself. Between the head wound and the loss of his hand, it would take him a very long time to heal. If he ever healed completely. They'd all seen the lurching monsters leftover from injuries not even the parasite could fully repair.

"Do you want me to take his head?"

Lyle scowled at Cam, who shrugged. "It would be

a mercy. We can't throw him in with the others. You know the weak ones don't survive. They'll tear apart the wagon trying to get to him and we can't shackle him now anyway."

"Separate him from the others as best you can," Lyle said. "We're keeping him alive until his hand grows back."

Cam's eyes widened. "That could take more than a year. He's not a pet."

"See that he makes it back alive. He gets his chance just like everyone else."

TWO

IT WASN'T EVERY DAY that a federation flagship visited a small border town like Split Creek and the entire community had turned out to marvel at the spectacle of it. The monthlong gathering of the eastern and western councils was to begin in less than a week and the ship was coming to pick up the fort's delegation to the assembly. The *Goliath* was far too large to land inside Fort Dougan's courtyard and the nearest level plot was Johnson's sheep pasture, located midway between the fort and the town. Though all of the livestock had been relocated to another field before the plot was tidied up for the occasion, it still smelled like sheep. Sheep…and other things that didn't bear thinking about.

Jane wrinkled her nose and lifted the hem of her skirts as she stepped onto the path leading down to the newly constructed landing pad. Red-and-yellow flags, mounted on posts, circled the landing area so that it could be easily spotted from the air. The flags snapped and twisted in the breeze adding to the carnival atmosphere of the gathering.

Everyone was dressed in their Sunday best, in lace and frills, wide-brimmed sun hats. Few of the men owned suits but their shirts were clean and their boots polished. They sat on blankets and on sturdy wooden benches which had been hauled out for the occasion. The wise had arrived early with picnic lunches to claim a spot in the shade and their children darted through the spectators playing tag. There wasn't any room left beneath the wide-spreading boughs of the old oak trees at the top of the hill overlooking the pasture, but then, Jane hadn't really come to see the ship.

Ahead of her, Toby Mason tugged at his mother's skirt and pointed. Jane squinted up at the sky. Right on schedule. When she'd left the women's barracks at the fort, the ship had been nothing but a speck on the horizon. Now you could clearly see the shape of it, but not the details. It was big and coming their way at a brisk clip. When the crowd hushed, you could make out the faint sound of the engines.

Jane turned her attention from the ship and began to push forward again, poking Willie Braxton in the back when he planted his feet in the middle of the path to gape at the sky. Once she managed to slip past him, she spotted the small platform where the delegation waited with their luggage.

The delegation consisted of only three people—Captain Jones, Abby, who was a Ranger, and Jake, Abby's husband. Abby would be serving as Cap's guard and Jake, who'd been successfully cured of the Reaper infection last year, was going as living proof that the cure actually did work.

Cap looked surly as ever, clearly not pleased by the hoopla. He'd stripped off his formal dress jacket in the heat and tossed it over one of the trunks behind him. He was a large man, imposing and stern, but his expression didn't scare her. She had a soft spot for the grizzled captain who'd been kind to her when Cam brought her to the fort last year. Bruised and battered with nothing but the clothes on her back, she'd expected Cap to send her away. Instead, he'd given her a job and a place at the fort. A home. He might look like a bear and he might growl like one, but there was a good man beneath it all.

Abby—possibly the only woman *not* decked out in her finest—sat on one of the other trunks, her legs crossed, kicking her foot impatiently as she watched the ship. She looked surly too, though she smiled brightly when Jake bent to whisper something in her ear. Newly wed, the two of them were practically joined at the hip.

Down there was where she needed to be. Cam would want to see his friends off and while everyone else might have come to gape at the ship, she'd come to see Cam. As if summoned by her thoughts, the sun came out from behind the clouds just then and lit upon him in the crowd. It was his hair. He wasn't wearing a hat today and his guinea-gold curls caught the light, making him glow like a beacon. He was at the bottom of the incline, not very far ahead of her. Though she was tempted to call out, she held her tongue and quickened her pace.

Now that she'd caught a glimpse of him, he was easy enough to track even though he was dressed in brown like most of the other Rangers. It helped that he was walking beside Lyle, who stood taller than most men. The time or two she lost sight of Cam, she could still see the lieutenant pacing beside him and she was right—they were making a beeline for the waiting delegation.

She didn't particularly relish the thought of approaching him while he was surrounded by his friends but he'd taken to avoiding her. Not eating in the mess hall during her assigned hours and rarely spending time at the town's lone saloon, a place he used to visit frequently. He was the whole reason she'd agreed to come live in this godforsaken town in the first place, the least he could do was be civil.

Once off the path and onto the cut grass of the field, the crowd split up, people moving away to find friends and family. She had no family here and very few friends so there was nothing to distract her. Not breaking stride, she opened her umbrella to shield her skin from the bright afternoon sun. She freckled and then burned, there was no tanning her skin to protect it. The curse of being a redhead.

"Dirty breeders."

A woman's voice. It was pitched low, but there was no mistaking that Jane was meant to hear it. How could she miss it when the speaker was staring right at her from only a few feet away?

The muscles in her neck tightened but she controlled her reaction before it went any further than that, forced herself to keep walking even as she looked down her nose to meet Mrs. Boyd's sneer with a smile. Of course it was Mrs. Boyd, one of the sharpest thorns in her side.

She was one of the most respectable women in town as well as the cruelest. Last year, when the captain allowed Jake and Abby to marry in a break with Ranger tradition, women started looking at the Rangers as potential spouses. Mrs. Boyd hoped Cam would court her eldest, a good Christian woman. Unlike the trash who chased after the Rangers hoping to conceive a star-marked child.

All children were tested at birth with an injection that formed a starburst-shaped scar in the immune and all the immune were drafted by the forts to be Rangers. Only Rangers begat Rangers and the children were usually male. In order to keep the birthrate up, the forts paid out a huge child price for the birth and rearing of every star-marked child. Scrapers, the people rich enough to live up in the mountain cities, saw women like Jane as no different from prostitutes, but people on the plains tended to be more tolerant. After all, their lives depended on the arrangement.

On the one hand, Jane understood Mrs. Boyd's disapproval of her kind. If Cap let one of his Rangers marry, it stood to reason that he might let others do the same. Jane stood in the way of her plans for her daughter. And there was the principle of the thing. Mrs. Boyd was big on principles. She had very high standards that she adhered to assiduously. And that would be fine...if she didn't expect everyone else to live by her rules too.

It was the umbrella she objected to this time around. Jane saw how her beady little eyes lingered on it. The stripes, cream and emerald, marked the owner as available, which Jane was. It was a design that whores often used to mark they were open for business, but it was also common for single women in the cities to use the color combination to mark themselves as women seeking a husband. This one had been a gift from a dear friend. The people of Split Creek knew that she wasn't a whore and she'd needed the umbrella to shield her skin from the sun. She wasn't going to get rid of it just to please a few self-righteous women who wouldn't even look her in the eye when she bumped into them on the street.

But a confrontation just now was out of the question. For one thing, she didn't have time for it. For another, it wouldn't do a damned bit of good. People were stubborn in their opinions, particularly in the ones that kept them on top.

Before the cure, no one had cared if you were a married woman or a whore, what your skin color or your lineage was. Those things mattered up in the Scraper cities, but the only thing that mattered on the plains was whether or not you were star-marked. The Rangers were special, everyone else was just trying to survive.

Now that there was a cure, things seemed to be changing and not always for the better. The city council wanted the brothel moved out of town and she'd heard some rumblings about the dark-skinned captain that she didn't like one bit. All the old prejudices were coming out, like a mold that'd been there all along and was only waiting for the right conditions to start spreading.

That's why Mrs. Boyd thought she had the right to look down her nose at her. Mrs. Teak, too, sitting right beside her on the old quilt. They didn't have that right. They'd never had it in the first place.

Jane ignored the whispers that followed her through the crowd, tugging on her attention the same way the breeze teased her skirts. She kept her eyes on her quarry and made her way to the platform. The smell of newly cut wood nearly masked the smell of sheep.

Cam and Lyle had already arrived and settled in to conversations. Lyle with the captain, Cam with Abby. Jake stood quietly behind his wife like a guard, legs braced and his arms crossed over his chest. He was the only one who noticed Jane approach and he nodded politely as she stepped onto the rough platform.

She twirled her umbrella and angled it to block the sun. The movement caught Cam's eye just as she'd hoped it would, but he only scowled. Abby turned to greet her.

"Jane! You decided to come, after all."

Jane smiled at her friend, one of the few she counted as such here at the fort. "How could I miss it? I would have been the only one and everyone would have felt the need to tell me about it. Repeatedly."

Cam's eyes narrowed on her face. It wasn't a friendly look, but she forced a smile as if it was nothing out of the ordinary. Unfortunately, that look wasn't really out of the ordinary of late.

"You didn't come out here to see an airship," he said, with a hard note of underlying suspicion. When Abby kicked him in the shin, he glared at Jane as if it was her fault he was being an ass.

"Not the ship, maybe. But I did want to see the delegation off. Same as you, I imagine."

A muscle jumped in his jaw as he clenched his teeth. They were straight teeth, all there, and mostly still white. When he smiled it made him even more handsome. Being a Ranger meant his body stayed fit. Tan skin. Golden hair and blue eyes as bright as the summer sky. Sometimes, she wondered if this all might be a little easier if he was just a little less handsome.

He looked as if he wanted to argue with her, but instead gave a small shake of his head and resumed his conversation with Abby. Every so often, he'd dart a look her way but all in all he seemed determined to ignore her. For now, she was willing to let him do just that.

She turned her attention to Jake. As dark as Cam was fair, his black eyes were steady as he responded to her proper hello. "Nice of you to stop by, Miss Fisher."

When she'd first met Abby's husband, he'd scared her. Not only because he used to eat people when he was a Reaper but because he was the type that was near impossible to read. She'd grown accustomed to that though, and she respected the way he treated Abby, as though the sun rose and set with her.

After she and Jake exhausted all pleasantries about the fine weather and the turnout, they fell into a surprisingly comfortable silence, watching as the ship made its final approach. It was an older model, opulent in the showy way of the pirate barons from a half century past. The engine sounded new though, smooth and deep. She could feel the rumble of it in her bones. A familiar ache hit her in the chest and she gripped the handle of her umbrella tighter. Jake noticed her reaction. When his curious gaze met hers, she shrugged.

"The ship. It's been such a long time since I've seen one this close."

"I forgot that you came from the city. Any last-minute advice for us?"

She didn't like to talk about her time in the mountains but she felt honor-bound to warn him. "It's a different world up there. They're more interested in shine than truth. Everyone will pretend they're happy to see you, but you can't trust they'll do the right thing just because they seem sympathetic."

"They're threatening to cut funding to the forts. We need them sympathetic."

"Just don't mistake sympathy for intent," she said. "The fort tax has never been popular and if they can find some way to weasel out of it, they will."

He gave a short laugh. "Without the forts to protect the farms and supply lines, they don't eat."

She thought of Eyrion, the enormous houses staffed by armies of servants. The people they'd be dealing with up there weren't ever going to go hungry. The problem was that Scrapers didn't have to worry about Reaper attacks. They might depend on the Rangers to keep the farmers and ranchers alive but they didn't see the danger up close and personal.

"You'd probably have better luck convincing them to pay up if you brought along a live Reaper instead of a..." She trailed off, trying to figure out a graceful way to pull her foot out of her mouth.

"A former Reaper like me," Jake finished, not sounding particularly bothered. The corner of his mouth tilted up. "I'm not terrifying enough for you, Miss Fisher?"

"You don't terrify me, Jake."

"I'm losing my touch, then. Maybe I should put a little extra work into my glower."

"Just be careful." Her gaze lingered on Abby, her reckless friend who didn't have a subtle bone in her body. She lowered her voice. "Watch out for her."

"We'll stay out of trouble," he reassured her. "State dinners and meetings listening to long-winded Scrappers drone on about things they don't understand. Cap only wanted me along because he thought some people might be swayed by the testimony of a cured Reaper and Abby wouldn't let me go alone."

No, she wouldn't. Theirs was a love match, as unlikely as that seemed. She and Cam had more of a hate relationship but they were just as tightly bound. That Cam chafed at the binding was unfortunate, but it didn't change facts.

The bulk of the airship blocked out the sun and she looked up along with everyone else to watch it glide into position. The ship was a beauty, an incredible work of fine engineering and sheer artistry. Brass gleamed in the sunlight and the wooden hull, centered perfectly above the landing pad and slowly lowering, was polished and waxed to a shine. The drag sails made a mighty clap as they caught wind and the sound from the engines deepened.

The crew was well trained, as was to be expected, and they were showing off. Apparently not trusting the local men to properly anchor the ship, they dropped rope while still about twenty feet up. Down came two dozen men, smartly dressed in dark green uniforms. As soon as their feet touched the ground, they turned and, still holding on to the ropes they'd descended upon, began to spread out in a perfectly expanding circle, dragging the ship lower until they reached the anchors which had been placed around the field. Once the ship was tied off, folding iron stairs were lowered from a hatch in the hull.

The Goliath's captain was the first down, raising his hand in greeting to the gathered crowd.

"Well." Abby slapped her thighs and stood. "I suppose that means it's time to go. Thanks for coming to see us off, Cam. Jane."

Cam accepted her hug and Jane looked away, pretending not to notice Abby whisper something sharp in his ear. Abby shouldn't get involved. She truly didn't wish to drive a wedge between Cam and his friends. Jake shook Cam's hand and inclined his head toward Jane before tossing his leather bag over his shoulder and following Abby toward the ship.

And then Jane was standing alone with Cam. Before he could escape, she slipped her hand through his arm. The muscle flexed beneath her fingertips and she thought he meant to pull away, but he didn't.

"I only wish to speak with you."

"Really? That's all you want?"

Impossible as it was to miss the bite in his words he

stayed by her side, watching as the crew finished securing the ship and loading the brass bound leather trunks into the storage hold.

"A gentleman would offer to escort me home."

"I'm not a gentleman."

"A kind man, then."

"Kind? You never stop playing games, do you?" He lowered his voice, though there was no one near enough to hear them over the sound of the engines. "You came here to corner me after I told you I'm done with you. No more, Jane. I mean it."

"It wouldn't cost you a thing."

A muscle in his jaw jumped. "You think it wouldn't cost me?"

"One night."

"You're crazy."

She couldn't help but flinch at that. It's what everyone thought, she knew it. Cam noticed her reaction and his expression softened. "It's over, Jane. It's past time you accepted that."

The crew already had the luggage mostly stowed. The captain was ushering the delegation toward the waiting stairs himself. As soon as the ship lifted off, Cam would run again, and this time he'd be even more determined to avoid her. *Why did he have to be so stubborn?*

Lyle stood watching the ship but she could tell he was well aware of what was happening behind him. Him she could read and he was trying very hard right now to give them space. He wasn't happy about it either, her confronting his friend in such a public place. Lyle was in charge of the fort while the captain was away. It wouldn't do her any good to get on his bad side. The captain might be sympathetic to her situation but that didn't mean Lyle would be.

"I don't understand your reluctance, I truly do not. It's such a small thing."

He gave her a hard look. *Men.*

"You know I didn't mean it like that." The only thing that kept her from laughing was the hurt look on his face. "Is that what you want? Flattery?"

"What I want is for you to go away. Stop hunting me down like I'm a damned Reaper."

Didn't he think she would if she could? Before she could think of way to convince him, the ship lifted off to whoops and cheers from the crowd. Slowly and steadily, it gained altitude until it cleared the trees and then turned to the west, taking her hope of getting Cam to seriously consider her offer with it.

Once the ship was on its way, Cam tried to pull his arm free. She tightened her hold and he sighed. "Let go of me."

"Please. Just *talk* to me."

"I'm done talking."

He moved to brush past her and she reached out to stop him. His hand shot out and wrapped around her wrist. She jerked away just as he released her. He didn't intend to let her fall, she knew that about him. No matter how sour he'd turned, she'd never known him to intentionally hurt someone weaker than himself.

But he let go faster than she anticipated. The resistance she'd expected simply wasn't there and she sucked in a surprised gasp as she fell, losing her balance and tumbling back faster than anyone around could catch her. Her heel slipped off the platform. Her full skirts and petticoats flew up in a flurry of lace and cotton and her breath went out in a whoosh as her tailbone struck the unforgiving ground.

A stunned silence fell over the crowd. Lyle spoke sharply to Cam who snapped something right back but she couldn't focus on the words. She could barely hear them over the pounding in her ears. She managed to sit up, pushing her skirts down to cover her exposed legs. The ship was only a mile up but hardly anyone seemed to be watching it. Everyone was watching her now, waiting to see what she'd do. They were all well aware of her pursuit of Cam. Some people had placed wagers on the outcome and were probably hoping to collect after this confrontation.

Except, there wasn't going to be a confrontation today because Cam turned and walked away. That was so unexpected she couldn't do anything but stare at his retreating back until Lyle blocked her view. Dark brown boots, worn but well cared for. Plain brown trousers and the bottom edge of the duster he always wore. She couldn't force her gaze any higher than that.

"Come on, Janie." He took her hand and pulled her up, nearly lifting her off her feet. Once she was steady, he tucked her hand around his arm and began to push through the crowd. "Let's get you home."

LYLE GUIDED HER deftly through the crowd. She'd expected everyone to disperse once the ship was gone but no one seemed in a hurry to be off. The band was playing, enthusiastically if not well, and Delilah, the saloon owner, was serving ale from a large barrel in the back of her wagon. There was already a line forming and Jane was sorely tempted to go stand in it. Lyle still had a firm grip on her arm though and his brisk pace said he had no intention of letting her go.

Instead of walking toward the road, he turned left down a narrow path of trampled grass. A deserted path. They weren't heading into town. She glanced up nervously. Lyle was handsome, not in the golden, dazzling way that Cam was, but appealing all the same. Strong jaw, straight nose. Gray eyes that were a little too piercing for her comfort. A big man.

"Where are you taking me?"

His jaw tightened but he didn't look her way or break his pace. "We need to talk."

The irony of the statement was not lost on her. It seemed to be a day for uncomfortable conversations all around. She thought about digging in her heels but decided against it. If Lyle wanted to have his say, she'd hear him out.

They walked for several minutes in silence, the sound of the crowd fading with every step. When they came to an old stone stile connecting the pasture to the one adjacent, he released her arm.

"Go on. Have a seat."

"I don't need to sit," she said crossly. "I can't imagine you have much to say."

He'd turned half-away but he glanced back at that, a fleeting smile creasing his face. "I'll come right to the point then." He pointed back down the path. "Whatever it was that happened back there...whatever is going on between you and Cam, it has to end."

She lifted her chin. "Maybe you should talk to Cam about that."

"He's at the end of his rope, Jane."

"I'd like to see him at the end of a rope."

Lyle studied her face for a moment and then shook his head slowly. "You don't mean that."

"Of course I don't." Some of the fight drained out of her and she walked to the stile. She sat down on one of the rough stone steps leading into the next pasture, the pressure on her bruised tailbone making her wince.

"Are you okay?"

"I flashed my garters at the whole town, broke my favorite umbrella and bruised my…" His eyes flickered with amusement and she gave him a sour look. "Pride," she finished. "Bruised my pride. It wasn't my best day."

Instead of trying to reassure her, Lyle grinned. "It was a sight to see."

She tried not to smile back, she truly did, but it was no use. The airship and the sheep pasture. The whole town set out in their Sunday best and her on her back with her skirts flying in the air. She buried her face in her hands and groaned. Mrs. Boyd and her cronies were probably still ripping her apart like coyotes with a fresh kill.

For some reason, that brought tears to her eyes and because she didn't want Lyle to see them, she kept her face buried as she heard him step closer. With a sigh, he sat down next to her on the step, close enough she could feel his warmth but not close enough to touch.

"It'll pass," he said gently. "There'll be another scandal in a week or so and everyone will forget about the color of your bloomers."

God. She'd worn the scarlet satin ones today. She groaned again. Lyle leaned closer and knocked his shoulder into hers companionably. "You've got to give up this thing with Cam though. He hasn't been himself lately and neither have you. Why do you want him anyway when there are a hundred men who would worship the ground you walk on?"

"Cam's a good man."

"One of the best," he agreed. "And he's like a brother to me which is why I can say for certain that the two of you don't suit. Never did. Never will."

"I think we suit just fine."

"You can say that even after today?"

"He was upset."

"Because you're hounding him."

"He'll come around." Or not. It was time to consider the possibility that he might not ever come around.

She sniffed a little and Lyle pressed a handkerchief into her hand. For some reason, that felt more humiliating than her fall. She took it anyway and blew her nose. She didn't like the soft cast to his eyes, didn't like it at all. The last thing she wanted from anyone was pity, particularly not from Lyle.

"Just tell me what's really going on here and give me the truth. I don't want to have to send you off. Meet me halfway and help me to understand it."

Send her off... Where would she go? She couldn't go home and standing here on the border between human and Reaper territory, there was quite literally nowhere left for her to run. But how to explain it all to Lyle? No good could possibly come of this conversation. Cam knew exactly what she wanted and that was bad enough.

"I think he cares beneath it all," she said carefully. "Don't you think that he might? He wouldn't have brought me back here if there wasn't...something."

Lyle shifted, angling his head to see her better. The brim of his hat blocked the sun, cutting a line of shadow across his face. The weight of his arm pressing to hers felt reassuring. "There are all sorts of caring, Janie. He doesn't want a wife. I bet if you asked him, he'd be pleased to see you happy with someone else."

"He was the one who asked me to come here."

"As a Ranger and a friend. I know him. He wouldn't have offered more."

"I don't want anyone else."

"Is this some kind of game then?" He frowned, his eyes narrowing. "You chase Cam so everyone else backs off?"

She didn't answer, just pressed her lips together and looked away. She should have kept her foolish mouth shut. He wasn't going to understand it. She barely did herself. She stared off across the plains, the grass rolling softly in the breeze, burned brown by the summer sun, the trees beyond gold and scarlet.

Lyle let that silence stretch for a moment and when he spoke again, his voice was gentle. "You don't need to do that. If people here thought you were available, I'm sure there'd be interest but you can say no. If you're unwilling, they will back the hell off."

The vehemence that crept into his tone at the end brought her attention back to his face. His expression was grim, hard as she'd ever seen it and she was touched by that. He'd misunderstood and she was tempted to correct him. But what was the point?

Earnest, that's what Lyle was, looking at her with those sharp gray eyes thinking he understood what was best for everyone involved. That he didn't know what the hell he was talking about didn't change the fact that he was going out of his way to make sure nobody got hurt. It was far too late for that but she didn't quite have the heart to tell him. It was none of his business anyway.

Nobody's business except hers and Cam's. She looked him square in the eye and gave him the plain truth. "I want Cam. It's as simple as that."

"You're playing a dangerous game. He's still a man. You might think this is safe or entertaining or whatever it is you get from it, but what are you going to do if he takes you up on your offer?"

That made her smile. "I'd have credited you with a better imagination than that, Lieutenant. Or at least a dirtier one."

"My imagination is just fine. Cam is used to women throwing themselves at him. You're beautiful but so are plenty others. He's not that desperate to get laid so if you're trying to wear him down that way, it's not likely to work."

"That's not what I'm trying to do."

"Are you trying to annoy him into bed?"

She didn't answer him right away. Instead, she took a good long look at his expression and then shook her head. "This is how everyone sees me, isn't it? Desperate and lonely and pathetic."

"I don't think you're pathetic."

Just desperate and lonely. "Well, that's a comfort."

"That's not how I meant it."

She knew it. He wasn't the type to wound a person for the pure sport of it.

"There's no shame in being lonely," he said.

That was entirely beside the point. "He'll change his mind."

Lyle started to reach for her, lifting his hand just an inch or two before checking the motion. It unnerved her. She didn't know what she would have done had he actually tried to give her a hug.

"I'm not unattractive."

"No," he agreed quietly.

"Not diseased or crazy."

Lyle held his tongue on that one.

"I'm not asking for more than he can give. I would walk away."

"Would you?"

She nodded without hesitation. She could tell by the expression on Lyle's face that he didn't believe her but, rather than argue the point, he simply waited for more.

"Why doesn't he want me?"

That startled a short, dry laugh from him. Something flickered in his eyes and he shook his head. "Honestly, Janie? I have no idea."

"He'll change his mind?" It shouldn't have come out as a question.

"Do you think you can wait until the captain returns from the assembly before poking at Cam again?"

"If Cam isn't man enough to stand up for himself—"

He groaned. "Just keep it between the pair of you. It's all I'm asking. No more scenes like today. No more trying to draw everyone else into your strategies and I'll gladly keep my nose out of your business. Think you can manage it?"

"I think you like my business just fine, Lieutenant. That's what I think."

She wanted the words back as soon as they were out. It was an ugly thing to say and she knew it. Especially when he'd always been respectful.

All the warmth and humor drained from his expression like water through a sieve and it made her feel like crap. She was tired, sore, sweating and covered in dirt.

Nothing about today had gone as she'd planned it. But that was no reason to take it out on Lyle.

"I'm sorry."

"You don't need to apologize to me."

"I do." She looked down at the ground. She needed to get away from him. From everyone. She felt bruised all over, body and soul. Lyle sat, patient and quiet, waiting for her answer, watching her with a strange gentle look on his face. But she didn't mistake that for lack of resolve. If he'd taken her out here to warn her to quit Cam or be sent from the fort then he meant it. She could appeal to the captain when he returned but the captain wasn't here now.

She climbed to her feet and shook out her wrinkled skirts. When she'd gathered her composure, she looked him in the eye.

"You don't have to worry about me, Lieutenant. I won't cause you any more trouble."

THREE

LYLE LET THE door slam closed behind him and shoved his hat onto his head. "Asshole."

Cam took one look at him and winced. "What's he done now?"

Arms crossed, Cam leaned against the hitching rail outside the large building they'd transformed from a storage barn into the laboratory and Reaper rehabilitation facility. He still refused to go inside the place and Lyle couldn't blame him.

The lab was in the new addition, with windows that looked out onto the main yard. But Welks hadn't been in the lab. His assistant, a curly-haired young woman named Minerva, had directed Lyle to the rehabilitation facility. Fancy name for a basement, really. Nothing but rows of metal beds filled with men recovering from the aftereffects of the serum injection. They were weak for the first few days after receiving the cure, like a bad flu. They had trouble keeping down solid food, were disoriented and often violent. It was a dark, foul-smelling dungeon of a place. He'd found Welks down there. Almost wished he hadn't. Now, Lyle wanted to go wash the stench of it off his body, out of his mind. His boots sounded hollow on the wooden porch as he crossed to Cam.

"We're down to our last six crates."

Cam shrugged. "Reapers will be running south soon.

We'll have time this winter to rebuild the stockpile and get the surplus out to the border towns before spring."

"Except Welks won't produce more serum until we pay him more money. He waits until Cap leaves for the assembly to try and renegotiate his contract."

"He thinks you'll be easier to deal with then Cap?"

"Apparently so."

Cam pushed off the rail. "Then he deserves what's coming to him."

Lyle blew out an exasperated breath. He appreciated Cam's confidence in him but he hadn't a damn clue how he was going to get Welks to do his damn job without threatening to shoot him. While drawing his gun on the man seemed the most satisfying option at the moment, he knew it would only make Welks dig in his heels harder. He guarded his secret formula like a dragon guarded gold. Which was incidentally exactly how he viewed the cure—his own personal pile of gold. Not for the first time, Lyle wished Cap back.

"Come on. I could use a drink."

He hopped off the wooden walkway and started for the captain's office. Cam fell in beside him and they cut through the training field to reach the small one-room structure that served as headquarters for fort business. Normally, they'd have made the trip into town but he wasn't fit company for anyone right now. Besides, he had to update today's entries in the log and he knew where Cap kept the good whiskey.

The office was sparsely furnished. Three chairs and a scarred wooden desk. A long bench beside the door. An old map on the wall and a large safe in the corner containing what remained of the yearly tax. Lyle knew exactly how much was left to see them through the last quarter and it was less than the amount Welks had just demanded of him to continue production of the serum. When Welks named his price, it had taken every last ounce of control for Lyle not to plant his fist in the doctor's face.

Dropping glasses onto the table, he pulled the cork from the bottle with his teeth and poured them each a dram. Nudging one of the tumblers in Cam's direction, he fell back into his chair. The setting sun sat above the wall at exactly the right angle to hit the sole window, painting a long rectangle of light on the dusty plank floor. He hated this office, hated the responsibility that fell on his shoulders when Cap was gone. Hated Welks too.

Cam sank into the chair across from him. "It's a little early for this, isn't it? You don't usually pull Cap's bottle until he's been gone a month or more."

"Special circumstances. He should have put you in charge this time."

"You have rank."

Lyle gave him a sour look. Rank didn't mean shit. The men respected Cam just as well as they did him. He'd been here two years longer, that's it. The title of lieutenant didn't even get him more pay, only more headache.

Cam took a drink and then closed his eyes to savor the smuggled whiskey. "Myself, I like it when Cap goes on holiday."

Lyle rubbed his face. He wanted a holiday. No, strike that. Most days what he wanted to do was get on his horse, start riding north and not ever look back.

Cam stretched his legs out in front of him, crossing his boots at the ankle. He looked relaxed but he'd been on edge lately, reckless. Some of that was the business with Janie but Lyle didn't think that was the whole of it. Since the cure, he'd felt that same itch under his skin. The world was changing and he no longer knew his place in it.

"I talked to Doc this morning," Lyle told him.

Cam folded the glass in his hands, resting it on his stomach. "Is he still pissed at you about the Reaper?"

"He doesn't think Cap should have let me off as easy as he did."

"He docked your pay for two weeks."

"I cut off a man's hand."

Cam scowled. "A *Reaper's* hand. It's growing back. I checked on him yesterday. He's in his own pen and I made sure he got a bucketful of scraps from the kitchens."

Reapers could sometimes regenerate a lost limb, though they were never as perfectly symmetrical as the original. Close though. He'd look as normal as a Ranger with a restoration and at least he'd have a fully functional hand. Welks hadn't seen the problem in what he'd done. The scientist had actually suggested they keep a few Reapers around for "harvest purposes." Lyle chased the bitter taste in his mouth down with another swallow of whiskey.

"The pens are full," Cam continued. "We'll need to build a new enclosure if Welks goes on strike. He picked a damn fine time to do it with Cap, Jake and Abby off on a wild-goose chase."

"It's not a wild-goose chase. Cap had to go with all the talk about cutting funding. The council needs to know the cure's not a quick fix, not with how many Reapers there are out there."

"It does seem like simpler times when we could just shoot them all," Cam readily agreed. "Cap might be interested in discussing policy, but you know Jake and Abby only went to dig up dirt on Williams."

"That's necessary too." Lyle leaned back in his chair, settling in for an argument. "Maybe we should have sent Jane along with them. She seems to know her way around Scrapers and it would've gotten her out of your hair."

"That's a rotten idea."

"Why? She's city-bred, isn't she?"

Cam's mouth pulled tight at the corners and he stared down at his glass. "She'd fallen a long way by the time I laid eyes on her. She wouldn't be welcome up there even if she was willing to go back."

Fallen. That's what they called Scrapers who'd lost money or position and were forced to move to the plains. It didn't happen often. Most of the people who lived in the cities were related to the founding families and they tended to take care of their own. The possibilities of what might have happened to Jane rattled around in his brain for a moment. Useless to speculate but he took a stab at it anyway. "She get involved with the wrong man?"

"You could say that."

"Does she have any connections that could help us get to Williams?"

Cam gave a short laugh. "If she had connections like that do you think she'd be down here? Besides, I don't see why you're all so set on going after Williams. It's a waste of time. You know we could have proof in our hands and it wouldn't make a damn bit of difference. We can't touch him anyway."

"We can. Eighty-seven people died at Fort Hill because he was worried about the cure hurting his business interests. He might have used Reapers to do the dirty work but he's still the man responsible. He's not getting away with that."

"We pardoned Welks, didn't we? For his part in it and for what he did to Abby. Where's the justice there? Scrapers have never had our best interests at heart, only their own. You're just pissed because you used to think otherwise."

Lyle waved a hand. "You're avoiding the question."

"I'm not. You're avoiding reality. It's a nest of snakes up there. Why hunt snakes just for being snakes?"

"I don't hunt anything for the hell of it. But I wouldn't hesitate to kill a poisonous snake that was set to bite me. That's plain good sense. We keep one eye on the mountains, one on the border and we don't get caught in the cross fire again. Jake's been able to help us understand how sentient Reapers think. Why can't Jane do the same with Scrapers?"

"That's really why you asked me here, isn't it? To pry into my business with Jane?" Cam lifted his glass. "You didn't need a drinking partner. You just wanted to soften the interrogation. Jane can't ever go back to the mountains so just drop it. Don't pull her into that mess."

"You're her knight in shining armor? Is that it?"

Cam looked out the window, light dimming. "That's not how she sees me."

"Cam."

"Let it go."

"I'm not pleased to be having this conversation either." Lyle shook his head. "Whatever is going on between you has become too public for me to ignore. I can't have you distracted now. Not with Cap gone, the men run ragged and Welks stirring up trouble. I'm trying to help the both of you here. Don't make me send her off."

Cam rubbed his face. He looked worn and Lyle felt a twinge of guilt for pushing him so hard. Just a twinge.

"Don't send her off," Cam said. "It wouldn't be right. You didn't say that to her did you?" He read the answer on Lyle's face. "Shit. I'll have to talk to her."

"I gave her the same speech I'm giving you now. I don't want to be involved, but it's gone too far. The townspeople have all sided with you and that can't be easy for her."

"There aren't any sides. It's a private disagreement."

"Not anymore it isn't."

Cam muttered a curse and shot him a glare. "If you're so worried about it, why don't *you* entertain her?"

Lyle couldn't help but flinch. "That would take care of your problem nicely, wouldn't it?"

"I see the way you look at her."

"You don't see shit."

Jane made him uncomfortable more than anything. Her fiery red hair and jaw-dropping body. The defiant glint in her dark eyes. The single-minded ferocity with which she chased after his best friend. All sorts of reasons it would be a bad idea for him to pursue her, not least of which that she'd given him no sign whatsoever that she would welcome such a thing. She'd told him that point-blank—she wanted Cam.

They were adults. He'd done what he could. He'd have to trust them to work it out and failing that, maybe see if he could have Janie placed in another fort. Hopefully, Cap would get back before it came to that. He downed the rest of his whiskey and set the glass aside. He'd just opened his mouth to dismiss Cam, but the clamor of the tower bell interrupted him.

Fuck. The alarm meant one of the towns in their territory had sent out a call for help. Dropping his head into his hands, he groaned. "It's too damned late in the season."

"Someone forgot to tell the Reapers that." Cam climbed to his feet. "Bright side, you don't have to deal with Welks today. Or worry about Jane."

FOUR

AT FIRST JANE hadn't paid the strangers much attention beyond noting their presence. It was her day off and she'd come into town to complete a few errands. The patrol was out, seeing to some trouble near Webster and the fort was unbearably quiet. The road into town had been deserted too and Split Creek was the same. She hadn't realized the Gavins were raising a barn today, but it wouldn't have changed her plans much if she had. All of the able-bodied men had been recruited to help and most of the young women had followed. If the town hadn't been so empty, she might not have noticed the strangers at all.

Once she did notice them, she couldn't help but think they were up to something unsavory. There was something off about the way they carried themselves, their hats angled down over their faces and the tension in their bodies even when slouched against the wall. They seemed nervous and watchful, and she kept a wary eye on them as she went about her business.

Rachel was expecting her third child and all of her dresses had needed to be let out but with two babies to look after, Jane couldn't imagine where she would find the time to do it. And so Jane had done it for her. A simple thing. It hadn't even taken up all of an evening. When she dropped the basket off at Rachel's cottage, Rachel tried to thank her by putting Macy in her lap and scurrying off into the kitchen to make tea. Macy was an adorable little thing with enormous brown eyes and curly black hair. When she smiled, she put her whole body into it, all gums and drool and chubby cheeks. Every time, Jane's heart tried to climb out of her chest. As soon as Rachel had her hands free again, she passed the baby back and hastily made her excuses. She used to love snuggling little babies, but that was…well, that was before.

After that, she stopped to visit with Harley who was out front on his porch where he would often spend the entire day chatting with anyone who bothered to stop for a minute. On his good days, Harley was a charming conversationalist who greeted her with a smile. On bad days, he often mistook her for his deceased wife, Mary. But even then he was a charming conversationalist. You just had to watch his hands. He tried to pat her rear as she passed him to take a seat in an empty chair and Jane shot him a suspicious look. She could never be sure but some days he seemed just a little sharper than others.

His eyes sparkled when he smiled. "Where were you off to, Mary? I missed you."

"I had errands to run." She sat beside him beneath the shade of his porch, listening to the creak of his rocker and watching the strangers just standing there outside the boardinghouse as if they were waiting for someone.

"Harley?"

Harley removed the cigar from between his remaining teeth. "What, love?"

"Those men over there—have you seen them before?"

Apparently Harley really was having one of his bad

days because he laughed, a dry wheezing sort of sound, then said, "Don't you recognize your own boys, Mary? Ah, your eyes are awful bad." He reached over and patted her arm. "Suppose that's why you took on an ugly dog like me."

She patted his hand absently, still watching the pair. The short one looked awfully familiar. She knew she'd seen him before. But where? "You're not a dog."

"Suppose it's been a while since I came sniffing at your skirts, eh?" His voice dropped. "Tonight I mean to..."

Oh dear God. Jane stood abruptly. "I need to check on Margie," she told him, cutting off whatever he'd been about to say and scooting off his porch before he could stop her. She'd tell John to check on his father this evening, make sure he had his supper and found his way to bed. She waved and called out. "I'll be gone for a while, Harley. Don't worry after me. You just stay here and John will be around later."

After she'd picked up a letter for Haddy from her people out east, she went to talk to John about Harley. She'd wanted to stop in to the general store anyway to see if he'd ordered the magazines she'd requested. The two men, the strangers, were still standing in the exact same spot. The taller of the pair had his back to the wall, arms crossed over his chest and though he looked as if he might be dozing, she saw the gleam of his eyes from beneath the brim of his hat.

The bell above the door jangled as she entered John's shop. He was busy helping Mrs. Weber at the counter so she pulled out the most recent fashion magazine and brought it to the table beside the front window. It was a favorite spot of the old men in Split Creek, a nice place to share a cup of coffee and talk about the weather. It afforded a good view of the town too. She could see the false fronts of the half dozen businesses opposite and all the way down to the small chapel at the end of the road. She had a perfect view of the two strangers loitering across the street outside the saloon.

Keeping one eye on the men, she flipped idly through the magazine. The edges were tattered, the pages starting to yellow. It was two years old and these dresses could not possibly still be in style. Not in the Scraper cities anyway. She'd seen one of the gowns, with the high bustle and the scooped neck, on Lily at the dance hall last week. Lily'd needed ruffles, not that plunging neckline that did nothing but show everyone she was as flat-chested as a boy. Jane suspected the poor girl had tried stuffing her corset. It had seemed…lumpy. Pity. Lily was tall and slender with a lovely face. She should work to keep the focus there. Try something with clean lines and a higher neck, maybe a front bodice panel in a richer fabric like crushed velvet or a fine scarf.

Turning the page, she paused, her fingertip tracing the lines of the gown on the right. A few months ago when she'd gone with Haddy to fetch medical supplies from the supply transport, she'd seen a lady descend from the pilot's compartment. She must have been someone important to have talked her way onto a medical airship. Usually they were full of young men feeling dangerous to be so near the border. Armed to the teeth and looking around nervously as if a Reaper might spring out of the shadows at any moment, they'd strut through the yard while the ships were being unloaded, laughing too loud and trying not to gape at the Rangers.

But this woman… She'd stood there quietly, bold

as the brassy highlights in her piled hair, taking it all in with a poise that had drawn the eye of every person on the landing pad. When she saw Jane staring, she'd winked and strolled away, reboarding the ship with the rest of the crew and the rowdy lot of young sightseeing Scrapers. They'd all braved the border and were ready to head back up and report how crude and dirty the fort was. Boast to their friends over delicate china and cut crystal about the adventure. About how exposed they felt on the open plains. Never mind they'd been here for less than an hour and behind the fort walls the entire time. Jane'd seen one man bend and gather up a fistful of red dust then wipe his hands on his black trousers just to dirty them up. She imagined him stepping off the ship and taking his sweetheart in his arms—*There, there. Nothing but a little tumble, darling.* Scrapers.

Jane had hated that woman. Because she'd been able to step aboard that ship and fly away from their dirty little town but more so because she saw in that lovely, confident woman how life might have gone if things had been just a little different. If her parents had lived. If they'd been employed by a better man. If she hadn't had to run. If… So many *ifs* they'd bury you if you weren't careful.

The woman had been wearing a dress like this one, slim through the hips but without the bustle and the sleeves had been different too. The puffs at the shoulders not nearly as large. And the fabric a simple ice blue trimmed with white lace that formed a V between her breasts, small pearl buttons on her jacket from breastbone to waistline. So elegant. Jane looked at the plate critically. She might be able to modify this pattern to make something similar, in green maybe, a bright spring green that would be perfect once the weather turned warm again.

John's customer was leaving. She nodded to Mrs. Weber politely as she passed and a moment later John came up beside her.

"Can I help you with anything, Jane?"

She didn't feel comfortable pointing through the window and so she only lifted her chin. "Across the street there. Do you know who those two men are?"

"Are you looking for an introduction? I thought you had your hands full out at the fort."

She ignored the taunt. "They seem familiar but I can't quite place where I've seen them before."

John shrugged. "They look like any other ranchers to me."

"They've been standing in that same spot for the last hour."

John raised his bushy eyebrows. "You've been paying them an awful lot of attention for someone who's not interested."

"I'm not interested in them the way you're suggesting. I expected better of you, John." Though truly, she hadn't. Harley was a charmer but his son had unfortunately fallen a long way from the tree…and then rolled down the hill some. She turned to face him fully. "Speaking of that, I stopped to speak with your father this morning and he's having another one of his bad days."

He crossed his arms over his barrel chest and scowled. "I don't need you to tell me how to handle my father."

She stood up and slid the magazine across the table in his direction. It was time for her to go home. She was being silly. Bored and seeing trouble where there was none. "Just keep an eye on him. I worry about him."

Harley had more bad days than good lately. She was worried he might get confused and wander off in the wrong direction. Just because the Reapers would be migrating south soon didn't mean there weren't any dangers out there in the wilderness. "Good day, Mr. Hanson."

John inclined his head. "Miss Fisher."

The bell rang as she pulled open the door. Shaking her head, she stepped outside into the bright fall day. She glanced once more at the ranchers. She wished she could see their faces more clearly, but both men had thick beards. They wore dark, well-worn coats cut in a style that had been all the rage in the foothills five years ago. She'd lived in the foothills for several years before coming to Fort Dougan. She might have passed one of them by on the street.

There was another possibility though, one that sent a chill down her spine when the taller of the two men turned suddenly and started walking toward the side alley. The second glanced back over his shoulder in a shifty sort of way and then followed.

Why were they moving now? And in a hurry no less. The street was empty, the stores closing up as people went home for the noon meal. She waved at Lily who was leaning on the railing laughing at some story that Harley was telling her. And then she crossed the street. She would just walk past the alley and stop to adjust the tie on her shoe. See if she could get a closer look to set her mind at ease.

But when she got there, the strangers were already through to the back lane. After a moment's hesitation, she followed, wincing every time the gravel crunched beneath her feet. Listening for voices, she crept slowly down the alley. She stayed pressed to the shadows nearest the wall of the bathhouse, glad she hadn't made her dress from taffeta, which made a horrible rustle whenever you moved. But satin, that slid over skin silently. Much better for stalking, satin.

When she reached the end of the alley, there was only an old wagon with a nag in the traces. Some supplies in the back covered up by a moth-eaten blanket. Probably just flour and sugar. The kinds of things an outlying ranch would need to stock up on before winter blew in.

Only John hadn't recognized the men so they hadn't picked up their supplies at the general store. She was still pondering the puzzle of it all when a third man slipped out the back door and hauled himself onto the wagon to take his seat.

This one must have been inside the whole time the other two were waiting. When he turned his head, the light caught his profile and the sight caused her to suck in a mouthful of air. *Him* she'd never forget. The thick shoulders and the hard stubbled jaw. She recognized the scent of his tobacco wafting toward her on the breeze.

Her stomach cramped with the need to retch and she pressed her hand to her mouth as she cringed back against the wall. He lifted the reins and clucked his tongue to urge the team forward. Jane closed her eyes, her legs and thoughts frozen with the shock of seeing Reginald Potts here so near the border.

These men weren't strangers after all and whatever else they might be, they sure as hell weren't innocent ranchers.

FIVE

LYLE MADE LILY repeat the story for Cam because it didn't make a damned bit of sense to him. So far, what he'd been able to gather was that three men had come into town early to drag the blacksmith out of bed. They'd busted a wheel on the road and were willing to pay extra to have it repaired immediately. The men had waited, patiently by all accounts, for the wheel to be fixed and when it was ready, they went on their way. It wasn't such an unusual story, except for the part where Jane had raised an alarm calling them outlaws and then chased them out of town.

When Lily was through, Lyle shook his head. "Jane told you to go to the fort for help and then she followed these men—*the ones she told you were dangerous*—all on her own."

Lily winced but she didn't deny it. "She sent me to the fort with the message and she followed the wagon. There was no one else. Everyone able was over at the Gavins' place to help raise the barn. The patrol was out and all of the Rangers you left behind were on duty."

When he swore, Lily shifted uneasily. "She said they were from Columbus Junction. That they knew her and wouldn't hurt her even if they saw her."

Lyle bit back an answer, reminding himself for the hundredth time that this wasn't Lily's fault. "What did they look like?"

He struggled to rein in his temper as Lily gave her description. She'd gotten an intimate look at one of the men while they waited and she said he had tattoos running up one arm. Cards mostly, which likely meant gang. She said he was quiet, courteous as things went.

Cam fidgeted as she spoke, scowling in the direction Lily said they'd left town. Lyle caught his eye. "Do they sound familiar to you?"

Cam nearly growled. "Three men of middling height wearing old Scraper clothes, one with tattoos? Are you serious? Could be anyone."

"Why would men from Columbus Junction be down here?"

Cam shook his head. "Hell if I know."

"That's where Janie came from?"

"She came from Eyrion, but Columbus Junction is where she landed."

"The man Janie was mixed up with when you met her, was he—" He broke off when he saw Lily's wide eyes. He took her gently by the arm and turned her toward the inn, thanking her for her help. After releasing her into her sister's care, Lyle walked toward the rail where their horses were tied, away from prying ears.

Columbus Junction was held by Stormking, the city-state run by pirates and thieves. Most of the smuggling operations ran through there, shipping goods to the fortified ports and across the ocean. They also dealt in exotic goods in demand within the cities—women, opium. Last year the patrol had caught a group trying to round up Reapers for some kind of Roman gladiator-type entertainment they were planning. Idiots. They were lucky Lyle's team had found them when they had—their ship was lifting off with Reapers clinging to the ropes. They could have infected a whole damned city. If there were men from Stormking here on the border, they were up to no good.

Cam joined him. They'd been riding all day, trying to make it home before nightfall only to be intercepted on the road with the news that there was trouble in Split Creek. Cam was covered head to toe in dust, just as Lyle was. And he was just as ill-tempered so Lyle came straight to the point. "I was willing to respect your silence on Jane when it didn't matter. It matters now. I need the rest of the story."

"We're wasting time. We should be out there tracking them down."

Lyle knew that. He could feel the time slipping away, but he felt this was important too. There were too many pieces of the puzzle missing. "Talk."

Cam looked as if he might rebel, but then blew out a sharp breath and looked away, down the street at the people gathered in little knots, chewing over the day's excitement.

"When Jane lived in Columbus Junction, she belonged to a man named Gideon Moore. You've heard of him?"

"What do you mean *belonged* to him?"

"You know what I mean." Cam ran a hand through his hair. "It was after I knew her or I would have kept my hands off. She had a child."

For a long moment, Lyle couldn't take his meaning and then it all came together. The connection between Janie and Cam. What a beautiful woman from the city was doing working in the fort kitchen. Why Janie couldn't seem to let Cam go. For the second time that day, it felt as though the ground dropped out from under his feet. "*Your* child."

Cam gave him a mulish look before staring down at his boots. The silence stretched and Lyle had to fist his hands to keep from pummeling the story out of his friend. His voice dropped to a furious whisper.

"Janie had your child and you never thought to mention it?"

"What point was there? I never got the chance to see him." Cam rubbed the back of his neck. "I didn't go to Jane, not past that one night, and she never sent word that she was pregnant. After the baby was born, she moved up to Columbus Junction and got involved with Gideon. When things turned bad, she tried to leave but he went after her. She made it about a month on the run when the child, Samuel, took ill with a fever. It was the dead of winter and she was in the middle of nowhere. Gideon dragged her back. By then, she'd sent a letter to me asking for help. When I got there, Samuel was gone and Gideon had Janie chained to the water pipe in the corner of his room. I had to bring her back here." He looked up, eyes burning. "Who needed to know that story? You tell me."

Lyle couldn't speak right away. Rage swelled inside him at the image of Janie in chains, but he pushed that aside because his anger wasn't going to help anyone right now. "You should have said something."

"Dead is dead. Better to let it rest."

Lyle understood that as well and as deeply as Cam. He also knew that most times the dead didn't rest peacefully. "So Jane saw Gideon's men, alerted the fort and then went after them on her own. That's why she thought they wouldn't hurt her if she got caught? Because she expected them to recognize her too? I trust that about as much as I'd trust a hungry Reaper."

Cam swore. "I don't know why the hell she'd go after them alone."

Lyle didn't either but he intended to find out. And then he was going to tan her hide for being so reckless. He unlooped the reins from the post and drew Smudge around. "You get back to the fort and I'll follow Jane."

"I'm going with you."

"No," he said sharply. "You need to check the Reaper cure."

Even in the deepening twilight, Lyle could see Cam pale. "Damn it."

"The only thing valuable enough to draw Scrapers from Stormking to the border is our stock of serum. Hopefully they were only here to scope out the place. Check the stock. Take a fresh patrol and meet us at the ford. I'll track Janie along the river and meet you there whether I find her or not."

He rode out of town at a brisk pace but had to slow when he caught sight of the trail of bent grass leading off the road. Leaning over the neck of his horse, Lyle followed Janie's trail down along the river wondering why she hadn't stuck to the main road. Judging by the tracks she made, she'd been wearing ridiculous shoes for this sort of path. He was trying to stay clearheaded but it was a trial, imagining all the things that could happen to a pretty and defenseless woman alone in the wilderness. When the light began to fail, he dismounted.

His mind was full of the information Cam had given him too. He couldn't seem to shake that image of her, dirty and scared and grieving, chained to a pipe. Who the hell would do that to a person?

Jane chasing after Cam made sense now—though not good sense. She wanted Cam because she wanted a baby. Not any baby. Cam's baby. Clearly, she was hurting. But it made the kind of sense a broken heart might find solace in.

When he saw the gouge her heel had made in the soft bank, his stomach tightened. She'd crossed the river, balancing on those slime-covered rocks. Why? The wagon would have traveled on the road to the ford and you couldn't see the road from here.

Had she been hiding from the men and betting she could cut them off or had she been heading for an arranged meeting place? He couldn't discount the possibility out of hand. It wasn't a possibility he liked much but she might have decided to finally give up on Cam. If they had come for the serum, she could have helped them from the inside. Maybe she was buying herself a new life away from the fort.

Remounting, he crossed the river, pausing for a moment to study the ground on the far side. She hadn't been trying to conceal her passage and even in the half dark he could make out her path. This side of the river was wooded and the ground was covered with fallen leaves, damp from the rain last night. Her narrow, square-heeled shoes and long skirts had disturbed the matted fall and all he had to do was glance down every few seconds to make sure he was still on her trail.

Smudge's ears rotated forward just before full dark and Lyle reined him in. He couldn't hear anything ahead but he trusted his horse. Cam and the patrol would reach the ford soon. He should go to meet them but he had the gut feeling that he was close and a driving need to know that Janie was unhurt. If there was a fight and something did happen to her, he'd never forgive himself for having turned back now.

After a moment's indecision, he dismounted, grabbed his rifle from its scabbard and slung a belt loaded with extra ammo over his shoulder. It was getting too dangerous to continue on the horse anyway, at least until the moon came up in another hour. So he ground-tied Smudge and went ahead to investigate on his own.

Janie couldn't be too much farther ahead of him. She'd only been missing a few hours and she'd been on foot. He walked for less than a mile and then spotted the campfire. About a half mile distant, an orange glow that cut bright and black as he moved between the trees. Lyle's gut twisted and he swore softly. "Where are you, Janie?"

Chambering a round, he moved in for a closer look. About fifty feet away from the campsite, he nearly tripped over a lump on the ground. Jane was lying flat on her stomach in the dip of a sinkhole, her skirts stained. Who staked out an enemy camp in satin? His first instinct was to pull her back but he couldn't be sure she wouldn't fight him. So he dropped beside her and put his lips to her ear.

"What the hell do you think you're doing?"

She turned her head to glare at him and they were close enough that the light from the fire touched her face. Her eyes didn't look right. Narrowed and too bright. She looked unhinged and all the relief Lyle felt on finding her, on her not being involved in whatever mischief these men were up to vanished like smoke.

"They took the serum."

He'd hoped to be wrong about that, but couldn't say he was particularly surprised. If those men had the cure then he needed to recover it. Now. Before they passed it off to someone else or it got destroyed in a firefight.

"You need to get back," he said gently. "I'll take care of this one."

"I'm not going anywhere."

She stared fixedly ahead and he glanced toward the fire again. Two men. They weren't making much of an effort to be quiet.

"Where's the third?"

"Gone," she whispered. "Nearly an hour ago."

Good. That was good. Two he could handle on his own. But first he had to see Jane to safety. With an ache in his chest, he placed his lips to her ear and whispered. "I know about Gideon Moore. About Samuel. If you're looking for revenge, this is not the way to go after it."

She turned her head so quickly, her chin clipped the tip of his nose. "What?"

Most of her face was in shadow but there was enough light for him to see the way her eyes teared up. He wished he hadn't been able to see it.

"Lyle…" This time she was the one to lean forward to put her mouth to his ear. Her breath tickled his skin. "I don't know what you think you know but it doesn't matter. I recognized the man driving the wagon in town as one of Gideon's. But he was never one of the inner circle, just a hired hand. He could be working for anyone now. And the serum's gone. They had a light ship come pick it up. I didn't get here in time."

Hell. She'd seen trouble and chased right after it. He reminded himself that it would raise a ruckus if he tried to throttle her now. His breath locked in his lungs. She could have been killed. "Get here in time to do what?"

"To get a good look at who was flying it." Her voice

shook with rage, not fear. "The ship wasn't familiar. If I'd recognized the pilot then I'd be able to tell you for certain who was behind the theft. I've been listening to them talk, hoping they drop a name."

"It didn't occur to you to go to the fort and let us handle this?"

"It occurred to me."

He growled and she glanced his way, annoyed.

"I sent Lily to the fort and clearly you got the message. You're here. Now, be quiet."

Lyle grit his teeth. He badly wanted to argue with her but he'd have to settle for shooting someone. Reaching over to put a hand on the back of her head, he lowered her face below the dip of the earth. When she pushed back, he leaned in close and breathed. "Stay put."

He felt her body coil up like a spring but she stayed still and she kept her head down. As an afterthought he took one of his pistols and pressed it to her hand. "Only if I'm dead. The rest of the patrol will be here soon."

He heard the sound of horses on the bridge. The two men would hear them any second too. Whether they decided to run or fight, he had a better chance of taking them alive if he handled it alone. He waited until she nodded and then he crept away from her, circling about a quarter way around the camp. He didn't want Janie to be in the line of fire but he didn't want to drive these two right toward her either.

They were idiots, half-drunk and lounging around the fire. Their mounts were staked a good distance away and Lyle could see a rifle tossed on the ground near the saddlebags, well out of reach. He'd have to assume that they both had pistols too but he didn't plan to give them a chance to use them. Carefully taking aim, Lyle picked off the first while still hiding in the tree line, catching him in the right shoulder and spinning him to the ground. The other scurried back from his injured friend. He climbed to his feet as Lyle walked into the camp, reached for his pistol but fumbled his draw.

"Real slow. I need you to take that gun and toss it that way." Lyle gestured with his chin.

The outlaw stared wide-eyed at his friend, still alive but choking on his own blood. He must have hit lung. Sloppy.

"You killed him."

"And you stole from me. I don't take kindly to men who take what's mine. You're next unless you do what I say and start talking." Lyle kept the rifle level, his finger on the trigger and rage in his eyes. With unsteady hands, the man slowly reached for his pistol. Keeping his finger well away from the trigger, he tossed the weapon aside and then lifted his hands.

"I'll tell you whatever you want to know. But I didn't steal anything from you. I went into town for flour and seed. Paid good money for it too. Too much money. You'll find it in the wagon."

Lyle took three long strides forward and drove the butt of his rifle into the man's face. "Have a seat."

Sprawled in the dirt, with blood streaming from his nose, the outlaw yelled, "Check the wagon. There's nothing in there but our own supplies."

That's when Janie ran in. When the thief saw the pistol clutched tightly in her shaking hands, his eyes rounded in terror. Lyle would have been terrified too. She looked like a fresh-bit Reaper. Hair mussed and straggly. Dirt on her cheeks and streaks of black mud on her dress. Little bits of grass were stuck to her gown and in her hair.

Lyle swore. "I told you to stay put."

"He has another gun. A hammerless pistol he keeps tucked in his pants."

Which the bastard reached for as the words left her mouth. Lyle lunged forward, slashing his hand down in a stunning blow to the man's wrist. It slowed him down enough for Lyle to use his bigger body to pin him down while he ripped the small weapon from his hands. He elbowed him in the gut for good measure, then climbed to his feet and turned on Janie. "How the hell did you know what he had in his pants?"

"I used to be a seamstress. He had me sew in those pockets when I lived in Columbus Junction."

The thief's reaction was damning as hell. He looked straight at Janie, studying her and then his face turned an odd shade of green. "Jane?"

"Reginald," she said. "Last time we met, this went a bit differently, didn't it? I've got the gun this time."

The man went cross-eyed staring at the barrel Janie shoved in his face. Carefully, moving slowly, Lyle put a hand to her shoulder and pulled her back. "We don't get the serum back if you shoot him."

"His name is Reginald Potts. He used to run with the Moore gang but that was several years ago and his kind will hire out to anyone." She narrowed her eyes at Potts. "Who are you working for now?"

Potts swallowed hard and then turned to Lyle for help. "I don't know what she's talking about. I might have gotten into some trouble in the past but I'm just a rancher now. Bought a plot twenty miles north, by the bend in the river. You need to take that thing away from her before someone gets hurt."

"I'm not the one who's going to get hurt," Lyle said. "I suggest you answer the lady's question."

With a grimace, Potts turned back to Janie. "Jane… I'm sorry for what happened to you and yours, truly I am. It's why I left. A lot of us did. Gideon went too far and we all knew it. But your quarrel is with him, not me. I was only following orders and I never laid a hand on you. You don't need to do this."

"You dragged me back to him," she said. "If we'd waited just a few days, Samuel would have been well enough to travel. I begged you."

It was clear that Potts understood exactly what she was talking about. Maybe even agreed with the accusation. It was clear, too, that the shrill note to her voice alarmed Potts greatly. As much as Lyle sympathized with Jane, he couldn't take a chance that she would slip and pull that trigger.

He didn't think she was as far gone as she appeared but it wasn't all an act, either. She was pissed as hell and he was glad not to be the one looking down the barrel of her gun. Despite appearances to the contrary, he'd bet money she wasn't going to kill their only way to track the serum. He'd bet everything. All-in, on Jane.

Letting his voice fall into an easy drawl, he said, "The lady asked you a question and it would be rude not to answer. You're new to the area so you might not know but we take manners very seriously down here. Who are you working for?"

Potts managed to draw his eyes away from the gun in Janie's hands long enough to say, "She's crazy."

Lyle shrugged, seeing no reason to correct him.

Potts's thick lips pressed together so hard they all but disappeared behind a fringe of whiskers. This close, Lyle could smell the stench coming off him—fear, piss and alcohol. Blood too. From the dead man lying to the other side of the fire. Squatting down so he could look the outlaw in the face, he said, "This is the border, Mr. Potts. There's no cell waiting at the end of this road, not even a hangman's noose. Do you know how we punish men who hurt women and children down here?"

Potts glared murder, but he was scared. Almost scared enough. All he needed was a little push. "I didn't hurt anybody."

Lyle let the moment stretch, keeping his gaze fixed on the prisoner. "You did. You hurt Jane and your actions may have caused the death of her son. But we're not talking about that right now. We're asking about the Reaper cure you stole from us. Who sent you to take it and where it is now? If you don't start talking, we're riding south. First group of Reapers we come across, I put a bullet in your gut. Fresh blood draws them in like flies to shit. They won't even stop to make sure you're dead before they start feeding. We clear?"

Satisfied with the way Potts's expression slackened a moment before he regained control of himself, Lyle stood. "Now answer the lady."

"Ah, hell." A droplet of sweat ran down his cheek and fell from his jaw into the dirt. Baby-killer or no, Potts had enough of a sense of shame that he couldn't look Janie in the face as he began to speak. Just stared down at his black-stained hands. "Gideon set it up. We were headed for the noose but he cut us a deal. We grab the crates while the patrol was out and bring them here.

That was the job. They were picked up by a ship but I don't know where they took it."

"What does Gideon want with the cure? Reapers never climb that high into the mountains."

"I don't know the answer to that. I get paid not to ask those kinds of questions."

When Lyle stepped forward, Potts's eyes went so wide, Lyle could see a ring of white all the way around the irises. He pressed his back into the rock and held up both hands.

"I don't know why he wanted it," he said. "Probably someone offered him enough money to make stealing it worth his while. He doesn't keep half the stuff he steals, just passes it along."

Potts turned his head when he finally heard the horses approaching. By the sound of it Cam had roused half the fort. Lyle looked at the dead man in disgust. Cam would give him hell for not waiting but he hadn't wanted to take the chance he'd lose both of these men in a shoot-out. Fat lot of good it did him—Potts likely knew more than he was telling them, but not much. A lowlife doing grunt work. And the cure gone. It was a heavy blow.

He gestured with his rifle for Potts to stand and it took the man two tries before he could get his shaking legs under him. Grabbing Potts by the shoulder, Lyle pushed him in the direction of the wagon. He'd strap him in the back and then he'd ride on the bench with Jane, have someone fetch Smudge for him.

As soon as he stepped away from the fire, the chill air raised the goose bumps on his bare forearms. He was cold but Janie had to be *freezing*. She was wearing a satin dress for God's sake, and a short-sleeved one at that. The temperature dropped quick this time of year after nightfall. He wished he had a coat to offer her but he'd left his behind with Smudge. He wished he could put an arm around her shoulders and draw her against his body, pull her into a warm soft bed and sleep for the next forty-eight hours. Well…maybe not sleep all that time.

Wishing was all he'd ever had where Jane was concerned.

As if she felt his eyes on her, she turned her head. "We should just kill him and go after the ship. It was small, not spec'd for the higher altitudes. There's no way they'll make Stormking in it. Columbus Junction would be a good stop."

"How do you know so much about airships?"

"Growing up in the city you get to know the basics and a friend of mine flew a ship that size. I picked up a lot from him too." The frown on her face deepened, suggesting there was more to the story. He didn't ask for more. There'd be time for that conversation later. Jane didn't confide things about herself easily. He strongly suspected he was going to have to press her for the answers he needed and he did not relish the prospect.

"We'll discuss our options when we get back to the fort," he said. "We need supplies. Hell, I don't even know where Columbus Junction is."

He didn't like the way her eyes shuttered. He didn't like the terrible coldness that settled over her expression. She walked three steps in silence before she said quietly, "I know exactly where it is."

"THEY CLEANED US OUT." Doc threw an empty crate against the wall of the dirt cellar and cursed again.

"We only had six crates of the stuff. It'll take us the rest of the winter to replace it."

And every town along the border was anxiously awaiting their promised delivery. Best of times, it was a slow-going process. The captain demanded they test every batch before it went out which meant even after it was produced, they needed to monitor the injected Reapers for a few weeks to make sure it was good. And now Welks was dragging his feet on production because he wanted more money.

Lyle ran a hand through his hair. "Come on."

Doc followed him up the stairs and past the stout door with the iron lock still hanging from the frame. It was nearing midnight and it was dark, the yard quiet. Out of habit he searched out the watchers on the walls to make sure they were in place and awake. The thieves had come in through the front gate with a delivery of food stores. Haddy had taken the shipment and everything was exactly as she'd ordered it. Nothing to raise her suspicion there. The men had accepted the offer to stay the night, which was common. Sometime before dawn, they'd disabled the guard, picked the lock to the storage cellar and cleaned them out. When it came time to switch guards, one of the Rangers found Ben tied and gagged in the locked room. By the time the Rangers pried the door open and figured out what happened, it was nearly noon. By then, Lily had come to the fort with her cryptic message and riders were sent out to notify the returning patrol and search the surrounding roads.

One of those scouts spotted the fleeing airship, flying low to the tree line and heading for the mountains. He located the camp but had to return to the fort for backup. Bad luck. Bad timing all around.

Lyle glanced at Doc. "How is Ben doing?"

"Has a knot on the back of his head and he's steaming pissed but he'll be fine in a day or two. Are you going to punish him?"

Hell. "I'm going to have to."

Their boots echoed hollowly as they climbed the porch steps to Cap's office. A dim light shone through the curtained window at the front of the building. Lyle pushed open the door and Jane looked up immediately, coffee cup half raised to her mouth. Lyle had expected to find her in tears and he'd braced himself for that. But her gaze, while intent, was extraordinarily calm. Lovely and haunted. He'd always thought her beautiful, copper-red hair and pale skin with a smattering of freckles. Dark eyes tipped at the corners like a cat's and the sweetly bowed mouth he'd always wanted to taste. Even exhausted and bedraggled, she was a sight to see.

Lowering her cup to her lap, she gave him a slight nod which he returned before moving forward. Cam straightened from his perch on the edge of the big wooden desk that took up most of the room. Lyle crossed the room as Doc closed the door behind them.

"They didn't have inside help," Lyle said to Cam's questioning look. "They picked the lock, cleared us out and apparently only stopped in town because the wheel on the wagon started to crack. Leonard patched it in less than an hour and they were on their way before the guard changed."

Cam hitched his hip on the desk again. "It took them a while to get the lock on the cellar open—Welks didn't want to turn over the key—but the patrol was ready to ride out when I got here."

"We need to work on our response time and start searching every wagon that goes in or out of the fort."

"We need to track down the people who stole the cure and get it back," Cam snapped.

"That too." Lyle rubbed his forehead. "Welks says if he has to work from scratch starting with blood samples, it'll take twice as long to restock. They took everything except for the one sample that Minerva was working on in the lab and he's not sure it'll be enough to start a new batch."

He eyed the big chair behind the desk and wished Cap was here to handle this mess. It didn't seem right to sit there right now, so he leaned against the desk instead, positioning himself between Cam and Janie.

Doc pulled up another chair and sat down with a sigh, stretching out his legs and crossing them at the ankle. "So what now? We've got a skeleton crew as it is. A pen full of Reapers and no cure. We can't afford to send a patrol into the foothills to start some kind of gang war."

"We can't afford to lose the cure either," Cam said. "It's nearly winter. The Reapers will migrate south soon. I say we go in force to take back our serum."

"Reapers haven't left yet." Doc scowled. "This last attack was the second near Webster this month."

"A patrol wouldn't do you any good anyway," Jane said quietly. Lyle caught the sour look that crossed Cam's face when Jane spoke.

By Jane's expression, she'd seen it too. "Gideon Moore is the sheriff of Columbus Junction. It's not a border town. It's a Scraper city under the protection of Stormking. You have no jurisdiction there, Lieutenant."

"If Moore was behind this theft, then I say we do."

"So you'll go in guns blazing?" She lifted her chin. "While Cap is up on Eyrion trying to make sure you have the funding and support you need to distribute the cure?"

"Right now there's no cure to distribute."

"Gideon has half the men in that town deputized and they're all loyal to him. Or terrified of him. He won't go down without a fight and there are a lot of families in Columbus Junction to consider too. They're not all outlaws there."

Lyle frowned. "Those families are Gideon's responsibility, not mine. He should have considered that before he stole from us." As soon as he said it, he wished the words back. Feeling a blush climb up his neck, he said, "I don't want anyone innocent to get hurt, but we need that serum back."

Cam shook his head. "Are we sure they're Gideon's men?"

"The one we caught said so. Jane recognized the third who left with the ship, so I'd say yes. Gideon is involved. Though why someone living in the mountains wants the cure so bad is beyond me."

"Money," Doc suggested. "There's bound to be a black market for the stuff. Because Gideon is one of those men who lives in fear of being bitten? For the status of it. Hell, maybe he wants to expand his operation down on the plains. The cure is valuable. It was only a matter of time before someone put a price on it and we should have protected it better."

Lyle gripped the edge of the table and lowered his head for a moment, absorbing that like a blow. *He* should have protected it better. This had happened on his watch. "Yeah, I know that. And we'll fix what we can but what I want to know now is—how do I get it back?"

The room became so quiet Lyle could hear the sound of the moth beating itself on the glass surrounding one of the lanterns.

"I'll go."

He raised his head and locked his eyes on Jane. "No."

Stretching forward, she set her coffee cup on the edge of the desk and sat back in the wooden chair. "I know the town. I know Gideon. I'll be able to track down the serum, or at least find out what he knows about it."

"You barely made it out of Columbus Junction alive last time," Cam said sharply. "You're not going back."

"You can't keep me here."

"The hell I can't."

Jane's eyes went flinty. "Are you going to lock me up too? Don't pretend to care about what happens to me."

Lyle's mind had stopped working on the word "too," remembering what Cam had said about Gideon chaining Janie to a pipe. Fighting to stay calm himself, he was too slow to stop Cam from saying something stupid.

"I won't. I've never pretended about anything. If someone is stupid enough to chase down their own death, I won't kill myself trying to stop them."

She flinched, her whole body tightening as if bracing for the next blow. Cam crossed his arms over his chest and leaned forward. "That doesn't mean I *want* you to die. And I'm not locking you up. I sure as hell wouldn't do that to you."

Lyle wrapped a hand around Cam's arm and hauled him back. Not that he thought Cam would do anything to hurt Jane, not physically, but she didn't need Cam hammering at her with words either.

"Leave her be."

Cam glared. "I'll go to Columbus Junction. I know Gideon well enough and it's past time we had a reckoning."

"I thought you didn't believe he had anything to do with Samuel's death," Jane said.

This time Cam was the one to flinch. Lyle could feel the muscle beneath his palm go hard as a rock. "I don't. Accidents happen, Jane. All sorts. You trust in the wrong kind of people and you're bound to get hurt."

Jane's eyes narrowed. "You don't have to tell me that."

Lyle slapped his free hand on the desk. "Enough. You two can't be civil for longer than two minutes at a stretch." A wonder they hadn't killed each other while they waited for him and Doc.

Cam pointed. "That's why she should stay behind."

Jane started to rise from her chair but Lyle waved her down. She sat with a *hmph* and fixed her glare on Cam. "You've been calling me a liar, calling me crazy for the last year but you know that I'm not."

"I never called you any of those things."

"You let everyone believe it." Her voice shook but her spine was straight as a rod. "That I was nothing but a love-struck whore who followed you home."

Cam made a slicing motion with his arm. "How far is it from the truth? You wanted me to fuck you until you had another baby." The blood drained from Jane's face and Cam shook his head. "You can't replace a *person*, Jane."

"I hate you." The words ripped from her throat and

Lyle wanted to go to her. He glanced at Cam, the rock set of his jaw, the color flagging his cheeks and then over at Doc whose head rested against the back of his chair. His eyes were closed as if he could block out this conversation, not bear witness to these two people ripping their bloody hearts out and throwing the ruined pieces at each other. Lyle wished he could block it out too but he hesitated to stop them. From what he could tell, this conversation was long overdue.

Cam stared at her for a long time. "You still blame Gideon for what happened to Samuel. This isn't about you wanting to find out what happened to the serum. This is you wanting to find a way to punish Gideon and you plan to use Lyle to do it."

"No," Jane said. "I want to help get the serum back and if that hurts Gideon then good. If I'd wanted revenge, I'd have gone after him sooner than this."

"You wouldn't be able to keep your emotions out of it. It's too dangerous."

"She wouldn't be going alone," Lyle said quietly.

Doc opened his eyes and sat up, giving Lyle an "are you crazy?" look. Cam made it a matching set. He was surely going to regret this but there were so few options and none of them were any good.

Lyle turned to face Cam. "You're staying here until the captain returns. Janie knows that town and the people in it better than you do. Not just Gideon but the ones who might be willing to help us."

"You stay here then," Cam said. "And I'll take her with me."

Lyle raised his brows. "One or the other of you would not survive that trip. I don't for a second believe you two could work together. I'll go. The missing serum is my fault. My responsibility. You work with the scientists to replace what we lost. Don't run any patrols unless you have to. I'll send word if it looks like we'll need help." He glanced down to where Jane sat regarding him with an inscrutable look. "Is all of this okay by you? Be sure about it, Janie."

Before Cam could come up with another protest, Jane stood up, smoothing her skirts in an automatic gesture before turning for the door. "I'll pack my things."

Lyle couldn't judge how shaken she was. He wanted some reassurance that he was making the right decision by accepting her help, but all he saw was a slender woman, a seamstress with a flair for fashion and bigger balls than he had. He'd survived as a Ranger for a long time by trusting his instincts. His instincts told him Jane could handle this. No point in doubting them now.

After the door closed behind her, Cam stood up and got in his face. "Are you out of your mind, Lieutenant?"

"It's a solid plan," Lyle said. "If *your* emotions weren't tied up in it, you'd see that."

"My emotions? You're shitting me. I'm the only one with a clear head here."

"As little as I like putting Jane in harm's way, she's our best shot at getting the serum back. There's no way you can two partner up without someone ending with a bullet in their head. Probably you. I'll go. She trusts me."

"She's using you."

Doc's chair scraped as he stood up. "Well, boys, this is good night for me. Try not to hurt each other too bad. We can't afford to lose anyone else and I'm not patching anyone up until morning."

Lyle took Doc's departure as a blessing. He never

had a problem sharing his opinions so if he was ducking out now it meant he thought Lyle had made the right decision.

Cam didn't even wait for the door to close. "You're going to abandon your post?"

Lyle walked around the table to get some distance and then dropped into the captain's chair. If he was going to make the hard decisions, at least his ass could be comfortable while he was doing it. "This is not a desertion. I'm taking care of a problem. You're just as capable as I am of managing things here."

"I'm just as capable of tracking down the cure, with or without Jane's help. She wants to hurt Gideon and I get that. You think I don't fucking get that? But she's not thinking straight and neither are you."

Lyle sucked at his cheek as he chewed that over in his mind. Cam could be a hothead. He often jumped to conclusions but that didn't mean he wasn't right. It was annoying, actually, how often Cam hit things spot-on.

Cam set his fists on the edge of the desk and leaned in. "You belong here and I don't want Jane in danger. She's my responsibility. This whole thing is—"

"Janie is not your responsibility." They both started at the strength of that declaration. The silence that followed was damned uncomfortable. Lyle bit back a curse and steadied his tone. "The cure was stolen on my watch. If she can help me get it back—and I think she can—then I'm taking her up on that offer. If you go hunting, it makes perfect sense to take someone familiar with the terrain and your prey."

Cam pushed off the desk and began to pace. "The Moore gang is behind most of the black market trade on the mountains. Opium. Women. And Janie—" Cam fixed him with a look that could tan leather. "—doesn't fucking belong there. It's too dangerous for her to go back. She was Gideon's girl and he doesn't like to lose. You know she doesn't give a rat's ass about the cure. Whatever she might have said, she wants revenge."

Lyle remembered Janie lying in the dry grass staring at that campfire, hoping to hear a scrap of information. The white of her knuckles as she gripped the gun and pointed it at the outlaw. She was still tied to that town and those people. To Cam too. Maybe going back to Columbus Junction would help put the past behind her. Right now, she was like a raw and bleeding wound and he couldn't leave her like that. He didn't want her at risk but she knew what she was walking into better than he did.

"Janie wants to help. That's the bottom line. She's smart, capable and a woman grown."

Cam stopped pacing to stare him down. "You just want in between her thighs. I thought you cared about her. This is dangerous."

Lyle's hand started to curl into a fist but he forced it flat. "We live on the border. Getting out of bed in the morning is dangerous. I'll see her home safely."

"You see that you do."

SIX

Satin gloves, Abby snorted. Of what possible use could they be? They wouldn't protect your hands for rope work, couldn't possibly keep you warm. All they did was snag on her calluses and make her look like a fool. Everything about the ship seemed designed to draw attention to the fact she didn't belong up here.

She smoothed her hands over the slippery red satin of her skirts and then clasped them together when Jake turned around. He stood on the far side of the large cabin, holding a drink. The light glinted off the finely cut crystal as he raised it to his mouth. When he saw her, he went completely still. For the space of several heartbeats, he remained frozen in place. She couldn't help but smile at his reaction and that seemed to snap him out of it.

Setting his glass aside, he stepped toward her, leaving the airship captain's mouth hanging open midsentence. When Captain Reyes saw what had so captured Jake's attention, he closed his mouth with a snap and gave Abby a stiff nod. Reyes wasn't a bad sort for a Scraper. An elderly gentleman who'd been flying this route more than forty years, he was still trim-bodied and sharp-eyed. Her opinion of him had softened considerably when he'd deigned to converse with Jake even after it became widely known that Jake was a cured Reaper.

Her former Reaper of a husband cut directly through

another conversation to reach her, his attention never flickering from his prey. Her. The look on his face was one she'd only seen when they were alone. The bones in his cheeks, the line of his jaw seemed particularly sharp. There was a slight flush to his dark skin and his eyes were narrowed. To anyone else, he might seem angry. The Scrapers certainly seemed to think so. They stepped back as he passed, their conversation turning hushed and furtive. But Abby knew Jake wasn't angry. That wasn't it. Useful stuff, satin, after all.

"You're wearing a dress."

Something she hadn't done since their wedding day. If she'd have known it would have this effect on him, she would surely have worn one sooner. His gaze swept down her body, leaving a trail of fire in its wake. She looked down too, heat rising to her cheeks.

"To be honest, I wasn't sure you'd even recognize me in this getup." She waved a hand toward the door. "The maid said I needed to dress for dinner and apparently Cap arranged to put this in my rooms."

She caught the odd expression that flashed over his features and frowned up at him. "It was you, wasn't it? Not Cap?"

She couldn't even say why she was hurt by that, but it stung. Before she could place her hands on her hips, he caught one of them and brought it to his lips. It was hardly an intimate gesture. She was wearing the damned gloves, for heaven's sake, but it felt as if they were standing naked among strangers. It always felt that way when Jake touched her. As if it woke up every tiny part of her body.

"I knew about it," he said, giving her fingers a gentle squeeze. "Cap mentioned he'd ordered appropriate clothes for us to wear for the meetings we had to attend. I had the maid take them from the trunk, but I didn't see them first. I never imagined…"

"That he'd put me in this." Her heart beat a little more heavily. "I know. I look ridiculous."

"Stunning, Abby. You look stunning." He lowered his voice. "If we didn't have to dine with the rest of the ship, I'd take you back to our rooms now and find out exactly what's going on beneath those skirts that makes them flare out like that."

She elbowed him and he grunted softly. "Behave yourself."

"Or?"

"I'll come up with something."

He glanced down. "You're not wearing your guns."

There'd been no place to put them. Cap joined them then, sparing her the need to reply. His bulk blocked the light from the chandelier behind him. She'd never seen him look so imposing. Black hair and beard neatly clipped. The wool suit he wore smelled faintly of sandalwood and spice. He smiled at her and his dark eyes glittered with repressed amusement. "My, don't you look lovely tonight, Abigail."

"As do you, Captain." She smiled. "If I didn't know better, I'd think you a born Scraper."

His smile thinned a bit and only belatedly did she realize he'd take that as an insult. "I didn't mean…" Well, crap. How did she mean it?

Waving his hand to dismiss her apology, he turned his body so that his back was no longer to the room. "Would you like something to drink? The bourbon is excellent although I believe we'll be heading into dinner soon, so perhaps something lighter?"

"There's a dining room on board the ship?" Startled, she looked around the cabin. Polished wood walls. Chandeliers powered by gaslight. Chandeliers, on what was basically a big floating wagon. Just a way to get from one place to another. "I thought surely they would just drag the tables in here. How many rooms *are* there?"

"They're not carrying cargo," Jake said, taking a sip of whiskey that made his mouth tighten. "The entire ship is designed purely for comfort. The engine's below but this floor is filled with private parlors and sleeping quarters. Reyes told me the kitchen is primitive because of the concern for fire but I imagine it'll still beat anything we could find in the mess hall."

She snorted. "Sure beats cooking over a campfire."

"I doubt any of the people here would appreciate the comparison."

There were a dozen Scrapers in the cabin—two servants, the captain, four boisterous young men returning from their first trip into border territory and already half-drunk. The other five she didn't recognize but judging by the looks of them, they were either council members on their way to the assembly or wealthy citizens from Eyrion heading home.

Her gaze rested on a thickset man who stared fixedly back at her. Perfectly groomed. Balding. His trimmed mustache only partially concealed the sneer directed her way. She'd never seen him before in her life but he seemed to have taken a dislike to her already. Tipping her head, she asked, "Who is that one?"

"Jonas Slater," Jake answered, scowling at poor Jonas until he looked away. "He's from the eastern range. Cold Mountain. They're poor, overpopulated and far enough south they see Reaper attacks at least once a year. He's a very vocal opponent of the fort tax. Would you like an introduction?"

"No." Slater didn't look like anyone Abby would care to know better. "If he's seen a Reaper attack firsthand, why on earth would he oppose the fort tax?"

"I didn't say he'd personally witnessed a Reaper attack. His people were attacked, but at the lower elevations. His territory can't afford the tax but current law requires they pay in the same portion as Eyrion."

"Poor is better than dead."

"Slater's plan is to disband the forts and then hire some of the out of work Rangers to serve as guards. And he wants us to hand over the secret to making the cure too."

"Good luck to him prying it out of Welks's head."

"I mentioned that," Jake said. "He didn't seem to think it would be much of a problem."

"It's almost tempting to hand Welks over." Her lips curled in a small smile. "When did you learn all this?"

Jake's soft breath of laughter stirred her hair. "I've been waiting for you to finish dressing for some time."

The gown had been a bitch to get into. Putting a corset on was like trying to hog-tie *yourself.* It was on the tip of her tongue to complain about it, but Cap was standing right beside her now and she didn't think he'd appreciate the comment. "What else did I miss?"

Cap answered. "Slater doesn't have a great deal of influence."

"So we don't have to worry about him."

Cap's brows rose slightly. "I wouldn't say that exactly, but no. He is not my biggest concern."

"Who is?"

"Here? Rosenthal from the eastern council, representing Alleghania. Bellamy from the west. Karst is always difficult but he doesn't have much influence. The most powerful delegates are already on Eyrion."

"We have the cure in hand," she said. "Do we really need their approval?"

Cap looked down at her then, a frown pinching his brows. "It's why we're here, Abby."

"It's *one* reason we're here. Bottom line? I don't care which way they vote. It doesn't change what we have to do."

"You ought to care. They pay your wages."

Cap looked over her head at Jake for support, but Jake only shrugged. "I'm with Abby. Parade me in front of whoever you need to, but I came for Williams's head."

Cap didn't like that one bit. He settled a glare first on Jake and then her. "The relationship between the Rangers and the city-states has always been a partnership."

"Until they went after the forts," Abby said.

Cap's frown deepened. "There's more than one way to take down a fort, Abby. You remember that."

If they hadn't been surrounded by Scrapers, she might have argued with him. But this wasn't the time or place. She wasn't about to question his authority when they were surrounded by the enemy. She turned away from his fierce look.

Cap had wanted Jake along for the ride as proof that the serum worked and she'd only agreed to come because someone had to watch their backs. Now, she wondered if she'd done the right thing. She was no diplomat, that was for damn sure. She didn't belong in a place like this. Didn't belong in these clothes or with any of these people.

As if he knew the direction of her thoughts, Jake's palm brushed the curve of her waist and settled on her hip, a warm and comforting weight. He didn't say anything, just exerted a small pressure so that her leg leaned up against his. Sometimes she couldn't tell if he was taking comfort from her or giving it. Mostly, she supposed it didn't matter.

The door opened and another of the crew entered, wearing the dark green livery that was finer than anything she owned. Abby shifted her weight, thinking they were being called in to dinner but rather than make an announcement, the man held the door open for a woman to enter. Tall and stunningly beautiful, she wore a gown that even Abby recognized as the height of fashion. If it wasn't, this woman would make it so as soon as the Scrapers in the capital set eyes on her.

Midnight-blue silk wrapped her torso like a second skin, outlining a narrow but well-proportioned figure. The material flared out around her hips before draping down in a simple fall of unadorned material. It wasn't flashy. None of the feathers or trim Abby had seen other Scrapers wear, though the neckline was lower than what was considered acceptable down in the border territories. A single diamond the size of a half dollar had been pinned to the lowest point, between and just above her breasts, nestled in her bosom as gently as a robin's egg in its nest.

The woman stepped forward enough for the crewman to close the door behind her but then paused, her gaze sweeping unhurriedly about the room. When she lit upon Abby, her brows lifted slightly before moving on. Dark skin, dark eyes and black hair that had been brushed to a shine before being pulled up in a style so elaborate it would have been impossible for her to accomplish on her own. Clearly, the woman had servants to help her with her grooming. But then again, maybe Scraper women had joints that worked differently from normal people.

The room had fallen silent. Two men split away from their groups to join her but she finished her sweep of the room before focusing her attention on either of them.

"*Españoles*?" Abby looked to Cap for confirmation.

"Yes. Her family stayed in Nueva España after the plague struck, retreating into the mountains. Santa Ana. You've heard of it?" She nodded. None of the northern cities had ever fallen to Reaper attack but over the past two centuries several of the cities of Nueva España had been destroyed, the most recent was Santa Ana, and that two generations ago. "They managed to flee before the attack." He lowered his voice conspiratorially. "Legend has it their ships were so loaded with gold they had to toss some of the crew overboard just to clear the foothills."

Abby had heard that legend before. It was one of Doc's favorites. "She's a Tirado."

Cap nodded. "Maricel Tirado. Head of the family since Sebastian's death, though there are rumors that may be challenged."

"Because she's a woman."

Cap's eyes tracked Maricel as she gracefully made her way through the crowd. "You know how they are here."

"As if you don't think the same."

He shrugged. "I'm curious to see if she can hold the position. I expect not, but I wouldn't mind being proven wrong." His smile was brief. "It won't be the first time. Don't look at me like that. I don't wish her to fail."

"You wouldn't lift a finger to help her though either, would you?"

"You have to see the world as it is to have any hope of changing it. Maricel Tirado's fight is not my fight."

She shook her head. "You've been spending too much time with Doc lately. You're starting to sound just like him."

Jake frowned. "The Tirados settled on Ballonet with the rest of the shipping families, didn't they?"

Abby nodded. "They did. I thought Farley was the Ballonet representative."

Cap's eyes widened in surprise. "You *were* listening during the briefing."

"I always listen. I just don't always happen to agree with you."

"Maricel can't sit on the council. She's not descended from a founding family, another strike against her." Cap finished off his glass of whiskey and set it aside. "She does own the ship, though, along with half of Ballonet."

And she certainly owned the attention of every man in the room. Abby wasn't sure whether to be jealous or impressed. The sound of the dinner bell saved her from having to choose.

ABBY WAS SEATED beside Karst, much to her consternation. Karst was the councilman representing Koln, the poorest territory on the western range, where most of the mills and slaughterhouses were located. Koln had never been much of a friend to the people on the border, possibly because they lived so close and had to look down on someone. Cap was to the right of the Tirado woman and while he seemed to be at his charming best, he kept casting warning looks in Abby's direction. Jake was positioned directly across from her. He didn't like crowds, even as small as this one, and he'd withdrawn into himself.

With a delegate on one side of him and one of the youngsters on the other, Jake remained silent unless someone asked him a question. He listened though. She was willing to bet he was tracking most of the conversations taking place up and down the length of the table. His mouth lifted when Karst brought up the subject of the mills.

It brought a grimly amused smile to her lips too. Especially when he suggested that moving the mills to the foothills was done for the sake of the forts…so Rangers didn't have to station guards there. "You didn't do that for our sake," she told him. "You're squeezing the farmers and ranchers."

Karst drew back from her, apparently repelled by her bluntness when everyone else within earshot had simply nodded at his dumbass comment. "Three mills lost in the space of five years. The slaughterhouse at Howardsville completely abandoned. That represents a significant financial loss."

"More than money was lost in those attacks," she reminded him.

He sniffed. "Of course. But that is exactly my point. It's not safe on the plains. Much better to move the facilities north or higher into the mountains."

"Beyond the reach of the average farmer who needs to count on you for transportation. Now you have all these middlemen—"

"There were always middlemen."

Did he think she was stupid? "There are more of them now, squeezing every bit of profit out."

"Someone needs to move the goods. Production was up this year."

"And prices are dropping. You're still cutting terraces into the mountains even though there's no need for them now that we have a cure."

His brows rose. "I'll tell you what we no longer have a need for now that we have a cure. Rangers."

Too late, Abby realized that conversation around the table had ground to a halt as everyone honed in on them. Karst's pronouncement dropped into the middle of the quiet room like a pebble in a still lake. A ripple of hushed response followed it and then stilled.

She drew in a deep breath. But before she could answer, Jake spoke. "I don't think that you realize how many Reapers there are, Mr. Karst."

"Surely you don't think things can continue as they have been."

Jake was unmoved by Karst's obvious spite. "That's why we're here. To discuss the repercussions. To choose a plan to move forward."

"The local sheriffs can stock the serum and inject the infected immediately rather than waiting for the Rangers to show up."

"The men," Abby said, pausing as attention shifted her way. "The men can be injected and maybe saved. The women still die as soon as they're bitten. The cure's a wonderful thing but it can't fix dead."

Most of the Scrapers ignored the comment, seemingly annoyed with her bad manners at bringing up such an unpleasant fact. The Tirado woman held her gaze for a moment and then gave a slight nod of approval.

Karst waved a dismissive hand. "Of course, there will still be a need for the star-marked for the foreseeable future. To guard the food supply and protect the towns. We can begin to reclaim the lost mines and—"

Bellamy, an older man with jowls and a perpetually flushed face, leaned forward to cut Karst off. "This is precipitous. I've seen no evidence that a cure even exists. Even if it does, who among us truly believes that a Reaper, *a flesh-eating monster*, can truly be redeemed?"

This time, everyone looked at Jake who silently endured the scrutiny for several moments before speaking. "I assure you, councilman. Rumors of the cure were not exaggerated in the least. The serum works."

"We've no one to vouch for your previous condition. By all accounts, you acted as any other man before the cure was administered."

Abby bristled, but Jake remained still. A heavy stillness that should have alarmed the Scrapers. They regarded him curiously awaiting his response.

"I was infected for a long time. It took more than a century before I was able to fight the parasite for control of my body. Decades to gain the kind of restraint I needed to work with the Rangers. Right now, there aren't very many sentient Reapers out there. The longer you wait to distribute the cure, the greater their numbers will be. And the more difficult it will be to eliminate them."

Bellamy raised his brows. "Perhaps we should simply wait for some of the older Reapers to regain sentience. If they're able to control themselves and the younger Reapers then the problem takes care of itself."

Abby had to bite her tongue not to speak. Jake shot Karst a disgusted look. "Sentient Reapers pose more of a threat to you, not less. That they're able to control themselves doesn't mean they will."

"According to you."

Jake shook his head. "You don't have to take my word for it. Any of your scientists will corroborate my story."

Bellamy opened his mouth to speak again but Miss Tirado placed a slender hand on his forearm to forestall him.

"Please," she said, in a rich voice with just the slightest hint of an accent. "This is neither the time nor place for this discussion. The assembly meets in less than a week." Her gaze swept the table. "Perhaps it's best to save the debate until then."

ABBY STOPPED WALKING as a man separated himself from the shadows. Tall for a Scraper male but just as bulky as the others. Overfed, the lot of them. Like cattle raised for the slaughter. This one was in his prime, with a straight back and thick blond hair smoothed neatly back from a high forehead. She'd been introduced to him earlier, although his Christian name slipped her mind. Karst's son. The light from the gaslight affixed to the wall farther down the corridor reflected off the sheen of whatever oil he'd used on his hair.

"Mr. Karst." She nodded and took a step nearer but remained out of his reach.

"It's considered unwise for a woman in polite society to wander about unaccompanied."

She managed not to smirk. "Of course. Who knows what kind of trouble we might get up to?"

Rather than rise to that bait, he looked pointedly over her shoulder. "Your husband?"

"Has stepped out for a breath of air. I was just going to find him. Did you want to speak to him?"

He made a crude sound. "Of course not. What would I possibly have to say to a Reaper?"

"He's not a Reaper."

"Flesh-eater. Rapist. Scourge of the plains." His eyes narrowed. "The only thing I can't figure out is what that makes you?"

A flash of heat struck her cheeks but she bit back a response, stepping forward to move past him. He stretched an arm, palm flat to the door, blocking her way. Her impulse was to break his arm. She could do that. For Cap's sake, for the sake of their mission, she managed to restrain herself.

Leveling her meanest look at him, she said, "I don't much care for your attitude."

"I don't much care for yours. My father has been a councilman for nearly thirty years. My grandfather was one of the founders of Koln."

"I'm not interested in your family tree. Stand aside."

He didn't budge. Instead, with his eyes locked on hers, he leaned close enough that she almost choked on the smell of alcohol when he exhaled. Pickled. Her hands curled into fists at her sides. If he so much as touched her and she'd deck him and damn the consequences.

"You think I'll take orders from you? You're here because your superior wants to display the tame Reaper to the assembly. You're no better than a Breeder. A freak female Ranger, depraved enough to spread her legs for a Reaper."

"My husband is not a Reaper," she ground out. "Not anymore."

Karst straightened, stepping aside to let her pass. "Call him what you will. He's your dog, Ranger. Make sure you keep him chained."

Her hand moved of its own volition, reaching for a weapon that wasn't there. Karst noted the motion and the corner of his mouth lifted in a smirk before he turned his back on her and walked away.

She was so angry she couldn't even breathe. Couldn't force herself to reach for the handle on the door until she saw him turn the corner. Bastard. She was still shaking when she stepped out onto the deck. The narrow walkway wrapped the midsection of the gondola like a belt. The railing was high, nearly coming up to her chest, but the wind, while not strong, was bitterly cold. It helped, the cold, to cool her blood, to slap her awake from the powerless feeling that had locked her in place when she was standing in front of Karst junior.

What could she have done? Nothing. Cap would peel a strip from her hide if she beat a councilman's son.

With one hand on the rail, she walked as quickly as possible toward the stern where there would be some shelter. When she spotted Jake, standing with his back to her looking out into the night, she came up short.

Even though she wanted nothing more than to feel his arms wrap around her, she couldn't run to him like this. He might not be a Reaper anymore but he was still a man. Protective and occasionally thickheaded. Not the kind to let an insult to her pass without rising to her defense. Normally, she appreciated that about him. Here it could only lead to trouble. She took a deep, slow breath and let it out. Only when she had a handle on herself did she move forward again.

Jake's hands were braced on either side of him, his

face lifted to the heavens as the snow drifted down. He didn't turn around but she knew he was aware of her presence. Reaper senses or no, Jake always seemed to know when she was nearby.

"Snow."

The infected fled south in the early winter, as soon as the temperature began to drop. Last year when the first fat flakes fell from the sky, he'd wept like a baby.

He glanced over his shoulder and smiled. "It's too cold out here for you in that dress."

"You'll keep me warm." She sidled up next to him and leaned on the rail. It was beautiful. The silvery slopes slipping beneath them as they passed through. Every so often a glimpse of bare, craggy rock. She closed her eyes as they hit a cloud bank. She didn't know how they managed to fly in this weather.

She stuck out her tongue to catch a snowflake and felt Jake's eyes on her. Swallowing a laugh, she cast him a wry look. "Sorry. Not very ladylike of me, is it?"

"I like your tongue. Like it particularly when you use it for creative purposes."

"My tongue almost got us thrown off the ship earlier."

She stopped when he laughed. It was *that* kind of laugh. The one she'd spent the whole night ignoring. Not something to be shared but something hurled at you, like a rock. She could take that crap from the Scrappers if she had to, but not from Jake. She started to pull away but Jake caught her arm.

"Whoa, wait a minute. I'm not laughing at you."

"Don't lie to me."

His smile disappeared as he studied her face. "Don't do this. I didn't mean it to hurt and you know that, Abby.

Those people in there…they have nothing to do with us. Don't let them get to you."

She stared at him for several heartbeats and then nodded. The muscles in her shoulders and neck eased a bit and it felt as though all of her energy drained right out of her with the fight. It wasn't Jake she wanted to be fighting anyway.

Jake took her hand, the bad one, and twined his fingers through hers. The corner of his mouth twitched in a smile which he suppressed. The glint in his eyes told her the direction of his thoughts even before he pulled her closer.

"Bellamy is an ass." His voice was a deep rumble. Even as a Reaper, there'd always been something about Jake that steadied her. He fit her in front of him so they were both looking out. His arms came around her and he pressed a kiss to the side of her neck.

"Karst is worse," she said, tacking his son to her mental list too.

"They use words to get what they want just like you use weapons. They fight dirty. Don't let them get to you."

"I won't." She swallowed. "Not so long as you're on my side."

"Always." He dropped a kiss to the top of her head. "This will be done before you know it and we'll be back home safe and sound."

Home. Where the only thing they had to worry about were flesh-eating monsters.

SEVEN

JANE HAD SWORN to herself that she'd never go back to Columbus Junction. It had been her home for less than ten months, but it had left scars years deep. Funny that she'd considered it a safe haven at one time. A neat, quiet little town at the base of the mountains but high enough north that they'd only seen Reapers once in the past twenty years. With the child price for Samuel she'd been able to afford a small cottage of her own and she'd felt welcome there. Of course, some welcomed her more than others. Gideon, for example, he'd liked her right off.

"I've never seen you ride," Lyle said, interrupting her unhappy memories. One of the young recruits led out the most docile mare they kept in the stables. "It's a long trip for someone not accustomed to being in the saddle."

Lyle's big hand was wrapped around the top post of the fence surrounding the stable's pen. His big body was relaxed but the lines around his mouth told a different story. He was under a great deal of stress, the poor lieutenant. She didn't want to add to his trouble so she mustered up a smile. "I can handle it."

He didn't look convinced.

"I know how to ride," she told him. "Don't try to put me on one of your retired mounts. I might be sore for a few days, but we can't afford to lose any more time than we already have."

He scratched at his chin. He hadn't shaved this morning and there were some whiskers coming in a purer shade of blond than the hair on his head. It was hit or miss with Lyle, who only seemed to shave when the mood struck him. "It's not too late to take a ship."

She shook her head. A piece of hair came loose from her braid and she tucked it behind her ear. "You said there were no scheduled transports for another fortnight. Even if we could hire a ship, it would only make Gideon suspicious. He pays close attention to the ships coming in and out of the city."

"He'll be suspicious anyway, especially once he sees you."

"I don't think so," she said. "I know the way Gideon's mind works and he never believed he'd done wrong by me, even at the end. He planned to marry me. Fed me, sheltered me, showered me with gifts."

"He imprisoned you," Lyle said, a catch in his voice. "And those gifts were bought with dirty money. He—"

"I'm not defending him, Lieutenant," she said. "I'm only telling you how he thinks. In Gideon's mind, I was the one who wronged him by running and he was in the right claiming what was his. If he sees me riding in to Columbus Junction, he's more likely to believe that Cam got tired of me and I've come crawling back than that I'm tracking the serum."

"Let him believe you want to reconcile?"

She nodded. "And that I've hired you to escort me home."

"I don't like it."

She didn't much like it herself but it was a solid plan. "It will let us get close to him."

The breeze picked up, lifting silt from the enclosure and pushing it several yards before dropping it and moving on to play with her skirts. She shivered. And because Lyle missed nothing, he stepped toward her and touched her arm just above her elbow. His warmth seeped right through the thin cotton sleeve and she shivered again. Beneath the brim of his hat, his gray eyes turned troubled. "You're sure you want to do this?"

"I'm sure I *need* to do this. If you tried to go alone, I'd follow."

He looked as if he wanted to call her bluff, but she wasn't bluffing. Lyle was a strong man and, in many ways, a hard one but he wasn't as ruthless as Gideon. She'd taken one look at his face last night and had known right away that he intended to go after the cure. And while she'd have worried about anyone going to Columbus Junction, she wasn't letting Lyle go in there alone. Not to face down a man like Gideon Moore.

Turning away from his searching look, she watched the boy take the mare for a turn around the pen. She was a pretty thing with a smooth gait. Fine for a ride to Split Creek or New Providence, but definitely past her prime. "How about the black gelding that came in last month?"

"Lightning?"

"Is that what you called him?" It was a good name. Ranger mounts were bred for stamina but Lightning was smaller than most which made him an uncomfortable fit for many of the men. He was young and fast and Jane had been itching to ride him since she first set eyes on the lovely gelding.

But Lyle shook his head. "Too young. He's not ready to ride that far at the speed we need to travel." He considered it for a moment and then nodded at the stable hand. "Go ahead and saddle up Samson." The boy's eyes widened at the order but he knew better than to argue. He turned the mare around and headed back for the stable door. While they waited, Lyle leaned against the fence post and ran a considering gaze over her body. "I thought you were going to borrow some of Abby's clothes."

"I have my own clothing, thank you." She spread her narrow skirts a bit to show him how they were split so she could ride. They were brown and a nice sturdy cotton. What more did he want? "Abby admired them. Before she left, she asked me if I could make her a pair."

"I was hoping you might be able to pass for a boy."

The glint in his eyes teased a smile from her. "You should have known better than that. I haven't been able to pass for a boy since I was twelve years old."

"I suppose not."

She glanced over her shoulder, noting that they were alone in the yard. Well, as alone as you could be at the fort. There were always men moving about their business but no one was paying them any particular attention. She'd said her goodbyes to Haddy and Amelia before she'd come to meet Lyle. She hadn't really expected anyone else to see her off, but she had expected someone would come for Lyle. At least the man he was leaving in charge of the fort.

"Are you and Cam still fighting?"

"We're not fighting. He thinks I should handle things differently. I have rank. End of story."

She frowned at that, but really didn't have any choice but to let it go. The young Ranger returned a few moments later, leading Samson. The horse was saddled and already loaded with her gear. True to his namesake, Samson had a lovely mane of thick black hair. She'd watched Seth work him in the yard often enough to get a feel for him. She liked the way he moved, fluid as water, but she also recognized that he had the personality of a trickster. Even as she thought it, he put his heavy hoof down hard in a puddle that was half manure and splattered the stable boy's pants to the knee. She swore he did it on purpose. Something about the way his ears twitched when the boy cursed.

Lyle laughed. "You're sure you can handle him?"

"I'm sure."

She mounted up smoothly and adjusted her skirts so they fell properly. Lyle's hand closed over her calf. It was just a friendly touch. She was wearing boots and he was wearing gloves, for goodness sake. But every part of her was aware of that light pressure on her leg.

"Let me know when you need to stop."

"I will."

"If you push yourself too hard too early, it will only slow us down in the long run."

"I told you I won't slow you down." She frowned. "Are you sure you're not the one having second thoughts?"

He smiled crookedly. "Second, third…it's what kept me up last night. Tell me I'm making the right decision here."

"It's not your decision. It's mine." She nudged Samson toward the gates with her knees, leaving Lyle to follow. He was at her side before she'd reached the bridge, moving as if he was part of his horse. She'd always admired that about Lyle. There was nothing flashy about him. He just made everything he did look easy. As if life was a river and he could float along on top while she fought the current. He was so sure of his place in the world and she envied that.

They rode slowly through town, nodding to people who paused along the way to wish them well. Past the last house, the road angled north, away from the border. This particular road ended at Fort Hill, which was no longer standing. From there, they'd head directly west. Two weeks if the weather held and they were able to keep a good pace.

"You *are* a good rider," Lyle said, after they'd traveled a few miles.

She didn't answer. "I told you so" seemed wrong and she couldn't think of anything more diplomatic.

"Did you learn in Columbus Junction?"

"No." He likely suspected as much. The mountain cities, even the ones in the foothills like Columbus Junction, had little use for horses. It was all about the airships there. They provided supplies from the plains and transportation between all civilized communities in the Rockies and east in the Appalachians. Still, some of the older families in the cities kept horses in order to display their wealth. Up in the capital city, where land was at a premium, to have a field dedicated to an animal you could hardly ride anywhere told everyone exactly how much money you had to throw around.

Lyle caught her eye and a slow smile spread across his face. It was the smile she'd seen him use to charm the women in town and she felt a pang because this was the first time he'd ever directed it at her. When she'd first come to the fort some of the men had propositioned her, but Lyle never had. Even if he hadn't understood then why she wanted Cam, he respected the fact that she did indeed want him. There was a dimple in his cheek. She'd never noticed it before.

"Give me something, sweetheart. I need to know what we're riding into and you know I won't hold your past against you."

"Won't you?"

It came out sharper than she'd intended and with a well of disappointment she watched as that lovely, charming smile dimmed. Lyle's eyes turned serious. He considered her for a long moment before speaking and though she wanted to look away, she didn't let herself.

"The man who was Lieutenant when I joined the patrol, the man whose job I have now, he had a saying—'It's all right to look back every once in a while, just don't stop and stare.' That's how most Rangers feel. Past is past. Whatever you were involved in when you lived in Columbus Junction, that's not who you are now. And the now is what matters."

"I think you're about to find out just how real the past can be for some people," she said quietly.

"Then tell me about it. I need to know."

She sighed.

"It'll be an awfully long trip if you won't talk to me."

"I don't even know where to start."

"How about with when you got to Columbus Junction? I get the impression you weren't born there."

She winced, but truly, it was as good a place as any. "You've probably guessed most of it."

"And Cam told me some, but I'd like to hear it from you."

She looked away from him, trying to decide how to phrase it. In the end, there wasn't any good way to tell this story and so she just started talking. "When

I first came down to the plains, I lived with my aunt near Baxter. After she died, I couldn't afford to keep her place alone." And she'd hated Baxter anyway. She might have been able to stay if she'd worked her fingers to the bone, but she'd wanted more. Which was kind of funny when you thought about it. "I followed camp until I conceived a child and then once Samuel was born, I used the child price from the fort to get as far up as I could afford." She smiled wryly. "Which wasn't very far. Columbus Junction."

"Practically on the border."

"Near enough." It had seemed like a safe haven when she'd first moved there. People didn't ask questions. They hadn't judged her for being a breeder like the people higher up would have done. And the money from the fort went far enough that she could live on just that income. What she'd earned from taking in work as a seamstress, she'd saved.

"How old was Samuel then?" Lyle had turned his head to look down at the trail. Prying, but he was doing it gently. Still hurt, but she appreciated his effort.

"When we first got there? Only about four months old. He looked like Cam. That hair. Pale gold and curly." He'd had Cam's eyes too. It hurt to look at Cam sometimes because of it. She frowned down at her hands resting on the pommel. "I'm sorry about last night."

"Which part of last night are you sorry about? Not getting yourself to the fort as soon as you recognized one of Moore's gang? Chasing down a band of armed outlaws on foot in your Sunday best? You regret saving my life when Reginald tried to draw on me?"

"I'm sorry you had to witness that fight. I know you

and Cam are close. And I'm sorry to be the cause of any trouble between you."

He didn't accept her apology but he didn't reject it either. She knew he was still angry about her following Gideon's men. She could hear the bite in his voice whenever he mentioned it.

"You're not the problem."

She didn't believe that. She'd heard their raised voices as she walked away from Cap's office. She'd hated that. The two men were as close as brothers and she'd never wanted to do anything to mess that up. "I'm *not* sorry I went after the serum. Maybe it was a little reckless, but I was careful."

He looked at her, hard enough to make her wince.

"I didn't get caught, did I?"

A slow shake of his head. "Don't do anything like that again. We're working together but you're here only as a guide. No running headlong into trouble you're not trained to handle."

"I took Reginald's pistol," she told him. "I know how to use that one but I'd like for you to teach me how to use the rifle too. It will take us at least a fortnight to reach Columbus Junction. Do you think there'll be time for that?"

She half expected him to say no. To leave her unarmed and dependent on him to protect her. Cam would have said no, but Lyle nodded. "We'll make the time."

She nodded her thanks and when she picked up her story again, the words came easier. "I learned to ride on Eyrion. That's where I was born. My father ran the stables for a rich man named Anson Stark."

He gave a low whistle. "A capital city girl. No wonder you seem out of place in our little town. Your father still there?"

She shook her head. No. Her father had been a good man, maybe overly protective of her. He'd never have let her live down here. Giving up his ranch and taking the job for Stark had been for her sake. She often wondered how her life would have been different if her parents had stayed on the plains.

"My parents passed away within a few months of each other when I was sixteen. Their employer asked me to stay on, but I…" *Didn't want to worry about Mr. Stark cornering me in a dark hall? Didn't like the way he would occasionally reach out and touch my hair?* She turned away from Lyle's curious look and said, "I decided to move to the plains to live with my aunt instead. When she died, I found Cam."

"I'm sorry about your parents," Lyle said, soft and sincere. She knew he meant it and she appreciated the way he didn't keep digging in that direction. She'd told him all she intended to about that part of her story. The rest of what he needed to know was about Gideon. They had time though—two weeks of it—to work up to that.

Silence fell between them as they passed Foley's ranch. It was a small farm but prosperous. He raised cattle which he butchered to feed the fort and kept a vegetable garden large enough for his extensive family. The cornstalks were still standing though they'd long since turned a deep golden brown and were no longer producing. Mary had given her a basket filled with the last of their tomato crop yesterday for Haddy to can. They were entirely self-sufficient except for wheat. Bread was in short supply since the only mills still in operation were in the foothills now. A hard distance to transport especially when the mills took such a high cut on the price.

When they came to a rise in the road and she saw all that open land stretching out before them, the mountains rising up in the distance, she thought seriously about turning back. Lyle didn't even pause to take in the view.

"How did you end up with someone like Gideon Moore?"

She nudged her horse forward to keep pace with him. "I didn't know who he was at first. I thought he was a prosperous businessman. That his money came entirely from trade." *Trade.* God, she'd been such an idiot. "I suppose he did get his money from trade, just not any kind I'd ever imagined. When I found out, I tried to leave."

Lyle's eyes narrowed. "And he locked you up."

"Not then. Not until…after. And then it was for my own good, don't you know? I was mad with grief and he was worried that I might harm myself. I managed to get a letter to Cam and he came to the rescue. Very gallant, don't you think?"

"Why didn't you tell anyone at the fort? You let everyone go on thinking that you were a stray whore who followed him home."

"Is that what you thought?" She held his gaze for a moment, couldn't read his expression, and then shrugged because it really didn't matter. "It's not so far from the truth. Some women chase Rangers and call it duty but I never hid behind words like that."

She didn't quite hear all of what he muttered under his breath but she caught Cam's name. "We're spread so thin we're barely holding on to the borders. There's no shame in what you did. We need more Rangers coming in. It's the only way we'll survive."

Maybe if she'd been raised on the plains she would have believed that but she'd grown up in a Scraper city and the rules were very different there. None of the other women down here shared her mind-set. Well, except maybe for Mrs. Boyd. But she knew that the Scraper people called them all Breeders. They'd call even Mrs. Boyd that just for living down here. It didn't matter that Mrs. Boyd had probably never slept with a Ranger in her life.

Breeder. Jane had never been able to shake the dirty way it made her feel. If she'd never heard that word, never heard a Scraper say it with a sneer in their voice then, she thought, things would be different. If she could scour the memory from her brain, she would. All sorts of memories she'd scour away if she could.

"My mother was a whore." Lyle glanced at her and then away. "Before she had me. And she was a good mother. She was a good person."

"I'm sure she was." He sounded tetchy about it but she had no reason to doubt him. She'd lived with whores and she'd lived with Scrapers. There were good and bad people everywhere, in every kind of occupation.

"What else did Cam tell you about me?"

Lyle looked back at the trail, absently shooed a fly that was honing in on Smudge's ear. "That you ran away from Gideon but he sent men to drag you back. Potts must have been one of them."

She swallowed hard and nodded.

"Cam said that Samuel caught a fever on the trip back."

"It was early March and a cold one. Gideon couldn't

spare a ship at the time so we were in a wagon. It snowed and we got stuck for days." Nearly two years had passed since then. Should it still hit her so hard? Blinking, she cleared her throat. "Samuel didn't make it."

"I'm sorry about your boy."

She could hear the pity in his voice. That was the real reason she hadn't told anyone her story when she came to the fort. She hadn't wanted the constant aching reminder of what she'd lost, hearing it in their voices, seeing it in their eyes. The air felt thick in her lungs and she blew it out. "You know, I didn't think Rangers ever got sick. I thought the immunity to Reaper bite meant they were immune to almost everything else."

"Rangers don't get sick, not generally, but it does happen. Every once in a while, someone who's been fighting Reapers for decades will have a reaction during a restoration. I came down with a cold once."

"Once?"

"When I was about seven. We're not invincible." She looked over at him and he laughed. "What? You've lived at the fort long enough to see the truth of that for yourself."

She looked long and hard at him and shook her head. "I know you're not invincible, Lieutenant."

Why else did he think she was here?

EIGHT

LYLE DECIDED IT would be best if he treated Janie like any other young recruit under his care so he began to teach her the tricks and tools she'd need to survive if something were to happen to him. As they rode, he pointed out landmarks and directions to towns and homesteads where she might expect to find help. He set up targets for her to practice shooting each morning and then taught her how to clean and care for the weapon at night. He also taught her how to trap and cook rabbit which wasn't a skill she seemed particularly excited to learn but at least she wouldn't ever go hungry. Passing so near the border, they met only one other traveler. A man he didn't recognize heading to Split Creek with a delivery of corn for the granary.

The first few nights they camped under the open skies and on the afternoon of the third day, they made New Providence. Fortunate timing as storm clouds opened up immediately after they stabled the horses. Janie had still looked good enough to eat, even with her hair darkened to brown and plastered to her cheeks. She'd been covered in dust from the road and the water droplets tracked wavering lines across her pale skin.

Lyle had thought that on the road she'd be less appealing. Sweaty, bedraggled and rumpled. She wasn't though. The messier she got, the more vulnerable she looked and he was starting to wonder if all of her fine clothes were just another tool she used to keep people at arm's length. Though why the hell she wanted to do that was still a mystery to him. You'd think being a woman alone in the world, she'd welcome every kindness offered to her. But not Janie. Contrary, that's what she was. Of course, the same contrariness that kept her out of his reach also kept her in the saddle day after day so he probably shouldn't complain much.

The night in New Providence did her a world of good. Hot baths, a warm meal and soft beds. Janie turned in early. They set out at dawn the next day and made good progress, covering nearly twenty miles. It was early afternoon and they had only a little farther to go before they'd reach the spot where he planned to rest for the night. A flat area near a slow turn in the river where they could catch some fresh fish for dinner. Far enough from the road that it would be difficult to see their fire after nightfall. And there was a thick stand of pines that would serve both as an adequate shield and block for the mounting wind.

"How much longer do you think?" Jane asked curiously. "We could camp here, couldn't we?"

There was a smudge of dust along her jawline but rather than make her look dirty, it made her seem… touchable. His fingers itched to do just that but he kept them resting easy on his saddle horn.

"It's too near the road," he said and pointed. "We're almost there though."

"That copse of trees?"

He nodded. "Just the other side of that and we're done for the day. I want a fire before the sun drops."

"A fire tonight? You're spoiling me, Lieutenant." Her

smile hit him square in the chest just like it always did and he couldn't help but smile back at her.

"If you're lucky, I'll even gut your fish for you."

He found himself looking forward to that quiet time with Jane when the night settled around them shutting all the world out. The ground would be soft and the river full. Jane would sleep beside him tonight though he had no ambition beyond the nearness of her body. She was in no shape for that, not yet.

She held her cards close to her chest but he knew this road was hard for her. Cam thought she was after revenge but Lyle thought this—going to Columbus Junction and facing down Gideon—was something she needed to do in order to say goodbye to her son. The way forward was something Janie needed to decide for herself, but until she sorted it out, he was damned well going to keep his hands off her.

She was under his command, even if they were only a patrol of two. He'd never taken advantage of anyone under him, not in any way. And he didn't intend to start now.

He realized that he was staring again, at the delicate profile and the way the sinking sun lit the red in her hair and made her pale skin warm as honey. Before he could turn away, Janie glanced over and caught him staring…again.

Her lips twitched and she shook her head. "I'm tired, not made of glass. You really need to stop worrying about me so much."

Just as well she thought that was his problem.

"I keep a close eye on everyone out for their first time."

She gave him a funny look. "Abby said the first time she rode patrol, you put a snake in her bedroll."

He grinned. "Everyone else wanted to go easy on her because she was a girl. I didn't want her to feel left out."

"She might not have minded."

Abby had screamed so loudly it had drawn the attention of the Reapers they were hunting. They'd stormed the camp shortly after and Abby had made her first kill. He didn't think Jane would appreciate that part of the story so he kept it to himself.

She shook her head and he returned his attention to the land around them. This part of their trip was an easy ride through pleasant countryside, sparsely populated and seldom harassed by Reapers even during the height of summer. He wasn't expecting trouble here. But when one of Smudge's ears suddenly flicked forward, Lyle straightened in the saddle.

The road they were on was a narrow dirt track, with trampled grass missed by wagon wheels down the center. It rose up ahead to the peak of a gentle hill, shaded on either side by a sentinel pair of old oaks. This time of year, the leaves were mostly gone. Those that remained were crisp and brown. They twisted in the breeze and when the wind gusted, a handful drifted down to scatter across the road. Whatever had alerted Smudge and caused the crows to call out an alarm was out of sight, over that hill.

"Jane—"

"I know," she said quietly. "I don't hear horses, though, or a wagon."

Which is why they'd nearly missed them. Wasn't Reapers. Smudge would be far more disturbed by the presence of Reapers than he currently was. Janie's mount, younger and not as seasoned, did a skittish little side step before she reined him in. Removing his rifle from its scabbard and setting it across his lap, Lyle winced at the sight of a pistol ready in Jane's small hand, even knowing it was a necessity.

She had a rifle too. She'd been practicing but though her aim was fine, she couldn't reload fast enough to be of much use in a close fight. The revolver would be better and it was of some comfort to him to be riding with a partner who kept their wits about them when trouble came their way.

"Hold back."

She nodded without the slightest hesitation and reined in Samson. No sense in them both being targets at the top of the hill. He could hear voices now, still a ways off. Out of firing range, if he was a good judge. And he was.

Dismounting to be on the safe side, he passed Jane the reins and walked with his rifle to the ridge, coming up behind the tree to the right. From there, he had a good view of the road below and the fairly large party of men who were headed their way. About a half dozen of them, still a few miles off. Big but lightly armed and most of them on foot. One poor old mule carried the weight of their equipment. The picks, shovels and carbide lamps marked them as coming from Oro.

He went back to Jane and mounted, directing Smudge back onto the road.

"It's a group of miners," he told Jane. "Could be trouble but it's not likely. Either way, we might as well meet it head-on."

She frowned. Scared, he thought, but he didn't see any sign of panic.

"What are they doing out here? The nearest mine is twenty miles in the opposite direction."

He urged Smudge forward. "Let's go find out."

On their way, he let her know how he intended to handle it and she listened carefully, asking questions that reassured him she wasn't going to do anything to place herself in danger. He might have known she could handle herself…he *had* known it else he never would have let her come along in the first place. But this was the first time that confidence would be tested.

Despite the turn of the season, the grass was nearly waist high on the flat stretch of field to their left. To the right, in the direction of the river, the terrain turned hilly and wooded. That was the direction they'd flee if they needed to make a break for it. On horseback, it shouldn't be hard to outdistance the miners.

When the men saw them coming, they paused to confer for a few minutes before moving forward again. As they approached, Lyle paid particular attention to the weapons that were drawn. Only three firearms. Two pistols and a shotgun. The rest gripped the tools of their trade, pickaxes and shovels. Altogether it was enough to do plenty of damage if it turned ugly. Normally, a meeting on the road like this wouldn't cause him so much as a twinge of concern. But there was Jane to consider now.

The miners stopped about twenty yards off. One man—the biggest—edged to the front of the group. His face was clean but his clothes were dirty. Gray speckled the black of his beard.

Lyle held up one hand in greeting and rested the other on the stock of his rifle. "You can rest easy," he said. "We're Rangers."

Pale eyes flicked over to Jane and lingered a little too long. "The both of you?"

"I'm a Ranger and she's none of your damn business." He felt more than saw Janie startle at the tone of his voice. But the miner's gaze snapped back to him and that's what was important. "What are you doing here? There are no mines in this direction."

One of the men shifted his feet but the leader was silent for a moment. "We came from Dickinson. The owners decided to abandon the shaft. Three Reaper scares this summer and they're shutting down the whole operation."

Lyle frowned. Dickinson was one of the most southerly mines. Iron. Owned by the Oliver family. It had never been particularly productive, but in his experience, miners were willing to risk a good deal to strip every last scrap from a shaft. "Where are you headed now?"

"We heard Fort Dougan is where they're making the cure." The miner nodded. "It's down this road, ain't it? We figure if we can get our hands on some—"

Lyle cut him off with a shake of his head. "That's not happening."

"We have money."

"It's not for sale. Our supplies are low and the Reapers haven't moved south yet."

The miner seemed taken aback by that. "Word is you planned to send out a supply to all the border towns. I don't see why the mines should get left out. How many people are getting bit nowadays? And it's almost winter. Surely you can spare it."

It wasn't a matter of people getting bit. That was still rare, thank God. It was a matter of rounding up and injecting old Reapers. And by the suspicious turn to his mouth, this man knew it. Lyle didn't care to be baited. No reason for a civilian to carry the serum if he only meant to use it to push south of the border for profit. The Rangers would like to push the Reapers farther south too, but they'd do it while making sure everyone else stayed safe in the process.

Lyle stared at the man until he dropped his gaze and then said, "Enough people get bit to keep us busy. If you're looking for work, I heard news of a strike near Ferromonte. It's still Oro—claimed territory but they're hiring."

The miner spat into the dirt. "Scrapers don't pay shit. They put their murderers and thieves in the hole to spare them the cost of a rope."

Likely true but also not his problem. Having failed to convince the miners that it was in their best interest to turn back, there didn't seem to be much point in lingering. Not with the sun beginning to set and the men watching Jane with increasing speculation. He should have pressed harder to disguise her as a young recruit. Chopped off her hair and put her in baggy clothes. Problem was she'd still probably look as beautiful as ever and it wouldn't have done anything more than piss her off.

"Good luck to you then," Lyle said, moving his mount to one side so they could pass. Jane moved behind him, positioning herself so that he always had a clear shot if he needed to take it. It took some new Rangers years to develop that kind of awareness.

The group passed by and the looks some of the younger men darted his way made him uneasy. Desperate men, young and stupid, always made him uneasy. At least Reapers were fairly predictable.

He and Jane sat watching until the last man crested the hill.

When they were gone, Jane holstered her gun and urged Samson forward, seemingly eager to move on. Lyle ran an eye over her to reassure himself that she hadn't been too badly spooked, but she seemed fine. More than fine. Dark leather belt and boots, and a buff-colored skirt that matched her wide-brimmed hat. Berry-red shirt that had been tailored to perfectly hug her curves. Pretty as a picture. No wonder the miners had stared.

She was worrying at her lower lip again. It was a habit he sincerely wished she'd quit because it didn't do anything but draw his attention to her mouth. She did it when she was thinking through a puzzle, which was fairly often. She didn't have a restful mind.

"What do you think will happen to those men?" She asked. "The miners. Do you think they'll actually go to Ferromonte?"

He shook his head. "They're still headed for Dougan despite the warning. Cam will have to turn them away. People always think there's something better down the road that's blocked."

She rubbed her cheek with her sleeve. Seeing the spot of dirt on the fabric, she reached for her handkerchief and wiped the smudge from her jaw and then the sweat from her face.

"They were telling the truth about Scraper wages, I can tell you that." She squinted up at the sun and then ducked her head so the brim of her hat caught the brunt of it. "People down here speak as if everyone on the mountain is rich but that's not true. The ones wealthy enough to board an airship and visit the forts or the ones your delegations meet when they go up, those Scrapers have money. Most of the people up there are still working for food and shelter just like the people down here."

"Is that why you didn't try to go back? Not many people move *down* the mountain. I'd always wondered."

"I didn't like someone else having power over me."

Of course she wouldn't. Jane was born to be a queen, anyone could see that. "I'd like to meet the kind of fool who would think they could slip a leash around your neck."

He didn't like the change that came over her face. Her dark eyes flickered with some strong emotion before hardening again into ice. All the life leeching right out of her, leaving her faded like cloth left too long in the sun. He realized his mistake and wished the words back but it was too late.

"Anyone can lose a fight," he said quietly. "It's all about whether you climb back to your feet."

She looked at him curiously. "Have you ever? Lost a fight, I mean."

"I've been knocked down more times than I can count."

She tipped her head slightly to the side. "I can't imagine that. It's always seemed to me that you could handle anything."

"Mostly when I was younger. I was scrawny and didn't know when to keep my mouth shut." A slight flush came to his skin. "Unfortunately, only one of those things has changed."

"I didn't get back up. I just ran away from my old life. I don't know if going back will do me any good but I have to do it. I need to know I'm not that woman anymore. The thing is I'm afraid I still am the same, underneath it all."

"You're not," he said immediately.

She raised her brows, a smile dancing around the edges of her mouth. "You know me so well, do you?"

"Enough. Besides, you have a lot going for you now that you didn't back then."

"What's that?"

"People who care about you at your back. A family and a home at the end of the road. Me. I'm here too, with you the whole way. I won't let you forget who you are."

She gave him a long searching look and then nodded sharply before lifting her chin toward the copse of trees in the distance. "Race you there?"

"You're on."

NINE

When Jane woke up the fire had died down to embers and the moon had long since set. The stars were thick and the sky was black. She and Lyle had stretched out beside the fire, their heads close. The steady sound of his breathing was a comfort, more reassuring than a lullaby. She'd been tempted to ask him to lie beside her, for the warmth, but she'd chickened out in the end. Smart is what it was, not cowardly. Lyle was attracted to her, she knew it, as much as he tried to hold himself back. And he still thought she was a little crazy for chasing after Cam for so long. And he pitied her too.

Lyle could have any woman he wanted with a wink and a smile. Why on earth would he want to entangle himself in the mess that was her life?

The way things had happened in Columbus Junction—her discovering exactly what kind of business Gideon was involved in, being on the run and that terrible sickness at the end—had all happened so fast. A matter of weeks. One moment she'd had Samuel in her arms, planning her wedding to the most powerful man in town. And the next moment, she'd had nothing, not even control of her own mind. Most of that time she barely remembered at all. Still pictures and bits of conversations, visible only through a fog. There was her life before, with Samuel. Her life now. And the dark space in between.

She needed to find a way to tie the frayed pieces together. To make sense of it all. And this was her chance to do that.

If she'd gone back to Columbus Junction alone to ask questions, she'd have ended locked up again in Gideon's bedroom…or worse. With Lyle, she could go back with a clear head, confront Gideon for what he'd done, visit the small grave. Maybe it would help. Maybe. At least this time she was armed.

She lay on her back and stared up at the stars, pulling the rough blanket up under her chin. In the distance, an owl hooted. A lonely sound so sudden and clear and piercing that she held her breath in the silence that followed, hoping it would come again. When it didn't, she sighed and rolled to her side to push herself up. Before she'd even shrugged free of the blanket, Lyle reached out and grabbed hold of her wrist.

"Don't." He was wide-awake, jaw set and expression grim. "Lay down, Janie."

She tugged at his grip but it held. "I need to relieve myself. I'll be back in a minute."

Slowly, he drew her down so that her arm was outstretched. He wasn't trying to pull her toward him, not exactly. She'd always thought that if Lyle decided he was interested in pursuing her, he'd try to charm his way in, not just yank her into his bedroll. She didn't know if she was more disturbed by his action or by how bad she wanted to go. Her heart picked up and her breathing shallowed out as warmth suffused her whole body. She started to move in his direction but his frown stopped her.

"That wasn't an owl." His voice was pitched low. "I don't know who's out there, but you need to stay put."

All the warmth in her blood went cold. She gave a tight nod and he released her. He shifted slightly and she saw the glint of metal as he slid his rifle closer. Then he turned his head slightly as if to catch a sound.

"There's more than one. If they rush us, you go for the horses. Samson will carry you bareback and he's fast. Just hold on tight and let him run."

She wouldn't leave him behind but now didn't seem the time to argue. "The miners?"

His mouth tightened and he hesitated for a moment before shaking his head. "Not the miners." And because he was Lyle and seemed to have the uncanny ability to see right through her, he said, "I mean it. If they attack, you run."

If they attack. Why else would someone sneak up on you in the middle of the night? She ducked her head to avoid Lyle's sharp-eyed gaze. She couldn't promise to run. She wouldn't leave Lyle alone in a fight if her staying might make a difference.

"Jane."

She flashed him an annoyed look. "Don't you think we should be quiet?"

"They already know where we are."

She bit her lip as she considered that. "Should we call out? Let them know we're not going down without a fight?"

He made a strangled sound. "We do not want to force a confrontation here. We play possum and hope they get bored and move on."

She turned her head to try to see his expression. There wasn't much light to go by and the dim red glow there was made his face seem unfamiliar. The glint of his eyes, the sharp outline of his cheek. That set to his expressive mouth. This was a side of him she'd never seen, not even when he was interrogating Reginald. Scared…*shit*. If Lyle was worried then there was a good chance they weren't making it out of this. Letting out a shaky breath, she whispered, "Reapers. You're talking about Reapers."

"No, honey. Not Reapers. These are men."

But they were hunting like Reapers. That's what he wasn't saying and suddenly the pieces snapped together. She'd heard rumors about cured Reapers who formed packs. Outlaws operating on the fringes. There'd been sporadic reports of them stealing unguarded livestock and harassing people on the road. They weren't Reapers anymore but they weren't normal either. Doc had gone on a rant last time she'd seen him at the saloon, shouting at one of the scientists that they were sending the cured men off too quickly and with no means of making an honest living. Welks had argued that the cure was enough and what the injected did with that gift was their responsibility. She'd agreed with that sentiment then. Here, in the dark, her opinion was taking a different turn.

She reached out for Lyle. Her fingers scraped through the dirt separating them, searching for something solid to touch. She couldn't even have said what she was reaching for until his hand found hers, his strong fingers closing around hers and squeezing tight.

"It'll be all right."

He couldn't know that, but she didn't mind him saying it. In fact, she grabbed on to it like a rope he could use to pull her to safety. His hand. His words. His breathing, just as even and steady as it had been when she thought he was asleep. She'd always liked that about him, that he was like a big steady ship that could ride out any wave that crashed against him. She'd always thought she could handle anything that came her way too. Until Samuel had been ripped away from her and she hadn't known what to do. Lyle…she didn't think anything could take Lyle down. Kill him, maybe, but not destroy the person he was on the inside.

The sound of a twig snapping echoed loud as a gunshot in the stillness of the night. She flinched and Lyle's hand tightened on hers. It was so quiet. Her ears strained to pick up the sound of movement but there was nothing, not even a breeze to rattle the dry leaves in the branches. That must have been how Lyle knew the hoot hadn't come from a real owl. Owls were shy creatures. Hunters. They wouldn't have lingered where even the rodents were too afraid to stir.

A scrape and a brief shuffling noise came from the left and she turned her head. "Steady," Lyle breathed and she closed her eyes. It wasn't like her to play possum. If she'd been the kind of person to stay still and let trouble take aim, she would still be up in the Scraper city now, probably in Anson Stark's bed. While a lot of people would say that was better than lying here in the dirt, ready prey to a pack of half-Reaper men, those cowards were dead wrong.

Moving slow and shifting her body as little as possible, she slid her hand down to the gun still strapped to her belt. Lyle had chastised her for wearing it while she slept but now she was happy she hadn't listened to him. Holding her breath, she eased it out of the holster and dragged it up until her arm lay in a more natural position. When she opened her eyes, Lyle was staring at her. Clearly, he knew what she was doing. Clearly, he wasn't pleased.

Screw him. He had a rifle in his hand and two revolvers strapped to his hips. Holding her gaze, he lifted three fingers and pointed toward the horses. Three of them, after the horses, or using the sound they made as cover. She nodded her understanding and focused her attention in that direction. Cold seeped from the ground into her body until she shook with it.

The waiting was awful. The stars cast just enough light for her to pick out the sheen from the horses' coats. They were restless. When Samson pushed against Smudge's shoulder, the creak of rope sounded loud in the echoing silence. No breeze. No rodents in the bush. No airships sliding through the still night. She wanted to scream into the dark just to break the silence and end the wait.

When a pile of ash shifted in what remained of the fire, she startled, turning her head. At the same moment, Lyle surged to his feet, bringing his rifle up and firing before she could even climb to her knees. The flash of light from the barrel showed four men rushing toward them, crouched low to the ground but moving fast. She saw the one out front jerk violently but was blind again before he even hit the ground.

When she turned, the other three were right there. Lyle shot the second in the gut and then tossed his rifle down to draw his pistol. He shot the third in the head. She took a step back, raising her gun to take aim at the fourth. Lyle, looking as calm as a mountain lake, smoothly pivoted, arm extended and fired at the last man.

There was a flash of light, a percussive crack from

the gun, and the man dropped. Four men dead in the time it would take her to thread a needle. She raised her hand to her mouth and a sob broke from her lips. Lyle had taken care of them all but she was shaking and sweating as if she'd fought them all single-handedly. She hadn't done anything. Her gun felt as if it weighed a hundred pounds as she slowly lowered it.

"Jane."

The edge of concern in Lyle's voice chilled her blood. She stilled at the sound but before she could figure out what had him scared, a thick arm wrapped around her neck and pulled her back, nearly lifting her from her feet. Startled, the gun flew from her hand, skittering away over the hard rock. Damn it.

She twisted hard to the right, driving her elbow into the man's gut. He grunted but only tightened his hold. How had he managed to sneak up on her when he smelled like a corpse? How had she not noticed the stench?

Bracing her legs, she pushed off and back, hoping to unbalance him but it was no use. He was too big and he simply picked her up by her neck, cutting off her air supply and making her vision go black at the edges.

Lyle's scowl was fearsome. He held up both hands in a placating gesture but his eyes were burning, boring right into her. He was pissed and she didn't blame him. He'd taken out the whole gang except one. She hadn't helped him one bit, had only managed to get herself caught and put them both in danger. She hadn't even held on to her weapon. Truly, she wouldn't be surprised if Lyle just let this man drag her off.

Lyle's glare shifted to fix on the man holding her captive. "Let her go and I let you go."

The man grunted again, but the band around her neck eased ever so slightly. She pulled in a breath, a trickle of air really, not enough to fill her lungs but hopefully enough to keep her alive.

"Stop," the man growled. "You stop moving or she dies. I'm going to back up nice and slow here. You're going to drop that gun."

Lyle hesitated. "And then?"

"And then?" The man sounded startled that Lyle hadn't instantly obeyed him.

"You can't think I'm going to let you walk away with her. Better I shoot her now and put her out of her misery."

The man hesitated, but only briefly before grunting in disbelief. "You won't shoot her."

The gun moved as if it were a part of Lyle's body, the butt slipping into his palm effortlessly. Her mouth went dry and she couldn't see anything except his finger on the trigger. She didn't dare look at Lyle's face. He was bluffing. He had to be.

But possibly not. If he let this man drag her away, she was as good as dead and she would be in for a world of misery before he finally got around to killing her. Fumbling, she reached back with both hands, scratching a furrow down the man's cheek with her left hand before he choked the air out of her again.

"Bitch. I'll kill you—"

"Let her go." She'd never heard Lyle's voice so hard. It got the outlaw's attention too. He jerked her back against him and locked her left arm behind her. But the pressure on her neck eased a little bit, just enough for her to suck in another breath. Her right hand was still free and that was what mattered.

"She's more trouble than she's worth."

Lyle was still pointing the gun at the man's head, rock steady, not even a quiver of movement. "Right now, she's worth your life. One more chance. Let. Her. Go."

"I don't—"

Jane stabbed down and back with the pin she'd grabbed from her hair. If he released her even for an instant, then Lyle could shoot. The metal sank deep into the meaty part of his thigh and she felt a surge of triumph. He cursed and she threw all of her weight forward. It hurt because he didn't let her go right away. If anything, he held on tighter. There was an awful pressure in her throat cutting off all of her air. She clawed and kicked at him, nearly blind, stars sparking in her field of vision. When he released her, she dropped like a rock. The gunshot sounded at the same time her forehead cracked against the ground.

She felt a splatter of droplets hit her back, like the first fat drops of a hard summer rain. She cringed, curling in on herself before struggling to rise to her knees.

"Jane?" Lyle knelt beside her, his strong arms wrapping her up and pulling her up against his chest. She felt his lips brush her temple and then bury in her hair. "It's all right. They're all gone."

"I'm sorry," she said shakily.

Pulling back, he stared down at her, brows drawn together and gray eyes sharp. One hand still held a gun, his other was warm on her back. "What the hell are you sorry for?"

"I dropped my gun and I let that bastard sneak up on me. I should have—"

"Come here." He repositioned himself, resting his back against a rock and wrapping his arms around her, not seeming to mind in the least that she was covered in blood. She noticed that he didn't holster his gun. Instead, he set it on the ground beside his hip, then cupped the back of her head and pulled it to rest on his shoulder. "You have nothing to be sorry for. We're both alive and that's the important thing. Things happen in a fight you can't predict or change. You just have to roll with it. You stabbed him with a hairpin and that's the only reason I was able to get a shot. I say you did good."

"Is he really dead?"

"They all are."

Good. She curled against him, taking comfort in his warmth and solid presence. While any other time she might have been embarrassed by their position, she needed this and didn't plan on moving until he made her. Luckily for her, Lyle didn't seem in any hurry to let her go. There was still work to do. They'd need to check the area to be certain it was safe to rest. They'd need to get rid of the bodies. But when she shivered, Lyle stroked his open hand down her back.

"Shh, there you go. It's all over."

When he inhaled, she rose with the movement of his chest. He smelled so good. Not like soap and perfume but good. And that was a little disturbing, considering they'd been on the road for days now. She smelled like sweat and blood. Those fat droplets landing on her back and in her hair…

"I need to bathe."

"It's dark, sweetheart. How about we wait until morning?"

His palm settled on the back of her head and he smoothed it lightly down her hair. She would start purring like a cat if he continued to touch her so. "I want to wash off the blood."

"Later. You're not doing anything but sitting here with me for a little while. I need a few minutes to catch my breath and I think you do too."

He shifted her in his arms and leaned over to grab a blanket. Once he had it tucked around her body, he pressed her head back against his shoulder so she was staring into the dying flames. "The bodies."

"I'll take care of them here in a second."

"I can help," she said. "I'm not a child you have to soothe back to sleep."

"I know you're not a child." There was an odd catch to his deep voice. Another shiver chased down her spine and he followed it with his hand.

"Lyle?"

"Hmm?"

"Would you really have shot me?"

"That was a bluff," he said. "Surely you knew that."

"There was some comfort in the thought of it. I wouldn't want you to have let him drag me away."

He was silent for a long time, fingers playing with the ends of her hair. "It worked out for the best, thanks to you. But even if he'd taken you, I'd have found a way to get you back."

She lifted her head from his shoulder. His face was only inches away, the right side dark, the left harshly lit by the fire. But his eyes were what captured her attention. Glittering and sharp, at odds with the gentle way he was holding her. He stared at her mouth and then met her gaze.

"One way or another. I'd have found you."

The moment stretched. She highly doubted this was

the way he comforted the other Rangers when they were frightened. Lyle was always so careful with her. Even out on the road when they were working together to settle the horses or to cook a meal, he rarely touched her. They'd had an unspoken agreement. He kept his distance so they could focus on their mission and she kept her distance because of Cam, the past behind her and Gideon at the end of the road up ahead. None of that seemed to matter just now. There was nothing between them now but a few inches of chill night air.

She could feel the shudder of his exhalation against her lips and when he drew in a deeper breath to speak, she tipped forward to stop the words with a kiss. It was barely even a kiss. Just a small tentative brush of her mouth to his. His lips were surprisingly soft. Warm. He didn't move at all but then, she imagined she'd surprised him. Pressing a hand to his chest, she felt him inhale sharply as she slipped the tip of her tongue between his parted lips to open him wider. She tasted him, sank into his warmth, brushed her thumb across the whiskers on his jaw and cradled his cheek. When he didn't respond, she pulled away.

The look on his face told her everything she needed to know. His hands hadn't moved from her back. They were still and heavy. He'd only been trying to comfort her because she was frightened. He was being kind. Because he was a good man who looked out for other people. And she'd taken advantage of that.

"Janie."

She turned her face away and started to disentangle herself. "I'm sorry."

"It's not that I don't want you, I do."

She knew that. Knew why he'd want to keep his

hands off her too. It made all sorts of sense and she never would have kissed him if she'd been thinking clearly. His grip on her arm tightened when she moved to get up.

"I won't take you here, not like this. Not with you shaking like a leaf and the dead lying all around us."

She pulled the blanket with her, wrapping it around her shoulders as she stood up. "I don't know why I did that."

"Don't you?"

Because she liked him. Because when she was scared and tired, Lyle had gathered her up in his strong arms. He'd been kind to her and he'd killed for her. "I wanted to thank you."

His brows drew together. "You wanted to thank me with a kiss?"

She turned away from his frown and saw the boots of one of the dead men not more than six feet away. She swayed, bile rising in her throat. She swallowed it down and heard Lyle climb to his feet behind her.

"You go down to the river and clean up," he said gently. "I'll take care of this."

"I can help."

He gave a short laugh. "You're turning green again. Go before you puke in the bedroll. They'll be gone by the time you get back."

"Thank you."

Before she stepped away, he reached out and caught her chin, lifted her face until she was looking directly into his stormy eyes. He brushed his thumb over her lower lip. "You can thank me later."

TEN

You can thank me later. He wished he hadn't said that because it was all he could think about from that point on. Janie in his arms trembling with spent emotion. The soft weight of her body. The way she'd turned toward him, lifting her face and then that kiss...God, that kiss.

When she came back from washing in the river with her hair soaked through and her bare toes peeking out from beneath the hem of her skirts, he'd wrapped her up in his blankets and set her back before the fire. She fell asleep before he did but woke up first the next morning. He'd startled awake to the sound of gunfire and found Janie by the river where she'd set up the targets, her hair bound back in a braid, bruises beneath her eyes and on her neck. Her clothing was slightly stained but all tucked in and proper. As he watched from the tree line, she hit every target she took aim at.

No sign of the vulnerable woman he'd rocked to sleep the night before. No sign of the temptress who'd invited him to love her, either. While he didn't truly regret not taking her in a campsite filled with cooling corpses, he regretted the circumstance that had forced him to turn her away. And the distance that put between them.

"Are you hungry?" he asked when she finally lowered her weapon and turned to find him standing there.

"No," she said, her expression calm and completely

composed. "The horses are ready. I've already packed everything."

"You could have woken me."

Cradling the gun so the muzzle pointed toward the ground, she walked to join him. "You needed the sleep."

"I suppose I did. Thank you for that."

She shrugged. "I figured if you weren't awake by the time I was ready for practice then the sound would surely wake you. We should be off soon."

"Give me a few minutes to wash up."

They left without eating which was just as well. When the wind shifted, it carried with it the unmistakable scent of something beginning to rot. He'd dumped the bodies a fair distance away in a ditch and covered them as best he could in the middle of the night but it was hardly a Christian burial. Even if he'd had the inclination, he hadn't the time for it. They rode at a brisk pace that didn't allow for much conversation, stopping at midday to give the horses a rest and share some dried meat. He got Janie to take a nip from his flask, hoping it would chase some of the shadows from her eyes. She thanked him then but didn't speak to him again until they reached the ruins of Fort Hill later that day.

He'd always liked the land around Fort Hill. It was the northernmost fort and nearest to the mountains. Rolling hills and a strong flowing river nearby. Good timber to the west too. Eventually someone would claim the land to farm but likely not for another generation or two when people's memory of the massacre that had occurred here began to fade.

Standing so close to the ruins—the charred wood and the rusted scraps of metal that still littered the ground—Lyle's memory of the massacre was still fresh in his mind. The great black billow of smoke from the fire that had burned for a full week. The utter destruction of the fort and all the people in it. His horror when he found a scrap of Abby's shirt and thought she'd died in the blaze.

He glanced at Jane. "Do you mind if we make a quick stop?"

"Here?"

"It's not really haunted," he said. "We'll find somewhere else to camp tonight. I want to pay my respects. It'll only take a few minutes. You can ride on if you like and I'll catch up."

"I don't mind waiting."

They followed the old road north. The dirt track was slowly being overtaken by weeds. Before the Reaper attack, they'd kept the land around the fort clear for a mile in every direction, burning back the weeds each fall so they could see anyone coming. Not that it had done them much good. Not against a sentient Reaper armed with explosives and information from the Scrappers who'd wanted the cure destroyed.

The grass was knee-high now, nearly obscuring the last of the standing support beams. Saplings were sprouting up here and there within what remained of the fort structure. He couldn't help but think of Dougan. They'd been attacked too, just a few months after Hill, but they'd managed to live through it. Abby, Cap, Cam and Janie too. All of them had nearly shared in the same fate as the poor souls buried here.

The graveyard was about a mile past the fort, at the top of a gentle slope overlooking the river. There weren't actually individual graves, just the one marker—a large square granite slab carved with the names of the dead.

Reapers had eaten the flesh off the corpses, leaving only the bones behind and there'd been no way to sort them out.

With the grass so high, it took him a moment to spot it. Maybe later, when this was all done, he'd see if Cap would let him take a team up here to tend to the place. That seemed more right to him than hiring a local farmer to do the job. Dismounting, he walked up to the monument. Some of the names were familiar but most he didn't recognize. Captain Schmitt, who he'd never really gotten along with. Lou Creston, the quartermaster and Jack Bender, Lou's close friend. Lou and Jack had just put in for a transfer to Dougan because Schmitt disapproved of their relationship. If Hill had fallen a few weeks later, both of them might now still be alive. Andrew and Ellison Ford had been twins, barely fifteen and such awful shots, Lyle had been genuinely worried for his own safety the one time he'd joined them for target practice. His gaze swept over the other names—nearly a hundred of them. Rangers, scientists and the unmarked workers who kept the fort running.

Rangers didn't have family like normal people did. Until Cap made the exception for Jake and Abby, they hadn't even been allowed to marry, let alone come to know any children they might father. If he was to die, no one would care except for the people back at the fort. Lyle's mother had passed away years ago and she was the only family he'd ever known.

He felt a little hollow looking at the lonely place with the ruins below and the grave marker already overgrown with grass. Bowing his head, he said a silent prayer, asking for peace for the men who'd died and a blessing for Fort Dougan, that the men under his command never meet the same fate. That they could get the cure out to the people who needed it and turn back the plague.

After a few moments, he heard the swish of grass and the rustle of Janie's skirts. She didn't say anything, just placed her hand on his arm and waited. When he was done, he turned to look down the slope at the surrounding countryside. In full summer, you wouldn't be able to see the river from here, but with the trees bare, it sparkled in the distance.

"It's very quiet here," he said finally. "Peaceful, don't you think?"

"I've never passed this way before. It's not what I expected."

He turned his head. "Expected?"

"Jake mentions this place every once in a while but he makes it sound like a prison."

"It was one for him."

"Welks speaks of it with nostalgia, not sadness. More like he mourns the place instead of the people."

"Welks hadn't been here for very long and he isn't the kind of man who makes friends easily."

"It only makes Abby angry. She never talks about what happened." She looked down at the marker. "You knew these people."

"Some of them." He covered her hand with his. "We should be going."

"I'm sorry."

"So am I."

He wished things were different, but wishing wasn't going to get them anywhere. They needed the cure back, continued funding and Williams's head on a spike. They could put it down there where the fort used to stand.

The remainder of the trip to Columbus Junction was uneventful. Lyle's skin began to itch well before they hit the first slopes of the great mountains, same as it did when he was hunting a Reaper pack. A tingling in his blood, an awareness that he was headed for danger. The ride became more treacherous with the rockiness of the terrain and the increase in ground cover. Their pace slowed but it didn't stop them from reaching their destination on the afternoon of the fifth day after passing through the ruins of Fort Hill.

Janie grew quieter the closer they got which gave him plenty of time to reconsider his decision to bring her along. She could get hurt. No use denying the possibility. And while he'd been willing to accept that risk back at the fort, it seemed an altogether different thing to him as they rode down the narrow street into the town where she'd once been imprisoned.

Chained. To a fucking pipe. By the man in charge of this town.

He hated the mountains. Crowded, noisy and all the cities smelled like shit. Not shit from normal livestock but like filth left to rot in the street. And there were eyes everywhere. In the buildings rising up three, four stories on either side of them and in the airships hovering above, as thick in the sky as flies around fresh meat.

The streets were narrow, land being at a premium. When Scrapers needed room to expand, they brought in the mountain planers to cut the terraces directly into the stone. Well, first the blast crews to do the crude work and then the noisy metal beasts that ground the rock into flat level steps that people could build their homes on. It was like this all up and down the Rockies. Every inch of stable rock claimed, bought and sold for more money than he would see in twenty lifetimes. Doc was born in the east and he said the Appalachians were the same, only older. More crowded and not as secure because they didn't reach the same heights.

Columbus Junction was one of the poorest towns under Stormking, barely above the foothills. Nothing more than an outlaw camp really. And the people there had no say over how it was run. The sheriff—Gideon Moore—was appointed directly by the Stormking council, the council elected by the landowners on the mountain.

You had to be a descendent of one of the founding families in order to be on the council and they didn't give a crap what happened down here so long as things continued to run smoothly. Stormking was deeper into the mountains, as high above Columbus Junction as Columbus Junction was above the plains. That was how they built their cities here. The most important people at the highest point, the riffraff straggling down the sides.

The people like him born on the plains…well, they didn't even bear thinking about, did they? He shifted in his saddle to glance over at Janie. Her back was straight and her expression calm but there was a haunted look in her eyes that was worrisome.

"We need to leave the horses at the stable," she told him grimly. "Riders are uncommon enough to draw attention. And then we're going to need to talk."

She'd talked a lot on their way here. Stories about Columbus Junction and Gideon Moore, all of which he knew had to have been hard for her to relate and some he wished he didn't have to hear. He'd have said she'd already told him everything he needed to know. If there was more, something she had to screw up her courage to tell him, it couldn't be good.

They stabled their horses, Lyle having to pay for the service. On patrol, everything he needed was provided by the forts or the towns they protected. He was a Ranger. It came as something of a shock when the stablemaster demanded payment. Scowling, he'd turned to dig through his saddlebag for the coin. They'd decided to take only one bag of essentials with them to their lodging but it was still stuffed fit to burst the seams. It took a moment and he might have cursed a time or two during the course of his search. But when he caught Janie's stifled smile, he decided that alone was worth the inconvenience.

That was worrisome too.

Dangerous for him to get distracted from his purpose here, even for a moment. And Janie was a distraction from the top of her coppery head to her perfect tiny toes.

When they stepped onto the walkway outside the stable, she threaded her arm through his. "Welcome to the real world, Lieutenant."

He smiled and covered her hand with his own. Her fingertips felt cold, fragile. "My world is just as real as yours, sweetheart."

"Except this isn't my world. Not anymore." She tugged his arm. "Come on. This way."

She surprised him by directing him away from the center of town. It was hard to say if the people who watched them as they passed did so because they were strangers or if it was because of Janie. Even coated with the dust from the road, she was still a beautiful woman. For all sorts of reasons, he'd like to get her off the streets as soon as possible.

He bent his head and lowered his voice. "Mind telling me about where we're going? A lot of eyes in this town and none of them friendly."

"The blonde we just passed looked awful friendly."

He hadn't noticed, but it was easy enough to spot who she was talking about when he glanced over his shoulder. A tall willowy woman with elaborately styled blond hair, a purple hat perched on top like a strange little bird. He smiled at Jane. "You're jealous."

"Just paying attention. You'd do well to do the same."

By the way her lips compressed, she wasn't happy with the topic and pushing it would do nothing but distract him further so he let it drop. "Where are we headed?"

"Somewhere safe."

"Safe?"

She tilted her head slightly. "Reasonably so. It won't take Gideon long to learn that we're here, but we can't stay at one of the establishments he owns, can we?"

He wondered at her evasion as they walked. Toward the outskirts, past the stink of the butcher's and the smoke from the blacksmith's, down a dark narrow lane where no respectable citizen would ever roam. And he understood her reluctance to give him a name. The place she was taking him to likely didn't even have one. This was the part of town that catered to unaccepted vice, the businesses too unsavory to be allowed a storefront. A devil's alley.

Every hair on his head rose and he shifted his coat back to give him easy access to his gun. He didn't ask any more questions though, just followed her lead. He trusted her to know the best way to proceed though he could hardly credit that she'd ever stepped foot in a place like this.

He knew she'd fallen on rough times after leaving Eyrion, but even a place like Columbus Junction would have some respectable society. And Janie had been poised to marry a wealthy man. When she'd spoken of the small cottage she'd purchased with the child price from Samuel, it had been with pride in her voice. There were no quaint homes in this part of town.

She stopped outside a clapboard house, by far the dingiest they'd seen. Narrow and wedged between two larger buildings, it was three stories high. If the wood had ever been painted, there was no sign of it now. Someone had hung their laundry from the railing on the balcony off the second floor and ladies' bloomers and shifts flapped in the breeze. The tinny sound of a player piano floated through the open door and there was a man curled in a fetal position sleeping half-underneath the stairs. It was a brothel, that's what it was. And, by the looks of it, not a particularly prosperous one.

Keeping one eye on the street, Lyle looked questioningly at Janie. She gave him a bare sliver of a smile and then started up the steps. "We're home."

Before that sunk in, she was already at the door. He closed his mouth and followed her. The place was a shithole, a hundred times worse than he'd imagined it. Janie, always fastidious, so careful about her clothes and her hair. He shook his head. He couldn't picture her living here. It looked unstable, dirty. He could smell the sharp reek of gin from the stoop. All in all, he'd rather sleep in the stables. And this, this was what she considered a safe place.

When he hesitated at the threshold, she grabbed his

hand and tugged him forward. His chest locked up but then he shoved the pity aside. She wouldn't like that, not even a little. She was a survivor. No shame in that. She was tough, brave, smart. She'd survived this place once, she could do it again. He'd make sure she made it home safely. To her real home.

The smell was worse inside but it looked marginally more respectable. The walls had been papered over, a wine-red patterned with ivy that would hide stains. Dark, even with the windows open and the glow from the gas lamps hanging from the walls.

Every male eye turned in their direction as Janie leaned over the bar to speak to the barkeep. Lyle put one hand on her waist and the other on his gun, glaring everyone down until they went back to what they were doing. He couldn't hear what she said but when the barkeep stepped away, Janie touched his arm and tipped her head to the side. "This way."

They passed through a door behind the bar, down a dim hallway and into a back room. It appeared to be a private sitting room, smallish and dimly lit with faded scarlet silk on the wall. No windows. A tall woman with dark hair, dressed with a shabby gentility that perfectly matched her surroundings, rose from the settee.

With a soft cry of surprise, she opened her arms to Jane. Even as Jane rushed forward to greet her friend, the madam's shrewd eyes fixed on him. Lyle glanced down the hall to be sure they hadn't been followed and then closed the door behind him. He watched the reunion with his hand resting lightly on the butt of his gun. By the time the pair separated and he heard Janie laugh at something her friend said, he'd relaxed enough to step forward.

Jane turned toward him and wiped at the tears on her cheek. "Lyle, this is my friend Rose. She's offered to let us stay."

Lyle still wasn't convinced that was their best option but he nodded. "Thank you. We appreciate your hospitality."

Rose's lips quirked at that but she didn't call him on his bluff. Instead, she moved forward, her eyes sweeping down his body in appreciative perusal.

"Well now, aren't you a big strapping man?"

He was reasonably certain that Rose was one too. Removing his hat, he ran a hand through his hair. "Ma'am. A pleasure."

Rose pursed her lips and widened her eyes at Jane. "A gentleman to boot. Where did you find this one, lovie?"

"At the fort. He's a Ranger." Jane sat down on the settee, pulled off her boots and tucked her feet up under her skirts. *Sure, Janie, just make yourself comfortable while I'm inspected like cattle.* When Jane met his eyes, she just smiled, eyes dancing with amusement.

Rose circled him slowly. "Is it true what they say about Rangers?"

"What's that, ma'am?"

She leaned forward, until her chest was pressed to his. "That they always walk around with their guns half-cocked and ready for action."

Lyle took her hand and removed it, gently, from his ass. "Half-cocked, ma'am?" He grinned. "No, I would never say that."

Rose smiled and called over her shoulder. "Jane, would you mind ringing for tea?"

Janie frowned at that, looking uncertain for the first time since they arrived. Was she worried about what

Lyle might do in her absence or was she worried about Rose? After a moment's hesitation, she headed for the door in her stocking feet, sparing him a warning glance before she closed it behind her.

Rose stepped away. "What the hell were you thinking bringing that girl back here?"

Lyle tilted his head. "It was her idea to come."

"She'll only take a minute or two so I'm going to tell you all you need to know. Don't let Gideon see her. Take her out of here before you stir up trouble you're not ready to handle."

He paused a moment to consider how far he could trust her. "I can't do that. We didn't come here on a holiday."

"Whatever your purpose in coming isn't worth that girl's life."

Lyle was inclined to agree with that but he couldn't change his decision now. "Gideon sent men to the fort."

Her face went ghost-white beneath all the cosmetics. "After Jane?"

He shook his head. "After the Reaper cure. He wiped out our entire stock. Jane knows the town and she's only here as a guide. She seems to think she can get Gideon to see us alone."

Rose laughed bitterly. "Oh, he'll want to see her all right. He was pissed when she ran off. If he finds her again, he'll take it out of her skin."

Lyle's hand clenched on the butt of his pistol and Rose gave him a sad look. She shook her head. "You've got no authority, Ranger. He probably already knows you're here. He'll take Janie. He'll kill you and toss your body down the mountain. Did you see that drop at the edge of town? It's called Bettie's Leap." She tipped her head in its direction. "Bettie may have been the first to go but she certainly wasn't the last."

"Why are you telling me this and not Janie?"

"Janie." Her eyes narrowed on him and then she laughed again. "*Janie* is as stubborn as a mule, in case you hadn't noticed yet. If she's worked up the courage to come back into town, she's not backing down on my say-so."

"Tell me about Gideon."

"He's a bastard, mean as they come though he hides it better than most."

"I need more than that."

The exasperated look she shot him reminded him very much of Jane. "That's all *you* need to know about Gideon Moore. Stay away from him."

He opened his mouth to ask another question, but before she could speak, the doorknob turned. Janie walked in and Rose turned away to help her with the tray of sandwiches and iced tea. He was having second thoughts about Janie's plan. Not that he didn't believe it would work. But he was worried that Janie underestimated the danger to herself. Or that she simply didn't care how much danger she was placing herself in. He cared. He cared very much. And Rose's reaction only added to his misgivings.

Walking around the table to pick up a sandwich, he sat beside Jane on the settee.

A tight knot of fear settled in his gut. She'd said it had been bad but he hadn't truly comprehended the extent of it until he saw this place. What he hadn't taken into account was his reaction to it all, the rage stirring inside him. He wanted to turn around, throw Janie on a horse and get the hell out of Columbus Junction. Not ever look back. He wanted to dismantle the whole damn town stone by stone. Mostly, he wanted to hunt down Gideon Moore and put a bullet in his head.

And he couldn't do any of those things. Not if he expected to find out what happened to the cure. Not if wanted to keep Janie alive. He couldn't kill Gideon without putting Janie in even more danger than she was already in.

And he wasn't letting her get hurt again. Not on his watch.

ELEVEN

LYLE DIDN'T ASK HER any more questions as she led him to their room, not about her life here or about Gideon. She wondered what exactly Rose had said to him. She hated people meddling in her life and Lyle already handled her with kid gloves, as if she was something fine and breakable when she knew she wasn't either of those things. That's why she'd hurried back to Rose's office after shouting an order for tea into the kitchens.

Now, she fully expected him to tuck her into bed and try to sneak out to handle it all himself. It's what Cam would have done, she knew. If Cam had let her stand her ground and fight Gideon the first time, she wouldn't need to be here now.

She pushed open the door but Lyle didn't immediately follow her into the shabby room. From the doorway, he looked around the small space. The wallpaper, a pale green scattered with tiny pink rosebuds, was worn but unstained. The curtains that covered the one small window were new and the linens appeared to have been freshly laundered.

It was amazing, really, that Lyle could blush at the sight of a bed. He stared at it with a strange expression on his face, a slight flush reaching the base of his neck. Jane bit back a smile. She knew he wasn't inexperienced. Rangers never were. The safety of the border depended upon the birth of as many star-marked children as possible and the forts paid the women who bore those children extraordinarily well. They were encouraged to spread their affections widely.

She wondered what would happen if she unbuttoned her dress and let it fall to the floor. Her fingers flirted with her collar but she didn't quite have the gumption to dare it.

"It's not much," she said.

His head tilted in that assessing way that told her he was mulling over something that piqued his interest. "This was your room?"

"For a time."

Stepping inside, he gently closed the door behind him. And they were alone. Oh, they'd been alone for the entire trip but this was different somehow. The tiny room, the closed door. The smell of sex that seemed to have seeped into the walls and linens.

And now *she* was the one blushing.

She touched the brass finial on the bedpost. "Rose let me stay here after the first time I tried to leave. She's the one who sent word to Cam that I was in trouble. Never even made it all the way out of town that first time. Here, let me see that."

She took the saddlebag from him and set it on the wooden chair in the corner. Busying herself with unfastening the buckles, she ignored the way the springs on the bed squeaked as he sat down upon the mattress.

"That can wait, can't it?" His voice was strained. "There's nothing to unpack and you should rest now while you can. We'll have to head out after dinner."

"Trying to lure me into bed, Lieutenant?"

The silence that followed was uncomfortable. She pulled her spare dress from the pack and shook it out, turning around and lifting it to show him how awfully wrinkled it was. "I should iron it."

"I bet Rose would have someone do it for you."

"If you asked, no doubt any of the girls would jump to the task. But it would be rude to ask." Rose and her employees worked hard enough. She laid the dress over the back of the chair. It might do. She could spritz some water on it before they went out. She'd want to wear a cloak in any case. All that anyone would see was a glimpse of the satin and that should be enough for Gideon's guards to let her into the saloon.

"What are you thinking?"

She smiled. "I was wondering if Rose would let me borrow one of her wigs. The longer I go without being recognized the better. I don't want Gideon to realize it's me until I'm standing right in front of him."

He removed his hat and set it on the small table beside the bed. When he ran his hand through his hair, a few pieces stuck up strangely. Her fingers itched to smooth them down.

"I'd rather you stay in tonight," he said "No one knows who I am. I can go play a few hands of cards and get the lay of the land before we start asking questions. All we want to do is verify that Gideon is the one who stole the serum, find out where it is if we can."

"They'll know you're a Ranger." It was in the way he carried himself. His clothes and his guns. "They'll wonder why you're here alone, especially if we're right and they were the ones to steal the serum. The plan was to let Gideon believe I'm moving back into town and you're my escort home. That, he won't question as closely."

After all, his last words to her were a promise that

he'd be waiting when she was ready to crawl back. Gideon would be suspicious. But he was arrogant, too, and he'd appreciate the thought of her begging him for shelter. She was reluctant to explain it to Lyle in those terms and hoped he'd just continue to trust her.

She smoothed the wrinkles from her dress with the palm of her hand. "You think it's foolish of me to want to help. That I think this is some kind of game, but I don't."

There was a long pause that ended with his sigh. "I know you don't think it's a game. I'm worried for you."

She glanced over her shoulder to find him seated on the edge of the bed, leaning slightly forward with his hands clasped between his knees. Watching her. She stopped fussing with the dress and crossed the room to stand in front of him. "You don't need to worry about me."

She brushed back a lock of hair that had fallen across his forehead and then froze at the hungry look in his eyes. He didn't reach for her though, didn't give her any sort of sign that he wanted more. Letting her hand fall to her side, she mustered a small smile.

"Do you mind moving over? I think I would like to lay down for a spell, after all."

He stood up as though the bed was on fire. She didn't even have time to step back. And then, when his body brushed against hers, she didn't *want* to move away. Lyle might be confused about what he wanted from her, but she wasn't. Not anymore.

She'd had some time to think about the night they'd been attacked on the road. To wonder if Lyle would have taken her up on her offer if they hadn't been sitting in the middle of a battlefield. She wanted to know.

"I'll let you have the bed," he said. "I might go take a walk around—"

"Stay." The word slipped out on its own but she saw him flinch as it hit. To her, it felt good that it was out there. Right.

Lyle didn't pretend not to understand what she was offering. "Janie…"

"Please." She reached out to catch his hand. "I want you to stay with me."

"It would feel like taking advantage." The corner of his mouth turned up. "Especially in this place."

"I'll pay you if it makes you feel better."

He let out a long shuddering breath that held just a hint of laughter and then reached up to cup her cheek. "I'm not cheap."

She turned her head and ran her lips along the calloused edge of his thumb. "There's no doubt in my mind you'll be costly."

Every time she let herself care about someone it cost her dearly. But it didn't change the fact that she wanted him. She edged a little closer. The heat of him sank through the layer of skirts to touch her skin and she used her grip on his hip to steady herself as she lifted onto her toes, letting her nipples graze against his chest with the motion.

She reached up to wrap her arms around his neck, her fingertips toying with the ends of his hair. She'd always liked his hair. Brown and sun-beaten gold with just the slightest bit of a wave to it. She'd always wondered how it would feel against her skin. His eyes hooded and he breathed a curse. But he bent his head, his breath fanning across her cheek. She wet her lips.

"You're killing me, Janie." He stroked her cheekbone in the gentlest of caresses. "Why are you asking me to your bed?"

A million ways she could answer that question. This place made her reckless. Either one of them might not make it out of Columbus Junction alive. There was plain, base want. The sight of him on her bed made her skin hot and her bloomers wet. So many reasons why. But because this was Lyle, who she not only respected but liked, she gave him the most honest answer she could. "I don't want to be alone right now."

He froze for a tic, studying her face. Then he bent his head to brush his lips across her temple. Her eyelids fluttered closed at that butterfly touch but he didn't linger. Sinking his hand into her hair, he angled her face up, placed a kiss to the corner of her eye before drifting lower to find her lips. He teased her mouth wide with his tongue and then dipped inside to stroke hers. He knew how to kiss and she'd expected that. What she hadn't accounted for was her response. The heat that surged through her blood. The way her breasts seemed to swell and her sex ached ever so sweetly.

One of his hands left her hair to stroke down her neck. He massaged her there gently and then his fingers dipped inside the neckline of her gown. All the while his mouth moved on hers unhurriedly, so calm and controlled that his groan took her by surprise. She wanted to hear it again.

He slipped the first couple of buttons free before she even noticed it. The cool air on her heated skin made her pull slightly away to look down and then she started to help him. When her fingers fumbled at the buttons, he moved her hands aside and made quick work of the rest.

That blush touched his neck again as he looked down

at her. Though her shift was made of very simple cotton, she'd sewn lace trim across the top. It was a cream color only a shade lighter than her skin. Lyle stared at the tops of her breasts with a particularly intent expression that made her shiver.

He looked up. "Are you cold?"

Shaking her head, she pushed her gown from her shoulders and let it pool around her waist. His palms fit against her there and pushed the mass down over her hips. He left her standing in her shift and reached down to pull back the blankets. "In."

She climbed in, scooting over as he sat down to pull off his boots. They fell to the floor with successive thunks and then he stood to shove off his denim trousers. The shirt, he pulled over his head.

Then he was slipping into bed with her. Lyle. Strong and lean and blazing hot where his skin brushed up against hers. Full of interesting textures. The hair on his legs and the jut of his hip. The muscles firm and plump and strong as they gathered her in.

"Do you want me to take off my shift?"

He made a strangled noise. "Keep it on. We're going to get some rest and if you take it off...just keep it on."

"Rest?"

"I'm not leaving you alone. I'm not taking advantage either."

"Lyle."

"Sleep." He tucked an arm behind his head, shifting the bed and her body as he settled in. "This isn't done. We're not done here."

"You want me." It wasn't a question. She knew that he did.

"We're going to face Gideon soon."

"And what?" She frowned when she realized what he was getting at. "You think this is about Gideon?"

He didn't answer right away. He smoothed a hand over her hair, stroking from the crown of her head to the ends that curled midway down her back. He was careful not to get caught in any of the tangles and she gradually felt her muscles begin to relax.

"I know you're scared." Lyle's voice was a low rumble. She could feel the vibration of it against her breasts. "Cam told me how he found you here. Chained to a pipe in Gideon's bedroom. You don't have to be ashamed to talk to me about that. I know it's not pretty."

The hard edge that came to Lyle's voice when he spoke Gideon's name unnerved her and she lay there listening to his heartbeat until her own slowed down. This is what she'd been afraid of, him rushing into Columbus Junction with his guns drawn, hunting Gideon as if he was just another Reaper. Lyle was brave. He was a good fighter and he was no idiot, but he'd never faced an enemy like Gideon. Reapers came right for your throat. Gideon was as slippery as a slug. She didn't want to see Lyle get hurt. She wasn't going to let that happen.

"You think I'm completely innocent? I'm not. Gideon wanted me and I knew it. He made sure that I knew it. When he staked his claim, no one else would help me, except Rose. She's very strong. I don't think she's afraid to stand up to anyone."

"I believe you."

"I worry about her."

His lips brushed the top of her head. "You worry too much about everyone else and not enough about yourself."

"He offered me everything I needed—a roof over

my head, food, a place in what passes for society here so I took him up on his offer. That part was my fault. I could have left then, when it was still early. But I was a coward and so tired of running."

A rumble worked its way up from his chest and he said, "He took advantage of you. He had all the power and you had nothing. He knew exactly what he was doing and you only did what you had to do to survive it."

She shook her head. "That may be true but I knew what kind of man he was. Maybe I didn't know *exactly* where the money was coming from but I knew enough to make me suspicious."

"You didn't do anything wrong."

She was shocked to silence by his sharp tone. Easy to forget that he was a fighter and lieutenant, a leader of men when he was always so gentle with her. And she realized then that Lyle would never take advantage of that power. He would never use it to hurt someone weaker than himself. Something inside her turned liquid and threatened to well up like a ground spring.

"I made bad decisions. There's no denying Gideon is a devil but I'm no angel. You're wrong to make me out as one."

"I'm not confused about who you are."

"Then you can stop acting like I'm a living, breathing tragedy. You're always watching me like you're waiting for me to fall apart."

"I don't see you as a tragedy." His hand slipped beneath her hair and curved around the back of her neck. "Last month, I watched a good friend of mine ride straight into a Reaper swarm because he was tired of fighting. That was tragic. I can't imagine you ever giving up like that."

She closed her eyes, letting that sink in. Not just the words but the warm approval behind them. No wonder everyone looked up to Lyle like they did. He had a way of making a person feel like they were worth something.

"And I don't watch you because I'm waiting for you to fall apart, sweetheart. I watch because I like the way you look."

She stroked her hand down his flat abdomen, her fingertips bumping over the edge of his waistband and brushing the head of his hard cock. He groaned and his body shifted as if he wanted to press against her. But he restrained himself. He caught her wrist, forcing her hand back up to his chest and twining his fingers through hers. *Exasperating man.*

"Why?"

"Because I'm responsible for you."

"You're not doing a very good job of taking care of me right now."

His fingers tightened on hers. "Do you really want this? Or am I just a distraction?"

"Does it matter?"

"It matters."

She lifted her head so she could see his face, look him in the eyes. "I want you."

And she almost had him. She saw the way his eyes flickered down to her mouth for a moment before lifting again. She felt the way his muscles flexed beneath her. That wasn't his gun tenting the sheets.

"A few weeks ago you told me the same thing about Cam."

She flinched. Nothing like the truth to draw blood. "I don't love him."

"I know that. But have you given up on your plan to have him?"

She had. But for some reason she couldn't seem to spit out the words. It seemed like a betrayal somehow. As if she was giving up on Samuel too.

Lyle's hand curved behind her neck again, his thumb set just beneath her jaw, keeping her face angled to him. He studied her a moment before pressing his lips to hers lightly. Then, with a sigh, he settled back and pulled her back down against him.

"Get some sleep. This will keep until later."

TWELVE

LYLE FIGURED THE easiest way to get them in to see Gideon was to let Gideon haul them in. But that would give him far too much power over the situation for Lyle's comfort. So he kissed Janie awake only a few hours after she'd fallen asleep and helped her get dressed. She was drowsy and tousled and he fought against the urge to push her back down to the bed and melt into her.

She wanted him. Wanted the comfort of his body anyway, and that was understandable considering the stress she was under. The stress she was under was the same reason he couldn't take her up on her offer. She wanted the solace of mindless sex and he couldn't give that to her. Well, he *could*. He'd been damn close to giving her just that, but it wouldn't have been right.

"What time is it?"

"Ten. Any idea where Gideon would be this time of night?"

Janie smiled wryly and held up her hands. "Somewhere a lot like this would be my guess. Is it Thursday? Then that's a card game. Top o' the World Saloon."

He nodded. "Can we lure him out? Is he alone on the way back to his house? All we need is a few seconds to snatch him."

Janie stared down at the floorboards for a minute or two while he pulled his gun belt on. She was still looking down when she said quietly, "You know I can get him alone. This was always the plan. I don't see why you're so set on changing things now. I lure him someplace quiet and we find out what happened to the cure. It's not like he'll hold out on giving us the answers we need. He won't regard anyone's hide as more sacred than his own."

"No," he said firmly.

"I can do it. They'll kill you if you try and I know how to manage him."

"No." He knelt down right in front of her so she couldn't hide from him again. This was too important. He knew she had words to say to Gideon but Lyle didn't want to risk a confrontation if it wasn't necessary. Their opinions on what was necessary did not align.

She looked up and he hated the blank expression on her face, the flat look to her eyes. "He's never alone and he won't leave the saloon tonight. He lives upstairs. You *need* me to draw him out."

"There has to be a time when he's without his guards."

She rubbed a hand over her face. "I don't know anymore."

"When he sleeps? When he shits?"

"All inside. There will be guards outside his personal suite and on the balcony."

"How about when he fucks?"

He regretted the words as soon as they were out of his mouth. Janie jerked beneath his hands and fixed him with a glare that should have set him on fire.

"Not always," she said quietly. "Not even then."

His hands flexed on her thighs. She shoved him away and he stood up.

"I won't be in the saloon for more than a few minutes. You'll hide in the cellar and I'll get Gideon there."

"He'll want you to go upstairs."

"And I have a perfectly good reason for refusing that request. The cellar is the only other place where we'll be able to have a private conversation. He conducts some of his business there. It's how he was able to keep so much of it from me for so long. Tonight, *I'll* be the business he doesn't want anyone knowing about."

He muttered a curse under his breath and Janie decided not to hear it. "There's an outside door to the back alley so we'll be able to slip out without anyone the wiser. It's perfect. I'm telling you it will work. I *know* him."

Lyle paced toward the door. He didn't like it. He didn't want her alone with that bastard even for a second. But they didn't have many choices and Jane had gotten them this far, hadn't she? Turning to face her, he leaned back against the wall. "How about you send him a note to meet you in the cellar alone? I can be waiting for him. You wouldn't really have to show up at all."

She shook her head. "It would make him too suspicious. It has to be his idea or he won't come. Or won't come alone, for certain."

"Then maybe we don't target Gideon. Who else would know his business?"

"About the theft itself? Any number of people. About where the serum is now? Gideon for sure, possibly Flynn. He was Gideon's pilot when I left although I can't be sure they're still working together..." She shook her head. "But it's stupid to change course now when we have a perfectly good plan already worked out. I don't know why you're balking."

Lyle crossed his arms over his chest and watched her sitting there on the bed, looking small and vulnerable and, God, braver than any man he'd ever served with. He had to honor that. Nobody ever saw the value of her and he couldn't reject it. She was braced for a fight too. Every line in her body wound tense. A shocking change from the soft and drowsy woman who'd been snuggled up in his arms such a short time ago. Even knowing she'd taken care of herself this far, he didn't like to see her all armored up. And he sure as hell didn't want her to see him as just another person she had to fight her way through.

When he nodded, her eyes widened.

"Your call, then," he said, already regretting the words. "You're right. I said we'd do this your way. Let's do it your way."

Not giving him a chance to change his mind, she stood up, all business, straightening her skirts and then moving over to the mirror. She made a horrified noise before sitting down on the little upholstered stool and pulling out pins.

"We don't have much time," he said.

"It will only take a minute or two."

Or twenty. But he had a few things to arrange himself so he let her finish up while he slipped out the door.

ROSE KNOCKED ONCE before entering the room. She'd never been one to respect a closed door or even a locked one. Jane met her gaze in the mirror and continued to try to fix the mess of her hair. She'd gotten all of the knots out but what was left behind was a frizzy mess.

"What have you done?" Clucking her tongue, Rose

came up behind her and took the comb right out of her hands. "Here, let me."

Jane sat meekly as Rose expertly began to smooth and pin back the errant locks. It had been a long time since someone had taken care of her. Since she'd *let* someone take care of her. Except for Lyle. But then, that stubborn, *exasperating* man seemed to have a knack for bringing out all her weaknesses. She couldn't afford to be weak now, not tonight.

"You didn't come here to fix my hair," she said.

Rose smoothed back a strand that had fallen over her forehead. "No, I suppose not. Although I did always like to play with your hair. I could make such a wig of this."

"Don't even think it," Jane said fiercely but smiled as she said it. It was an old threat and an old conversation. Familiar and maybe a little bittersweet, considering she was unlikely to see Rose again once she left this place. This time when she left Columbus Junction, she wasn't ever looking back. She reached to touch Rose's hand. "I missed you, Rosie."

"I missed you too, turtledove." Rose bent to kiss her cheek. When she straightened, she lifted the hair iron and began to curl the loose ends. "My one comfort has been knowing you were safe. I imagined you holed up with that nice young man who descended on the town like an avenging angel to sweep you away to safety."

Jane smiled sadly and then had to look away from her reflection. That's how she'd seen Cam too, at least at first. "Things don't always turn out the way you expect them to."

"I suppose not, especially where men are concerned. Why did you come back, Jane? You know nothing good can come of it."

"You know why I came back."

"You caught dust fever and couldn't stand to live another day on the plains? Got homesick? Missed me and Flynn, your old life here? That cold bastard of a man who nearly killed you?"

Jane's fingers curled in her skirts. "Gideon wins, every time. And if he thinks he's going to lose, he cheats. You know he won't let Lyle walk away with the serum, not while he's still standing."

"He let you walk away."

"There was nothing left of me then. No point in putting a bullet in my head. At the time, I wouldn't have minded if he had." She smiled. "Gideon knew that and there was Cam to consider. I was broken, of no use to him and not worth picking a fight with the Rangers."

Rose tugged hard at a piece of hair and Jane winced. "You think he'll want that fight now?"

"If he sent men in to steal the serum, he's already decided it's worth it."

Rose's eyes locked on her in the mirror. "And what exactly are you planning to do about that?"

"What I should have done in the first place."

"You can't—"

"I can and I will. Cam saved my life and Lyle..." She shook her head. "Well, I'm not letting any of them get hurt. They're my family now and I'm not standing aside while Gideon goes after them too."

"I don't think the good lieutenant will make an easy target, not even for Gideon."

Jane shook her head. "He's a good man, a just man. He lives like there are rules. Gideon will hide behind a tree and shoot him in the back. No, he won't even do it himself. He has the money to keep hiring people until the job's done."

"Gideon could just as easily shoot you." Rose tipped her head toward the door. "And that one has no idea what you're really doing here. Do you even know what you're doing here?"

"I'm just cleaning up an old mess. You don't leave broken glass on the floor where anyone can get hurt."

"You left it there for a good long time, Jane, without a second thought as to who might be stepping in it."

She scowled. Rose always did like to get philosophical about stupid things. What did it matter why she'd decided to take care of Gideon? "It's time, that's all."

Rose laughed. When Jane stood up and threw a glare at her, she only laughed harder. "I need to go."

"Are you sleeping with that fine specimen of a man then? Is that what this is about? You're here as his little guardian angel." When Jane crossed her arms, Rose's smile widened. "Well, my, my. Rangers must truly be as good in the sack as the rumors say. Good enough to risk your life for, is he?"

"I'm not sleeping with him." When Rose's brows lifted, she added, "Don't give me that look. I offered."

"And he said no?"

Jane wished she had something more solid to throw at her than a hairbrush.

Shaking her head, Rose leaned forward to check her reflection in the mirror. "That is a pity. He's welcome to sample the house if he's a mind to."

"I'll be sure to pass that along." She'd swallow her tongue first. "If all goes well, we'll be back in a few hours."

Jane pushed back the chair and stood up. Just like

Rose to ruin a moment. She never had liked goodbyes. When Jane had her hand on the doorknob, Rose called her name. Jane paused, looking back over her shoulder.

"Love isn't worth dying for. You should know that by now."

Rose was being dramatic. This was only a job she had to get done. It was time for her to move on and to do that she had to take care of unfinished business with Gideon.

"Don't worry about me. I know exactly what I'm doing."

Rose pursed her lips and turned back to the vanity, sweeping up the extra hairpins in the palm of her hand and dropping them in a cut-glass jar. "That's what you said last time."

THIRTEEN

TOP O' THE WORLD was top tier Columbus Junction which was hardly top o' the world. It was dirt-grubbing-bottom in terms of quality of men that was for certain. Lyle disabled the guard in the back alley with a clip to the back of his head, tied and gagged him in seconds and then broke the lock to the cellar. Dumping him inside, he lent Jane a hand down the rickety wooden stairs. She moved aside to light their small lantern while he checked the basement to be sure no one else was lurking about. There was no one. No sign of the missing crates of serum either.

Once reassured that it was clear, Jane gave him a sharp nod before turning toward the stairs again. She'd have to pass down a short alley and walk through the front doors of the saloon by herself. It was possibly the hardest thing he'd ever done to stand there and watch as she left him to face Gideon alone.

If she'd balked at all, if she'd so much as glanced over her shoulder, he would have come up with a new plan. Tucked her away at Rose's while he staked out the place. Tried to bribe a few of Gideon's shadier associates. But all of that would take time they didn't have and Jane was certain she knew Gideon well enough to make this work. It was the reason he'd allowed her to come along. Her knowledge of the town. Her familiarity with Gideon. No point in second-guessing himself now. Or her.

Jane's step never faltered. Spine straight, jaw clenched and eyes forward, she didn't so much as glance back at him. Grit. He was so proud of her and scared to death, worried that he was making a terrible mistake. As soon as she was gone, he blew out the light and settled in the pitch-black cellar for the blind wait.

Time seemed to slow even as his heartbeat ratcheted up. Something scurried across his foot and he kicked the little rodent into a crate. Or something that sounded wooden anyway. There were no windows down here and he couldn't see his hand if he held it up in front of his face. The sound coming from above was muffled too. The heavy stomp of boot heels on the wooden planks drowned out the sound of anything else.

It occurred to him that they could take Janie away and he'd never know it. Drag her upstairs kicking and screaming, put her in chains again. They might have done so already.

His hand tightened on his gun. They might have her spread out on the bar as they took turns at her. A sick sliding feeling in his gut made him clench his jaw. When someone shouted directly above him, Lyle was halfway to the stairs before he could calm himself.

The door at the top opened and he drew up short. There was the flare of a match being lit and he heard Janie's voice. That settled him as quick as a dunk in ice-cold water. She was safe. She sounded irritated but not frightened. The knock in his chest settled into a steadier beat and he withdrew again into the shadows.

"I want privacy," she said. "I don't care how dirty it is, we won't be down here for long. You know I hate having everyone know our business and you already let them think I'm dragging you off so you can fuck me. Thanks for that."

"We could always go up to my room."

"Where you kept me chained for three weeks? I never want to see that place again."

"Now, Jane." Gideon sounded hurt. "That was for your own good. The doctor suggested the asylum in Silent Falls but I refused to send you. I couldn't let you hurt yourself, could I? And I was right you'd come around eventually. Look at you now."

She started down the stairs. Lyle crouched behind the crate and watched her descend. The light from her lantern lit her face but the man behind her was nothing more than a hulking shadow. Big. Of course Gideon would be a big man. He had the hard, wide body Lyle associated with the men who drove wagons for the fort. One thick hand swung into the circle of light as he put it on Janie's shoulder and spun her around.

He touched Jane as if he had a right to and that pissed Lyle off to no end. And that was before he saw the small cut to her lip she'd acquired during her brief visit to the saloon. The cure, he reminded himself. They were here for the fucking cure.

"Things didn't work out with that Ranger of yours? I told you there was no reason he'd want to hold on to one whore when he had every woman from here to Appalachia spreading their legs every time he so much as winked at them."

Janie, cool as ice, lifted one copper brow. "Jealous, are you?"

Gideon laughed and finally shifted so Lyle could see his face. He'd expected ugly but was disappointed.

Gideon didn't *look* like a monster. Just a man, even-featured with dark eyes and a cruel turn to his mouth. Women would likely think him handsome. "You know I never did mind sharing."

Gideon's smile widened at Jane's flinch and Lyle gathered himself to move.

Step away, asshole. He was still too close to Janie. And Lyle was too far away to get there before Gideon could snatch her to his chest to use her as a shield. He only needed Janie to put another foot or two between them before he could make a move.

"And Jane, dearest?" Instead of backing away when he moved closer, Jane stood her ground. Gideon took her chin between thumb and forefinger and forced her gaze up. The asshole had his hands on her. The blood roared in Lyle's ears. Janie's glare was all raw, searing hatred but she didn't try to pull away.

"This time I'm making sure you don't go nowhere. Not if I have to tie you to the bed."

Janie shoved his arm away and walked toward the corner. Lyle eased from his hiding place. Even as he moved, he could see the spark in Gideon's eyes when he saw that she'd trapped herself. But Gideon didn't see Lyle coming until the gun was a few inches from his temple. He froze at the rolling click of the hammer and then moved his hand toward his weapon.

"Do it and I pull the trigger," Lyle said softly, almost hoping that he did. "Just give me the excuse."

Slowly, Gideon's hand pulled away from his hip.

"Drop the belt and back up over there." Lyle jerked his chin toward the chair.

"You shoot here and my men will be down before the smoke clears."

"Just in time to bury your sorry ass. Now sit."

Gideon followed directions but Lyle could see the animal cunning in his eyes as he searched for a way out. Janie walked toward the door to fetch the rope as Gideon settled in to the wooden chair near the center of the room. His smile was easy and confident. Janie had mentioned his arrogance. A man like Gideon wouldn't believe he could possibly be in any danger inside his own home which was a shame. Might slow things down. Lyle would have to find a way to convince him.

Gideon gave a low whistle and shook his head. "She's under your skin, ain't she? Sweet piece of ass but crazy as a blood-drunk Reaper. She doesn't want you she just wants what you can do for her."

That was a load of horseshit. Janie was possibly the most independent woman he'd ever known. She hated to have to rely on anyone.

"We're not here to talk about Jane," Lyle said. "We're here to talk about the serum."

But Gideon kept pushing. "I bet you have rank too. She wouldn't pick any common soldier given the choice." His eyes narrowed. "And you're not the one who came for her last time. How long did it take for her to throw him over? My bet is she wanted him right up to the moment you crooked your finger at her. She's not as innocent as she looks. Cold inside. I'm sure you've seen that. Something is broke in there."

"Shut up," Lyle gritted out, glancing up as Janie held up the rope. She was asking if she should bind Gideon's hands, but Lyle didn't want her to have to touch the man at all. Not even to tie him down. He held out his free hand and after a moment's hesitation, she gave him the coil of rope.

Gideon kept his attention fixed on Lyle. "You wanted me to talk and I'm telling you what you need to know. You need to stop and think about what you're doing, friend. You come in to my house and threaten me and I'm not letting either one of you walk out of here. I'm giving you a chance—one chance, right now—to change your mind. You can't trust anything that woman's told you." Gideon's voice dropped to a conspiratorial whisper. "She killed her own baby, did she tell you that?"

Janie gave a startled cry and Lyle gestured her forward, gave her a firm look and placed the gun in her hands, folding her fingers around the butt and pointing it at Gideon. He needed both hands to finish off the knot anyway. And maybe this would keep Gideon polite.

Lyle tied the rope maybe a little tighter than he needed to and then stepped back to take his gun from Janie's hands. Her skin was cold where they touched. Cold and with a faint tremor she couldn't quite get a handle on. Understandable, considering what this man had done to her.

He wanted to wrap an arm around her shoulders and pull her in, reassure her that he knew Gideon was just shooting off his mouth to save his own skin. Tell her that she was the bravest woman he'd ever met, and he'd known some very fine women over the years. He tried to put some of that into the look he gave her as he nodded for her to fall back. Then, he turned to face Gideon.

"Now we talk."

"You could have made an appointment."

"If you think that group of boys up there will keep you safe, you think again. I can kill you without the gun. You can't hear shit from down here anyway. Sure as hell no one will hear you scream. Even if they did come after us, I shoot things for a living. I'm fairly confident I can handle a dozen half-drunk fools who like to wave their guns around but couldn't hit the side of a barn. Once I kill the first three or four, the rest will scatter for cover. Your men don't have the kind of loyalty that will make them keep coming after me." Not that he wanted a shoot-out, but he was prepared for it if necessary. Four revolvers on his person. Extra ammo, if needed. Janie was armed too and over the past few weeks, she'd turned into a surprisingly decent shot. The horses were ready to go at the bottom of Bettie's Leap.

Lyle leaned in closer, holding Gideon's gaze and enjoying the flicker of doubt he saw there.

"And just so we're clear," he said softly. "I know Janie. You're not driving a wedge between us. She's a fine woman, brave, smart and worth more than a million of you. I don't have time for your bullshit games. I'm giving you one chance, right now. You cooperate and I let you live. I give you my word as a Ranger on that."

Gideon's smirk faded a bit but his eyes were still hard. "Just tell me what you want to know so I can get back to my game." His gaze slid over Lyle's shoulder. "She ain't worth any of this shit."

"You sent men to steal from me," Lyle said, keeping his voice even. "I want my property back. You can hand it over or tell me where it is, I don't care which."

Gideon frowned. If Lyle hadn't seen the flinch at the corners of his eyes, he might have believed what he said next. "I don't know what the hell you're talking about. You're a Ranger which means you have no jurisdiction here. It also means you don't own anything worth stealing."

"The Reaper cure. Welks's serum. You've heard of it, I'm sure."

"Everyone's heard of it. Why would I need Reaper cure up here?"

Lyle took a knife from his boot sheath and slid it along Gideon's thigh. "Excellent question. Answer that one too. And here's another while you're at it—what kind of man endangers an infant's life just to prove a point?"

"You're not going to cut me so why don't we just—"

Lyle pressed his forearm to Gideon's neck to cut off the shout he made as the knife sliced open his thigh. Deep enough to hurt, close enough to his dick to give fair warning that he meant business. Gideon's face turned an interesting shade of purple before Lyle eased back just enough for him to draw a breath.

"Give us the information we want and I let you go. I give you my word on that," Lyle promised in a low voice. "But believe me when I say that I have no problem whatsoever cutting the information out of you piece by piece."

"You don't have the time for that."

Lyle nodded. "Everyone thinks you're screwing Jane right now. How much time do you usually take at that?"

Gideon looked over Lyle's shoulder and whatever he saw on Janie's face made up his mind. "Always knew the bitch was dangerous." He didn't take his eyes off Jane and that raised Lyle's hackles. "You don't want to talk to me anyway. You want Flynn."

"What does Flynn have to do with anything?" Jane asked. "He does what you tell him to do."

Gideon snorted. "You always were blind to what you didn't want to see. Flynn belongs to Corrigan, always has. He does what I tell him to do because that's the way Corrigan wants it."

Lyle glanced up at Jane to see if she could verify that and she took a step forward, eyes narrowed at Gideon. "The ship that Flynn's flying now? What's it look like?"

"A new cutter with a scarlet tail. Small and fast. Just like you." Gideon smirked and turned his attention to Lyle. "I've never had another woman come so easy or so often. She does enjoy a good hard—"

Lyle pressed the edge of his knife against Gideon's leg, a friendly reminder to keep him on course. Jane had mentioned Flynn as the pilot she suspected of taking off with their supply. Corrigan, he recognized as a Scraper businessman. From one of the founding families on Oro, if he remembered correctly.

It was possible that Corrigan was actually behind the theft. More likely that Gideon was trying to lead them offtrack. The thud of a boot heel directly overhead sent dust drifting down from the ceiling, reminding him that they were running out of time.

Jane brushed a fleck of dust from her shoulder. "Why does Corrigan want the serum?"

"Don't know," Gideon said. "Don't care. I was not at all involved in that operation."

"Reginald Potts pointed to you."

"Did he now?"

"Where is it, Gideon?"

Lyle put a little pressure on the knife, enough to split through the fabric. Gideon flinched a bit as he felt the cold steel but he kept talking to Janie. "Flynn is who you want to talk to. He's upstairs right now. Would you like me to fetch him? He always did have an eye for you. I'm sure you can come up with a way to make him talk."

"You're not going anywhere," Lyle said.

Gideon raised his brows. "You can't take me out of here and they'll come looking soon. Shoot and it'll be sooner. Either way, you're going to need time to get out of town too."

Lyle didn't need to be reminded of the time slipping away from them while Gideon laid a false trail.

While he was still contemplating how far he wanted to go with this, Jane circled behind Gideon and slit his throat. It happened so fast Lyle couldn't do anything but stare. At her hands. The blood. The blank expression on her pale face as she wiped the blade clean. Gideon was dead, or good as. His eyes were bulging and a sick gurgling noise was coming from the gaping wound in his neck.

Lyle didn't even know where she'd pulled the knife from. He hadn't realized she was carrying one. As she stepped back from the quickly spreading pool beneath the chair, she looked directly at him and flinched at whatever she saw on his face.

"Jane…" His voice came out in a harsh whisper. *"What the hell?"*

"It had to be done," she said, calm as can be. In fact, she looked more settled than she had been since they'd stepped foot in this godforsaken town. "He was right about the gunfire. And if we want to get out of here, we need to go now. We have our answer. We need Flynn. It was his ship I saw in that clearing. Gideon described it exactly. He wasn't going to be of any further help."

Be that as it may, she hadn't needed to go and slit the man's throat. However much of a bastard Gideon had been, they'd come for answers, not murder.

"You said you weren't after revenge." And he was the idiot who'd believed her.

"I'm not," she said. "This wasn't about revenge."

"Then what was it?"

"You heard him. We couldn't leave him alive. He'd have chased us down and sent word to Corrigan. We'd have lost any chance we had of recovering the serum. Gideon would have put a bullet in your head."

"You don't know what might have happened."

"You're right. He might've hanged you instead."

Lyle bit back a curse as the door above creaked open. Jane reached over and shuttered the lantern. Giving wide berth to the chair at the center of the room, Lyle crossed to meet her. Wary of the knife, he found her hand in the darkness and pulled her toward the cellar door. He didn't want a gunfight if it could be avoided.

The man at the top of the stairs cleared his throat. "I'm sorry to disturb you, boss but…well, this needs your attention. Mr. Moore?"

"Billy," Jane whispered. "Gideon's secretary. He'll come down."

There was no point in waiting. Lyle pushed the cellar door and the hinges squealed like a stuck pig. Shoving Jane into the alley, he scrambled up behind her.

"This way." The whisper came from a small figure crouched in a shadow near the wall. Reflexively, Lyle pointed his gun in that direction until their guide revealed himself, armpit-high and skinny as a rail. The boy started down the alley without waiting to see if they meant to follow. Lowering his gun, Lyle pushed Jane after the street rat.

When Jane looked back at him questioningly, he

shrugged. "Rose sent him just in case. Said he could get us out quick and send word if there was trouble."

"He's only a boy," she hissed.

"I noticed that too."

At the end of the alley, the boy turned left into an open lot that was littered with debris. Pieces of rusted-out metal and stone. Broken glass crunched even beneath his light weight as he scurried through. When Jane saw the direction he headed, she stopped walking so suddenly that Lyle almost ran her down. "We need to go back and talk to Flynn."

"Hell no. I'm getting you out of here and sending word to the captain and the fort. We'll come back with a full patrol. We got the answers we were looking for. That's enough. This goes deeper than we thought, Janie, and it's too dangerous."

She crossed her arms. "Too dangerous for me, you mean."

Damn. There was no time for this argument. An alarm hadn't gone up yet but they had only seconds to clear out before Gideon's men flooded the streets. He grabbed Janie's arm and tugged her forward.

"It's too dangerous for you and me both," he said. "There are smart risks and there are stupid ones. Staying here is a stupid one. If we fail now, no one will ever know what happened."

Janie glared at him but kept moving. The boy waited at the mouth of another alley, hunched and darting anxious looks their way. If they didn't hurry, Lyle guessed that he'd bolt. So he pressed viciously.

"I took a chance bringing you. Everyone said you were crazy but I believed in you. I trusted you. Don't prove me wrong any more than you already have."

He felt the flinch in her arm but she didn't fold as meekly. "Flynn will talk to me. He's not…he's nothing like Gideon."

"A good friend of yours, is he? A smuggler working for Gideon with ties to Scrapers even higher up? A friend of yours who stood by while Gideon ran you and your son down like dogs?"

"He tried to help." Her voice cracked and he felt a twinge of guilt that he had to ignore. He needed to get her out of town as quickly as possible. She was not thinking straight. She'd just murdered a man for fuck's sake.

At the next turn, she dug in her heels and turned to him. They were at an intersection of two alleyways. Lyle could smell stable and sewer. The only light came from a window in one of the houses hemming them in. He could see the pale shadow of her face and the gleam in her eyes. A trail of water seeping down the stone wall behind her.

"He'll talk to me," she said in a fierce whisper. "We go to his ship. It's the one place we can be sure he'll come back to. If things go bad, he'll get us out."

Lyle shook his head. "I trust you but I won't trust in a stranger. Especially not one with ties to this place."

The alarm went up, loud even from where they stood. The rumble of men's voices and then someone fired their shotgun into the sky. Like a flash, the boy was gone. "Damn it, Janie. He was going to see us down the hill the back way."

She laughed. "Back way? It's only a rope over the Leap. I can manage that for you if it comes to it. Have a little faith in me. I left a letter with Rose. She'll see it gets back to the fort if we don't. We should go talk to

Flynn before we lose him for good. You know as well as I do that there'll be no tracking a smuggler pilot who doesn't want to be found. He's right here *now.* We can't pass that up. If I'd wanted safe, I'd have stayed at the fort. We came here to get the serum back. Let's do that."

Lyle sighed caught somewhere between pride and irritation that her plan was better than his. "Gideon was bluffing. That's what I think. He knew exactly how to get under your skin to buy time until someone came looking for him. If this Flynn is a good man do you really think he'd be working with someone like Gideon?"

She shook her head and looked away. Half her face was in shadow but the part he could see made him want to tuck her into his arms and run away from this mess. After he shot Flynn and anyone else who'd ever dared to lay a hand on her. He should have been the one to kill Gideon. He hadn't wanted that burden for her.

"I never said he was a *good* man."

"All right. We stay and find out if Gideon was telling the truth about Flynn. My plan was to outrun them. What's yours?"

"First we need to check the landing pad for Flynn's ship. I didn't see Flynn in the saloon but he might have been in a back room or upstairs. Knowing him, he was probably the one who sent Billy to fetch Gideon. And if Gideon was telling the truth, there's a chance the serum is still here. We don't have much time. Flynn will slip anchor at the first sign of trouble. Are you with me or not?"

"I'm with you." So help him God.

FOURTEEN

GIDEON MOORE WAS DEAD. Whatever happened next—whether she escaped Columbus Junction alive or they caught and hung her—she'd accomplished that much. What stabbed at her like a knife in her side was the memory of the way Lyle had looked at her right after she'd done it. Gideon's blood flowing out in a big messy wave and Lyle frozen, half reaching for her with the most appalled expression she'd ever seen on his face.

Just a few moments earlier, he'd been telling Gideon that she was smart and brave. He'd said it so casually that she knew he meant it, that it wasn't a line to charm his way under her skirts. He'd said it as if it was the plain, unvarnished truth and she hadn't known what to make of that. She wondered what he'd say about her if asked again.

Cold. Black-hearted. Murderer.

Maybe now he'd agree with Gideon that there was something broken inside her. She reminded herself that it didn't matter what Lyle thought so long as he was still alive. And then she forced herself to take another step.

"Which way?" Lyle peeked around the corner, sweeping his gaze left to right. "We're clear here."

She slipped under his arm and went left, leading the way deeper into town. She could hear some shouting coming from the direction of the saloon and she started to run, keeping to the shadows as much as possible but not making too much of an effort at invisibility. Speed was more important.

With Lyle a breath behind, she turned the corner, not breaking stride as she looked around to get her bearings. Straight ahead she could see the town square. There were three ships docked on the wide, flat space, as many as Columbus Junction could handle at one time. The tower rose up from the center of the square, gleaming and cold in the harsh glare of gaslight. The towers were built for the safety of the airships, to mark the location of the landing pads. Always kept lit just like the lighthouses in the port cities. Every town worth putting on a map had one.

Only the bubbled tops of the ships were visible from this distance. One was certainly a cargo ship, judging by the size. Either of the other two might have been Flynn's. She'd need to be much closer to be sure. Hopefully, he hadn't already left.

Behind the town square the mountains rose high, sprinkled with lights all the way up to the cloud cover.

"Guards?" Lyle loped along beside her. She was winded and had a stitch in her side but he was barely out of breath.

"Ships provide their own. It's a quiet town, the captains usually give most of them leave. This late at night, not even the maintenance crews will be there." She grabbed his arm and made a hard right, gasping her way down an alley and leaning against the wall at the far end to catch her breath. "The smaller ships are toward the back of the square."

Lyle nodded. "Could you tell if either of them was the one you saw?"

She shook her head. "Not from here. They're about the right size though."

He looked down the dark alley and then back at her. "We're a good distance from the Leap. If this goes bad…"

"If they catch us near the ships, we cut the lines."

"They'll shoot us down," he said.

"No." They wouldn't, of that she was absolutely certain. A Scraper would view such an act as sacrilege of the highest order. "The ships are worth more than we are. Theft, the owner will have to deal with. If they shoot us down, they'll have to pay up to replace it."

He accepted her word on that with a nod. "Do you know how to fly one of those things? Because I sure as hell don't."

"I do." She almost smiled at the look on his face. For the sake of honesty, she added. "Enough not to crash into the mountain anyway. If we can get back onto the plains, we'll have a better chance."

"Without a crew?"

"You're thinking of the cargo ships. With the smaller models, the cables release on a lever and are self-retracting. All of the controls can be accessed by the pilot."

She pushed off the wall and they circled the square without incident. In the distance, she could hear men, still behind them and a ways off. With luck, they'd search the stables and then the roads leading out of town.

Distracted, she didn't hear the footsteps around the corner until it was too late. And then a man was there, dead smack in front of her, too close to avoid. She ran right into him as Lyle's fingers caught in the back of her dress and tried to haul her back, hard hands clamped on her shoulders to steady her.

She caught a flash of the quick smile she would recognize anywhere, even in a dim alley on a dark night. Cassius Flynn. His hair was longer than she remembered, black as his leather vest. His shirtsleeves were rolled back and his arms were bare. Collar open, she could see the inked wing tip of the crow tattoo that started at his neck before curving down past his collarbone.

"Janie," he said with a touch of wonder. "By God, the very woman I was looking for. I heard Billy talking about the redheaded beauty who lured Gideon away from the table and I wondered." Before she could react, he caught her up in a bear hug that pinned her arms to her sides. He spun her away from Lyle and then abruptly dropped her to her feet. It seemed like a thoughtless action. An overexuberant hug, but she knew Flynn better than that. He didn't recognize Lyle and was trying to get her away from him.

He met her glare with a smile. "It's good to see you again. You're the cause of this trouble tonight, aren't you? I knew—"

Whatever he was going to say was interrupted by the sound of Lyle cocking his gun. "Step away from her and over to the wall there. Janie, come back here."

Flynn's eyes met hers, laughing green that made her want to trust him even when she knew how dangerous it would be to do so. He was amused by the gun pointing at his head. Of course, he would be. If her arms weren't restrained she might have tried to whack some sense into him.

He didn't release her until he was sure she had her

balance. But then, rather than send her back to Lyle, he stepped *toward* the gun, blocking her body with his own.

"I don't believe we've met." His head tipped to one side as he gave Lyle a once-over. "A Ranger. But not the one who came for Janie last time."

"You're the man who stole my supply of Reaper cure."

"Am I, now?" Flynn placed his hands on his hips. It looked like a casual gesture but Jane saw how near his hand was to his holstered gun. She knew how quickly he could draw from that position.

She knocked his hand away and when he looked down at her, she said, "We don't have time for this."

Flynn shook his head and returned his attention to Lyle. "My hold is empty. I don't have it, whatever it is you're looking for."

"But you did."

"You're a long way from your patrol to be casting around accusations like that. Why would you think I have anything that belongs to you?

"Gideon pointed his finger at you right before Jane slit his throat."

Flynn looked down at her with a smile. "Good for you, sweetheart."

She simply didn't have it in her to smile back at that. Instead, she turned away to look back down the alley. The noise from the saloon was waking up the rest of the town. Lights were flickering on in the windows. Soon more people would spill out into the street to see what had happened. They truly didn't have the time for a pissing contest. Lyle, the steadiest and most sensible man she'd ever met, didn't seem to care.

All his attention was fixed on Flynn. "She's not your sweetheart."

Flynn cocked an eyebrow in her direction, but she shook her head. No time to explain her relationship to Lyle. Even if there was time, she didn't know what she'd say.

"We need to get out of here and you're going to help us."

Jane turned down the alley in the direction from which Flynn had come. "Jane—"

She held up a hand. "I'll find the ship on my own. You two have fifteen minutes to work this out and then I'm leaving with or without you."

Footsteps behind her told her all she needed to know.

"You can't take my ship." Flynn caught her elbow, but Lyle's growl made him drop it. They came to the end of the alley and she peered out, didn't see anyone and stepped out onto the wider road. Flynn's sigh followed her. "I knew I never should have taught you how to fly."

"Jane," Lyle said quietly. She glanced back at him. He was still holding his gun but it was no longer aimed directly at Flynn's head. "If you really can fly then we don't need him."

"We need to know where he dropped the cure and we don't have time to beat it out of him. You'll tell us though, won't you, Flynn? Gideon said you've been working for Corrigan."

Flynn rubbed a hand through his hair, leaving it tousled. A tell. "I'm sure Gideon would say just about anything to save his life."

Deciding his cooperation was more important than the truth at the moment, she didn't call him on his evasion. "We need a ride upstairs."

Lyle hadn't reholstered his pistol. Jane noticed but she didn't say anything. Truly, she didn't blame him. If she didn't know Flynn, she wouldn't trust him either. Heck, she *did* know Flynn and she only trusted him so far. He was charming. He had fine manners and a wicked sense of humor. He was also a criminal who'd had business dealings with Gideon. She didn't know what they were. It was possible that Gideon had told them the truth and Flynn was working for Corrigan. A Scraper businessman from the mining city-state of Oro who occasionally had need for a few items that could only be obtained on the black market. It was possible that Flynn had only run a few jobs for Gideon as payback.

Flynn had spent an awful lot of time in Columbus Junction though. Whatever he'd been up to then, it clearly couldn't have been anything good. She'd been hesitant to dig too deeply back then because she was afraid she wouldn't like what she found. Now, she wished she'd kept her eyes open instead of ignoring everything she didn't want to deal with.

They reached the ship without incident—the same red-tailed light ship she'd spied in the clearing outside Fort Dougan just a few weeks past. Flynn unlatched the curved door and lowered the steps. "Get inside. There are a few things I need to do before takeoff."

Lyle eyed Flynn suspiciously until the smuggler disappeared behind the ship. Then, he holstered his gun and gave Jane a hand up before climbing in behind her. "Is one of those things to alert the authorities, do you think?"

"I told you I trust him."

"That's not exactly what you said. You told me he

would know about the serum and that he's not a good man."

She brushed past him, drawing off her gloves. The right one was badly stained and she stared at it for a moment before tossing it aside.

"Well, then," she said quietly. "I'm not a particularly good woman either, but you've been content to deal with me these last weeks. Has that changed?"

Lyle muttered a curse but before he really got a chance to answer, Flynn swung aboard. It was a small space—no passenger appointments, a chair for the pilot and a bench along the wall opposite the door. Sturdy netting partitioned the control area from the storage compartment.

Hands wrapped around the metal support above the door, Flynn caught her gaze and lifted his chin in Lyle's direction. "Should I toss him out now or do we wait for more altitude?"

"Don't lay a finger on him."

Flynn's brows rose at the sharpness in her tone. He gave Lyle a long hard look but he didn't comment. When he moved toward the controls, she turned away, ignoring the bench to go look out the short bank of windows. She heard Flynn's chair creak as he sat down and started to adjust the gears, readying the ship for takeoff. She was familiar enough to know it would still be several minutes before they were ready to launch.

She should offer to help. It had been a long time but she'd remember the sequence well enough. Flynn had made some adjustments to the ship—the rear rudder was smaller than it should be and the engine sounded different, louder, than it should for a ship of this size. She was curious at his reasoning for the changes but she couldn't seem to get past the anger and hurt she felt at Lyle's rejection to ask. Lyle didn't seem to have the same problem. He came up behind her and placed a warm hand on her shoulder.

"What do the symbols on his arm mean?"

She kept her voice low as his. "The crow marks him as a pilot for hire. The others surely mean something as well though I don't know their significance."

"Can we trust him or not, Janie?"

It was just like Lyle to see trust as black-and-white. "Flynn does what's best for Flynn." Her lips curved. "And you might be surprised by what he thinks is best for him. He's not cruel though and he'll get us where we need to go."

"For a fee, I will," Flynn said, glancing at her with a quick smile. His ears always had been sharp. It would do not to forget that. "Don't forget about the fee."

"We're no burden," she said reasonably. "You were leaving Columbus Junction anyway."

Lyle touched his gun. "And we are letting you keep your head attached to your body. There aren't any bullets in you yet. I think you should take a minute to count your blessings."

Flynn shook his head. "Now, Lieutenant, no need to bring it to that level."

"Lieutenant?"

A soft question, but Jane heard the suspicion in it. That edge of menace that Lyle usually managed to hide quite well.

Flynn glanced back with a lift of his chin. "The plating on your weapon. Pearl grips and three stars make you a lieutenant."

Lyle grunted, but the tension in his shoulders eased slightly. "You're smarter than you look."

Rising from his chair, Flynn walked to the door. He'd already released the latch but he hurried the closing mechanism along with a sharp tug. When it sealed, he spun the lock to secure it. "I'm going to choose to take that as a compliment."

Flynn dropped into the pilot's seat and made a show of checking the gauges again, taking his sweet time. Too much time, Jane thought. Through the window, she had a good view of the wide main street. She could see the glow of torchlight at the end of that road. They had maybe ten minutes now.

Walking over to Flynn, she reached down and pulled the release lever for the cables, jerking it back between his thighs and making him flinch. There was a thunk below followed by a muted whirring noise from the rotation of the coiling mechanism.

He looked up at her in annoyance. "I wasn't stalling. The engine's been finicky lately. It needs the extra time to warm up."

It was possible he was telling the truth, but she fixed him with a warning look on the off chance he was keeping them there while Gideon's men closed in. "Remember I can fly this thing if I need to. You can take the second's chair if you want."

Ignoring his glare, she turned back to Lyle and pointed at the wall behind him. "Those leather bands are the passenger belts. Just loop your free arm through. The currents here are tricky and I don't trust him not to take advantage of the turbulence to disarm you."

She felt the lift in her gut, that slippery sliding feeling that used to make her smile.

"That's just the vents," Flynn said, more for Lyle's benefit than her own.

She helped Lyle to get strapped in, the tension easing out of her as they began to rise above the airfield. She hadn't misled Lyle, not exactly. It was unlikely that anyone would take the risk of shooting at them but it was always a possibility. She wouldn't feel truly safe until they cleared the tower.

When she looked up, Lyle's gray eyes were fixed on her. "How do you know so much about airships?"

"I taught her," Flynn said, leaning over to check one of the polished gauges. It was an awfully nice ship for a smuggler, newer than the one he'd been flying only a year ago. "Some people have the touch for it and some don't. Jane here took to the skies like a falcon." He glanced over his shoulder to smile at her. "You never mentioned me to your new friend? I'm hurt, love. I thought we meant more to each other than that."

She glared at him. He was purposefully trying to mislead Lyle. Flynn thought of her as a little sister. They'd grown up on the same estate. Her in a cottage near the stables. Flynn in the big house. There'd been too big of an age difference—too big of a class difference—for them to have been friends but Flynn had been fond of her father, much fonder than he was of Stark. Not that she blamed him for that. Stark had never been kind to his stepson.

Flynn ran away from the estate when she was eight and they hadn't seen each other again until he was running some job or another for Gideon. He'd tried to warn her away from Gideon when she was too stupid to take the advice. He'd also taught her how to fly.

She knew what he was trying to do now—drive a

wedge between her and Lyle to give him more control of his situation. Try to grab hold of any weakness and exploit it. A few hours ago she would have been certain it wouldn't work. Lyle had trusted her. But that was before he'd watched her kill a man. He hadn't been remotely pleased about that and she wouldn't know exactly where she stood with him until they had a chance to talk about it in private. Until then, she'd need to try to keep Flynn from stirring trouble.

"Flynn taught me to fly," she told Lyle. "Gideon put an end to the lessons when he realized it would give me another way out."

Flynn's expression sobered. "A handful of lessons do not a pilot make. You pop the wrong switch and you die. There's no room for mistakes, not up here."

Jane ignored that and turned to the window to check for pursuit. They were still drifting up. She could see the men gathered at the saloon, lanterns from the search parties. A few men stopped to point as the departing ship. They'd be out of range before those men made the square. The wind caught the gondola and Flynn reached over to flip a switch. She heard the hiss of steam running through the pipes overhead a second before the thrusters fired, correcting their slow spin.

"The only mistake I seem to make is with who I can rely on."

She heard Lyle's soft intake of breath but didn't have the courage to meet his gaze. She wasn't talking about him. She was talking about Flynn. Lyle was smart. He'd work out her meaning. Flynn fell into an uncustomary silence. He turned a valve that caused another surge of steam to rattle through the pipes above and the sound of the engine changed subtly. Once they cleared the tower, she leaned back in her seat.

"I'm sorry about Samuel, Jane," Flynn said softly, still staring at the controls. "Sorrier than I can say."

She might be a fool, but she believed he was sincere. Flynn and Rose were the only two people in Columbus Junction brave enough to befriend her. They'd both tried to help her and Samuel get out. "You were supposed to meet us."

"Gideon found me out. It was Ada Sloane, Rose's maid with the blond curls and the..."

Enormous breasts, yes. She knew exactly who Ada was. "She told Gideon everything. You'll have noticed she's no longer employed by your friend if you stopped by. Gideon had me thrown in jail for nearly a month after that. I might have hanged if he hadn't needed me for a job."

Janie released a pent breath and stared at her hands knotted in her lap. Ada. She'd suspected as much. Ada had never liked her. She'd been after Gideon's attention though God only knew why. Flynn though. She'd always considered Flynn a friend.

Her hands knotted together in her lap. "You could have found me later on."

"Not right away I couldn't. By the time I was free it was over. And what would I have said?" He looked back at her, green eyes glittering in the dim light. "Samuel was gone and you were safe. You should have stayed away."

She had been safe at the fort with Cam. She was the one who'd willingly come straight back into Hell. A shiver ran down her spine and she glanced up at Lyle sitting beside her, following the conversation with some interest. He met her gaze though his expression was shuttered and she couldn't tell what he was thinking.

When she looked away, Lyle turned his attention to Flynn. "She came to help track the serum you helped to steal. It wouldn't have been necessary for her to come back at all if not for that. Tell us what happened to the cure."

But Flynn didn't answer Lyle, he looked at her. "You need to get out of this one, Jane. I don't blame you for going after Gideon, but you need to cut line while you still can. The cure is gone. You're not getting it back."

"They can't steal from the forts and expect the Rangers to do nothing."

"You're not a Ranger." Flynn's gaze shifted to Lyle. "I thought the only use you had for women was breeding. You thought you'd just dangle her in front of Gideon to see if he'd bite? You use her as Reaper bait too?"

She felt the muscle in Lyle's arm tighten and she placed a hand on his thigh to forestall him. To Flynn, she said, "It was my decision to come here. Lyle needed a guide to get to Gideon and I had unfinished business with him. No one uses me for anything. Not anymore."

Flynn looked at her for a long moment and then turned back to his controls. "The order came from Corrigan. I work for him occasionally just like I did for Gideon. I'm not bound to Corrigan despite how much he might like to think so. He's a paying customer, that's all. Two weeks ago he gave the order to pick up six crates in a clearing two miles west of Fort Dougan. I landed at the balloon marker and delivered the shipment to a compound he has in the southern range. Easy in. Easy out. Good money. I didn't ask what was in the crates."

"But you knew."

A slight hesitation then Flynn gave a short nod.

"Do you know why they want the serum?"

Flynn flipped a lever and they began to climb more steeply, moving forward at a faster pace. He leaned over to tap at one of his gauges and then turned his chair around to face them.

"The mines," he said. "They want the serum for the mines."

Lyle shifted on his seat, leaning forward to rest his forearms on his thighs. "Which mines? They're shutting down Dickinson. The only other mines still producing are Ferromonte and Sterling."

Flynn's smile was brief. "That's the problem, isn't it? They're not the only mines that are still viable. They're just the only ones that are accessible north of the border. Now, for a man willing to take certain risks there's a fortune down there."

Janie felt the blood drain from her face as his meaning sank in. They meant to reopen the old mines south of the border, the ones lost to Reaper territory.

Lyle shook his head in disbelief. "That's suicide."

"Not if you're immune to Reaper infection, it isn't. Or if you have a serum to cure it."

Lyle scratched his jaw as he contemplated that for a moment. "How much time do we have before Gideon's people come looking for us?"

"You mistake matters," Flynn said. "The people of Columbus Junction were afraid of Gideon Moore. They weren't loyal to him and they sure as hell aren't going to try to avenge his sorry ass. They'll be busy fighting each other for his position, not looking for justice. Most would buy you a drink for the favor. Should keep them busy for a few days at least. If we're lucky it'll be over and done with quick before the whole town goes up in flames. People with children will move out until the dust settles. Your only concern is that Corrigan had an inside man. If he suspects Gideon's death had anything to do with the stolen serum, he'll want to stop you before word gets out about the mine."

"Then we'll just have to stop him first," Lyle said.

Flynn laughed at that, green eyes crinkling in true amusement. "Corrigan won't be worried about *you* ending his operation. He'll be worried that his competitors will get the same idea and drive down the price of silver."

FIFTEEN

THEY TOUCHED DOWN within two hours. The nearest telegraph station was in the small town of Canfield just a few miles higher than Columbus Junction to the northwest. Flynn didn't know the exact location of the mine Corrigan had opened up but he was able to give them the location of where he'd dropped the serum in Eagle Creek. Lyle was determined to get that information to the captain as quickly as possible. It was becoming increasingly apparent that this was something that was far beyond their ability to handle on their own. What he needed to do was to get Janie safe transport back to the fort.

They gagged Flynn and left him in the mechanical room where any thumps or rattling sounds he made might be attributed to cooling equipment. The best part of Lyle's day was whacking Flynn in the head to get him to stay still long enough to tie him up.

When they left the ship, Janie gave him an odd look. "You're grinning."

"Only think how cheerful I'll be if I get a chance to shoot him."

She shook her head. "He's helping us, you know."

"That's exactly what makes me suspicious. He was helping Corrigan and Gideon too. He was going to help you and Samuel to safety."

He didn't like Flynn, didn't trust him worth a damn.

But they needed him and he was Janie's friend. The sooner they could be rid of the man the better, in his opinion. Janie nodded and Lyle took her by the arm. It was a light touch, meant to comfort, but she shrugged free of him. "You heard Flynn. We were both betrayed. He could have died trying to help me."

"And yet here he is still working with the men who threw him into prison." He saw her flinch and felt bad for it. But he needed to know she was seeing things clearly. He'd thought they were on the same page right up until the moment she slit Gideon's throat. He didn't like the distance that put between them. He didn't like the way Flynn kept trying to drive it wider.

"Maybe your friend does feel bad about what happened and is trying to make it up to you now," he said. "But we can't depend on that. We're being cautious. I played it your way in Columbus Junction. Now we play it mine."

"I count Columbus Junction as a success."

He gave her a dark look. "We made it out alive and you got your revenge so I suppose for you it was."

"We got the information we needed. I told you revenge had nothing to do with it."

Lyle clenched his jaw against an argument and simply nodded. Jane, apparently, wasn't as keen to let it go. "If you think that's what I was after, you're dead wrong."

"Maybe you shouldn't go throwing words like *dead* around so casually."

"You killed five men on the road here."

He looked down the street to see if anyone had overheard that, but all was quiet. The townspeople were keeping a discreet eye on the strangers in their midst but no one looked nervous. There was a man leaning against a post near the saloon who seemed to be paying them particular attention. But that might have been Janie. She drew an unusual amount of attention wherever she went.

With a sigh, he turned to face her. "Those men were out to kill us."

She frowned down at her rumpled skirts and smoothed a pleat with her fingertips. "You have a rulebook in your head, is that it? About who's fair game and who's not."

"Just let it go."

"How can I let it go when you keep looking at me like I've grown horns?"

He wasn't going to be baited into a fight with her, not now. They needed to talk, that was the plain truth but not in full view of every stranger in town. He kept walking, eyes scanning the street for trouble.

"I can see why you might need rules with all the killing you have to do."

That was sadness in her voice, not accusation, and that drew his gaze down to her upturned face. There was a smudge on her cheek and her skin was uncharacteristically pale. Her lower lip was split and he had no idea when that'd happened. But her eyes drew him in. Dark and troubled. When he didn't answer, she looked away. "I hope your rules help you sleep at night, Lieutenant."

She stepped onto the walkway in front of the post office and brushed off her skirts. He held open the door so she could pass through and then followed her inside. Jane stood beside the door as he ordered a brief, carefully worded telegraph to be sent to both the captain on Eyrion and to Cam at the fort. If all went well, there would be a message waiting for them when they arrived in Eagle Creek telling them that help was on its way. At the very least, an acknowledgement that their message had been received. If something happened to him or Jane while they were tracking the serum, someone needed to be able to pick up where they left off.

The clerk kept darting furtive looks at Jane as he worked and Lyle couldn't tell if it was her beauty, her split lip or something else that drew his eye. He angled his body to block the view and fixed the clerk with a stern glare until the message was sent.

Once outside, he took Janie by the arm and led her back toward the inn, not letting her pull away from him this time. He was worried about her. The pallor of her skin and the way her eyes kept going distant and unfocused when she thought he wasn't looking. "Let's go have that talk," he said in a low voice.

"Here?"

"A quick stop." He pointed at the inn. A two-story structure that appeared older but well kept. The porch was newly swept, anyway.

"What about Flynn?"

"He isn't going anywhere. When's the last time you ate?"

She shook her head. "I'm not hungry."

Like a new recruit, running on fear and adrenaline. "Humor me then. I'm starving and I think we both could use the rest."

He drew her arm more tightly through his, and pulled her inside the open door of the small inn. "Come on."

The innkeeper was a matronly woman in a black dress and pristine apron. When he requested a private room, her frown was fierce but her protestation that she ran a respectable establishment ended abruptly when Lyle withdrew a wad of cash from beneath his vest. She led them to a private dining room off the kitchen that looked to have been last used to host a card game.

While he placed the order for food, Jane wandered to the window that overlooked the street. They were serving roast tonight which wasn't quite ready. Rather than wait for it, Lyle told the innkeeper that warmed-over stew would be just fine. More than food, what he wanted was a moment alone with Jane. She seemed confused on a few of the finer points of their relationship.

Jane, apparently, was of the same mind. As soon as the door closed behind the innkeeper, she spoke. "You're angry with me."

"Don't say that as a reproach," he said. "I've a right to be angry with you. Killing Gideon was never part of the plan."

It hadn't been part of his plan anyway. He strongly suspected that it had always been part of Jane's.

"He needed to be stopped."

"And if I'm angry with anyone, it's myself. I shouldn't have brought you here. I didn't realize that until it was too late to turn back."

"I knew full well what I was doing."

"No, Janie. I'm not buying that. You're not a killer." He remembered her shaking in his arms when they'd been attacked on the road. She was not a woman who was in any way comfortable with that kind of violence. He'd promised Cam he'd bring her home safely and he was doing a piss-poor job of shielding her.

"But you are," she said quietly. "So I don't see why you're so upset. You make your living at killing people."

"Not people."

Her eyes flashed. "Would it have made a difference to you if Gideon had been holding a gun and able to defend himself? That wouldn't have made things even, it just would have made me stupid."

"You're not stupid." She was smart and competent and brave as hell. It terrified him the way she went after what she wanted with no apologies. The danger had passed for the time being but Janie was still wound up tight as a top. He was well familiar with the aftermath of battle, bloody and not. He didn't want to fight with her now, but it was just the two of them and they needed to be able to work together, to trust each other. It was better to have this out here and now.

She rubbed at her forehead as if it ached. "You were right not to get involved with me. You should feel good about that."

"I don't feel good about any of this."

When he took a step nearer, she sidled away.

"You blamed Gideon for Samuel's death," he said. "That's why you did it. I understand that."

She shook her head. "That's not what this was about."

"What was it about then?"

"You were going to let him go." She pointed a finger at him. "Even knowing what he was capable of, you were going to let him live. Stealing a horse is a hanging offense. He stole your entire supply of Reaper cure. How many people died so we could have that? How many people will die because it's gone missing? It wasn't about revenge. It was about stopping him from doing more harm."

"It was still wrong, Janie. He was tied to a chair and I'd given him my word."

"The first time I ran, I let him live and he killed the

most important person in the world to me. He would have sent men to hunt you down and I wasn't going to let that happen again."

It took him a minute to think that through and when he realized what she was saying it hit him like a mule kick to the chest. "You did *not* kill a man for my sake."

Her lips thinned and even though he could see the truth in her eyes, she shook her head to deny it. "The world is a better place without Gideon in it."

"Agreed."

She was breathing hard, her hands balled up into fists and he wanted to go to her. He just wasn't sure she was ready for that. And then it didn't matter, because his feet were moving anyway, closing the distance all on their own. Janie moved too, stepping forward, her hands coming up around his neck as though they belonged just there.

He smoothed a palm down her spine to rest at her hip. She was trembling and he gathered her in closer.

"You hate me now."

Hate. Is that what she thought?

"I'm angry. Killing Gideon stirred up a hornet's nest we can't afford to deal with right now. A Ranger killing a sheriff will hurt Cap's campaign to keep them from cutting our funding."

"You didn't kill him." The words were muffled against his shirt. Soft. She'd stopped shaking, her fingers played with the ends of his hair. He pressed a kiss to the top of her head.

"That's how the story will come out though and you know it. I should have protected you from having to see Gideon again. I thought it might help you, but it only made things worse."

"I don't regret what I did."

"I don't like the way it played out, not anything about it. A dirty, ugly business and I wish you'd had no part in it. But Janie..." He threaded his fingers through the tangle of her hair and gently eased her head back, waited for her to meet his gaze. There was a hint of tears in her eyes but that was mostly defiance he was looking at. "I could never hate you. You're braver than I wish, stronger than I wish. You terrify and exasperate and frustrate me, but none of that is hate."

She weighed his words. He half wanted to know what was going on in her head, was half-grateful that he didn't.

"What is it then? Because damned if I can figure it out."

She was pressed right up against him. He could feel her every breath. She had to feel his erection, too, but she didn't shy away from it.

"You're a smart woman." He cupped her jaw, stroked his thumb across the smooth skin of her cheek. Her lashes lowered slightly and his heart ached with tenderness. "How can you be confused about where I stand?"

She made a helpless sound and her hand fisted as if she meant to throw a punch before she buried it in her skirts. "You are the exasperating one."

He was saved from responding to that by the knock at the door. The food. Lyle hesitated for a moment, tempted to ignore the intrusion. On the second knock, he untangled himself and opened the door. The innkeeper brought their meal herself, possibly to prevent her staff from reporting morality violations to the town committee. Not for the first time, Lyle found himself anxious to return home. He watched Jane as the innkeeper set down her tray and unloaded plates and napkins and silverware. A pitcher of cider and two sturdy glasses. Lyle held the door for her to leave, closed it and then shot the bolt home.

When he turned around, Janie was in the same spot he'd left her, staring at him. Her shoulders were hunched and her eyes held the same haunted look she'd had when she first came to the fort. He hated seeing it again. Hated knowing he'd had any part in putting it there.

"We should get back to the ship," she said. "I don't trust Flynn. If he manages to break free, he'll leave us here in a heartbeat."

And this was a man she counted as a friend. "The rope will hold."

Her lovely brown eyes narrowed as he walked toward her, abandoning the food on the table. Two steps brought him within touching distance. When he drew her into his arms, she welcomed him as if it was the most natural thing in the world.

"I thought you were hungry."

"I am but this is more important."

Her eyes remained troubled but there was just a hint of a smile on her lips. He kissed the corner of that sweet mouth as though he could seal it there. Her thighs brushed against his and her breasts pressed to his chest. He swore he could feel her nipples even through his vest. "What's more important?"

"You killed Gideon for the same reason you're here with me now. The same reason you volunteered to come in the first place. I may not be the quickest draw but I get there eventually."

"I don't know what you're talking about, Lieutenant."

"If it makes you feel better, you can always consider this a thank-you."

Her expression curdled into a scowl but before it could get all the way there, he bent his head and kissed her. Just a touch, a light press of flesh to flesh. Nothing more than a question. When her mouth opened beneath his, he groaned at the rush of warmth that flooded his body. His hands left her hips to frame her face. He angled her head to deepen the kiss and she responded with the same rising desperation he felt. He'd known it would be like this, touching her. Like opening a floodgate and he'd only wanted to be standing on solid ground first. He was just beginning to realize that there was no solid ground where Janie was concerned. He'd been falling since the moment he met her and it didn't seem as if he'd be hitting bottom anytime soon.

He'd been wrong, dead wrong to take her back to Columbus Junction but she'd survived it. Survived that place, Gideon, everything life had ever thrown at her. He could feel her pulse thrum beneath his thumb where it rested on her elegant neck. She gasped for air and he gave it to her. She was solidly, thrillingly, electrically alive and he just wanted to rest in the knowledge of it for a while. Flynn could fucking wait.

She pulled away and though her eyes were lust-darkened and her face flushed there was still a shadow of doubt in her eyes. "Back in Columbus Junction, I thought… What changed your mind about me?"

"Nothing, sweetheart. My mind's been made up for a good long while about you. I never wanted to get in the way of what you wanted. Didn't want to be a temporary comfort or another burden you had to carry. But don't be confused about where I stand. *Hate* is the last word I'd use to say how I feel about you." He touched a finger to her swollen lower lip. "You can turn me away but it'll be your choice if we walk out of here right now, not mine."

For a moment, he thought she'd do just that. The possibility that he might have missed his chance with her locked the air in his lungs. He couldn't remember ever being this nervous, not the first time or anytime since. When she turned her head to kiss his palm, the tightness in his chest eased and he reached to pull her closer.

"You won't regret this."

SHE COULDN'T HELP but smile at that even as his mouth captured hers in a fierce kiss. Pure hunger. She tasted it on his tongue, felt his need in the hard pressure of his hands. An arm banded tight around the base of her spine and he half carried, half pushed her back toward the corner of the room where they'd be hidden from the view of anyone who happened to glance through the curtained windows. She could hear people outside though. The rumble of a passing wagon. And closer, the clink of cutlery and glass from the nearby kitchen.

Not breaking the kiss, Lyle pushed her back until she hit the wall with a small thud. She half expected him to jerk down her skirts and drive inside her. He wanted to do that. She could feel the tension in the strong body pressed to hers.

She'd always admired his body even when she'd thought nothing would come of it. Solid. Everything about Lyle was solid and well-knit. His legs were long and his back straight. Thick layers of muscles wrapped his arms and shoulders. She wanted his shirt off, to feel his skin. But she'd take what she could get.

Muttering an apology, he fumbled at her skirts until he remembered they were split. With a groan, he pulled back and dropped to his knees. Her hands trembled as she unbuckled the belt at her waist. Before she had it completely unfastened, Lyle tugged at her skirts and bloomers, pulling them down over her hips and shoving them down over her boots and clear of her feet.

Rather than stand, he nudged her feet farther apart. His hands, palms warm and rough against her sensitive skin, stroked up the outside of her thighs. When he reached her hips, he lingered there for a moment and then his thumbs began a slow sweet descent down the seam of her thighs.

Lyle could be gentle. She'd known that about him. But sex for her had rarely had much gentleness to it and for some reason it took her by surprise now. They weren't even in a bed. He had every reason to take her hard and fast and none whatsoever to lean forward to brush his lips across her belly, to murmur her name so soft and low as he urged her to open for him.

His breath touched her first, hot and soft, then tongue, then lips and—oh God—that felt good. She reached down to touch the top of his head, her fingers slipping through the silky strands of hair. He spread her with his fingers as his mouth did wicked things. Delicious and wicked. Without the wall at her back, she would have melted into a puddle on the floor.

When he pushed his tongue inside her, she cried out and then bit her lip to seal in the sound. She felt the way his mouth moved as he smiled and then he did it again.

He looked up, his gaze meeting hers for just a moment before his head dipped low and he caught her clit between his teeth. Her whole body jerked and then his tongue stroked over the spot with a gentler pressure.

She could feel the scrape of his whiskers against her tender skin. She could feel the tension in his shoulders, the slight vibration of the pleased and hungry sounds he was making. Her body was shaking with a restraint she didn't truly understand. The pleasure was right there. She had only to let herself go. To accept it.

But a part of her couldn't relax while she was spread and exposed like this. It would be one thing if Lyle was just as vulnerable. But he was still fully clothed, on his knees in front of her with his hands on her bare hips.

He teased her, circling his tongue, increasing the pressure, building that tension to a fever pitch until it was too much. A losing battle. His mouth was amazing. His hands. Lyle. Lyle was loving her right now. When she'd expected him to shove her away after what she'd done.

Every muscle in her body locked tight. Her eyes opened but she didn't see a damned thing. It was as if time stopped in that moment. The whole world froze. Nothing there but her and Lyle. His wicked mouth and her twisting beneath his touch. He pressed two fingers inside her. Moved them slowly in and out until her muscles clamped down hard, and her whole body spasmed with her release.

He moved quickly, it seemed to her, riding up her torso. His pants were abrasive against her sensitive skin. He was still fully dressed and she wished he wasn't. He nuzzled at her neck. "Janie. You still with me?" He gave a shaky laugh. "Please say yes."

She lifted her face to look at him, feeling spent. Feeling scrubbed clean and wrung out. Lyle was staring down at her, those gray eyes sharp and focused, dangerously intent. It was the first time she'd seen him without even a hint of a smile on his face.

"What is it?"

She touched his cheek. "You look so serious. I'm sorry…"

She trailed off because he was shaking his head. "You don't apologize to me. Not ever, not for anything that happens between us when we're together like this. I…damn…that was beautiful. Knowing that I could make you come apart like that." He pushed her hair off her forehead and dropped a kiss to her cheek. "But it was maybe the hardest thing I've ever done not following you over the edge. I'm trying to hold off until you're ready to let me inside you. I'm not angry and if I was, you should kick me in the balls for being an asshole. You don't apologize for taking pleasure, not ever."

She reached down and grabbed hold of his cock through his clothes, still hard, and hot as a brand. He sucked in a mouthful of air and let it out in a hiss as she unfastened his trousers to let it fall heavy into her hand.

"I'm not tall enough for us to—"

Lyle's hand curled beneath her thighs and lifted her up. He'd done this before, of course he had, but best not to think on that overmuch. Perfectly positioned, she guided him inside her. She was so wet. Perfectly, achingly ready for him.

"Better?"

A slow smile spread over his face but faded as he pushed himself fully inside. Her flesh was still swollen and she could feel as it grudgingly gave way, could feel every inch of him as the thick heavy weight lodged deep. He groaned and dropped his head, as a lock of sandy hair came loose to brush against his cheek. Jane wrapped her arms around his shoulders and hitched her legs up over his hips.

He pulled out a bit and plunged in again, like a horse lunging through shoulder-high water. His muscles were moving hard beneath her fingertips, bunching and then releasing in heavy surges. She cried out as her body absorbed each blow.

He kissed her temple and slowed. "Sorry…sorry." He kissed her gently and tried to slow down. She could feel it. His muscles locked down tight against the instinctive flex of his body. He was moving in short, shallow strokes and his breath was uneven. She could feel the restraint shaking through his whole body.

"No," she said sharply and he pulled back looking at her like a kicked puppy. Did he think she wanted him to stop? "If I don't get to say sorry, then you don't either. You're not holding back. I don't want that. I want to feel you, Lyle. Make me feel you."

He hesitated a moment but she felt the second he accepted that because he took a ragged breath and rammed into her.

"Yes," she told him, urging him on.

And he did it again. Pulling out so slowly she could feel the drag of his skin as her body gave him up and then he surged forward again, his whole body flexing with the effort. She moved her hands up to his back, loving the feel of long muscles sliding under her fingertips. She loved the way he looked, raw and savage, jaw clenched tight, the light turning his wavy hair golden. Her golden knight. His broad shoulders filled her vision, his heavy arms supported her. She could feel that coil inside her winding up tight again. Bless the man, she could tell that he was working at it. She could feel the trembling in his big body as his movements went jerky and he pulled it back and his thrusts went long and smooth for a bit again until he was shaking all over and his thrusts became frantic. She tensed her thighs to absorb the shock and pressed her hips down to take all of him.

"Oh, God."

He was close. His cock seemed to swell a bit bigger, sliding hard and high inside her. His movements became urgent and uncontrolled. She did this. She did this to Lyle. A man who never got rattled by anything. Who stayed cool as mountain ice even when he was facing down Reapers. He wasn't cool now, or calm. He was riding the very edge of his control and he was about to lose it.

She came apart again right before his big body went rigid. He moved his hand, pushing her hip down to hold her trapped and tight against his body as he filled her. Her head tipped back and she cried out as Lyle hammered at her body until it shattered.

When she drifted back down to reality—the small room that smelled of smoke and liquor. Their cooling food. Her sore thighs. Lyle was brushing her hair back from her face, murmuring something as he kissed her chin, her neck. She blinked her eyes open and he looked down at her.

"Janie?"

He seemed to need some reassurance from her and so she tilted her head to kiss him lightly on the lips. "So serious, Lieutenant. You're not having regrets already, are you?"

His voice was rough. "Hell, no."

"Good." She smiled. "Me neither. Let's eat and get out of here."

SIXTEEN

FLYNN WAS NOT very happy with them when they returned and Lyle cut him loose. He'd managed to badly fray the rope binding his wrists. Another hour and he'd have been free. Lyle didn't regret a thing, considering the time well spent. Janie no longer looked as brittle as thin ice. And he...well, other than a desire to sleep for a few days, all was perfectly right with his world.

"Here." He shoved a tin bucket into Flynn's hands when the man quit cursing at him.

Flynn eyed it warily. "What is this?"

"Bread and cold meat. Janie wanted to bring you a slice of apple pie too but there was no good way to carry it. There are cookies in the sack."

His brows raised in disbelief. "You brought me cookies?"

Lyle tossed a flask and Flynn snatched it out of the air with quick hands.

"I told her you'd rather the gin."

Flynn settled back against the bench and set to his meal while Janie came up the steps into the ship. "We're ready to go."

Jane smiled brightly at Lyle and he could not help but smile back. Flynn looked from one to the other, muttered something unsavory under his breath and ripped a chunk of bread off the small loaf with his teeth. Jane dropped into the pilot's chair.

"You eat. I've got this."

Flynn was on his feet before she'd pulled the first lever. "The hell you do." A choking fit stopped him momentarily before he cleared his throat with a swallow of gin. "Up, Janie. I'm still the captain here. Nobody's hands on the ship but mine."

"She can fly it if she wants to," Lyle said, earning a smile from Janie and a scowl from Flynn. Both gratifying. "Don't be selfish."

"Are you going to share your toys too, Lieutenant?" Flynn glanced over his shoulder and laughed at whatever he saw on Lyle's face. "Yeah, I didn't think so."

Jane turned in the chair but didn't relinquish it immediately. "Tell me again why we shouldn't leave you in the cargo hold?"

"This is me helping you. I got you out of Columbus Junction and brought you here to send your message. I promised to take you to where I dropped the serum off and then we're even."

Jane stood up gracefully. Her hair was tangled worse than it had been when they went out and now there was a small tear near the hem of her skirts. Still she was as regal as a queen as she faced Flynn. "I thought we were friends."

The corner of Flynn's mouth curled. It only made him look more dangerous and Lyle stepped closer. "You don't want to be my friend, Jane. But a deal is a deal. I broke my end of the bargain once. This is me making it up to you. Believe me when I say I can't cross Corrigan right now." When she hesitated, his smile faded. "It's the best I can do."

"You mean the least you can do."

He grunted as he took his seat and tapped a stuck

gauge. "We'll have to agree to see it different." He looked over his shoulder at Lyle. "Right now I'm the best friend you've got. No more ropes."

Lyle rested his shoulder against one of the curved beams bracketing the door. "I don't make promises I can't keep."

FLYNN WAS TRUE to his word. They passed out of Stormking within the next hour and flew south through clear skies to the lower levels of Oro. Flynn set them down safely two miles away from Eagle Creek in a small clearing shielded by a rock formation that did in fact look oddly like an eagle lifting to flight. He said he'd give them twenty-four hours before taking off. This time they didn't tie him up. For one thing, they were out of sound rope. For another, there were no guarantees that they were coming back, not this way down the mountain. They'd sent the message to Cap by wire. Lyle planned to hole up with Jane at the inn, hopefully for several days and nights, while they waited for the cavalry to arrive.

Flynn stood framed in the doorway to his ship, one hand braced on the frame. "My contact is Ada." When Jane raised her brows, his expression soured. "Yes, that Ada. I told you I don't manage to hold on to my friends long. Enemies are another matter altogether." He downed the last of the gin and shook the flask just to be sure. If he could have fit his tongue through the hole in the top, Lyle imagined he'd have done it. "She meets me here when she knows I'm coming, but doesn't stay in the town but for occasional work at the brothel. If she sees you nosing around, she'll likely send word to Corrigan. Her house is about five miles farther up and I'm pretty sure she doesn't live alone."

"What does that mean?"

He shrugged. "Don't know. Just an impression I got. I never cared to ask. She calls them her 'special clientele.' Now you know everything I do about this godforsaken place. We're square?"

Janie nodded and moved toward Flynn. He straightened at her approach and watched her warily. She waved him down from the steps and he came, docile as a pup. And while Lyle didn't like it one bit, he managed to refrain from drawing his gun when Jane wrapped her arms around Flynn in a tight bear hug. The confused expression on Flynn's face almost made it worth the restraint.

"You take care of yourself, Flynn," Jane said to him.

Flynn patted her awkwardly on the shoulder, his eyes flicking up apprehensively to check that Lyle's gun was still holstered. Then, the corner of his mouth turned up and he bent his head to whisper something in Jane's ear. Whatever he said was too low for Lyle to make out. But Jane laughed. A moment later she was beside him again, and they stepped onto the dirt path Flynn said led down into town.

Once they were well past the clearing, he looked down at her. "What did Flynn say when we were leaving?"

Jane gave him a wide-eyed look that wasn't any kind of innocent. "A lady can't tell all of her secrets now, can she?"

"Then thank the good Lord you're not a lady. What the hell would I do with one of those?"

"I don't want to imagine it."

"What did he say?"

She shaded her eyes with a dainty hand and squinted up at him. "Are you jealous?"

He grimaced at the word. "I don't like your friend. I don't trust him and I want to know what he said."

"He did exactly what he said he'd do. He likely saved our lives getting us out of Columbus Junction like he did."

"Which he wouldn't have done if I hadn't pulled a gun on him."

"He was searching the back ways between the saloon and Devil's Alley for me when we found him." She smiled sweetly. "Because he likes me. He always has, you know."

Lyle growled and her smile widened. She stopped walking and tugged on his arm to pull him around. Lifting onto her toes, she placed a hand on his chest to steady herself as she kissed him sweetly on the mouth. When she pulled back, her cheeks were flushed and her eyes bright. Beautiful despite the lack of sleep and the small cut on her lip. "He said he likes you too."

SEVENTEEN

MOST SCRAPERS WOULD SAY that the only culture to be found on the whole godforsaken continent was in the capital cities. Art. Theater. Music. And while Abby would say that Scrapers were full of shit, even she had to admit that the music was something. She'd never heard anything to compare with the symphony she'd attended on her last trip up.

She wondered if she'd be able to take Jake to a performance before they left Eyrion, though it seemed unlikely. And there was music at the gala they were attending tonight, just as lovely if not quite as grand. She could hear it now, drifting out through the open doors of the balcony. She probably should have closed the doors behind her but she didn't think anyone would mind. It was so hot inside the ballroom, she'd been in honest danger of sweating her gown a darker color. She'd slipped outside for a breath of air and now stood looking out over the glittering city of glass and steel and wishing she was home.

"It is beautiful here, isn't it?"

She whirled around. "Jake."

He smirked at the gloved hand she'd raised to her throat and she lowered it quickly, fixing him with a stern look. "You have to stop sneaking up on me like that."

"Habit." He plucked the crystal-cut goblet from her

hand and sipped at her champagne. Despite her irritation, she couldn't help but smile at how grand he looked all dressed up. The fine wool pulled taut at his shoulders as he crossed his arms and leaned his hips against the railing. "I was sneaking away from the crowd, not trying to sneak up on you, if it's any consolation."

"It's stifling in there."

He looked up, trailing the smooth rock surface of the capital building with his gaze. "Some of that's the elevation." When she raised her brow, the corner of his mouth lifted in a smile. "The air's so thin it's hard to breathe."

She grinned. "And you're not the one wearing a corset."

His smile became positively wolfish. "I can help you out of it if you'd like."

"Later." She jerked her chin toward the ball. Light spilled onto the flagstones along with the sound of laughter. A group of brightly dressed women passed in front of the archway, saw them and then bent their heads together as they walked away, whispering. "How long do we have to stay?"

"Another hour at least."

"Is the captain still chasing after the Tirado heiress?"

Jake barked a laugh. "You make it sound like he's trying to get in her skirts. He's old enough to be her father."

She crossed her arms and leaned back beside him. "You're old enough to be my great-great…how many greats do you think it would be?"

He didn't answer the question. His jaw tightened a bit and she felt bad for bringing up his past. She didn't usually. Normally, she preferred to ignore the fact that he'd been a Reaper. That was impossible to do up here.

"He's trying to enlist Maricel Tirado's support. She's recently come into power and there are a lot of people within her own house who would have preferred to see her married off before that happened."

Or relinquish her post to a male relative, preferably one with an ancestor who was a founder. As hard as it was to imagine, women in the Scraper cities had even less of a say over their lives than women on the plains. The ones who had money often seemed the most trapped which was funny when you thought about it.

"I don't trust her," Abby said, lowering her voice even though there was little chance they could be overheard out here.

Jake's mouth lifted at the corner. "You don't trust any of these people."

"She wants something from us. I just can't see what it is yet."

"That's what Cap aims to find out."

Cap, who had Scraper views when it came to women. She shook her head. "I think I'd feel better about it if he was only trying to get under her skirts."

"You're in bad mood, aren't you?"

She rested her head against his shoulder. "It's this place. It brings out the worst in me."

He kissed the top of her head. "Cap wanted to know if we'd stay."

She started to laugh until she realized he wasn't joking. He finished off the glass and set it aside. "I take it that's a no."

"Would *you* want to stay?" She couldn't imagine it. Jake got antsy when he was around crowds of people for too long. But the expression on his face now was thoughtful.

"It might be good for the Rangers to have a presence up here. The council still controls your funding. And these people see me as enough of a curiosity they would welcome me here...at least for a while."

"You can't seriously be considering it."

He stared into the ballroom. Gaslight. Smiling people. The tables nearly bowed with the weight of all that food. "It's not such an awful place."

She shook her head. "How can you think that? How can you enjoy any of it when you know what it's like down there?"

He turned his head, looked straight at her and she knew all in a rush what it was that had him even considering such a ludicrous idea. "I'll stay at the fort if you want me to, but I'm not staying here."

He rotated his body enough to kiss her briefly. His hand touched her stomach and lingered there for a moment before falling away. Catching his hand, she led him back inside.

The largest chandelier she'd ever seen in her entire life hung from the high rotunda ceiling. Glittering crystal dangled from polished brass arms, powered by gas instead of candles just like everything else in the city. She was told there was more than fourteen miles of gas piping within the capital building alone. It boggled the mind.

"Headache?" Jake asked, placing a warm hand to the base of her spine to guide her toward the captain.

"Not yet." But it was coming, she could tell. Dancers spun through an elaborate sequence of steps at the center of the room, separating from their partners and then circling back to rejoin them a moment later. From where they stood, Abby could not see the musicians but the sound of the orchestra filled the room, nearly drowning out all conversation. That didn't stop people from clustering in corners and nooks, working out deals and gambling lives just like in any saloon she'd ever been in. The scenery was just prettier here. Gold and white and glittering.

Jake bent his head to her ear. "Do you see who Maricel is standing with?"

Taking a sip of her champagne, she looked about the room. Maricel was wearing a dark green silk, so thin it clung to every curve. Most of the other women were dressed in paler colors and blended in with the white walls and with each other. Abby's gown was a deep burgundy red because Jake had favored it, and she felt as if she stuck out like a sore thumb. A woman like Maricel probably dressed to stand out on purpose. "I see her."

"The older gentleman to her left is Williams. Cap pointed him out to me earlier with a warning to keep my distance." He squeezed her waist. "Let's go say hello, shall we?"

"And me without my guns."

"You can't shoot up the Founders Ball," Jake said, as they began to move through the crowd, smiling and nodding to the people they passed, being all cordial-like just as Cap had requested. "I don't know if you've heard, but this is the social event of the season."

They'd heard it a million times since they were granted the invitation, as if being allowed to attend was the highest honor. "If it meant I could get out of this corset sooner, then yes, damn straight I would."

Jake didn't laugh as she'd expected. Instead, his hand flexed briefly on her waist. "They would hang you," he said grimly. "Ranger or not. Remember we have to abide their laws here."

"You sound like Cap. You know I'm not stupid."

"I know you."

He did. If there was a way to take care of Williams, she might risk her neck to do it. She glanced up to meet his concerned frown. "Don't worry. I'm not going to hurt him."

For one thing, she didn't have a weapon. Unless you counted the glass in her hand. Tapping him on the chest, she said, "You don't do anything stupid either."

Because she knew Jake too. The corner of his mouth lifted just as the couple standing in their path moved out onto the dance floor. Jake guided her forward and smiled at Maricel, inclining his head in a slight bow. "Miss Tirado. It's a pleasure to see you again so soon."

Maricel allowed Jake to take her gloved hand. He bent his head to kiss the air above her knuckles. And what the hell was the point in that, Abby wondered for the umpteenth time. A kiss wasn't a kiss unless it landed on skin.

"Miss Tirado." Abby bared her teeth in what she hoped was a believable enough smile. "Quite the party you're throwing."

"I'm as much a guest here as you are." She touched the sleeve of the gentleman beside her. "The Williams family was among the original founders of Eyrion. And this gentleman here—" She gestured toward the man on her other side. "—is Daniel Farley. He's the councilman from Ballonet."

She nodded politely at Farley before turning her attention to her true quarry. "Mr. Williams," she said. "I've been looking forward to meeting you."

"Have you?"

Jake touched her elbow in warning but she didn't need it. She'd caught the look in Williams's eyes too—that flicker of disdain. But there was something else there as well, a sharpness, a *hunger* she was more used to seeing on Reapers than on humans. Williams didn't reach out to touch her but Farley extended his hand in greeting.

"The Ranger and the Reaper," Farley said. "I've read your story in the papers of course. I have to say, the pair of you are just as striking in person as I imagined. You're causing quite the stir at our little gathering."

Abby raised her brows at that. Hardly anyone had approached them. She'd gotten the distinct impression that they were unwelcome. Practically invisible, anyway.

"Usually these affairs are so dull," Farley said, sipping his champagne.

"Williams was just telling us of some coming excitement." Maricel said, a strained note to her voice. She ignored the warning look from Williams which Abby found interesting. "It's to be announced during the council meeting. We're to have an unusual visitor during the summer session."

Out of the corner of her eye, she was aware of Williams's scowl and that Farley was shaking his head, but Abby kept her attention fixed on Maricel. Hard dark eyes, intelligence and determination mixed in equal measure. "Williams has invited a sentient Reaper to address the council."

Abby blinked, thinking she must have misunderstood. But the look in Maricel's eyes convinced her otherwise. The woman was seriously pissed. And no wonder.

Behind her, Jake cursed viciously. "Are you out of your fucking minds?"

Williams caught Maricel's arm, his grip making her skin pale beneath his fingers. "That was to be a surprise, Maricel. You shouldn't have mentioned it. The details have not yet been finalized."

"Bringing a Reaper into the council isn't a surprise," Abby managed to get out. "It's an act of war."

"He's sentient and of some standing, as I understand it." Williams's gaze flickered briefly to Jake. "The leader of his kind. A man named Tomas."

Jake growled and Maricel appeared startled by the sound. "If he bites just one person, the infection could spread to everyone up here. You have to know that."

"Which is why I plan to request a Ranger to watch over him during the visit. To ensure our protection as well as his own."

They'd need more than just one Ranger. They'd need a whole patrol of them, especially if things went bad. She shook her head. "Maybe you could collar him?"

She looked to Jake and flinched at the expression on his face.

"He's already refused the collar," Williams said. "The guard he'll accept. One of them. We've wanted to open negotiations with the sentient for some time and this is an enormous gesture of goodwill on their part."

She stared daggers at Williams who had the good grace to look away. The attack on Fort Hill had been caused by Williams secretly working with the Reapers. This was his way of bringing everything aboveboard. Hard to accuse him of conspiring with Reapers when he could call it diplomacy and still get the results he wanted. Either way it was stupid and dangerous.

"Does Cap know about this?"

He couldn't, not yet. She glanced around the room but he was nowhere in sight. Williams had a faint smirk on his face. The bastard was enjoying her reaction to the news and she wished again for her gun.

Farley noticed the drift of her hand to where her holster should be. He smiled grimly. "You know what they say about strange bedfellows? There's a reason all weapons must be left at the doors."

Earlier in the week, Jake had pointed out that they weren't likely to be the only ones with an interest in seeing Williams fall. The trick was in figuring out who might be a willing ally. The kind of backstabbing Scrapers called politics didn't bother Jake much. He said it was the same way sentient Reapers operated so he was used to it. All of the people here had smiles on their faces and knives in their hands. She hated this place.

"Why would you risk such a thing?" Jake asked Williams.

He shrugged. "It's not such a risk. You were a sentient Reaper who was able not only to work with the Rangers to recover the cure but also charm this young woman here into becoming your wife. Proof that they can behave themselves. And it's important that we open the lines of communication between our two peoples. The sentient are ancient, with extensive knowledge of Nueva España and the southern territories lost to us."

"They're only interested in humans for food and reproduction. What could you possibly have to offer them in return?"

"Peace."

Jake snorted. "That's the last thing they'd be interested in."

Williams was the former Secretary of Defense. In that role, he'd worked closely with the forts to protect the border. Now, he was doing his damnedest to hand the plains over to Reapers on a fucking platter. He gave Jake a flatly patronizing smile. "We'll just have to see about that, won't we?"

Before Abby could jump on Williams and pummel the smile off his face, they were called in to dinner and Jake took her firmly by the arm.

"We have to find Cap and tell him what they're planning," she said as they took their place in the line. "They're idiots."

"Agreed."

Abby was so angry she shook with it. "How can he even consider inviting a Reaper up here? To Eyrion of all places? Why on earth would Tomas agree to come?"

Jake shook his head. "He'll have his reasons. He's not sane. It's impossible to guess what he's playing at. As far as what Williams hopes to gain? Access to the southern territories for one. Power. Wealth. He's already proven he's not afraid to make deals with the devil to get what he wants."

She glanced at Williams, smiling charmingly at the lovely young woman on his arm. "I want to kill that man."

Jake bent his head to brush his lips across her temple. "He's not the only one we need to worry about. And I'd rather keep my wife in one piece."

Before they made it in to the dining hall, Cap appeared in the doorway and walked briskly toward them. At the sight of his grim expression, Abby thought she knew exactly what he was coming to tell them.

"Come with me."

"You heard about Williams."

Cap gave her an odd look. "Williams? No. I just received a telegram from Lyle. There's trouble. Go back to your rooms, change and take whatever weapons you brought with you. Meet me in the main hall in an hour. We're leaving."

"How?"

Cap's mouth tightened. "I haven't figured that out yet." He paused at the door. "What is it about Williams?"

She shook her head. "You don't want to know."

EIGHTEEN

ORO WAS WHERE a lot of the old mining families had settled. It was the farthest south of the city-states that formed the federation and, because of that, the lower elevations were more sparsely populated than in some of the other territories. Eagle Creek was midlevel, a quiet respectable town that held the record as being the closest Scraper town to the border.

The inn at Eagle Creek was much grander than the one in Canfield. Newly painted, there was a balcony above the entrance where two finely dressed women sat on wrought-iron chairs, taking tea as they watched the comings and goings about town. The saloon could be accessed from the inn but also had a separate door that let onto the main road for patrons not staying overnight.

Their private quarters were decadent, with polished walnut furniture and red brocade covering the large bed. They had a sitting room partitioned from the sleeping area by glass-plated doors. A fireplace, painted white and trimmed with gold, filled one wall and a pair of large windows looked over the main street. They even had their own private bathing room with running water. It was a far finer place than any she'd ever stayed in. She found out later that it was the honeymoon suite. When she asked Lyle about that, he only gave her a small secretive smile and shrugged.

She was overwhelmed. After two weeks on the road

and then the many horrors of Columbus Junction, the beauty and quiet of this place made her never want to leave it. Lyle took the new accommodations in stride, just as he did everything else.

Two nights. Two nights they'd stayed without leaving their rooms, waiting for confirmation that Cap had received their telegram. It was the best time of Jane's life and that scared her deeply. Because no matter how wonderful it was to slip into that enormous bed with the cool sheets and the night breeze stirring the curtains. No matter how perfect it was to touch Lyle's shoulder in the middle of the still night and have him roll over meekly so she could ride him to exhaustion. No matter how *right* it felt to wake up in his arms, she knew it couldn't last. They'd leave this room and go back to the dirty old world—the real world—and she thought this time it would hurt even more to walk through it.

They'd slept late and she was still drowsing in bed when there was a tap on the door. Lyle sighed and kissed her lightly before rising to answer it. When he returned to the room, his trousers sagging slightly around his lean hips without the belt to hold it up, his shirt unbuttoned at the neck to reveal the smooth slab of muscle beneath, she could tell by the expression on his face that it was bad news.

He held up the thin paper and she sat up, pulling the sheet up around her breasts. "They're coming," he said.

"The captain?"

He nodded. "Tomorrow at dawn. I want you to stay here today and rest. If anything happens to me, one of us should be here to meet them."

They'd decided to wait to scout out Ada's house until the last possible moment in order to avoid alerting her to the fact that she'd been found. Lyle was far more experienced at scouting than she'd ever be but she still didn't want to let him go alone. He dropped the paper and envelope onto the bureau and came toward her.

"Don't give me that look." He touched the corner of her mouth and she refrained from biting him. He might like that.

"I've been resting since we got here."

"Is that what we've been doing?"

He sat and his weight on the mattress pulled her toward him. "I didn't go to all this trouble to let you go off on your own now," she said.

"Your job was seeing me through Columbus Junction. You did that at a cost I'd rather you hadn't paid. This next part is mine."

"The people here think we're newlyweds. They know we've been locked up here for days. What will they think if the first thing you do is go off looking for a whore?"

A smile played about his lips. "You're not jealous. And since when have you cared what anyone thinks?"

"I care if they get suspicious and warn her to run. I've invested too much in this to let it go without seeing it through. I'll tell them I'm looking for my sister."

"Who you didn't bother to ask after until now."

"We're estranged."

"You're demented."

"I'm not crazy." Her voice was sharper than it should have been in reaction to the gentle teasing. Lyle's eyes narrowed a bit but he didn't answer right away. Not in words. Slipping a hand beneath the fall of hair and cupping the back of her neck, he pulled her forward and pressed a kiss to her forehead.

"You're perfect is what you are. And I don't want to risk you."

Too late for that, but she held the blow. He couldn't have known how it would be in Columbus Junction and...she might be mistaken, but she thought his feeling about placing her at risk had changed somewhat over the past few days. She supposed it was normal for a man to be protective of the woman he was sleeping with. There were probably all sorts of biological reasons to explain it.

"I don't belong to you. You're not risking me. I am."

Rather than pull away or get angry, Lyle went still. He studied her face while he sorted through the implications in his head. It was against his nature to leap without looking while she tended in the opposite direction. She was right about this though. He'd see it that way too.

"While we're in town, you can accompany me," he conceded. "Drop a few questions about your estranged sister who may or may not have taken up residence in the area. Just a general description and you don't push. I'm scouting the house alone. I'm more comfortable in rough terrain than you are and you don't have the clothes to manage it."

She wanted to argue that. Surely she could find what she needed in the mercantile store. But, just as surely, that would raise suspicion. "You're used to giving orders."

"I'm used to having my orders obeyed without argument," he answered wryly.

"And how do I explain your absence?"

He smiled, sensing victory. He clearly didn't know her as well as he thought he did. "Why, that we're looking to settle here and I wanted to explore the area before making a decision."

She dropped her gaze to her hands, completely unable to smile back at that. "Give me a half hour to get dressed."

Spiraled curls shadowed her face and he gently smoothed them back, the rough skin on his fingers catching at the finer strands. When she lifted her face, he leaned forward to steal a kiss. "We have plenty of time."

IN THE END, it was easy enough to locate Ada. They went into the saloon and while Lyle was still scoping the place out along with everyone in it, Jane walked up to the barkeep and gave him her best smile. She told him her story about searching for her long-lost sister and asked if he might be able to help.

Pausing from drying the glass in his hands, he gave her a long, offensively thorough look and then slowly shook his head. "Ada? The name doesn't ring a bell. I don't think your sister is a customer. Sure I would have noticed someone looking like you in here."

She tipped her head to one side and Lyle came up beside her, too close. The man couldn't keep his distance. A touch of wariness came into the barkeep's eyes. That simply wouldn't do. She leaned forward to rest her elbows on the bar. Attention reclaimed. Little beads of sweat popped up on the barkeep's face.

She traced at a scratch in the wood. "Oh, she's a little thing. Her face is plain as a mouse and she's just as timid. She has blond hair, not red." Her eyes flicked up to catch the barkeep staring at her breasts. She smiled.

"But we do share certain physical attributes. She'd likely keep to herself."

"On the run?"

"Not from the law." At the flicker in his eyes, she said, "Not from me either. There was a death in the family. She's owed a small inheritance and I want to see that she gets what's coming to her."

"Blond, you said." He rubbed his jaw. "Could be Adelaide McKay, the little lady who runs the orphanage up the hill."

Had he said…? That couldn't be right. Ada was a whore. She didn't run an orphanage. She knew Gideon was involved in some shady business dealings but surely he didn't traffic in children. Her stomach turned.

"Orphanage," Jane repeated numbly. She'd never felt more at peace with her decision to slit Gideon's throat.

"A right blessing to those poor kids," he said, looking her in the face now and smiling. His expression had warmed. "You should see them when they come in, starving, ragged little things. Reaper orphans. I said to my wife when your sister first moved here that it would be trouble, their kind. I thought they'd be running wild in the streets. But I'm not too proud to tell you I was wrong. It might be a founder paying for the place, but it's your sister who's really saving those kids." He rapped his knuckles on the bar to emphasize the point.

She rocked back onto her heels and Lyle's warm hand splayed on the small of her back, steadying her. The man who'd been slumped in his chair to her other side met her stunned gaze in the chipped mirror hanging over the bar. He nodded. "An angel."

She couldn't say anything though both men were staring at her waiting for her response. It was Lyle who took up the conversation. "You said up the hill. Do you mind giving us the direction of the place?"

The barkeep gave him a suspicious look, but after glancing at Jane again, he slowly nodded. "Well, you follow Main out of town. Only a little over four miles. You'll see a tidy cottage with a little plot of land in the back. She's got amaryllis on a trellis beside the porch. Can't miss it. The sheriff will take you over, I wager. But he's over to Bert's place to help with the roof that collapsed in this last storm. Shouldn't be more than a day or two before he's back in town."

Jane waved that aside. "Oh, no. That won't be necessary. I'm sure we won't have any trouble finding it. No need to trouble anyone for such a small distance. And thank you kindly for your help."

They started walking back toward the inn and Lyle put a hand to her arm. "Slow down a bit, honey. You're drawing attention, storming like a thunderhead down Main Street."

"An orphanage," she spat. "They think nobody in their right mind would think to look in an orphanage for stolen goods because no one in their right mind would hide them there. How could they hide behind children? It's despicable."

"I know it." He rubbed at her back, a soothing gesture that only made her want to sit down in the dirt and cry.

He was looking around the quaint little town with its tidy shops and well-dressed citizens. Lyle had a two-day beard and the hem of her dress was stained with mud. They were getting a lot of curious stares but no one made a move to ask them their business. She supposed she should be grateful that the sheriff was out of town today but all she felt was a seething rage at the kind of people who would take advantage of defenseless children.

"Now, you don't have to walk *that* slow." Lyle grinned at her, looking rascally with his strong white smile and all that scruff on his face.

"How do we question her without putting those kids in danger?"

"We don't. I'm heading up the hill just to take a look at the place. You're staying here." She must have given herself away somehow because his eyes narrowed, the pale gray turning stormy. "We agreed on this. If I leave now, I'll be back by nightfall."

Still she hesitated. Lyle touched her cheek. "We're partners here, aren't we? I need to be able to depend on you. I need to be able to take you at your word."

She tried to gauge how serious he was. She was used to getting her way, at least where men were concerned. Lyle was used to getting his way too and he didn't look as if he was going to bend on this point. She glared at him and ignored the lift at the corner of his mouth. "Has anyone ever told you that you fight dirty?"

The tension left his shoulders with his shrug. "Maybe a time or two. Are you going to stay mad at me long?"

She turned and swept toward the inn, leaving him to follow. She didn't like staying behind and she wouldn't pretend to for Lyle's peace of mind. Even though she'd agreed to the plan and even knowing it made good sense. Anger was a lot easier to stew in than worry.

NINETEEN

UNLIKE THE GENTLE hills they'd viewed from Flynn's ship, this side of the mountain was all rock. Sheer cliffs and jagged peaks with narrow strips of wooded areas clinging to the slopes. The settlements were more sparsely populated because of it, with smaller homesteads planted on every patch of arable land. The sky was cloudless and the wind had sharp teeth. To the north, the mountains were snowcapped, but at this elevation it felt nearer to fall.

Lyle turned up the collar on his duster and quickened his pace. He didn't like leaving Janie behind, even for an afternoon. As beautiful as it was up here, he wanted to be back on the plains where he knew what he was doing, where he knew the dangers and how to handle them. Where people, their machines and their machinations weren't the dangerous things. It was a hell of a lot easier when Reapers were the only thing he had to worry about.

If the barkeep's directions were to be believed, he was almost to the house. He'd passed the creek with the stone bridge, used the death trap of a cable car and now he was nearly to the stand of pine that marked the location of the orphanage. This level was greener than the one below, which surprised him, considering. The size of it surprised him too. This much land would surely be worth a great deal of money. Not that Corrigan couldn't afford it, but he would have expected the neighbors to question it. Perhaps they did. Perhaps they were only wise enough not to voice those questions aloud.

As soon as he was able, he slipped off the main path and into the trees. There was a clearing ahead where the trail ended but he didn't want to go up and knock at the front door. He'd avoid being seen if it was at all possible. Pretend to be lost if he ran into anyone. He only wanted the lay of the land and to confirm that this was, in fact, where Ada lived. And that she was here still.

Circling around to the side of the house, he crept forward, listening for the sound of anyone moving about the property. The wind sighed through the trees, rustling the dry leaves still clinging to the branches. A crow called out a warning that was echoed by another farther up the mountain. He had to walk carefully on the leaves underfoot so as not to make too much noise. When Ada's house came into view, he paused to take stock of it.

It was a large two-story building with a wide porch that ran the full length of the front. A pair of windows above the porch roof, like eyes looking down the mountain. It was in reasonably good repair. A patch in the roof and a slight sag to the porch. It needed new paint but he imagined the weather took its toll up here in the mountains. From where he stood, near the front west corner, he could see the edge of a large garden stretching out behind it. Only one outbuilding, a small barn with an attached pen. A cow well past prime grazing in the yard and a scattering of chickens.

The land around the house was heavily wooded, and while it sat on fairly even ground, the area behind the house sloped up at a steep angle. It was from that direction that he heard the first sign of human occupation. Voices, young ones—sharp and bright—drifting down from a good distance up the hill.

Keeping one eye on the house, he followed the sound, working his way above them. After a short time, he found the children playing beside a deep but narrow ravine that likely carried runoff down the mountain in the spring. It was dry now. There were four children in total, all boys, the oldest about ten. The four huddled heads were bent together. They were speaking mostly in whispers but occasionally one of the kids would raise his voice above the others only to be immediately shushed.

Lyle knew enough about children to know they were up to no good. And that was before he got close enough to see the rope they'd attached to a half-rotted branch above the ravine.

He took stock in a glance and felt some relief that they appeared to be well cared for. All of them were wearing shoes, at least. There were no visible tears in the clothing they wore and just enough dirt for a day or two's worth of play. The eldest had red hair that gleamed bright as a copper penny in the dappled light through the trees. The youngest couldn't have been more than three.

It still pissed him off that Corrigan was using an orphanage as a front to hide his theft. He wondered if it was still possible the supply was here but it was more likely that Ada had only held it for a day or two before passing it into a new set of hands. He didn't want to endanger the kids in any way, but as this was their only lead, he needed to find out. Be sure that it wasn't still here.

He circled round, behind a stunted pine and an old oak, leaning away from the west wind. There was a blackberry bush clinging to the rock there. Careful to avoid the thorns, Lyle passed between it and a boulder to creep close enough to get a better look at the kids. Something niggled at him. And he, being a cautious man, could not ignore the sensation.

For one thing, they were climbing where they surely should not be climbing. Their awareness of this evidenced by the way they spoke in hushed voices. "I can swing you over to the other side. I know I can. I'll give you a good shove and then all you have to do is let go when you get there."

Sounded like a good way to break your neck, or at least an arm or leg. The ravine wasn't wide but it was deep, a big crack in the earth. And while the smart thing would be to leave them to it, distracted as they were, Lyle couldn't quite turn his back. He looked at the rope again. It was thin, more the kind of thing you'd use to lead an old cow around with than something you could trust your weight to. Frayed at the end. They'd tied it to a rock and thrown it. Wrapped it twice around the branch and then twisted it around the part of the rope that hung over the ravine. Might hold. The branch looked more suspicious than the rope, truth be told. It was about six inches around and eight feet in length. The end was broken off.

By the time he was level with their position, it was clear they meant to give it a try. Lyle watched with a sinking feeling in his stomach. One of the boys jumped up and grabbed the rope, his weight ripping it from the hands of the older boy. That one gave a shout and turned helplessly to watch the child swing out over the ravine. He spun once, twice before he reached the other side. The boys shouted at him to let go of the rope but he didn't heed them. Instead, he careened back in their direction, laughing wildly. The other boys scattered out of his path. Lyle didn't like the noise that branch was making. Didn't like the sway of it.

Cursing softly, he moved forward just as the boy started to swing back in the opposite direction. The branch snapped. Lyle lunged forward the final two feet as it dropped, thorns shredding through his denim trousers as he passed through the blackberry bush. The oldest boy was sprawled in the ground flat on his stomach. He had hold of the younger one by the sleeve. The daredevil was screaming his bloody head off and kicking his legs as he hung above the ravine.

Seams gave and the sleeve ripped off just as Lyle grabbed hold of his arm, catching him mid-tumble. He hauled the child over the side and fell back on his rump. The small circle of boys stared at him in shock and guilt was stamped plain on their pale faces. He imagined the expression he wore looked much the same.

He started to speak but the words died on his tongue before he could force them out. The sleeve had ripped at the shoulder and the starburst design that marked those immune to Reaper infection was clear as day, purple-black on his pale skin.

The sight of it punched the breath from Lyle's lungs like a horse kick to the chest. All he could do was stare at that mark. Not doubting his eyes, but not knowing how what he was seeing could possibly be right.

What the *hell* was a star-marked child doing out here?

The boy tried to twist away but Lyle tightened his

grip. He had no intention of letting go. He had no intention of letting any of these children out of his sight. For one thing, they'd surely tell Ada that had a stranger had been lurking about the place. For another…well, he just wasn't going to leave them behind. When he turned to the others, they stopped edging away from him, although they were clearly torn between wanting to help their friend and wanting to run for help.

"Are all of you star-marked?"

The redhead squared his body as though he was getting ready for a fight. "You have no business here, mister. This is our property and you need to leave it now."

"Answer the question." Lyle stood, hefting the struggling youngster up with him. "I won't hurt you. I promise you that, but I need to know. Do you have a mark like this on your arm?"

The boy hesitated, but only for a moment. "If you let Creed go, then I'll show you."

Lyle gave the boy a slight push toward the others and the redhead stepped forward. He rolled back his sleeve enough so that Lyle could see his mark on his arm. It was placed somewhat low for a star-mark, just a few inches above his elbow, as if the doctor administering the shot had been in a hurry and missed the muscle they usually aimed for. Misplaced or not, it was clearly a star-mark. Lyle had seen enough of them to know.

The boy stiffened up like a board but allowed the touch when Lyle grasped his wrist. Lyle turned his arm to brush his finger over the distinctive starburst pattern. Ever so slightly raised, it matched the one on Lyle's own arm exactly.

"Where's your family?"

"I don't have one," the boy said. "None of us do. That's why we're here."

Four boys. The oldest, ten. The youngest, three. All of them star-marked and watching him with open suspicion. If he didn't gain their trust somehow, he was going to have a hell of a time sneaking them down the mountain.

He shrugged free of his duster and it hit the ground with a rustle of dry leaves. Loosening his shirt enough to pull it aside, he showed them his mark, high on his left shoulder. Creed sucked a mouthful of air through his teeth. The eldest tipped his head to the side and studied his arm for a long moment before looking up. "You're a Ranger."

"You know what the mark means then?"

"Of course I do. I'm not stupid."

Lyle tried to restrain his grin. "Of course you aren't. You can call me Lyle, by the way. I'm a lieutenant with Fort Dougan."

That earned him a hesitant smile. "I'm Brandon. That's Creed and Will." He nodded toward the daredevil and then the dark-skinned boy. "James is the baby."

Will had scooped up the chubby little toddler at some point during the discussion. James had golden blond hair, bright blue eyes and a scowl that looked so shockingly familiar, Lyle's attention lingered for several seconds before he looked back at Brandon.

"How did you come to live here?"

"There was a Reaper attack when I was seven," he said. "I survived but the rest didn't. I don't remember very much of it. The sheriff found me on the road walking into town and he sent me here."

"The sheriff? Do you know his name?"

"No. He was from the next town over. His wife wanted to keep me but they sent me up here on an airship instead. There was a Scraper..." He trailed off with a frown. "Why do you need to know all this?"

"Because I'm a Ranger. Technically, that makes you, all of you, my responsibility."

"Ada's in charge of us."

Ada, who was working for Corrigan who, according to Flynn, had stolen the cure to expand his mining operation in Reaper territory. Lyle would bet every penny he owned that Corrigan meant these boys for the mines too. Who better to serve as guards for his operation in Reaper territory than his own little army of Rangers?

Lyle's gaze fell on the youngest again. "And him." He nodded toward James, who wasn't anywhere near old enough to be running wild in the woods. "When did—"

He didn't get to finish the question. Pain exploded in the back of his head as something hard and heavy cracked against his skull. Lyle reached for his gun, but it was too late. Darkness closed around his vision as he fell forward and everything was black by the time he hit the ground.

TWENTY

LYLE DIDN'T COME BACK from scouting Ada's orphanage.

Jane sat up all night on the plush velvet settee staring out the window. From that position she had a splendid view of Main Street, the side alley down which Lyle had disappeared earlier that morning and the mountain stretching up, a jagged black shape that blocked out the stars. When it started to rain about midnight, she rose and stood at the window, eyes on the road, crystal beads of water sliding beneath her fingertips pressed to the glass. When her breath began to fog her view, she retreated, poured herself a glass of whiskey and resumed her vigil from the settee.

He might already be dead. Corrigan's men might have captured him. Or he might have simply slipped and fallen. He wasn't familiar with the land here. One misplaced step on a narrow trail could send you sliding off a cliff. He wouldn't know to watch for the snakes that liked to sun themselves on the rock. Or the bears and mountain lions. He could be lying feverish or broken in a crevice somewhere even now. She rose, paced to the window again and peered out a while longer at the darkness. She wouldn't find him at night, in the dark, in this weather. She would only kill herself and then there would be no one to look in the morning. She should rest now while she had the chance.

But the cycle kept repeating itself all night. Before

the sun was fully up, she was on the trail. She'd left a note behind for the captain, Abby and Jake. It brought them fully up-to-date on the situation and what she meant to do. She'd find Lyle and if she failed, the other Rangers would come looking for them both.

She rounded a bend in the trail and the fierce and blazing light of the morning sun hit her full in the face. The storm clouds had broken up early and a stiff southerly wind shoved them off toward the plains. The rain might have been what kept the captain from flying in to the rescue but she wasn't waiting in Eagle Creek a moment longer than she had to.

Letting out a deep breath, she adjusted the brim of her hat to block the glare and leaped over a sluggish brown stream. The rock above was slick and stained a rust color by the sewers from the next level up. They let their shit leak right down the mountain. There was a metaphor somewhere in that. The view in the opposite direction was spectacular. Thin strips of clouds streaked across a sky so blue it made her heart ache. A rocky outcrop several dozen feet below hid Eagle Creek from view, making it seem as if she was all alone up here. She could see forever. Gray rock giving way by bits to the smooth flat stretch of the plains, a sea of green and gold. And she was still only in what was considered the foothills. The people here were poor, though not as wretched as the ones forced to live on the border.

Those people down there were her people now, the ones on the plains and in the forts. Damned if she was going to let some entitled piece of Scraper shit steal from people who had so little. Lyle…she wasn't letting them take Lyle away from her either.

She kept a brisk pace as the path widened and meandered through another settlement. This one was a small collection of homes built on the high slope with a terrace cut into the hillside below. The narrow fields were already prepped for frost. No one was in the field today but she could feel eyes from the buildings above her as she passed. She kept her head down and breathed a sigh of relief once she crossed the stone bridge and the trail began to curve upward again more steeply.

As she rounded the next bend, she lost her footing and cursed. Her boots were made for riding, with sturdy heels and smooth thin soles. Not made for climbing mountains but she hadn't been able to find another pair her size in the mercantile store. She'd gone shopping yesterday afternoon…just in case. Trousers and a belt. A workman's leather jacket. Extra ammunition for her pistol and the heavier .45 Flynn had given her with a warning to watch her back. The gun hung from the belt at her waist. Black-barreled with mahogany inserts. It was a business weapon, not a showpiece.

Flynn would be long gone by now and she had no way to get hold of him, not that he would come at her request if called. She couldn't blame him for that. He was in deep with Corrigan, had betrayed him already by bringing her and Lyle as far as he had. She was well and truly on her own until she found Lyle or Cap arrived with whatever Rangers he could call in on such short notice.

It was a bit of a climb. When Scraper folk said five miles out of town they were talking about trails that wound around the mountain. Every patch of flat earth was tilled and planted and the homes were built flush up to the rock, tall narrow structures anchored directly into the mountain face. The path she was on was well tended though. There were even guardrails where the trail wandered close to the cliff's edge. Sturdy poles of wrought iron.

It was a Sunday which meant that there were few people out and about their business though the morning was fine. As she passed through one cluster of homes, she could distantly hear the sound of people singing from the church.

It took her a full hour to reach the abrupt end of the trail from Eagle Creek and the carts leading to the next level.

The cable car was locked above her, out of reach of mischievous children. She set to work on the winch, grimacing at the metallic grind as one of the gears slipped. In the richer cities, the carts were steam powered. All you needed to do was press a button and the oiled gears and cables did all the work. This one worked on hydrogen like some of the older ships. They kept the balloon filled, the woven wicker basket tethered to a cable as thick as her wrist. When you wanted to go up, you reeled it to your level using the winch then floated up to the top on a guide. It was hot and dirty work that she'd become unused to. This town, she guessed, was about fifteen levels or more down. Only two steam cable carts had separated the city proper from the house she'd grown up in.

Funny how she'd never questioned that luxury until it was gone. Funny how little she thought about the city now. When she'd first left home, it had felt like the end of the world. She couldn't imagine going back to that life. The prospect of living in a town like Columbus Junction or Eagle Creek was just as bad.

She set the winch when the bottom of the cart was

level with her knees. Hopping aboard, the wicker basket swayed beneath her feet. There was a broomstick of a lever inside which she forced forward to release the cable brake. Up she floated, watching the jagged cliff slip past.

Lyle would have come this way just yesterday. She wondered how he'd managed the contraption, having likely never encountered anything like it. It couldn't mean anything good that he hadn't returned. If she was smart, she'd disappear just like Flynn had. Run away far and fast. Start over. Even if she returned to the fort, no one would blame her for leaving Lyle behind. She looked up at the swiftly approaching landing, her eyes tearing up from the bright glare of the sun. There was a rattling clank from the upper anchor and the basket jerked to a stop, rocking gently.

Lyle would tell her she was stubborn and reckless and too ballsy for her own good. And maybe she was all of those things. But as stupid as it was to go after Lyle, she couldn't turn back…not without knowing what had happened to him. There was still a chance. With a deep breath, Jane set the brake and stepped from the cart.

A woman waited at the top for the ride down, a young child tugging on her plain-spun skirts. She started to smile at Jane until she got a good look at her—at her rough clothes and the gun at her belt—and she immediately bent and lifted her child onto her hip. It was uncommon for a woman—anyone really—to walk around openly armed so high up in the mountains. At the highest elevations, there were city ordinances preventing such thing.

"Good morning," Jane said. "It's a lovely day, isn't it?"

The woman nodded her head in agreement but then

hurried past to climb into the cart. As the door closed behind her with a clank, Jane swore she heard "Breeder" muttered like a curse. She couldn't help but smile at that. That's exactly what she was. And she was fine with that. She sure as hell didn't belong up here anymore.

Not ten steps up the trail, a gust of wind blew down the mountain, carrying with it the sound of male voices. She hesitated but in the end she decided to move forward. Truly there was nowhere to run or hide.

She reconsidered her decision to keep climbing as soon as she saw the men—five of them—rounding the rocky outcrop straight ahead. They weren't wearing uniforms but they might as well have been. They were dressed nearly identically in dark woolen trousers and fine shirts. Their vests were plain black cotton. The sturdy soled boots that would see them up and down the mountain without losing their footing. The rifles they carried were perfectly well kept, even she could see that. Gleaming stocks and polished barrels. It was a special design, long-barreled and created especially for long distances. For…say, if you wanted to hide high behind a rock and shoot a person dead from miles away. Riflemen. They were the last law on the mountain, the deliverers of justice if not the deciders of it.

They were also the first people you'd run to if there was trouble. If one of the carts malfunctioned or if a mountain lion claimed territory too close to town. They were rope-trained for rescue. She'd seen them work once when a man had taken a fall on one of the trails near Columbus Junction. He'd been trapped, injured, on a ledge below town and they'd called in riflemen to attempt a rescue. It was an amazing sight. They were like spiders on the sheer cliffs.

It gave her pause to see them here because they were also cocky sons of bitches. Unlike the lawmen on the plains, these men didn't belong to the people they served. They were paid and owned by the city founders. Each group sponsored by an individual benefactor, generally the one who had the most financial interest in the area.

What marked them even above the weapons they wore was their facial hair. Sideburns extending down to the jawline and a neat thin mustache from the corner of one lip to the other. It was a style that had gone out of fashion years ago but for some reason Corrigan's people couldn't quite seem to let it go. If Corrigan had something to protect here, an aboveboard businessman like himself would ensure he had riflemen here to protect his investment. Lawfully sanctioned gunmen that he owned.

The leader stepped forward, his rifle slung loosely in the crook of his arm. That didn't fool her a bit. He could aim and fire faster than she could run and if he couldn't, then one of the men standing behind him surely could. "Ma'am."

He was the tallest of the group. Black hair, pale skin, gray eyes. He touched the wide brim of his hat as a brief courtesy which was then quickly negated by the way he looked her over. She noticed that his attention lingered on her gun and that his eyes were a little harder when they finally made their way back up to her face.

"Rifleman." She managed not to spit the word. What awful luck she'd had lately.

"It's a fine day today, isn't it?"

"Lovely." She wondered if these men were the reason Lyle hadn't returned. Even as unsettling as the thought was, it gave her hope. Riflemen were less likely to put a bullet in the head of a Ranger without asking questions first. If they'd found him, they might have only locked him in a cell somewhere. "I wonder if you might be able to help me."

"We'd be happy to assist you in any way you require." He took a step closer and she had to force herself to stand her ground. "Might I ask why you're so heavily armed? That's an awful big weapon for a little thing like yourself."

Well, since he worded it that way, she chose to ignore the question. "I'm trying to locate my sister. Her name is Ada McKay. She moved into this area about a year and a half ago and we lost touch shortly after. I'm trying to find her."

He considered that for a moment. The man directly behind him shifted slightly and while she couldn't see him clearly, she thought he was drawing his gun. Damn. The leader scratched his jaw. "There is an Ada who lives in the area but she's never mentioned a sister."

Jane snorted. "She wouldn't have. She's estranged from the family and we didn't part on good terms. Our father died last month and he left her some money in his will. This is my last attempt to satisfy the lawyer that I did my part to reach her and then I'm through. Can I have your name in case they need to verify that I was actually here?"

She almost had him. She could see it in his eyes, the thoughts bouncing around inside his brain. A young, attractive woman obviously out of her element. Traveling alone so maybe she thought she needed the gun. Even *with* the gun, Jane doubted that she looked particularly dangerous. People did tend to underestimate her. She wasn't above using that to her advantage when it was necessary.

"Joe Lassiter. Marshal of Westin. Have them contact me if they need the proof and I'll give it."

Her knees trembled just a little she was so relieved. Especially when, with those words, the posture of all the riflemen changed. Shoulders easing, their hands fell away from their guns. She'd have to walk right through them which would take some bravery but she could do it. It seemed there were no bounds to what she could accomplish when she put her mind to it.

She was only a few feet away from the first rifleman when she heard the soft whump-whump of a propeller high above, descending from the northern slope. Her stomach slid right down to her toes. She quickened her pace before glancing up at the sky. What she saw there nearly made her stumble. It was the Tirado flagship, the *Goliath*, descending toward Eagle Creek. Brass trim caught the sunlight and glinted merrily as the ponderous unwieldy beast slipped through the sky. The weaponry mounted fore and aft hadn't been in place when the ship had picked up the fort's delegation for the assembly.

When she lowered her gaze, Marshal Joe Lassiter of Westin moved to block her path and his men closed ranks behind him.

"I'm sorry, ma'am. You'll come with us back to the compound. I believe I do have a few more questions for you to answer, after all." The thing that scared her was that he actually did sound regretful.

They relieved her of her weapons but they didn't cuff her. Not that they needed to. Five big, heavily armed men surrounding her front and back on this narrow little trail. The only way to escape was to make a run for the ledge and she sure as hell wasn't that desperate. It wasn't a long trek. About a half mile up. They turned right when Ada's place was up and to the left. All she could see in that direction was more dirt and rock, a few scrubby trees clinging to the rock. A glimmering puddle in the cup of the rock from the rains last night. As she watched a bird splashed right into it. Loosening the scarf at her neck to let the air cool the prickle of sweat from her skin, she wished she could do the same.

One of the men, who'd introduced himself as Carlo, noticed her distress and offered her water which she accepted. He had the slender build of youth though she estimated him at about her own age. Like all of the riflemen, he moved easily over the rough terrain.

She drank from his flask and handed the water back to him. "Worried that I'll pass out and you'll have to carry me the rest of the way up?"

"You're awfully suspicious."

"Oh?" She raised her brows. "Did I accost you on the road and take away your weapons?"

"You haven't been accosted," he said mildly. "We're only…delaying your journey for a bit. Cooperate with the marshal and I'm sure you'll be on your way in no time."

"Where exactly is that you're taking me?"

"Our station is ahead. You can rest there while we check out your report with Ada and then you'll be on your way. It shouldn't take long at all." He'd slung her gun belt over his shoulder. Touching the butt of her pistol, he said, "This is a lot of firepower for a woman visiting family."

"You're awfully suspicious."

He smiled at that. "It is my job."

"I mentioned my sister and I are estranged. I can't be certain of my welcome with Ada."

"Ada's never mentioned a sister," he said thoughtfully. "Are you a bounty hunter?"

When she didn't answer, he smiled. "We'll find out soon enough but I admit the curiosity is killing me."

"Now if only that were true."

He laughed. "No reason to be mean about it. We're only doing our job. Keeping the community safe."

"Keeping Corrigan's interests safe."

"That too."

"This is a little outside his normal territory, isn't it?"

"It is," he agreed easily. "But it still belongs to Oro. What do you know of Corrigan's territory?"

She shrugged for an answer and fell silent, preserving her breath for a steep stretch. She ignored the hand he offered and when they reached the top, she could see the gate to the compound that must be their headquarters ahead. From the way the trail had curved around, she suspected if you looked out over the edge you'd be able to see most of the trail below leading all the way down to Eagle Creek.

"You don't want to jump."

"I wouldn't jump." He made a small sound, more like a grunt than agreement. She gave him a sharp look. "And why would you care?"

His mouth thinned in a narrow smile. "We're responsible for the maintenance of the trail too. Jumpers are messy."

Shoving aside that gruesome image, she focused on the clearing they entered once they passed through the plain wrought-iron gate. The gate would have been an oddity on the plains, but not so much here. Iron and stone were the preferred construction materials on the mountains.

The compound itself was small, consisting of only three buildings. A main house, a barn and a small stone, one-story building that was for business. That was the one they led her into. Most of the men had continued on toward the house. But the leader accompanied her, as well as Carlo and another man who had yet to speak a word. He was big and intimidating as hell, standing by the door grim-faced and silent like a guard dog. She imagined that was his job—to intimidate and so she dismissed him for the time being. Lassiter removed his hat and hung it up on a peg before gesturing her toward a small wooden chair near the center of the room and taking the seat behind the desk himself.

He didn't waste any time getting down to business. "Your name?"

Had she given one? Best to stick as close to the truth as possible. "Jane." And because this was trouble if she'd ever seen it, she added a belated but sincerely respectful, "sir."

That seemed to please him. He leaned back in his creaky old chair and folded his hands over his belly. "And do you have a last name, Jane?"

"Fisher." Because she was nobody. If he recognized that name then he'd beaten it out of Lyle and she was already lost.

"Ah."

Her blood went cold but if she paled a bit, that was the only reaction she was giving him. He might be playing with her. It didn't mean that Lyle was gone.

He let the silence stretch and she could hear the chickens out in the yard and the low murmur of men's voices coming from the direction of the house. A breeze came through the door and stirred the loose edge of one of the wanted posters nailed to a board on the wall.

"All right then, Miss Fisher. Let's hear your story again. About your sister Ada."

She told it, being sure to keep it consistent with what she'd said on the trail and in town, just in case he decided to check. There was a tremor in her voice and surely he could hear that but it could only help her. Men like him liked to believe that women were weak. It was a fine line though. She wanted him to believe she was weak enough not to pose a threat, but not so weak that she needed an escort up to Ada's.

"We've had trouble here lately."

"Trouble?" A numb feeling settled in the center of her chest.

He nodded. "Outlaws and such, taking advantage of the good citizens we protect. You would think now that they'd discovered a cure, people would flood down to the plains to claim land but that simply hasn't been the case. We have more people abandoning their stakes to move in with family until its safe again. You came from the plains."

It wasn't a question so she didn't deny it. She shrugged. "It's not really worth chasing after Rangers anymore if there won't be a child price, is there?"

"They haven't said they'll discontinue that."

"But they're not making promises anymore either. There are former Reapers banding together to stir up trouble, that's why I travel armed. But I don't see what that has to do with anything here."

"Just yesterday we found a Ranger walking the very same trail we found you on. Two months and no one's taken that path. Now it's a highway. There's that, and the Ballonet gunship making a visit to a quiet town like Eagle Creek. I want to know what's afoot, Miss Fisher, and I think you can tell me."

She couldn't have told him anything just then even if she'd wanted to. It was as if her brain was collecting the words that spilled out of his mouth but couldn't quite make sense of them. Nothing after he'd said the word *Ranger*. She wanted to ask—badly—about what had happened to Lyle. But she couldn't risk it. Not quite yet.

"I'm sure I don't know."

And she held to that line for the next hour they questioned her, with the guard dog glowering at her and Carlo lurking silently in the shadows by the wall. Lassiter grew increasingly frustrated until he stood abruptly, nearly overturning his chair. She gripped the edge of her seat, bracing herself, but he walked to the door, said a quiet word to Carlo and then left.

Carlo didn't ask her any questions about Ada or Columbus Junction or the Tirado flagship. In fact, he barely spoke as he locked her in one of the tiny cells in the back of the jail. When she demanded to be released, he gave her a hard look and told her they weren't nearly finished with her yet. Several hours had passed since then, and now she was actually beginning to look forward to their return.

Lyle. She needed to know what had happened to him.

They'd left the door open, probably as much to prevent even the illusion of privacy as for airflow. The four windows were tiny slits in the stone. It was a small stuffy space that would be sweltering in the full heat of summer. At first she paced the cell, wondering if they'd kept Lyle in here, examining the stone for some sign of him. There were names scratched there but none were familiar. She sniffed at the blanket as though a bloodhound but it only smelled old and musty, like old sweat and barn. Then, she slid back onto the bed, across the straw mattress. The cotton covering it was worn and sharp pieces poked through in spots. With her back to the wall, she watched the sun move across the stone. She drew her knees up to her chest and tried very hard not to think about anything but how to get out.

It was at least an hour after sunset when she heard footsteps crossing the plank wood that served as a porch. One pair of footsteps. The bright rattle of keys. She held her breath until she saw Carlo in the doorway and then let it out slow.

He set something down on the desk. A bowl, she thought, and had it confirmed when the scent of stew reached her a second later. He lit the lantern, tightened the wick to a low burn and then unlocked her cell. The door swung smoothly open and he held it wide.

"I have a few questions for you and I've brought food."

She climbed to her feet but didn't move forward. There was nothing she could use as a weapon. The iron bed was a solid piece, soldered together rather than screwed and for all of her many fine attributes, she lacked the strength to pry the bars from her cage.

"Ma'am," he prodded and she stepped forward. She had to turn her body to avoid touching him as she passed to the chair and he seemed to find that amusing. She wondered how amusing he'd find it if she kneed him in the groin. But he was armed and she'd try polite first. Not that polite had served her well in the past.

Eying him warily, she took a bite of the stew. Reassured by the taste, she set to work at shoving it down her throat, aware of the eyes watching her. She needed the sustenance, especially if she wanted a shot at escape. When she was done, she pushed the bowl aside toward her left hand. He remained to her right. If she needed to, she could get more momentum from that direction, the better to brain him with.

Carlo sat on the edge of the desk so close that his boot touched her leg. When she withdrew as far as the chair allowed, his brows rose. “I’m not interested in you, Jane.”

“You’re interested.”

He smiled. “You’ve a high opinion of yourself.”

That wasn’t fair. She was attractive to men. It was the plain truth. She’d only be stupid if she denied it. “What do you want, Carlo?”

“For you to tell me what happened in Columbus Junction.”

He’d pieced together that she’d come from Columbus Junction, had he? She shrugged. “There was some disturbance at the saloon. Who can say? We heard shots. When men took to the streets, we got out of town.”

“We?”

“My hired pilot and I.”

“Where is he now?”

She shrugged. “Gone. I had enough money to get here but no farther. It’ll be a long walk home.”

“That’s what happened?”

“That’s what happened.”

Dark eyes studied her face. “I can help you, you know. All I need is for you to be honest with me.”

“I’ve heard that kind of offer before.”

Annoyance flickered over his fine features. Truly

too refined for a man's. He reminded her of Cam in that way, though his coloring was darker. His skin olive rather than golden. He was probably used to women falling over themselves to please him. Just like Cam. "I told you I'm not interested in anything but your story."

"Tell me what happened to the Ranger." She blurted it out and knew it was a mistake as soon as she said it.

His eyes narrowed with something close to smugness. "The Ranger we found on the trail?"

She nodded. "If you want information, I'm willing to trade. What was he doing all the way up here?"

"Why do you want to know?"

"Curiosity," she said without hesitation, having anticipated the question. "It's unusual, you have to admit."

"I do. We found it unusual."

More than anything, she wanted to get out of this conversation. Now. Even before she had her answer, while there was still some hope that Lyle was out there somewhere in the world safe and maybe even looking for her by now. It wasn't fair. She'd only just found him. Gideon had been like a burr. Lyle…she'd barely had hold of him. She didn't even really have him. A few nights. She'd known going in that he'd move on eventually. But not this way.

Carlo leaned in closer. "No one is coming to save you, if that's what you're hoping." He turned the keys in his hands. Four of them. Heavy iron. The sound scraped her ears. "You came here with him, didn't you? That's the only explanation. Somehow you sent word to Tirado when he didn't return. What I don't understand is how you managed that so quickly."

He paused but she'd be damned if she gave him anything. *No one is coming to save you.* She didn't want those words to mean what she thought they might. She gritted her teeth against the pain rising up in her chest. "What happened to the Ranger?"

He shook his head. "What do you think happened? The two of you against Corrigan. You had to know that couldn't end well."

"I don't know what you're talking about," she said, and then cleared her throat because her voice was hoarse. "I came here looking for my sister Ada, not looking to take on Corrigan."

Lyle...he couldn't possibly be dead. She'd feel it, wouldn't she?

"Lassiter sent a man down to Eagle Creek to check on the ship and your story. You know what I think he'll find?"

She grabbed the bowl and swung it hard. A narrow upward arc that connected with the side of his head. She was nearly as surprised as he was by the action. The blow caught him in the temple and he rolled sideways off the desk, landing on his feet like a cat. But he was stunned.

Blood trickled from the gash in his forehead. Even in the dim light, she could see that his eyes weren't entirely focused on her. That didn't stop him from reaching for his gun. And she was too angry to have the good sense to run. She dove at him, knocking him off balance and sending them both to the floor in a tangle of limbs.

He tried to lift his hands to defend himself but the space was too narrow. And she still had that heavy piece of crockery in her hands. This time when she hit him, he jerked once and lay still. Her hand was raised to strike again before she noticed that he wasn't fighting back.

Breathing hard, she checked to see that he was still

alive and decided to leave him that way. She'd lost the desire to bash his head in and a gunshot would be too loud. She took his gun though and wasted no more than the few minutes to be sure that the yard was clear before she slipped through the door into the night.

She didn't go down which is where they would expect her to run. Instead, she took the branch she'd seen that led up. Taking a chance. It would probably be safer to go back to where they'd found her and follow the trail from there. This narrow path looked like a shortcut and she was betting that the riflemen had plenty of those that they could use to cut people off.

The path was a terror in the dark though. The moon was covered by clouds and the trail was so steep she practically scraped her nose climbing up. There was a storm coming in and the air was damp, heavier than it ever felt at this elevation. She used her hands and her ears as much as her eyes for feeling her way forward.

Pausing at the top of the first long stretch, she listened for pursuit. From this angle she could actually see the rifleman's compound below. She crouched down behind a rock so as not to make a target of herself just in case it was true what they said about riflemen being able to shoot the wings off a fly in a tornado. It looked quiet. Lights glimmering in two of the windows. The barn doors shut up tight for the night. But there was no light coming from the prison and she'd left the lantern on so that the others would think Carlo was still interrogating her.

While she was still considering that, she heard a slight sound from below her on the trail. Soft. Maybe a single stone coming loose and rattling down the rock. It might have been anything—a rodent or just gravity tugging it down. Not wanting to take any chances, she bolted.

At the next turn in the trail, the moon flickered out from behind the clouds and she risked a glance down. Nothing to be seen. This trail was more of a groove in the rock face carved from rainwater. If those clouds opened up, she might just be washed out. The man behind her was more of a concern though. If there was actually a man following her and it wasn't just a trick of her imagination. Why would there be just one rifleman tracking her?

Surely if they'd found her missing, the entire compound would have been roused. The thought that there might be more out there, moving to surround her made her push away from the ledge. She touched the gun wedged into her waistband to reassure herself that it was still there and climbed the final distance to the level where the innkeeper had said Ada was living. This had to be it. South face about five miles up. This was the first level ground sizable enough to support a claim.

She didn't linger on the edge. Instead, she broke through the stand of pine that served as a windbreak and ran toward the mountain. The home would be there beneath the shelter of the rock. She thought she could see the hulking shape of it in the darkness, the roofline blacker than the night. She passed through a sizable garden, well past harvest. Though the moon was shining high above, the cloud layer was thick. Only a faint eerily cool light managed to break through. It painted the soil black and the chaff so white it seemed as though she was walking through a field of bones. The house was very still.

Why were there no lights? She slowed and then

stopped completely. Pressing a hand to the stitch in her side, she tried to catch her breath. Surely, the riflemen wouldn't have hurt Ada or the children in her care.

Hearing a sound, she turned away from the mountains. The pine trees were a black jagged line against the night sky. She drew her gun a moment before a shape separated itself from the shadows, hands raised to his sides so she could see he was unarmed. Her heart rose. Her whole body felt light enough to rise into the sky.

And because she was a fool who never seemed to be able to give up hope, she called out softly, "Lyle?"

The clouds parted just then enough to let a sliver of moonlight through and her heart sunk. That wasn't Lyle. Carlo, still alive, after all. He'd come to and then he'd followed her alone, likely to avoid the embarrassment of having to tell his friends that he'd been beaten up by a woman. She cocked the gun and he stopped.

"You're not going to shoot an unarmed man."

"Try me."

"You don't understand," he said. "I told you I was trying to help you. You'd have been safe if you'd only stayed put."

"Inside my nice little cell? You can keep your safety and your help. I don't need either."

He sighed at the same time the door to the house squealed open behind her. And as if the entire world was working against her, the clouds chose that moment to break up enough for the clear cool light of the full moon to spill out over the clearing. She could clearly see the ugly gash on Carlo's forehead and the frown on his face as he stared at whoever was behind her.

"Lower your weapon, Ranger."

That was a woman's voice. Not Ada's. She remembered Ada well enough to be sure of that.

"I'm not a Ranger," Jane called out, keeping her eyes fixed on Carlo. "And I don't take orders from people I don't know. Especially not Scrapers."

The woman made an annoyed sound and Jane heard her take a step closer. "You're completely surrounded. Lower your weapon or you die."

For a reckless, hopeless instant Jane considered not backing down. Why? Why should she keep fighting? It never did her any good. Lyle was gone. There was nothing left for her here.

But it just wasn't in her to start shooting. Slowly, she lowered the gun and turned around.

TWENTY-ONE

LYLE'S HEAD FELT as if someone had driven a railroad spike into it. A fierce pounding pain in his left temple and a dry fuzzy taste in his mouth. It was like the worst hangover he'd ever had in his life times a thousand. Each time his heart beat, he saw a red flare behind his closed lids and no matter how hard he willed himself toward unconsciousness, it wouldn't come.

Little by little, he became aware of his surroundings.

That wasn't his heart beating, after all. The steady percussive noise was a mechanical thump loud enough to vibrate through his body where it was pressed to the floor. His head, right shoulder and thigh were on hard wood, his back to a softer support. Not a person or pillow.

He was still alive. That was something. Though at the moment, that gift was of dubious worth.

Accepting the inevitable, he slit open his eyes and swallowed the bile that rose in his throat. Another fucking airship. By the looks of it, he was in the cargo hold of a light ship like Flynn's. That support at his back was netting. If this was Flynn's ship, the rat bastard was going to die, friend of Janie's or no.

His hands were tied behind him which explained why he couldn't feel his arms. Numb. That was going to hurt like a bitch when he was cut free. If he was cut free. There was crusted blood on his cheek and grit in his eyes. Just as he opened his mouth to curse a blue streak he snapped it closed. Because it seemed he wasn't alone, after all.

The four kids he'd found by the ravine were huddled together like a mass of puppies, sound asleep. Their mistress, Ada he presumed, pressed a hand to the youngest one's back and lifted her chin as she met his gaze. Fear. That's what he was looking at. Not malice, but the kind of fear that made a man quake in his boots. She was holding her ground for the kids' sakes. It concerned him what she might be so afraid of. Certainly not him. Tied up, beaten to a pulp and on the verge of vomiting.

Small in stature, she didn't look much older than the little ones she watched over. Thick blond hair and dark eyes. He wondered if she was the one who'd bashed his head in. Possibly. He'd been distracted, talking to the boys. But if Ada had dragged him down the hill and tied him up all on her own, he'd eat his boots.

"Ma'am."

She startled at the sound even though she'd been staring at him. Her throat flexed as she swallowed but her voice was steady when she spoke. "You're a Ranger."

It wasn't really a question but he nodded anyway. Her wariness concerned him. He'd assumed that she was working with whoever had abducted him. "And you're Ada."

She sucked in a breath at the name but nodded. "How did you find us?"

"We were tracking the stolen serum."

"I don't know anything about a serum," she said it so vehemently that he might have believed her if not for the fact that she was leaning against one of the fort's crates. That was Doc's handwriting right there on the box. It was possible she didn't know it. It was also possible the serum had already been removed from those crates. He shifted, groaning at the way his stiff muscles tightened.

The smallest child, James, rolled over and nuzzled his little face into the crook of Brandon's arm. "That may be, but you do know that these are star-marked children. Children that you placed in danger."

Her arms tightened around the children and his brows rose.

"Protective of them, are you? That's somewhat ironic, don't you think?"

"I take good care of them. As good as I would my own." She glared at him something fierce. "Nobody was in danger until you came along. This is your fault."

He sighed. "How did they come to be in your care?"

"I run an orphanage."

"Star-marked children don't go to orphanages."

"They're Reaper orphans. They had to go somewhere."

"Is that what Gideon told you when he plucked you out of Rose's brothel and sent you to work for Corrigan?"

Her mouth pressed into a thin line. Nope. Wasn't answering that one, but she didn't really need to. A person didn't ask questions of men like Moore and Corrigan without getting hurt. Hadn't Janie said that?

The thought of Janie sitting alone right now in Eagle Creek, waiting for him to come back tugged at his heart. She'd be safe there. The captain was due to arrive today. Even if the captain didn't come personally, he'd send help. She might worry but she'd stay out of trouble. She was a survivor, Janie. If he made it out of this...well, best not to get ahead of himself.

"Where are they taking us?"

At first, he didn't think she was going to answer that one either. But then she tipped her head back against the wall and closed her eyes. Her throat contracted as she swallowed and she said one word, bitter and bleak. "Hell."

TWENTY-TWO

JANE TURNED AROUND to find a veritable army closing in on her from the surrounding woods. Just as well she hadn't started shooting. She would have been dead before she fired a second shot.

Standing docile as a lamb while they disarmed her, she fixed her attention on the small group standing on the porch. Someone unshuttered a lantern and it lit their bodies in silhouette. The woman at the center of the group, presumably the one who'd spoken to her, was clearly a Scraper. Her posture was straight as a rail and the gown she wore was cut to perfectly fit every curve of her body. Her hair was coiled above her head in an elaborate coiffure and when she stepped forward, she did so with the cultivated grace of an aristocrat.

"Jane!"

From the direction of the barn, Abby jogged toward her, holstering her gun as she approached. Jane looked back at the woman. The Tirado ship. These Scrapers must be the ones Cap had hitched a ride with yesterday. She didn't see any sign of the ship so they must have climbed up after getting her message or landed on another level.

Abby's hug was tight enough to make her ribs ache. Jane received it awkwardly at first, but when Abby whispered fiercely, "I am so happy we found you," she hugged her back tighter. Blinking away tears, she saw

Jake coming up behind Abby with Cap beside him. No longer dressed in his Scraper clothes, Cap was a Ranger once more. Brown leather duster and a rifle crooked in his arm. Carlo passed them by to intercept the Scraper woman and she wondered at that.

"He's working for her," Abby told her. "Carlo Juarez. He's been keeping an eye on Corrigan's operations in this area for the Tirado family."

"A spy?"

Abby nodded. "Cap had trouble finding us a ride until he approached Maricel over there and mentioned Corrigan's name. Apparently there's bad blood between the families."

That was an understatement. The Tirado-Corrigan feud was legendary. When Santa Ana was overrun by Reapers, the Tirado family had escaped Nueva España in the airships they were famous for even then.

Oro turned them away, denying them refuge, and the Tirados lost two ships and half their family on the way up to Ballonet. The Corrigans had been the ones to force them away and the Tirados never forgave them for it. They'd worked at cross-purposes ever since, adding injury to injury. Sebastian Tirado had died just a few months before Jane left Columbus Junction and even then there'd been rumors that Daniel Corrigan had something to do with it. If Cap had presented Maricel Tirado with the opportunity to help catch Corrigan red-handed stealing from the forts in exchange for a little help, it was no wonder she'd jumped at the chance.

"Jane." Abby took her hands, half to grab her attention, half to steady her. "Where's Lyle?"

"He didn't come back." She looked at the dark cabin. The door was hanging open and the windows were black. Now that the danger was past, she felt empty inside. "I had hoped to find him here."

"We got your message and came here immediately. They'd already cleared out, and in a hurry by the looks of it. Carlo was to meet us here to report in. You must have been the reason he was delayed."

Carlo joined his mistress and was conferring quietly with her. Every once in a while he'd glance back at Jane. His dark eyes were black in the moonlight and there was nothing friendly in his expression.

"Where's the ship?"

"Still down on the Eagle Creek landing pad. We couldn't land anywhere near here. Had to take a light ship up in groups. It should be back any minute now."

The Scrapers approached and Abby released Jane's arms so she could face them. She didn't go far though. Abby and Jake caged her in on either side, Abby to her left, Jake to her right, and Jane had that strange feeling again. A sting to her eyes and heavy ache centered in her chest. But then, she was tired and sick with worry. No wonder she felt ill. It had been a bitch of a day.

Maricel was even more imposing close-up. A pair of servants in the dark green uniforms of the Tirados held lanterns a few steps behind her. She was beautiful with black hair and dark eyes that glittered in the dim light. It wasn't a soft or touchable kind of beauty, hard-edged as the mountains rising behind her. She dismissed Jane with a glance and fixed her attention on Cap, coming straight to the point. "Carlo knows where they've taken your man, but it's not welcome news."

When Jane shivered, Jake placed a hand on her back to steady her. "Just tell us where he is and we'll go fetch him."

The corner of her mouth lifted in a smirk. "Through miles of Reaper-infested territory? Only two of you are immune and even Rangers can be killed."

Cap shifted. "Reaper-infested territory?"

Maricel nodded and gestured for Carlo to speak. "We won't be able to get in easily. There's no place to land. Last I heard the place was still swarming with Reapers. We should go in strength. More ships. More Rangers if possible. And a hell of a lot more ammunition. We'll be fighting Reapers on one side and Corrigan's men on the other."

Jane didn't know what the hell he was talking about, where they had taken Lyle or why. There was only one thing she knew.

"If we wait, Lyle will be dead," she said.

Maricel turned her dark eyes on Jane and her lips thinned as if she was annoyed by the interruption. Of course, a Scraper would see Jane as less even than a servant. *Breeder.* Maricel didn't have to say it, the opinion was plain in her expression.

"We will pass above the site to see if there's another alternative. But this isn't the time or place for this conversation. The riflemen will come to investigate soon and I don't wish to lose any of my men to a scuffle. We'll leave now and discuss the rest aboard ship." Maricel turned to the captain. "If the girl's not a Ranger we should leave her behind. I can have a ship return her to your fort directly."

Cap seemed to consider that. Before she could protest, Jake took her by the arm. "Technically, I'm not a Ranger either. I say Jane comes with us."

Despite the fact that he was no longer a Reaper, people generally didn't argue with Jake. Not if they knew what was good for them. Whatever else she might be, Maricel was no fool—or she simply didn't care whether Jane survived the trip or not. With a stiff nod, she turned away and as if that were a signal, the lightship dropped through the cloud layer. It set down gently beside the house and Maricel walked toward it, lifting her skirts as she passed through the fields. Scrapers. Assuming everyone else would just fall in line and follow.

Jane turned to the captain. "She's on our side, right? You trust her?"

Cap's expression didn't change by so much as a flicker. "I don't know that it applies, Miss Fisher. She has a lot of people who depend on her. I trust that she'll do what's in their best interests. At the moment, that appears to involve helping us find Lyle and the serum."

"She's not interested in Lyle or the serum."

Cap took her arm to lead her toward the waiting ship. "But she is keenly interested in seeing Corrigan fail."

THE TIRADO GUNSHIP was nothing like Flynn's. Jane followed Abby down a short stairwell and into a wood-paneled foyer that would have been at home in any mansion on Eyrion. A marble-topped table held a cut-crystal decanter and gleaming glasses. The settees—three of them—were upholstered in luscious green velvet and there was even a phonograph in the corner. It would have to be a smooth ride indeed for a phonograph to be able to function without skipping. Of course, the size of this airship meant that it would be slow to maneuver and not easily tossed around by the wind.

It was about the same size as the cargo ships that transported cattle and grain to the Scraper-owned butchers and mills in the foothill cities except this ship didn't smell like shit. Its entire purpose was to show off the wealth of its owner. This was likely its first meaningful voyage. Those guns up on the deck had probably never been fired except during the ceremonial parade on Founding Day.

For a rescue mission like this one, Jane would have picked Flynn over Maricel any day. Except Flynn was gone. And even if he'd been standing right in front of her, he'd have laughed in her face if she'd suggested he fly her into Reaper territory.

The shutters were closed up tight, but the room was cast in a warm golden light from the sconces set every few feet along the wall. A servant had offered her a change of clothes but she'd declined. She didn't want to dress in Tirado colors. She had no wish to be beholden to Maricel in any way. Jake filed in behind her and touched her arm when she paused near the center of the room. "You go sit. I could use a drink. Do you want one?"

She nodded gratefully and took a seat on the settee beside Cap. Abby took the chair across from them and Jake joined them a moment later with a stack of priceless crystal in one hand and the decanter in his other. He passed out the glasses and poured. "No point in running back and forth."

The whiskey was smooth, the expensive stuff imported from Europe. Of course it was. Nothing but the best on this ship. Jane settled back and cupped the glass between her hands, lowering it to her lap when she began to shake.

She felt the change in the engines…subtle. They were on the opposite side of the ship from the mechanical equipment here and the walls were well insulated to sound. It was curious, feeling the liftoff without the external stimuli. No view. No wind. Only that distant hum and the sensation of motion. She looked up to find the Cap's eyes steady on her. The concern she saw there tugged at her heart. She'd always liked Cap and he'd been fair to her. But they weren't particularly close. He'd always been Cam's friend, not hers. That's how she'd always seen it anyway, but wondered if maybe she'd been wrong about that too.

"What happened, Jane? Why weren't you with Lyle?"

"That was Lyle's doing," she said, stuffing her annoyance. She should have fought harder to join him. She'd been flattered by his protectiveness and…well, she hadn't wanted to drive him away. *Compromise*, she knew what the word meant. Next time, she wasn't letting him walk into trouble alone, no matter how he felt about it. "He didn't want me slowing him down."

Abby made a sound but Cap just watched her steadily, weighing that. He was a quiet man, smart as a whip. He took time to think things through. "He wanted me to wait for you but there was no point in that, was there? You made it to Ada's just fine. When he didn't come back, I bought a gun and I followed him."

She expected them to tell her how stupid a decision that had been. But Abby lifted her glass in a salute before taking a long pull on her whiskey and even Jake smiled.

Feeling bolder, she straightened in her seat. "The riflemen cut me off on the trail up and took me back for questioning. I managed to escape from Maricel's spy when he came to my cell after nightfall and the rest you know."

"When he came to your cell?" Cap's eyes narrowed.

"That's what I thought too, but looking back I think he might actually have only been after information." She shook her head. "Maybe he was trying to help, I don't know."

"That cut to his head?" Jake asked, touching his temple. "That was you?"

"A bowl of stew." She shared a grin with Abby before turning back to the Captain. "Now it's your turn. Did you get a chance to search the house? Was there any sign of Lyle there? And if it really was an orphanage, what happened to the kids? *Why* are we heading into Reaper territory?"

"It's all about the mines." A voice came from the doorway and she looked up to find Carlo standing there. Clean-shaven and dressed in the dark green livery of the crew, Carlo didn't look anything like the rifleman who'd shoved her into the cell earlier that day. Only the bandage on his forehead marked him as the same man. "Everything with Oro is about the mines."

He went to the sideboard and, finding the decanter missing, pulled a bottle from the cabinet beneath. He was silent as he poured a dram into a crystal glass. When he joined them, he didn't take a seat. He rested a narrow hand on the back of Abby's chair.

Ignoring Jake's dark look, Carlo took a drink and continued. "The building was an orphanage, that much is true. We discovered it last year. Corrigan's been collecting star-marked children and caring for them. They weren't in any real danger or we would have alerted you."

"You should have alerted us anyway," Cap growled. "There are no star-marked orphans. Every Reaper-immune child belongs to the fort. I've never heard of a child who didn't have kin willing to raise them for the child price."

Carlo shrugged, his expression cool. "The riflemen said the children were found in homesteads attacked in the raids after Fort Hill fell."

"The riflemen who belong to Corrigan?"

Rather than answer, Carlo lifted his glass and took another long swallow. He winced and then said, "It took about a year for us to figure out why he wanted them. At first, we thought he'd figured out a way to milk the forts for the child price but he never collected."

Why would a man like Corrigan need that money? The child price was a fortune to someone like her but to Corrigan it would be a drop in the bucket. Carlo's eyes shifted to hers and it was as if he read her mind. He shrugged. "You'd be surprised at how many pies he has a finger in. He's creative in his enterprises if nothing else. And he likes a long shot. A gambler at heart. His family wealth might have come from the mines but he has more in common with the scum on Stormking."

There was a sneer in his voice but when no one seemed sympathetic to his disdain, his features smoothed. "Turned out he wanted the children for the same reason he stole your serum. And apparently when Ada reported a Ranger on her doorstep, Corrigan decided to relocate the children permanently."

Cap set his glass down on the marble table with a gentle click. He clasped his hands between his knees and leaned forward. "And why exactly does Corrigan want the serum? The star-marked children?"

"He's reopened Calder's Tomb."

That name didn't mean a thing to her but by the change that came over Jake and Abby, it was familiar to both of them. And Cap… He looked outwardly calm, but Jane was sitting right next to him and could feel the coiled tension in his big body. It took effort not to lean away from him.

Abby cleared her throat. "I thought it was just a story. You never know with Doc, which ones are true and which not."

Carlo shook his head. "It's not a story."

"What?" Jane demanded when no one spoke right away. "What is Calder's Tomb?"

"Seventy years ago the border was nearly a hundred miles farther south than it is now," Cap said quietly. "The Calder Mine was barely north of the line even then. A silver mine, a productive one. Calder owned the stake and he oversaw the operation from on-site which was unusual for a Scraper. That reassured the men working there that it was safe…even after the forts issued a warning for them to clear out." He shook his head and took up his drink again. "It was a long summer. More Rangers were lost during that summer than in any other on record. Calder didn't evacuate in time and the mine was overrun. Two hundred men were trapped. The next winter when the Reapers retreated south, they went in looking for survivors. There was nothing left but broken equipment. Not even any bones left to bury. That's when they started calling it Calder's Tomb. It's a cursed place."

Carlo smirked. "It's a valuable place. They'd hit a new vein the month before the mine fell. That's why the old fool refused to evacuate."

"Calder's Tomb is still twenty miles into Reaper territory. It won't be safe to go that far south for another two months. Even in February it's a risk. In a mild winter, Reapers can survive there in the caves…and mines. They're taking a hell of a risk, no matter how well they lock themselves in."

Carlo nodded in agreement. "Corrigan owns the stake now. The mine belonged to his maternal great-grandfather, Benedict Calder. He has the airships to get in and out and a smaller mine worked by convicts with an unusually high mortality rate. He's been sending the strongest miners south to work the Tomb. He has a few Ranger deserters he's paying a fortune to protect his investment. The star-marked children at his orphanage were meant to replace them. The mine has been profitable for him and he's looking to expand."

"He intended to raise the children into guards," Jane finished for him softly. "But with the serum, he won't need them anymore, will he?"

Carlo looked annoyed by the interruption but he did have fine manners. His brows rose in polite query.

Jane had to fight the urge to slap the smirk off his face. "Will Corrigan take the children back to the mine or just get rid of the evidence?"

"Both," Abby said, her skin pale but her eyes glittering with anger. "The star-marked children were always meant to go to the mine as guards. He's just sending them in early. Bringing them there now takes care of his problem either way."

And Lyle. He wasn't anything more than a complication. When Corrigan realized how troublesome the fool man could be, there'd be no reason for him to keep Lyle alive at all.

A LOW CLOUD LAYER hugged the mountain, dirty and gray. The weak morning sun was at their backs as they made their approach, the hull slicing through the clouds and sending swirls of mist spiraling down the length of the ship. Jane wrapped her arms around her torso to stave off a shiver. Her coat was back at the prison with Marshal Lassiter. She hadn't taken the time to grab it during her escape and regretted it now. She could have stayed below where the others were ironing out the details of their plan but as soon as the first rays of the sun had slivered through the window, she'd left the stuffy room. She found the steep metal stairwell and then headed up to the deck to find a quiet spot near the bow. It had been a very long time since she'd been aboard a ship of this size. Not since she'd traveled with her father and mother on a special excursion to see the basilica on Tabor shortly before her mother died. Nearly twelve years ago now.

As always, she was struck by the sensation of life—the warmth in the wood and the sweet curve of the metallic balloon above, the power of the engine thumping away like a heartbeat at the center of the ship. She could barely hear it from here but she could feel it, vibrating through the soles of her feet. She could feel the small jolt too as they hit the cloud bank and then slowed. She gripped the rail and leaned slightly forward. The clouds thinned and then disappeared completely as they descended.

Still several hundred feet about the ground, the Reapers who scurried from their shadow seemed as insignificant as ants. Her fingertips tightened on the rail. There *were* a great many of them. Far more than she'd ever seen gathered in one place. Some of them loped on hands and feet like animals over the broken terrain but most ran upright. Some were clothed but most were not. They were deeper in Reaper territory now. She supposed it made sense that these were older than the newly turned ones that lingered on the plains.

When she looked farther out she could see where the land began to rise into the mountains. The rock formed a great wall. No trees. Carlo had said they'd cleared the area of wood around the mines to fuel the steam engines of the machinery they used and were now flying in coal. That's what had originally alerted the Tirado spies that Corrigan was up to something. Their coal usage had increased so dramatically the Tirados were compelled to investigate.

The natural wall had been reinforced by a man-made structure of wood and brick that sealed up the gaps in the natural stone. There would be watchmen on that wall who would have already spotted their ship. Beyond that patchwork bluff was Calder's Mine, a high narrow slit in the side of the mountain. Silver. Strange that something so beautiful should come from someplace so ugly.

"They'll know we're coming."

She startled, inhaling sharply as she turned her head to find Carlo just a few feet behind her. She was half surprised he hadn't taken the opportunity to shove her over the railing.

She shrugged. "No way for us to see them without them seeing us too."

He took a step forward. "May I join you?"

"Can I stop you?"

He ignored the snub and leaned against the rail beside her, silent for a time. He was good at silence, she'd noticed that. His body was as still as a statue. It made her want to hold up a mirror to his nose just to see if he was breathing. His attention was fixed below at the ground rushing beneath them and that great wall looming larger with every second. He cursed under his breath and shook his head. "We haven't been able to find a place to land."

If there was a landing pad, it was behind the wall and likely too small to accommodate a ship of this size. Setting down this side of the wall would only get them swarmed by Reapers. "There has to be a way in."

"You sound like Maricel. She's determined to retrieve your serum and as many of Corrigan's men as she can take alive. She doesn't take 'no' for an answer either."

"It's your job to land the ship?"

"It's my job to see that she gets what she wants."

Rather than answer, Jane turned back to scouring the ground, looking for a good place to land. Reapers scurried for cover as they passed. "Jake says Reapers have the capacity to learn. That sentience doesn't come on them all at once, it's a gradual awakening. I always thought they were senseless but they know well enough to be afraid of the ship. Someone's been firing at them."

"I'm sure they have. Corrigan's ships are smaller. Behind that wall is a courtyard big enough to hold a cutter."

"We could rope in."

He shook his head. "I could rope in. Maybe a handful of others could manage it but I have no interest in storming this particular castle alone."

"How many men do you think Corrigan has down there?" She looked directly at him for the first time. Dark eyes stared back at her, calm and unflinching. "How many who are willing to die for him? I bet they have their hands full keeping the miners in line. I'm in. Abby, Jake and the captain said they'll go too."

"You'll be more of a burden than a help." The amusement in his tone was irksome.

"I can shoot." Thanks to Lyle. He'd taught her to defend herself.

Carlo placed his hand on her back and she stiffened. When she turned her head to glare at him, his hand fell away. "Your Ranger might already be dead. Take that into consideration as you decide how much you're willing to risk."

She knew how much she was willing to risk to get Lyle back. Everything. The thought of going back to the fort without him…well, she just wasn't going to do that.

"Were you there?"

He frowned. "I don't follow."

"When they took him, were you there? Did you help them do it?"

"He was still alive when we put him on the ship. He had a knot on his head no worse than the one you gave me."

But he would have known then that he was sending Lyle to die. An innocent man. A good man. She shook her head. "I don't know why you're even talking to me then. We are not going to be friends."

He set his forearms to the railing and leaned forward. "Friends." His mouth pulled tight and then he shook his head. "No. We're not. You blew my cover. I'd been working on it for two years. Do you know what that's like?"

Did she know what it was like to pretend to be someone she wasn't, to live a lie? Why, yes, actually she did but she had no interest in a heart-to-heart with Carlo.

It was his choice to take on that job. He'd had other choices. "I won't apologize for escaping."

"That's not—" He muttered something under his breath. "We're working together now. I want to know you won't try to bash me over the head again when I'm not looking."

"You were looking the first time." She smiled sweetly at him but he didn't smile back.

"I told Maricel I'd go in," Carlo said. "The captain doesn't want you along but, as I understand it, he has no true authority over you."

"He doesn't." She'd leave her job at the fort if she needed to.

"None of the crew is willing to take the risk and I won't force them. It's my call. I ask again—are you capable of working with me?"

Her smile faded and she studied his composed features for a long time before turning back to watching the ground slide beneath them. She nodded. "Just stay out of my way."

TWENTY-THREE

HELL TURNED OUT to be cold, dark and almost eerily silent once the ship was secured and the engines cut off. Two men dragged Lyle from the hold. Once outside, they unceremoniously threw him to the ground. His hands were still bound behind his back so there was nothing to break his fall. His cheek scraped against the grit and rock. He could feel the warmth of blood trickle down his cheek toward his ear when he turned his head.

One of the men nudged him in the side with his boot. "Stay down until we tell you to get up."

"He's not a deserter," Lyle heard someone say behind him.

"A Ranger," the guard spat. "What the hell does he want us to do with a Ranger?"

"I expect he'll tell us when he gets here. Corrigan sent word he's coming down to take care of the problem himself."

The other laughed. "When's the last time you saw a Scraper take care of any problem by himself?"

Lyle turned his head to see the pilot. Rough around the edges with a bulbous veiny nose. He was half relieved it wasn't Flynn. Only half because while he would have been pissed at Flynn's betrayal, he also would have had some hope that Flynn might feel bad enough about it to let someone know where they were being held.

The guards were a bit gentler with the kids as they led them off the ship. Someone grabbed his biceps and hauled him to his feet. It was night and he couldn't see much of his surroundings. He had the impression of being inside a large bowl formed of black rock, with walls looming on every side, before they were ushered quickly inside the mine. The opening nothing but a tall narrow slit in the face of the mountain.

Once inside, the guards didn't pause to let them catch their breath. Not that he'd want to breathe too deeply. It smelled like the inside of a cattle ship. Like animals packed together in too close quarters. As they walked down the main tunnel, he could hear the workers too. There were man-made doors branching off the main shaft to either side. From the sound of it, they were little more than cells though he didn't see evidence of doors. Possibly Corrigan kept his miners chained to their beds. Possibly they were docile enough because there simply wasn't anyplace for them to run to even if they did escape. Lyle made note of the mystery and as they passed deeper into the mountain, they turned from the main shaft. The tunnels became narrower the farther they went. And darker.

In the main tunnel, there were carbide lanterns hanging from hooks on the wall every fifty feet or so. Down here, the only light came from the lantern carried by one of the guards. Lyle tripped and stumbled hard into the wall. The guard roughly righted him only to push him forward, nearly sending him careening into another wall. Behind him, Ada whimpered. He didn't know what had caused the sound, but to draw the attention of the guards, he stopped walking.

"What do you plan to do with us?"

The guard pushed his shoulder. “Shut up and keep walking.”

“They’ll come for me.”

“Do you truly believe that? I don’t.”

“They will. I might be able to manage a pardon for you.” He looked at the man, who was about his own age. He looked as if he’d led a harder life than Lyle had, which was a trick. “If you were once a Ranger, then you know how it works.”

The man’s lip curled, but he didn’t respond to that which only confirmed Lyle’s suspicion that he was a deserter. It didn’t happen often. The Ranger life appealed to most young men who were called to it and they were all raised to believe it was their noble duty to go out and defend the border. They were compensated decently enough too. But the older you got, the more friends you saw die, the more Reapers you killed, it started to wear on you after a while.

Apparently, Corrigan had managed to track down a few of those deserters to serve as guards in his mine. Not a bad idea, really. The kids were likely meant to replace them when they came of age. Lyle wasn’t going to let that happen. He just had to figure out a way out of this mess.

After another ten minutes or so, the guards stopped before a door. It was one of the first actual doors Lyle had seen since they entered the mine. The rock was braced by wood timbers that had been used as the frame. The door was heavy and there was a length of wood that could be used to bar the door from the outside.

One of the guards removed the bar, and Lyle said,

"My hands have gone numb. You're going to cut the rope, right? I don't want to lose my hands."

"That's the least of your worries." The guard shoved him inside. He stumbled, grunted as he landed again on the ground, this time taking the brunt of his weight on his shoulder. The kids were ushered in behind him.

"Wait," Ada cried out, as the light withdrew. The guard paused. "They're children and they're frightened. At least leave us a light."

Lyle rolled and managed to work himself to a seated position. Ada carried James, still drowsy and half-asleep. Brandon had a hand on each of the other boys' shoulders. The guard glanced to the door and through it Lyle heard the sound of a flint strike. The guard set his lantern down on the rock and then withdrew.

"We'll bring you something to eat in the morning."

Ada turned, startled. "You're leaving us here with him?"

The guard glanced at Lyle and shrugged. "He can't cause trouble like that and there's nowhere else to hold him. Try and get some sleep. You'll be fine."

Ada watched as the door swung closed and then slowly turned around. She looked at the children and nodded firmly. "We'll be fine. Come on boys, you heard the man. Let's try and get some sleep."

Creed spoke, a tremble in his voice. "Why'd you bring us here, Ada? I don't like this place."

Ada's gaze flashed to his, accusing, before returning to Creed. "Believe me. It wasn't my idea, but we'll make the best of the situation. Let's think of it as an adventure."

"An adventure?"

Ada sat down with her back against the wall, drawing James onto her lap and pressing his head against her shoulder. She started talking to the other kids about mines and airships and eventually they settled down a bit. Lyle tipped his head back against the wall and tried to find a comfortable position to ease the tension in his shoulders. It was difficult to think of a way out of this mess when he couldn't even feel his hands.

Brandon came to sit next to him. He was a good kid, intelligent and even-tempered, always looking out for the younger ones.

"What's really going on, Lieutenant?"

"You don't happen to have a knife tucked away anywhere, do you?"

Brandon shook his head. His skin was pale and his eyes wide but his voice remained steady enough. "We weren't being raised for the forts, were we?"

"I don't believe so, no."

"Then she—" Brandon lifted his chin to indicate Ada. "She's in on it, isn't she?"

Ada, seeming to realize she was being talked about, looked up in annoyance, before answering a question Creed had asked her. She was trying to get them back to sleep though Lyle didn't see much a chance of that considering how wound up they were. He sure as hell couldn't sleep just now, tired as he was.

"I think Ada cares for you," Lyle said slowly. "But the man she's working for, a Scraper named Corrigan, owns the mines and needs star-marked guards to protect it. My guess is he's raising you to work for him."

"I'm not working for him."

Brandon might not have much of a say in the matter, not unless the border moved far enough south where he might stand a chance at escape. That could take most of his lifetime.

Brandon leaned back against the wall. "We're in Reaper territory, aren't we?"

"Yeah."

"How are we going to get out of here?"

His voice cracked at the end. For all his bravery in the face of being shoved onto an airship and taken away from home to this dark cold place, Brandon was still just a kid.

Lyle sighed. "It's the truth that the Rangers will come for me. I had a partner awaiting my return in Eagle Creek. She'll get word to my captain and he'll find a way to get down here."

"Rangers don't fly airships."

Lyle turned his head to look Brandon in the eye. He'd seen the same expression on the faces of raw recruits countless times before and he responded as he would to any young man facing his first mission. "Rangers do whatever the hell needs doing. They'll get here. We just need to hold out until then."

And pray. Prayer never hurt either. Maybe that was the reason he was still alive when so many of the people he'd trained with had died. He wasn't ready to die yet. He wasn't ready to give up his life, or Janie, or any of the kids here.

Ada rose and joined them, settling cross-legged on the ground in front of Lyle. Lyle studied the little boy in her arms. James. Blond hair and fair skin. His eyes were closed now but Lyle remembered the color of them exactly. He'd spent a lot of time looking into eyes exactly that shade of blue. He was trying very badly not to get his hopes up about James but if what he suspected was true... There was that ache in his chest again. *If* this beautiful little boy was really Samuel, he wanted to be with Janie when she set eyes on the chubby little toddler. To comfort her if he was wrong and share in her joy if he was right. It hurt how much he wanted it to be true. It hurt knowing he might not ever see Janie again.

"Did Corrigan send you James?"

Ada's lips pressed together and for a moment Lyle didn't think she'd answer him but then she nodded. "Holson flew him in last year." She paused. "A little longer ago than that maybe. It was midwinter and I gave him hell for risking the boy that time of year. He was very sick and for a time I didn't think he'd make it."

"He had a fever," Lyle said.

Ada nodded. "A lung infection. He had trouble breathing. The man who brought him to me had given him a curative to keep him from coughing. I think it was the snake oil that nearly killed him. It stopped the cough but sent him into such a deep sleep I thought he'd never wake from it. His lips had turned blue."

"Ada." He looked at the frowning young woman. "How could you not have questioned what was going on with these kids? Did you just not want to know?"

"I was hired to take care of orphans."

"They're not all orphans. I'm pretty sure I know who James's parents are and they're both still alive."

What remaining color Ada had in her cheeks drained away. Oddly, it made Lyle feel just a little bit better knowing Ada didn't know that part.

"You *think* you know who his parents are," she said finally. "He was a baby when he came to me, looked nothing like the boy he is now. You might see a similarity but that doesn't mean anything."

No, he couldn't be sure about it. Not yet. Maybe he'd never be completely sure of it. "If something happens to me, you need to bring this boy to Jane Fisher and tell her my suspicion. Let her decide the truth of it for herself. I'd say you owe her at least that much."

"Jane..." Ada made a small sound of protest. "Red hair? She used to live in Columbus Junction."

Lyle nodded.

"I didn't know the baby was hers," Ada whispered, looking down into James's face. "I thought she ran away from Gideon."

"She tried to." Lyle lifted his chin toward the sleeping child. "This is how Gideon punished her. You should know that Gideon's dead now. If you were hoping for rescue from that quarter, it's not coming."

She swallowed and Lyle was surprised to see her eyes well with tears. She nodded. "I wouldn't have expected rescue from Gideon."

Ada had to know she didn't have a much better chance of making it out alive than he did. Whatever Corrigan had been paying her to care for the boys, she'd surely never counted on ending up in Reaper territory, surrounded by a bunch of miners whose only choice had been this work or the noose.

Beside him, Brandon stirred. "I'll tell them even if she doesn't...or can't. One of us has to make it out this and they won't hurt a baby."

Ada's mouth twisted a bit, echoing Lyle's thoughts. Corrigan would likely sacrifice his own child for the profit this mine could turn for him. Shaking her head, Ada passed the sleeping James to Brandon and then turned to Lyle.

"I need you to turn around."

Lyle eyed her suspiciously. "Why?"

"Just do it."

When he didn't budge, Ada rolled her eyes and then reached beneath her skirts to pull out a long thin blade. Gesturing with it, she said, "Don't worry. I'm not going to stick you."

"I'm not sure I believe you."

But with his hands bound, he didn't have much of a chance against anyone armed, even Ada, so he did as she asked. He couldn't suppress the groan that ripped from his mouth at the dart of pain shooting from his shoulder to his neck but he managed to turn enough for Ada to slice through the rope. It took her a minute. Her blade was made for sliding in between a man's ribs not for sawing through strong rope but she got the job done. Blood rushed into Lyle's hands when he finally moved his arms and the pain was so sharp and bright that his vision went black at the edges for several seconds. When the sensation finally passed, he gave Ada a wry look.

"You don't happen to have any other weapons stashed up there, do you?"

She pressed the handle of the blade into his hands. "Find a way to get us out of here, Ranger."

TWENTY-FOUR

MANY TIMES DURING the course of her life Jane had found herself asking how she'd come to that particular point. When she'd first left her home on Eyrion, worried that at any moment Anson Stark was going to order her into his bed. When she was chained by the ankle to the pipe in the corner of Gideon's room. When she'd ridden with Cam to the tiny fort on the very edge of the border. But she'd never felt more out of place than she did right now.

Jake tugged at the rope around her waist to test the knot. "You have the knife I gave you?"

She'd attached the sheath to the gun belt Carlo provided with the rest of her gear. She wrapped her hand around the hilt and Jake nodded. He clearly wasn't happy she was coming along either. She didn't deny it was a dangerous thing for her to do. But it was dangerous for all of them and they needed every gun they could get.

"Keep it in reach. You may have to cut yourself loose." He studied her face. "You're sure about this?"

Not really, no. But she couldn't tell him that. What she wanted to do and what she had to do were two completely different things. They usually were. "I'm going."

He looked as if he wanted to say more but stepped back as Abby moved to join them. She handed Jane a pair of leather gloves that were dyed a deep dark green. So finely made that there was only one person aboard ship they could have come from. When Jane looked at her questioningly, Abby shrugged. "Don't worry. They were offered. I didn't steal them."

"They're worth more than I make in a year," Jane said.

"You need them to protect your hands from the rope. Don't even think of pocketing them for later."

It was tempting. Jane smoothed her thumb over the buttery leather, barely able to resist the urge to rub her cheek against it. She could build an entire outfit around the gloves. It was a sin to destroy something so lovely.

Abby shook her head. "It'll be easier to pull the trigger if you still have skin on your hands."

There was that. She pulled on the gloves. Behind Abby, the captain holstered a third gun. He smiled grimly when he caught her eye. "Five minutes."

Everything was in place. The railing was shorter on this stretch of deck and there was an iron contraption of wheels and gears mounted directly to the ship that would lower them into the mining compound. Men with rifles lined the deck to either side, ready to provide cover fire but they were depending upon the thick morning fog to do most of the work of shielding them from view. The engines had been silenced a few miles back and they were using a sophisticated system of rudders and sailcloth wings to control their glide in. With luck, the watchers on the wall wouldn't see them coming at all until it was too late.

The silence that fell over the ship as they approached the mountain was so complete she could hear her own heartbeat. Her hands began to sweat inside the leather gloves and she closed her eyes a moment to send up a prayer to a God who'd never bothered to listen to her before. Maybe he'd intervene for Lyle's sake, a good man who deserved to live. That didn't make a difference, she knew. But it should.

Jake rested his foot on the rail and leaned out, testing the give in the rope. Abby touched the gun at her hip but Jane couldn't do anything but stare at the approaching mountain. The fog meant she couldn't see more than the hazy black shape of the rock, growing larger by the second. A gust of window sheered down the mountain face and caused the ship to tremble.

She felt more than heard the vibration of a gear turning below her feet. Then the flap of a sail quickly silenced as it caught wind. The pull of the wind turned them slightly, placing them on course once again. The ship was remarkably responsive for its size. Even on the smaller vessels a controlled glide was difficult to maintain with any accuracy. You had to know your ship. You had to be able to navigate wind currents like an eagle. The crew needed to work together in perfect coordination. Silent, perfect coordination. Her respect for Maricel's people nudged up the tiniest bit.

An unnaturally straight line appeared ahead and below them and Jake touched her arm. The wall. Her throat felt so tight she could hardly breathe. For a second she considered backing out. She wasn't trained to fight like the others. Lyle would *not* want her to do this. He'd never in a million years ask such a thing of her. But she knew if their positions were reversed, he'd be the first one to come running. And she wanted him back. Even if she couldn't keep him forever, she wanted him back.

One of the crewmen assisted her over the side and after a short, wrenching drop she was hanging suspended above the sharp, rocky ground. It was difficult to see and that was likely a blessing. They weren't above the compound yet. The plan was to lower them just inside the gates. There were only six star-marked guards in Corrigan's employ and the snipers aboard ship would be responsible for taking them out.

The miners were generally locked in cells and chained for work so that the outnumbered guards could control them. They weren't expected to be an issue, assuming Carlo's information was sound. Maricel Tirado had produced an old map of the mine so they knew where the offices and storage rooms were located.

What they didn't know was how many human guards Corrigan had been able to talk into joining him now that he had the serum. They didn't know where he'd keep Lyle. There was no way to retreat if things went bad.

Jane clung to the rope with one hand, and the knife with her other as she was slowly lowered above open ground. There were Reapers down there. A lot of them. She'd seen them when they'd passed overhead yesterday. And while they were hidden now, she still knew they were there. The Reapers would be aware of the attack before the human watchers. She'd heard they could smell human blood miles off. That they could track you down by the sound of your beating heart. Her hand clenched on the rope when it jerked and she had to force herself to ease her grip lest they cramp. The Reapers were less of a threat to her than Corrigan's men, so long as she made it over the gate.

A stiff breeze caught hold of her and sent her swaying. The rope creaked against the wood above and for a brief moment, she thought she might careen right into Abby who was directly to her left. Before she made contact, she swung back the other way, spinning so that she faced away from the mountain. That wind… The fog seemed less dense already. The sky was beginning to lighten as the sun rose. Soon they'd be visible. So much of this plan depended on timing and luck but it was their only option, except to wait for reinforcements and if they did that then Lyle would surely die.

Slowly, she spun back toward the gate. Its black shape grew more distinct as she came closer. Less than a hundred feet now. The nearer she came, the faster it seemed to approach. Almost there.

She fisted her hand around the hilt of her knife. Cap had told her not to draw it until her feet hit the ground. It would be too easy to cut herself in a fall. But she wanted to be ready. The gate passed silently below her feet and she held her breath as the crewmen above let out the rope quickly now, lowering them down with a speed that made her stomach bottom out. So fast that she only received hazy impressions of the compound around her. The sheer rock face ahead. A wooden tower. Mound of black rock and what looked to be some sort of machinery big as a shed, coming up fast. She wouldn't touch ground before she hit it.

The machine looked new—huge, gunmetal-gray and silent as a sleeping dragon. All cogs and wheels and smokestacks. That was going to hurt like hell, if she survived the initial impact. Judging the distance to the machine and the ground, she drew her knife. Sending up another silent prayer, she cut line just as the first shot was fired.

The sound of it reverberated through the canyon, bouncing off the rock face and the wooden walls. Stopping her heart entirely for a long beat. Her feet hit the ground hard, stinging her ankles and making her legs collapse under her. She dropped the knife when she hit and rolled to absorb some of the force of the landing. It stole her breath and she came up to her hands and knees still trying to suck in air.

Before she'd quite managed to catch her breath again, a hard hand grabbed her arm and yanked her up. Carlo.

"This way," he said and dragged her back, out of the open courtyard and toward the gate. Multiple booms filled the compound as they ran, seeming to shake the mountain. A brief silence fell as they reached cover and the men above reloaded.

"So much for the element of surprise," she said, pulling her gun from its holster.

Carlo didn't answer. He'd placed his hand on the gate. Before she could ask what he was doing, she felt the jolt through the thick slab of wood against her back. Their eyes met.

"Reapers," he whispered.

The howling that arose from the other side of the gate lifted every hair on her neck. She pushed away from the wall and stared at it. It had seemed so imposing from the air, now...not so much. At least the gunfire was no longer directed wholly at them. Corrigan's men had to shoot over the wall in order to keep the Reapers from swarming the gate. They had to worry about getting picked off by the snipers aboard ship too.

Her mouth dried. "We have to get inside."

Carlo set off at a jog toward the slit in the mountain that was the mine. The workers lived inside the mines in case the wall ever fell. They slept there, worked there, died there. That's where Lyle would be now. *Somewhere* inside.

She followed Carlo, staying close to the wall. In the

open space between wall and mountain, the air was hazy with fog and gun smoke. It was still that gray time before sunrise and the darkness provided some cover, as well. To their right, wood turned to mortared stone and then solid bedrock.

After less than fifty feet, Carlo stopped running abruptly, holding his arm out to catch her. She still nearly ran into the shape ahead of her. It was Abby, Jake a half step behind her. The captain was there too. He turned when they paused to guard their back.

Abby shook her head. "We can't get in, not that way. Too many."

Carlo frowned. "Our information said there were only a half dozen star-marked guards. By the sound of it, most are on the wall now."

"They've armed the miners," Abby said. "I don't know what they promised them in return for fighting but there are at least thirty and they know those tunnels. We don't have enough ammunition to fight through them all."

Carlo swore. "The ship will be back for the second pass any minute now. We can grab rope and let them haul us out."

Jane didn't get a chance to mull that over. Apparently the decision wasn't up for a vote. While she was still staring at the mine, Carlo took her by the arm again and started to run in the opposite direction. She tried to pull free but his grip only tightened. When she dug in her heels, he lifted her off her feet and jerked her close. "You don't have a chance in there alone," he growled into her face. "Those miners won't be any kinder to you than the Reapers."

She shoved him back. "What do you care?"

He gave her a hard look. "You're a member of my crew."

She wasn't arguing with the bullshit of that right now. They were running out of time. Abby nudged her in the back and she started forward again. The sky had cleared enough for them to see the bulk of the ship glide overhead again. This time the engines were humming and the men on deck were shooting back at the watchers on the wall. She did not relish the thought of hanging by rope in the middle of a gun battle. The engines on the *Goliath* had powerful lift. It would take them only seconds to fly out of range at full power but it only took a half second to get shot too. The ropes were dangling loose near the center of the courtyard, the ship hovering almost perfectly still overhead save for a slight drift toward the wall. She ran for the nearest rope.

They'd let out more rope than necessary or had flown in slightly lower than planned. There was a good deal of play in the rope and its end trailed behind her in the dirt as she turned around. Carlo had grabbed hold of another and was busy fastening it about his waist. When Jane pulled her rope toward the gate, Abby looked up with a confused expression on her face. Jane ignored it when Abby called her name. No time to argue about this.

Dropping to her knees, she quickly tied the rope around a wooden beam that was set to brace a weak spot in the wall to the left of the gate. Her fingers worked the rope, remembering the familiar pattern. A constrictor hitch. She'd learned that one from her father though she doubted it had ever occurred to Jeremiah Fisher that his daughter would have cause to use that knowledge in such a situation.

Abby came up behind her as Jane stood, wiping the

dirt from her hands on her breeches. Abby's scowl was fierce and she still held on to the end of her rope with one hand.

"What the hell are you doing?"

Jane pulled her gun from the holster. "Do you want me to tie it around your waist? I can do it so it won't slip. You don't have much time. They said ninety seconds and Maricel runs a tight ship."

Abby looked at the knot and then the gate. She cursed. "You'll kill every man in there, including Lyle."

Maybe. She'd gotten a good look at the mine entrance through Caleb's spyglass yesterday. The opening to the mine was rigged to collapse and if they'd done that as a last resort, she'd bet there was another way out. "Twenty-four hours and watch for a signal. Convince them to wait that long."

Abby looked set to argue but a shout from Carlo told them they were out of time. The sound of the engine changed, becoming deeper and louder and the rope in Abby's hand tightened. With a curse, she dropped it and turned to look at Jake. He looked fit to kill something.

The wooden brace that supported most of the weight of the gate groaned ominously and Jane turned her back on it and began to run toward the mountain. She heard the pound of Abby's footsteps behind her but didn't spare the time to look back. She'd made her decision, Abby could make her own.

Leaping over a scrap of metal, she ran full-out. If the rope held and the ship held, Reapers would be flooding the yard within moments. She'd seen how fast they could move. The opening to the mineshaft was still a hundred yards away. Big men, chosen for their size and strength and armed with the pickaxes and hammers and shovels of their trade stood before it. No guns that she could see, which was a mercy. Even if they'd had guns to spare, Corrigan's men wouldn't trust their captives with weapons that could be used against them.

The engines dug deep and the heavy whump of the propellers beat in time with her heart. The ship rose. The rope held and the great log wrenched free. There was a tremendous crash and when she risked a glance back she saw a huge chunk of the wall tumble to the ground. Reapers were already pushing through the gap. The sound of gunfire, from the ship and from the wall, was like a mighty wave of thunder. The log swung wildly below the listing ship, crashing into things and causing more damage to the wall. Two Reapers clung to the wood and more lifted their arms to grab for it. They'd pull the ship down if they could, but she couldn't worry about that now. The crew was sound. They'd be able to cut the rope long before it came to that.

Already the miners had broken to flee back into the mountain, screaming about Reapers. She had to make it to the mine before they blocked the entrance. Forty feet out she was hit hard from behind. She grunted as she hit the ground, a solid weight landing on her back and driving her into the dirt. The ground itself seemed to shake and gunfire sounded from almost directly behind her. She struggled until she recognized the voice shouting in her ear. Jake.

"They cut the rope," he said as he hauled her up. The wooden beam hanging from the ship lay not a dozen feet ahead of her, directly in her path. She'd have been crushed beneath its weight if she'd kept running. There was a dead Reaper a hand's breadth away to her right and Abby was firing at another that was headed their way. A clean shot between the eyes. Jane swallowed hard and turned away from the sight of it.

The only Reapers she'd seen up close were the ones the Rangers dragged back to the fort to be injected with Welks's serum. Those were terrifying enough, snarling through the bars of their cages. A whole 'nother level of terrifying when they were loose, hungry and coming for your blood.

"You should be aboard ship."

Jake scowled. "And leave you here?" Not *her*, Jake likely would have left her behind but not Abby.

She couldn't take offense to that. If it had been anyone down here but Lyle she wouldn't be here either. Abby ran ahead of Jake, at first moving cautiously with her gun raised but as the Reapers gained ground behind her and it became apparent that none of the miners had stood their ground, she simply ran full-out. Jane did her best to keep up, but both Jake and Abby had longer legs than she did and were clearly more accustomed to sprinting over broken ground. Her bones ached from the falls she'd taken that day. Her ankle complained with every step. Her breath came in sharp short pants but she kept pushing forward. There wasn't a choice.

She didn't need to look behind her to know how close the Reapers were. They weren't quiet as they chased down their prey. The gunfire had slowed. The pauses between those great teeth-rattling booms grew longer until they stopped coming altogether. Those men on the wall—the ones Cap called deserters—were all dead. Because of her.

Gritting her teeth, she ran harder, pushing through the pain and then crying out when she heard a deep rumble coming from the direction of the mountain.

They'd released the great boulders suspended above the main entrance by an iron net. The right side sagged before the left and a rock the size of a horse fell directly in their path, nearly crushing Abby as it bounced and rolled to the right. Almost there. Not more than a dozen feet and they'd be within the shadow of the tunnel. An egg-sized stone pelted her hard in the shoulder. It threw her off balance for a moment but she caught herself before she fell and lunged back to her feet.

Jake hooked an arm around her waist right before she reached the tunnel, pulling her back as another large boulder dropped in front of them. They dodged to the left and it was only pure dumb luck that sent the rock right.

And then they were inside.

Abby stood several feet ahead, both guns drawn and pointing into the darkness. Jane pressed her hand to damp rock and struggled to draw air into her abused lungs. Jake shoved both of them farther into the cave as rock continued to fall behind them.

"It won't be long before the rest of it falls."

Until then, they had the Reapers to worry about. Because the only thing worse than being trapped inside a mine was being trapped inside a mine with a bunch of Reapers. Jake took out the front-runner and a falling boulder crushed the legs of another. There weren't many of them, not yet. But she'd seen dozens outside the walls yesterday.

"The miners have cleared out," Abby called over her shoulder. "I say we do the same." She gestured toward the branching tunnels. The branch to the right was barely a crack in the wall but there was a faint glow coming from that direction. The other way was black as pitch. Right lead to the sleeping quarters for the miners and beyond that to the storage rooms.

"We can't run headlong after the miners," she said. She didn't want a fight. She only wanted to find Lyle and then get the hell out.

Abby turned to face her. A streak of dirt on her cheekbone. Guns still pointed toward the tunnels. "They don't know we made it in. They'll run."

A Reaper approached the entrance. Jane cringed back against the wall. The thing was crouched down on all fours, sniffing the air. Rock covered the lower half of the mine four feet deep and the Reaper eyed it warily but he still moved cautiously forward. Following his nose. Their scent. The blood rushed from her head and Jane suddenly felt light-headed. Naked and filthy and moving in jerky motions that weren't human. Jake had been like this? She could barely credit it.

Jake took aim but the Reaper must have seen the movement because it snarled and darted to the left even as Jake pulled the trigger. He fired again as the Reaper leaped forward, its fingers grasping the top of the rock. The bullet struck true, dead between the eyes. Momentum brought the creature half over the wall of rock before it fell in a sprawl.

The netting holding back the avalanche finally broke then, releasing several tons of debris to fall in a mighty rush to cover the entrance to the mine. The noise was deafening. The darkness sudden and complete. She stumbled back as far as she was able, falling into Abby and then Jake. They half tripped, half pulled each other into the farthest recess of the cave, instinctively moving toward the faint glow that marked the right-hand branch.

In the darkness, Jane imagined she could feel the

weight of the mountain pressing down on her—heavy and apt to fall down upon them at any moment. The air was so thick with dust she choked on it. She reached out and found Abby's hand which wrapped around hers in a tight squeeze.

"Was this the limit of your plan, Jane?" Jake asked, his voice cool as ever but with a sharp edge to it that brought a rush of blood to her face.

"I'm hoping there's another way out."

His growl told her his opinion of that.

"I didn't ask you to come," she said sharply.

When she tried to pull her hand free, Abby's hold tightened. She was fearsomely strong. Jane had always admired that about her.

"We stick together," Abby said, tugging her back. "No choice but to go forward. I'll lead."

Another growl from Jake.

"Let me go first," Jane said, moving forward but keeping her hand in Abby's. "This was my idea." She took the hat from her head and tossed it aside. "Besides, they're men who've been locked down here for God knows how long. They're more likely to hesitate if they see me first. No one ever considers me a threat."

"Well, they don't know you now, do they?" Jake asked, but he didn't try to hold her back when she started forward so she took that for agreement.

It was the truth. Even with a gun in her hands, most men would hesitate to shoot her outright. So long as they weren't panicked and expecting a Reaper to come running down the tunnel. They'd shoot Jake without question, and Abby was sometimes mistaken for a man. This way they had surprise on their side if they ran into any miners. And if Reapers managed to break through the rockfall, they'd come from behind. Jake and Abby were far better equipped to deal with Reapers than she was.

She took the right branch, ducking her head beneath the rock ledge and sighing in relief when beyond that, the tunnel opened up so that even Jake could stand upright. The light ahead seemed to grow brighter which either meant it was stationary or her eyes were beginning to adjust to the gloom. Through the gloves, the stone felt cold beneath her palm. The ground, in this part of the mine at least, was well-worn and smooth. Carlo had said the miners slept in cells within the mine in case the wall should fail and they needed to seal themselves inside. If they had a way to seal themselves inside then it only stood to reason that they had a way out, as well.

After the first few cautious steps, she picked up her pace. The sound of their shuffling footsteps filled the cave but all around them the mountain seemed to tremble. Either the rockslide the miners had rigged to seal the entrance had triggered an avalanche or the ship was firing its cannons on the horde of Reapers. That might buy them time in the short run but the sound would also draw in more Reapers to see what was going on. Every thud and tremor was a reminder that they were running out of time. Lyle was down here somewhere. She'd find him. She had to.

LYLE TOOK ONE last look into the wide and terrified eyes of the children before handing their guardian the broken pickax he'd found in a garbage pile in one of the abandoned tunnels. The oil from the lantern was running low and they'd turned the wick down as far as they could without snuffing it out. The dim light left most of Ada's narrow face in shadow. Her eyes gleamed bright with unshed tears. He felt a grudging respect for the woman, little more than a child herself really.

"I'll see what's going on and I'll be back for you."

She nodded, clutching the flimsy weapon to her chest but he could tell she didn't quite believe him. Why should she? The armed guard had already abandoned them, leaving them locked up together in a cell with only a guttering lantern and no food. The mountain was shaking as if it was about to tumble down on their heads and, as far as Ada knew, he was her enemy.

He'd been able to use Ada's knife to pry open the rusted hinge on the old door to get them out. He wasn't entirely sure they were any safer out of the cell than in it. The guard who'd promised them breakfast in the morning had never returned and even buried as they were in the mountain, they could hear some disturbance above, an intermittent rumbling vibration like the sound of distant thunder.

Nodding to the boys, he replaced the door on its frame, took up his knife again and tried to remember the way they'd come in. He'd been groggy then, still suffering from the effects of his head injury. The guards hadn't been gentle. He'd fallen more than once and his memory of the twists and turns leading down into this big hole in the ground were hazy.

Passing the knife into his right hand, he pressed his left to the wall so he could feel his way in the dark. He remembered that there were lanterns mounted on the walls of the main passages and he thought he saw a glimmer of light up ahead. The light might indicate a way out or it could be from one of the carbide lamps the miners carried. Impossible to tell until he got closer.

It was too soon for the Rangers to have realized he

was missing let alone mount a rescue. Janie…well, damn. Hopefully, she was still safe in Eagle Creek awaiting his return. It would take time for Cap to engage the services of a passenger airship and get to her. Time to figure out where he'd disappeared to, if they ever figured that out at all.

He felt a twinge of regret at that. He'd finally gotten close to Jane. She'd let him in, had begun to trust him, and it hurt to think that in the end he'd failed her too.

He crept forward, staying close to the wall and walking slowly across the slightly uneven ground. Some of the passages were more even than others. When he came to a turn, he eased around it. He took one quick look down the tunnel and then a longer one when he saw the way was clear. A lamp hung from a hook pounded into the stone, lighting the empty intersection of two wide passageways.

Both of them disappeared into darkness within just a few feet but the one on the left looked as if it climbed upward so he took that one. He left the lamp behind with some regret but he wouldn't be able to move much faster with it and it would only announce his presence to anyone who might be lurking in the tunnels down here. Besides, it would serve as a beacon once it was time to make his way back to Ada and the kids.

A faint sound came to him and at first he tried to ignore it. Clank. Clank. Clank. Growing louder as he walked. A steady beat of metal to rock and all he could think of was Doc and the ghost stories he liked to tell about his first patrol near the eastern range and the old coal mines there. They were deep, most abandoned now.

Reapers avoided them and Doc attributed that behavior to ghosts. Tommyknockers. Ghosts of miners who'd been buried in the earth, pounding on the rocks even after death. A chill worked down his spine even though he knew it was a bullshit story. It wasn't the dead warning him to turn back.

Still, it seemed like an eternity he walked through the darkness but was probably only a few minutes. It was painfully slow going. His eyes were open but blind. The sound growing louder as he walked. At first nothing but a faint vibration in the air, the tapping sound eventually turned into something he recognized. Gunfire. The rhythm of it was unmistakable.

He moved faster then, the air tasting cleaner the higher he went. At the sound of footsteps, he stopped and backtracked a dozen feet to a small turn he'd felt in the rock. He'd thought it was an alcove but when he traced it out with his hands, he realized it was an opening. The footsteps were definitely growing louder. Only one set of them and light. Hopefully it was someone he could overpower easily. Or someone who could tell him what the hell was going on and how to get the hell out of this place. Praying that the ground didn't fall out beneath his feet, he ducked inside the crevice, adjusted his grip on the hilt of his knife and waited.

JANE PICKED UP her pace. She could see somewhat now. The rooms that split from the main tunnel where the miners had made their living quarters were all empty. The hooks on the wall were rusted but sturdy enough to hold a heavy lamp. If they'd once done so, the miners had taken them when they fled. There were damp spots on the wall in places that looked black as tar and a glitter in a vein that traced the roof that under other circumstances she might have paused to marvel at.

Her attention was focused entirely on the light up ahead, growing stronger with every step. Everything they'd seen so far said the mines were well and truly abandoned. She couldn't hear anyone up ahead. On the one hand, she was glad that the miners were only trying to save their own skin and not hunting them. On the other, it would be a comfort to be with someone who knew the tunnels, even if that meant captivity.

Her attention was so focused on the light that she didn't see the man step out from the alcove to her right until it was too late. He grabbed her arm and swung her around so her back was to his chest, at the same time pressing a knife to her throat.

"Stop right there," he said in a gravelly voice. His whiskers caught in her hair and his smell nearly made her gag. He reminded her of those former Reapers who'd attacked them on the road to Columbus Junction, but this time Lyle wasn't here to save her. Abby and Jake both took aim at a point just over her shoulder but neither tried to move forward in the narrow space.

"Lower your weapons and I'm going to back up nice and slow. The boss just wants a word with you."

"Your boss," Jake said mildly. "And who might that be?"

Abby looked pissed but the lack of expression on Jake's face was downright terrifying. Jane imagined that this was how he'd looked as a Reaper about to tear someone's throat out. The man pulled her back with him, the blade at her throat loosening marginally as he moved. Jake and Abby slowly followed.

The light, when they reached the small cave at the end of the tunnel, was nearly blinding. And now she could hear other people, a handful of men by the way they moved, crawling out of the side tunnels to join them. Jane couldn't see who they were but by the way Jake scowled, that was probably a good thing.

"Corrigan," Abby said and Jane tried to turn her head. She yelped when the knife nicked her skin. The man holding her cursed and tightened his hold around her rib cage.

But he'd shifted enough that Jane could see for herself that it was truly Corrigan. She'd seen him once before when she was a girl and she'd gone with her mother to watch the beautiful, glittering crowd arrive for the Founder's Ball on Eyrion.

He was of middling height with brown hair and dark eyes. He'd filled out somewhat since she'd last seen him. But the sly look to his face, that smirk, was unforgettable. It had given her a chill then even as it did now.

Corrigan didn't waste any time getting to the point. "We'll get you out of the mines in exchange for passage on your ship.

"It's a Tirado ship," Abby said. Honest as a sunrise. Because of course it wouldn't occur to Abby that it might be better to lie in a situation like this. "I don't know if you could come up with enough money to convince her to save your worthless hide."

He tipped his head in Jane's direction. "I can give you your friend's life. The way through this rock which you'll never find on your own. I can give you the serum."

"Which you stole."

"Recovered," Corrigan said. "And I'd be happy to return it…for a lift out of here. Surely, a Ranger could convince Maricel that it would be the right thing to do."

Jake lowered his gun but Abby looked as though she

wanted to put a bullet in the man. And Jane couldn't let that happen. Not yet. She pulled at the arm holding the knife, twisting away. When the guard holding her reached for her again, Corrigan held up a hand to stop him. She got a dirty look from the guard for that but she ignored it, turning away and positioning herself directly in the line of fire. Behind her, Abby cursed in frustration.

"We can get you out," Jane said, raising her voice so the men with him heard the offer too. "It's a big ship. There's enough room for all the survivors if you show us the way out." Corrigan's eyes narrowed as if searching for the catch. So she gave it to him. "But we want the Ranger you captured too."

"What Ranger?"

Jane stepped aside enough for Abby to have a clear line to fire. She'd intended it as a threat but Corrigan only laughed. "You shoot me and nobody gets out. There's a bank vault seal on the escape tunnel and I'm the only one who knows the combination. And the other Ranger…I don't know where he is. The ship that brought him in arrived shortly before mine. The guards who secured him all died on the wall. He could be anywhere down here and we don't have the time to search. I have the serum. That will have to be enough."

Enough? She shook her head. "We can make more serum."

Corrigan held out his hands. "That's the offer."

"It's not good enough," Jane said. "I need a guide, someone who can bring me to where they might have chained him."

Most of the men surrounding Corrigan were too finely dressed to be miners. Only one of them looked the part, a small man with pale skin and hard hands. He shifted his feet uncomfortably and glanced to the tunnel that branched off to the right.

Corrigan's lips thinned. "The others are waiting by the escape tunnel for me. We only came back for the serum. Let's get to the door and you can ask for a volunteer." He dropped an insultingly speculative gaze down her body. "Depending on what you offer for payment, I'm sure you'll find someone to take you up on it."

"And then you leave us down here with a story about how we didn't make it out? Maricel won't lift a finger to help you."

He gestured toward the crate. "She will once she sees we have this." He gave a signal and two men stepped from the tunnel behind them, shotguns raised and pointed at Jake and Abby.

"And now we have you to bargain with as well," Corrigan said with a smirk. "No man left behind, isn't that the motto?"

"That's one of them," Abby sneered. "The other is, 'One bullet at a time'. Which is how we take care of unholy monsters like yourself."

Corrigan patted his chest. "I'm just a businessman, trying to make a living."

"A dishonest living." She glared at the man who took her gun, who looked abashed but followed orders anyway.

No one was paying any attention to Jane, even though she still had her weapons. Both were holstered. She'd told Jake the truth earlier—no one saw a pretty woman as a threat. Of course, she couldn't shoot them all, and it would do no one any good to shoot Corrigan when he was the only one who could get them out. She took a step back while the guards disarmed Jake and Abby.

Jake noticed what she was doing and frowned. He gave a small shake of his head just as her hand reached back to touch rock. Corrigan saw the motion and turned to look at her but before he could speak, she spun, ducked under the outstretched arm of the guard who lunged for her and darted down the dark tunnel.

Someone shouted and gave chase. Abby called out her name but she kept running. She knew she was risking her life on a stupid chance, on a guilty look on a miner's face when he looked down this tunnel. She knew the odds were against her finding Lyle, against getting him out in time to meet the ship when it came back to check for survivors. But she also knew it was the only chance she was going to get.

Corrigan had already written Lyle off for dead. He wasn't going to send anyone back for him. He'd only taken Abby and Jake because he thought he might need them for leverage in getting aboard Maricel's ship. Her shoulder clipped the rock as the tunnel curved and she grunted with the impact. She slowed just enough to trail her hand along the wall as she darted forward. She could no longer hear footsteps behind her. The man had likely been called back. She wasn't important. Not a Ranger. Not worth any use as a hostage. But still she ran as fast as she safely could. Time was not her friend.

There was a light ahead and that meant another intersection. Another choice that meant life or death for herself and for Lyle. This one empty and quiet with a well-cared-for lantern hanging on a rusted hook. She left it there as a beacon and took the right turn. The path became rougher. The tunnel narrowed and she was considering turning back when she tripped on an upraised rock.

She would have fallen to her knees if not for the arms that reached out to break her fall. Before she could regain her feet, she was lifted up and pressed back to the wall. In the dim light she could make out the features of the man looking down at her. A shudder ran through her body and his face blurred.

"Lyle," she whispered. "I found you."

She wrapped her arms around his neck and hugged him tight. After a moment, his hands closed around her waist and gathered her in.

"Jane," he whispered, lips moving against her temple. She inhaled, breathing him in. He didn't smell pretty but it was a comfort just the same. His chest moved beneath her fingertips. His heart beat there, strong and steady. He grabbed hold of her shoulder and pushed her back to look down at her. His face was a filthy mess and his scowl was terrifying. "What the hell are you doing here?"

She smiled and took his face between her hands to pull him down. At first he didn't kiss her back but eventually he relented. A groan slipped past his parted lips and she slipped her tongue inside. Her fingers threaded through his hair and she kissed him hard, letting that kiss scour away all the fear and heartache of the past few days. Eventually they parted and he pressed his forehead to hers. The scowl was gone but she could see the glitter of his eyes, all frustration and exasperation. "I left you safe and sound in Eagle Creek."

"And if you ever try to do something like that again I'll shoot you and spare myself the wondering what happened when you don't come back. I am not a pray-and-wait kind of woman."

His short laugh was cut off by the sound from farther down the tunnel. It might have been a footstep. It might have been a pebble falling.

"Come on. This way." He pulled her through a short narrow tunnel, barely a crack in the wall. It was pitch-black but as soon as the air changed, letting her know they'd stepped into a bigger cavern, he pressed her back to the wall and leaned against her. This time he initiated the kiss. It was just as demanding as hers had been but this time he took his time.

"Now tell me. You might not be a patient woman but you're not a gunslinger and you're not a bird. If Flynn dropped you here and took off, I will hunt him down and flay him alive."

"Maricel Tirado flew us down here. She's Corrigan's dearest enemy so Cap was able to talk her into lending a hand. The ship will come as soon as Abby lights the flare but the gate fell and they won't have time to linger with all the Reapers about. Abby and Jake are down here with Corrigan and a small group of his personal guard. I don't know how many of the miners survived. A good many of them, I think." She drew a deep breath. "And I'm scared out of my mind. I don't want to see another gun in my life, or another Reaper, but I had to come."

His big hand cupped her jaw and his thumb smoothed across her cheek. "I wish you'd stayed away."

"I wish lots of things different."

He grunted softly, as if she'd punched him in the stomach, and closed his eyes.

"Not you," she said in exasperation. "The only thing

I regret about you is that I didn't meet you before Cam or Gideon." Lifting onto her toes, she kissed him again. "I love you. Why else would I be down here?"

He just blinked and then stared at her, a touch dazed. There *was* an enormous lump on his head. When he lifted his hand to touch her cheek, she grabbed it and pulled him toward the tunnel. "Now, come on. We have to hurry or we'll miss the ship."

He squeezed her hand and allowed her to lead him out of the alcove but to her surprise, he turned right, downhill and away from the exit.

"First, we have to go get the kids."

TWENTY-FIVE

IT DIDN'T TAKE LONG to find the cell where Lyle had been locked up by the miners. The lantern had burned out while he'd been gone and the woman and her four charges were huddled in the corner of the room. They squealed in fright when Lyle pushed open the door. He had to lift it and set it aside because of the broken hinge.

"It's all right, Ada. It's just me…with a friend. We've found a way out but we have to hurry."

Ada was in no condition to help them along. Jane gripped her cold hand to help her up and it trembled so badly that she was afraid Ada would be unable to walk, let alone hold on to the child she carried. Jane relieved her of her burden and bid her to hold on to her gun belt. The eldest boy followed behind Ada, holding on to one of the younger children and Lyle brought up the rear carrying a fourth child. They made a peculiar caravan but they made it back to the intersection where they'd been ambushed without trouble.

It was empty, silent. Jane said a silent prayer as she lifted the lantern from its hook and started down the tunnel she hoped led in the right direction.

Less than twenty minutes later, after they'd hit two dead ends and had to backtrack, they reached a steel door that looked as if it hid the wealth of Eyrion. Gleaming brass fittings and a cyclical locking system fixed the front. The door was ajar and the room was echoingly empty. Jane dropped the lantern and darted forward. There was enough daylight peeking around the edges of the door to see by now and at least the room was empty and not crawling with Reapers. There might still be time.

Before she rushed out, Lyle called her name. She hesitated for a moment but then heard the heavy whump of a propeller and kept going. They were leaving.

Shifting the weight of the child on her hip, she drew her pistol, placed her back to the rock wall beside the door and looked outside. The sun had cleared the mountain and they were a good deal higher up here than the gates. It was a large clearing, large enough for a lightship but not the *Goliath*.

There was a sharp drop and judging by the position of the sun, this was the south face of the mountain. The fog had cleared and there was nobody standing in the clearing. The ship was above, steadily gaining altitude. Already the ropes and baskets they'd apparently used to lift the survivors were being pulled over the rails and stowed away. She ran outside, Lyle a step behind. She waved her hands and shouted but if anyone above saw her, they gave no sign of it. The ship didn't change course.

Lyle said her name. Quietly, in that calm steady voice she'd always so admired. It scared the hell out of her right now. It held a warning that made her raise her gun as she turned to answer him.

She didn't need to ask what was wrong. He'd set the child he was carrying on his feet and pushed him back toward the door. He didn't have a gun. They'd stripped him of weapons when they'd taken him captive. He held only a long knife, nicked in a few spots and he pointed with it toward the edge of the clearing.

There was a hand there, stretched above the ledge and grappling for purchase. As she watched, another joined it. With a grunt, the Reaper hauled himself over the edge and started running toward them as soon as his feet touched the ground. Tall, wide-bodied, with a snarl on his lips and death in his eyes. Jane pulled the trigger, hitting him square in the chest. He dropped but didn't stop moving. He'd be back on his feet within minutes.

Head shot. She needed to wait until she could get a head shot or they didn't stand a chance. Who was she kidding? They didn't stand a chance anyway. Not miles deep in Reaper territory with her two guns, a handful of ammunition and Lyle's knife.

The child she carried screamed and squirmed, trying to get away from her but she didn't dare let him go. Over her shoulder, she shouted for Ada and the other children to start climbing. She handed Lyle her extra gun and glanced again at the ship. It might have slowed. They'd likely heard the gunshot. But it was slow work to turn a ship of that size. And the Reapers would have heard the shot too.

Lyle walked over to the wounded Reaper and drove the knife into its head through the eye socket. Then he calmly turned back to her, shoved his weapon into the empty holster in his belt and stripped off his shirt.

She shook her head. "Now is hardly the time."

He smirked. "Just hand me your weapon. I'll need whatever ammunition you have too."

It spoke to how well she trusted Lyle that she didn't question that until after she'd handed him her gun. Glancing over his shoulder to make sure no other Reapers had managed to climb so high, he came around her, wrapping his shirt around her body to form a makeshift sling. “Those shots will draw them. They’ll already have been headed in this direction because of the ship.” He paused as he tied the knot tight and she could hear them already. The howls below were terrifying but the smaller sounds of exertion coming from closer scared her more. He strapped the child to her back. The poor thing had gone mute and still, clearly as terrified as she was. His little hands clung to her shirt and Lyle had to pry them loose as he adjusted the sling. The way the child hung on to her, she didn’t know that the sling was even necessary.

When he was done, Lyle stood in front of her. He had an ugly bruise on his cheek and his bottom lip was cut and swollen. Two days’ growth on his face but he was still the finest-looking man she’d ever seen.

He checked the ledge once more and then bent his head to kiss her. Just a press of his lips. He didn’t linger. But every part of her rose up, lifting toward that moment. His fingers against her neck. The scrape of his whiskers and the sigh of his breath as he pulled away. He looked into her eyes a moment longer and then placed a hand on her shoulder to turn her toward the mountain. “Climb.”

“I can help you hold them off.”

His brows lifted. “I can shoot better than you and we need to conserve our bullets. Find a ledge if you can. Otherwise just get to the highest point you can reach. They’ll get the ropes down to you.”

“You’ll follow us up.”

He smiled and dropped a kiss to the corner of her mouth. “Of course I will. Go on.”

He turned away not giving her a chance to argue and there was no time for it. The Reapers were drawing closer and the child on her back was trembling like a leaf. Lyle was right. He was the better shot. She knew that. But, *damn it*, she didn't want to leave him behind.

It didn't matter what she wanted though. He was taking this risk to save their lives and she had to honor that. Walking to the base of the mountain, she took one last look at Lyle who now stood at the edge of the cliff, aiming down at the nearest Reaper. She blew out a frustrated breath and then she began to climb.

The ship had seen them. When Jane paused to glance up at it, it was clearly closer than it had been only minutes ago. The gunmen aboard had begun to fire again, holding the Reapers at bay. They were lowering a small basket, like the ones used in the older models of cable cars, along with all of their ropes and harnesses. Still so far out of reach.

Her handhold crumbled beneath her grip and she returned her attention to the climb. Every time she heard the gunfire below her, she was reassured that Lyle was still living. He had both of her guns and she hadn't fired a single shot coming in. She should have counted. How many bullets did he have left before he ran out of ammunition?

She shoved the thought aside and focused on getting herself and the child clinging to her back to safety. He was the innocent one here. Damn Corrigan. And Moore. All of the Scrapers who didn't care who got hurt so long as they didn't have to see it and so long as the money kept rolling in.

She reached the ledge just as Ada was ushering the wide-eyed children into the basket. She helped get them settled and fastened herself into one of the waiting harnesses. Lyle had stopped shooting. Hopefully, that meant he was climbing. She couldn't see him past the jut of rock she was standing on and there was nothing she could do to help him now. Signaling that she was ready with a tug on the rope, she braced herself as the crew aboard ship began to pull her to safety.

Lyle.

She cast around, looking for a sign of him. He wasn't on the ledge below. Not near the mouth of the cave. The rope began to twist as she was wrenched higher and she kicked her legs, trying to turn around, craning her neck to see. There were Reapers everywhere. From this vantage, she could see them milling about in the courtyard beyond the busted walls, scaling the rock face toward the ledge where Lyle had been standing only moments before.

And then, there. On the face of the cliff above, she finally caught sight of him. There was a long bloody gash down his bare back. Reaching up, he dug his hand into a crevice and kicked at the clawing hand of the Reaper reaching for his boot. Both guns were holstered to free his hands although it was unlikely that he had any ammunition left. His foot slipped when he began to climb again and for a heart-stopping moment, Jane thought he would fall. Somehow, he managed to hold on to the rock with his fingertips and pull himself high enough to find another foothold.

One of the Reapers trying to grab him wasn't so lucky. Excited by Lyle's near fall, it lunged up, lost its hold and peeled off the cliff face. Screaming, arms and legs beating at the air, it fell backward into the pit. The other Reapers swarmed the body. She tore her eyes away from that, swallowing down bile and returning her attention to Lyle.

He was almost to the rope. Five feet. Three when the crew winched it lower. Jane held her breath, watching helplessly as Lyle continued to climb, the muscles in his shoulders bunching with the effort.

As Lyle finally reached the rope, the nearest Reaper made a last-ditch effort at grabbing hold of his ankles. A gunshot rang out from above and the Reaper jerked before falling away. They pulled Lyle clear immediately, raising him so quickly she worried he might lose his grip. He managed to hold on. Up, up, up he went and her breath left in a whoosh. Closing her eyes, she pressed her forehead to the rope, murmuring soft words of comfort to the child still clinging to her back as they were hauled the rest of the way up.

Once aboard the ship, one of the crewmen cut her free and a cheer went up from the crew as Lyle was hauled over the side behind her. She caught a glimpse of Corrigan out of the corner of her eye, surrounded by a ring of Tirado guards.

As she climbed to her feet, strong hands caught her by the shoulders and spun her around. The child on her back, sensing he was finally safe, let out an unholy wail and began to struggle to be put down. Rather than attempt to unknot the sash, Lyle cut through the cloth and lifted the child free.

She took the boy into her arms, hoisting him onto her hip. He seemed heavier there than he had on her back, but he was still just a very young, very frightened child. His little body was trembling and he ducked his head beneath her chin as though he meant to hide. She felt the old familiar ache begin to swell in her chest like it did every time she held a child, but this felt a little different. Maybe because this one was so young and frightened. It triggered every protective instinct she had.

Shifting him in her arms so she could see his face, the ache in her heart sharpened to painful intensity. He had guinea-gold curls and a tiny dimple in his chin. His tear-bright eyes were a pure true blue so piercingly familiar her legs buckled. If not for Lyle standing there to wrap his arms around both her and the boy, they both would have hit the deck hard.

Samuel... Samuel... Back from the dead.

Even knowing it couldn't possibly be true, the thought swelled in her mind and she couldn't force her way past it. The resemblance was utterly wrenching. She couldn't do anything but stare even as the little boy began to cry. She wanted to comfort him. She did. But every muscle in her body was locked up tight. On the outside she was frozen as a statue but inside a storm was raging, tearing her to shreds.

"I've got you," Lyle murmured into her hair. "It's all right. I've got you."

TWENTY-SIX

IT TOOK SEVERAL HOURS to see everyone settled. By then the ship was well on its way toward Fort Dougan. Home. Cam. Everything she owned in the whole world was there. Her job. The people she considered family. The idea of it just didn't seem to fit, no matter how she tried to wiggle into it. She'd changed. This trip with Lyle, what she'd done to Gideon. All of it had changed her.

And there was the boy. James, Ada had called him. Was it really her Samuel come back from the dead or just a child that resembled Cam? She couldn't wrap her head around that either. It was possible that this *was* Cam's child, but not by her. She rubbed her forehead. If he wasn't really Samuel, wouldn't it be a betrayal to pretend he was?

He was sleeping now with the other children, all of them clean, fed and tucked into the most enormous bed she'd ever seen. They hadn't wanted to be separated. The oldest, a ten-year-old named Brandon, had seemed particularly protective of the younger children. He'd asked about Ada too, who was being held in a separate room. They'd had to let her come reassure him that she was all right before he finally settled down to sleep.

Jane sat on the sofa beside Abby while Jake spoke quietly with Cap in the far corner. Lyle returned from the bar with three full glasses of whiskey which he set down on the marble-topped table beside her. When

Abby moved to get up, he waved her down and knelt in front of Jane.

"I know what you want to talk about," she whispered. "But I don't even want to hear you say it. I don't know how it could be possible."

"After seeing what Gideon was involved in, I think it's more than possible. We always knew he was trafficking in more than black-market whiskey."

"Whores and opium, yes. But this?"

"Those children are proof." Lyle placed his hands on either side of her hips, caging her in a loose embrace. His gray eyes were steady and bright. "You told me you were ill when Samuel passed. That you regretted never having seen his grave. I know Gideon drugged you when you got back to Columbus Junction. Isn't it possible that one of his men might have drugged you on the trail?"

"I saw him," she said, flinching from the memory of his still, little body cradle in her arms. He hadn't been breathing, she remembered that, even through the fog of sickness and grief. And then they'd taken him away.

This boy...James had that same angel-blond hair. Eyes the same shape and color as Cam's. He was the right age too. She'd rocked him to sleep earlier, tracing out his features looking for something more than hair color to pin her hope on but she simply couldn't trust herself to judge it rightly. A shudder ran through her body. She wanted to believe it so badly it hurt.

"He was deathly sick. He was having such trouble breathing his lips turned blue."

"You weren't yourself then," Lyle went on. "Sick and drugged, if Gideon had told you he was dead and then taken him away, you wouldn't have questioned the truth of it."

She shook her head. "Gideon was cruel, but I never would have thought he'd lie to me about that. Why would he have lied?"

"Because Corrigan wanted to open more mines, expand his operation before the border moved south and he had competition. Gideon was recruiting deserters from the fort to work as guards in Corrigan's mine. He was collecting star-marked orphans to raise as guards. Lyle's arms tightened. "Gideon wanted you and he knew as long as you had Samuel to fight for, you'd keep trying to escape him."

She wanted to believe him. She wanted it so bad. "I can't trust myself on this."

"Do you trust me?"

A tear leaked out from the corner of her eye, tickling her skin as it ran down her cheek. Absently, she wiped it aside. "You know that I do."

"He's your child," Lyle said gently. "I spoke with the rifleman from Eagle Creek, the one secretly working for Maricel."

"Carlo?"

He nodded. "He'd just started working for Corrigan when that child came in. A man named Holson delivered him. Does that name ring a bell?"

Her heart stuttered a beat. Holson was a pilot. He wasn't nearly as reliable as Flynn. But Gideon had hired him before on the jobs Flynn refused for one reason or another. If this child really was Samuel, it brought her some relief knowing that Flynn might truly not have known anything about it.

"He said the boy was still sick at the time," Lyle continued in his deep, even voice. "Feverish and squalling. They didn't think he'd last out the week. Ada tells the same story." He lifted her hands from her lap to cradle them. "There are too many coincidences for it to be otherwise. I'm sorry. Glad for you but sorry too."

Her head came up. "Why on earth would you be sorry? You don't have a single thing to be sorry about."

His hand tightened on hers. "I'm sorry because it was a line you thought Gideon wouldn't cross, but he did. That's always hard to face."

"That's nothing you ought to be sorry about. Gideon crossed all sorts of lines. And you should know by now that I can face hard facts when I need to."

A ghost of a smile touched his lips. "I know it."

Rocking back onto his heels, he stood. He pressed a glass of the whiskey into her hands and then lifted one of his own. "Let it sink in. Talk to Carlo and hear the story from him. We'll be back home soon and we can sort everything out there."

TWENTY-SEVEN

After everything, it took only three hours to make it back to the fort. By the time the iron stairs were lowered, Cam was there waiting for them at the bottom. Maricel had put one of her men down in Eagle Creek to send the telegram updating the fort on the situation. By the way Cam's eyes locked on Jane—on the child in her arms—they'd given a very thorough update.

Lyle stood back, watching as Cap thanked Maricel once again. Jake patted the side of the ship and hopped down but Abby lingered by his side. Lyle wanted to go to Jane, to be the one standing at her side. But he had no right to that place. Not yet. Maybe not ever.

It was hard to keep his distance. Hard, but necessary. She'd had a shock and it would take time for her to adjust to it. She'd need time to become reacquainted with her son. To speak with Cam and to recover from the stress of their mission.

Abby rested her hip against the rail. "What exactly happened on your trip?"

He pulled his attention from Jane to meet Abby's curious gaze. She tilted her head in Jane's direction. "You've been staring at her like she's candy-coated and you're a Reaper with a sweet tooth."

He shook his head. "I'm worried about her. She's been through hell and I couldn't protect her from any of it. If I'd have known it was going to be that bad, I never would have taken her with me."

"It's not your fault. She survived it and she got her child back." Abby cocked her head to the side. "Jane's tougher than she looks."

"That's the truth."

Abby made her way down the steps to the dirt road and he fell into pace beside her. Men were already loading the wagons with their trunks. Maricel was taking Corrigan, Ada and the surviving miners back up with her to Ballonet where they'd face charges for what they'd done. Lyle would rather have dumped them into the pit of Reapers swarming the mines but Maricel felt the need to make a show of it. Scrapers had their own ways of doing things. They wanted a trial.

Cap seemed encouraged by how willing Maricel had been to help. Lyle didn't put much stock in that. He'd seen the sparkle in Maricel's eyes when they'd put the manacles on Corrigan. Her reasons for helping the forts out this time around were entirely personal.

Abby looped an arm through his. "Do you think Cam will chase after Jane now that his son is here? That would be an interesting change, wouldn't it?"

It took every ounce of willpower not to shout a denial. He knew it was a possibility that with Samuel returned to her, Jane might change her mind about him. She might decide to set her sights on Cam again, to try and build a family with him. Maybe this time around, Cam would be willing. Whenever the thought came to him, he shoved it aside because it hurt too much to consider.

"If she stays at the fort," he said. "Cam might try

to keep her close. I don't know what Jane will decide to do."

Cam was holding Samuel and Jane had a shaky smile on her face. She looked happy. They both did. He let Abby lead him to where Cap and Jake stood several feet distant.

Cap pointed toward the wagon. "You checked the serum?"

Lyle nodded. "It's the same tinted glass Welks insisted on. I transferred everything to a locked trunk just to be sure it wasn't misplaced. Maricel asked for a sample. Said she might need it for evidence."

Cap grimaced. "I'll see that she gets it. I caused enough of a stir by leaving Eyrion before the assembly started. I can't afford to make an enemy out of Maricel too."

"She should be happy," Abby said, crossing her arms and lifting her chin toward the ship. "She got what she was after. Most of the Scrapers are just looking for an excuse to disband us anyway."

"And that is why we need to walk carefully now," Cap said.

Lyle couldn't help but glance over at Jane. No matter how bad recovering the cure hurt Ranger-Scraper politics, it'd been worth it. The whole thing beginning to end. He wouldn't have changed a damned thing. Abby elbowed him as she turned from the ship.

"Come on. Let's get the serum back to the fort."

TWENTY-EIGHT

FUNNY HOW A PERSON could jump off an airship, battle Reapers and face down a whole horde of personal demons and yet still be afraid to have a simple conversation with a man. It seemed to Jane that making it through the other side of all that alive should make her immune to fear. Clearly, that wasn't the case because it took her several days to work up the courage to visit Lyle after their return to the fort.

Oh, she'd been busy. And Lyle had understood when she'd asked him for time to see James settled. James now, not Samuel. So many changes for a little boy. She hadn't wanted to push a new name on him too. She became reacquainted with her son while Lyle attended to his work. She'd told him she'd come find him when she was ready to talk and then she'd found a reason, every day for more than a week, to avoid going to him.

James's return was a wonder that she was still struggling to accept. Her world felt tipped upside down and shaken about. She'd only just managed to start sleeping through the night without having to check on him a dozen times to make sure it wasn't all a dream. Yesterday, he'd called her mama. Cam was a frequent visitor, getting to know his son. With the way things worked, it was unusual for a Ranger to know their children but Cam was just as caught up in the delight of having James there as she was.

And then there was Lyle.

He was the reason she had James back in her arms in the first place. And she was scared down to her bones that he might not have a place for her in his life now that they were back at the fort. On the road, they'd been a team. Unstoppable.

But what if he didn't feel the same way now that he was home?

She paused before she crossed the busy yard. It was a sunny day and the patrol was in. Cap was speaking to the locksmith from Split Creek about some changes he wanted made to the door to Welks's lab and Garrett was leading the younger men through a training exercise. Lyle's quarters were just around the corner, his front door facing the gates. If he was even there today.

He wouldn't turn her away. She knew that. He might not be able to give her exactly what she wanted, but she thought he'd always be her friend. He'd told her that, that he'd always be on her side and he'd never given her any reason to doubt his word. Gathering up her courage, she stepped into the dirt road that led from the stables to the gates. After less than a dozen feet, she made a right turn and then nearly faltered when she saw Lyle standing on the short wooden porch.

Catching sight of her, he turned to watch her approach. He looked all neat and proper, dressed in a clean uniform and freshly shaved. The brim of his hat shadowed his face and she wished she could see his expression.

Her stomach churned and her mouth went dry. It seemed an enormous effort to keep moving forward. As if he sensed her difficulty, Lyle straightened, the board beneath his feet creaking as he came down the steps to meet her. The noise of the fort lessened behind her. She knew the men were all watching. It was a small community. She'd never entered Lyle's quarters before, but they'd spent several weeks in each other's company. People would wonder. She knew that Cam did.

Lyle was there before she could force herself to take the next step. His expression was mild, nearly tender and some of the tightness in her chest loosened.

"I came here to talk."

Lifting his hand to cradle her face, he skimmed his thumb along the edge of her bottom lip and studied her face. "You look upset, sweetheart. You didn't come to tell me goodbye, did you?"

She shook her head. "I don't want to say goodbye."

"Good."

He bent his head and touched his lips lightly to hers. She heard a commotion behind them. Garrett's sharp command, calling the men back to order. But that was in the back of her mind. Lyle's hands were warm on her cheek but his lips were cool. Careful. It was a gentle kiss meant to soothe, not arouse. But the promise of heat was there, simmering just below the surface. And she kissed him back, caught in the moment, not caring that they were standing in the middle of the fort with Rangers all around.

Lyle pulled back too soon. He grinned at her and pressed his hand low on her back to usher her toward the stairs. "Come on then. Let's go talk."

As he closed the door, she stood there for a moment looking around her uncertainly. It was a masculine place. Fort Dougan had been around for nearly a century and she wouldn't have been surprised to learn that this had been one of the original structures. The walls were bare wood, darkened by age and wood smoke from the small fireplace against the far wall. The shutters were pulled and it took her eyes a moment to adjust to the dim light. He had a square table near the front window and a pair of chairs. A porcelain washbasin on the bureau and a trunk pushed to the foot of his bed. The bed was large, to suit his frame, and an old quilt had been pulled up to cover the slightly rumpled blankets. She pulled her gaze away.

When she turned around, the corner of Lyle's mouth was turned up in a smile. But he didn't reach for her. Just stood there expectantly waiting to hear her out.

She shook her head. "You know people will talk about that kiss."

"I don't care what people say."

"Not even the captain? I know the rules. Cap let Abby and Jake stay together but that doesn't mean he'll turn a blind eye to everyone else. If we keep on as we were, it could cause trouble for you and I don't want that."

"Is that what you're worried about?" He stepped nearer, his thighs pressing into her skirts. "You don't have to be. I can handle Cap. What about Cam?"

Lyle lifted up her face so she had to look at him. His thumb stroked her cheek as light as a butterfly wing. It always amazed her how gently he could touch her when his hands were so hard.

"Are you interested in trying to build a family with him?"

"No."

"He's been spending a lot of time at the house."

"Because of James."

She and Cam had settled into a surprisingly easy

friendship. Apparently, Cam liked her much better when she wasn't trying to get into his pants.

"Where is James right now?"

"Sleeping. Haddy's watching him. All of the boys."

They had a houseful. Early on, there'd been some talk of fostering them out, but none of the children had wanted to be separated. And Haddy, Amelia…they'd all grown so attached. The boys had already lost Ada, the only mother most of them remembered. They'd worked out a schedule to keep the children at the fort while Cap looked for their families.

"I know there are all sorts of reasons for us not to be together," she said, then hesitated. She took a deep breath and then spit out what she had to say. "I know I can't expect you to be faithful." He made a rough sound and she continued, best to get this all out. "And I'm not sure I can handle that. But I want to be with you. No matter what it's going to cost me. And I need to know—" She was terrified to know. "—if you still want to be with me now that we're home."

"Cost you…" A slight smile played around his mouth. "You're insulting me, sweetheart."

"I'm telling you that I love you."

His hand slipped back beneath her hair to curve around the back of her neck. "I know that you do." He dipped his head and took her lips in a sweetly gentle kiss. "I love you too."

He bent and lifted her into his arms and started walking toward the bed. "We really should talk about this. It's important."

But there was no force behind it. Not when he was setting her gently down on that worn quilt and then climbing onto the bed after her. Stretching his big body out beside her, he set to work unfastening the line of buttons at the front of her dress. She kicked her shoes off and when they clattered to the wooden floor, Lyle smiled at her.

"Nothing to talk about." He kissed the tip of her nose. "You're staying at the fort, right?"

"Of course." This was her home. She hadn't really considered leaving it.

"And you're done with Cam."

That wasn't a question but she nodded anyway.

"And you want me?"

That *was* a question and the soft look in his eyes made her heart ache. She whispered, "So very much."

"Then here's how it will be." He pulled her bodice wider and bent his head to press a kiss to the base of her throat before slipping the fabric off her shoulders and down her arms. "You'll marry me."

He pushed and then tugged the simple cotton dress from her body while she processed that. Hope rising in her chest, heat surging through her blood. He tossed the dress aside and knelt between her legs, placing a hand on each of her stockinged calves. He pushed the fabric of her slip up her thighs. "It's a new world. If Abby can break the rules, so can I."

He leaned down and pressed a kiss to the seam at the top of her thighs. He pushed the fabric up to her waist and then tugged it over her head. She was nude, except for her stockings and garters but he didn't seem to be in a hurry to get rid of those.

"You have every right to expect me to be faithful. I'll expect the same." Arms braced on either side of her rib cage, he lowered himself to kiss her again, deeply. Thoroughly. When he pulled back, his eyes burned. "We'll give James brothers and sisters. And by the time they're grown, they'll be able to choose for themselves whether or not they want to fight Reapers. The cure changes everything. I keep hearing that from Cap, Doc, Welks. And I think some of those changes ought to benefit me."

She pulled at his shirt, tugging it loose from his waistband and he ducked his head to accommodate her tearing it the rest of the way off him. She skated her hands down the smooth warm skin on his back and sighed.

His hips settled between her legs and it was frustrating because he hadn't removed his trousers. She could feel his erection through the cloth but she wanted him bare. Wanted him inside her.

Gently, he brushed her hair back from her. "I think it's time we break some rules, don't you?"

"You should take your boots off first."

"Janie," he groaned. But she was too busy trying to shove his trousers down his hips to respond to the exasperation in his tone.

He loved her, even here, now that they were back at the fort and not staring death in the eye. That love was like one of the big cables they used to moor the airships to the earth. Anchored by that, she could ride out any storm. He wanted to build a life with her. This precious man who would be perfect if he'd only cooperate and take the rest of his clothes off.

Big hands caged her face and forced her gaze up. "Are you with me?"

She kissed him, long and fierce and deep. "Of course I am. I only stayed away these last days because I didn't want to hear you tell me all the reasons why we needed to keep our distance now."

He smiled and it was like sunrise on the plains, slow and golden and lighting up the whole world between one moment and the next. "You should have known better."

"Yes." She should have known better. She had. She'd only been scared because everything was so…perfect. James. Lyle. So perfect she was afraid to blink lest it all disappear. But Lyle was here, real and solid. And he loved her.

Lyle pulled away, rolling to sit on the edge of the bed and swore when his boots didn't come off as quickly as he'd like. Once they hit the floor, he stood up and shucked off his trousers before climbing back into bed with her. Gorgeous man, nude, beautifully made. Hers.

She opened her arms and he crawled above her, lowering his body and then sliding into her embrace. He nuzzled at her neck and then kissed her lips. But when he looked up, his eyes were very serious. "If I'd known what you were thinking, I'd have stormed into the women's barracks days ago and stolen you away. I thought you might have changed your mind, being back here. Having James again. Being with Cam."

She touched his cheek. "I never loved Cam."

"You still haven't told me you'll marry me."

"You didn't ask." She smiled when he blushed. "I was just going to let you have your way."

"Jane…"

"Lyle." She pressed her palm to his cheek. "You are the best man I've ever known. And I would be honored to be your wife."

She hooked her legs around his and wiggled just a little bit…there. His arms tightened around her and she thought she saw tears gather in his eyes before he buried his face in her neck.

"Good." With a sigh, he pressed inside her, filling her smoothly, completely. "You don't know how hard it's been keeping my distance these past few days. I think you enjoy testing my restraint."

She smiled, thinking of how he'd rejected her twice on the road, worried about taking advantage of her when she was facing down the demons of her past. Those old ghosts didn't have any kind of hold on her now. The past was well and truly in the past and all she could see now was a future with Lyle.

He filled her again and she clung to him, tangling her fingers in his hair and pulling his head down for a kiss. His mouth opened on hers, sweet and generous. His tongue bumping over her teeth to stroke hers.

Gentle mouth, firm hands. He angled his hips just so that he pressed against her clit with each thrust and when that didn't get the response from her he wanted, he curved a hand beneath her thigh to hike her leg higher. "There," he murmured when his next slow thrust pulled a moan from her and caused her to body to instinctively clench down on him. And the infernal man slowed then rather than rush her to climax. He drew out the moment, withdrawing so she felt every inch of his retreat. Filling her with smooth, lazy thrusts as if they had all the time in the world.

"I missed you. Six days. Do you know what torture that was?"

She knew he was paying her back for it now. By not pressing harder, moving faster or releasing his hold on her so that she could hurry him along. He must have read some of that frustration on her face because his smile widened. When he bent his head to kiss her, she took the opportunity to grab hold of him. Arching her back, she rolled him beneath her. She wouldn't have managed it if he hadn't already been off balance. His breath left him in a rush and he laughed.

"If you'd wanted to ride me, all you had to do was ask."

His warm hands gripped her hips, setting her in motion and guiding her until she'd found her own pace. Then his hands drifted higher, fingers tracing the bottom edge of her breasts a moment before his palms slipped up to cover them. She moaned, resting her hands on the ridges of his stomach. His muscled flexed there as he lifted his hips to meet her.

"You're beautiful," he whispered. "Have I told you that? I always thought you were beautiful. I hated that you wanted Cam. Tell me you're mine again."

Her eyes fluttered open and she looked down at him. His skin was flushed, his mouth set hard. But his eyes, dear Lord, his eyes burned as he lifted his gaze from her breasts to her face. She loved that look on his face, that she was the one to put it there. "No one else's."

He moved his hand lower, the backs of his knuckles grazing her belly. His fingers found her clit and pressed there lightly as she moved over him. She was close now and she was having trouble maintaining the pace. Every movement seemed as if it might cause her to fly apart and she wanted Lyle to come with her. He was determined though. She could see that too. He gripped her hip, leading her faster. His thumb stroking her with a firmer touch even as she tried to pull back from the edge. No use. She was falling. She closed her eyes and her head fell back. She clung to Lyle as a heavy wave of sheer pleasure crashed over her. A moan slipped from her parted lips and Lyle echoed it. He continued to move when she became incapable of it. Aftershocks rippled through her with every thrust and for a second she just floated there in pure mindless bliss.

"I love you, Janie."

The words tugged her back down. To the warm bed. Lyle's strong arms. To the soft words he whispered against her hair as he strained beneath her. Inside her. Around her.

Brought her back down to exactly where she was meant to be.

* * * * *